高等学校专业英语教材

物流专业英语教程

张庆英　主编
李　郁　副主编

电子工业出版社

Publishing House of Electronics Industry

北京·BEIJING

内 容 简 介

本书以物流的术语定义作为起点,对物流的基本内容、运输、仓储、配送、包装、装卸搬运、流通加工等各环节的内容进行了讨论,在物流信息管理的基础上,探讨了电子商务、B2B、B2C 等方面的内容。对供应链管理,供应链管理技术发展趋势、ERP 系统、MRP 系统以及第三方物流、第四方物流、国际物流、绿色物流、RFID 技术等方面的内容加以阐述。全书分 26 课,每课有 A、B 两篇,其中 A 篇为精读课文,B篇为阅读课文,课后包括生词、短语及注释,并列出了若干讨论主题。为了方便教学,本书另配有电子教案,向采纳本书作为教材的教师免费提供。

本书可以作为高校物流及相关专业的本科生专业英语教材及物流业从业人员的培训用书,也可供从事相关专业的工程技术人员学习参考。

图书在版编目(CIP)数据

物流专业英语教程/张庆英主编.—北京:电子工业出版社,2010.1

高等学校专业英语教材

ISBN 978-7-121-09879-6

Ⅰ. 物…　Ⅱ. 张…　Ⅲ. 物流－英语－高等学校－教材　Ⅳ. H31

中国版本图书馆 CIP 数据核字(2009)第 207159 号

策划编辑:杨丽娟
责任编辑:杨丽娟
印　　刷:北京市顺义兴华印刷厂
装　　订:三河市双峰印刷装订有限公司
出版发行:电子工业出版社
　　　　　北京市海淀区万寿路 173 信箱　　邮编　100036
开　　本:787×980　1/16　印张:22.25　字数:487 千字
印　　次:2010 年 1 月第 1 次印刷
印　　数:4 000 册　定价:33.00 元

凡所购买电子工业出版社图书有缺损问题,请向购买书店调换。若书店售缺,请与本社发行部联系,联系及邮购电话:(010)88254888。

质量投诉请发邮件至 zlts@phei.com.cn,盗版侵权举报请发邮件至 dbqq@phei.com.cn。

服务热线:(010)88258888。

前　言

本书以物流工程与供应链管理作为主线，涵盖了物流的基本概念和基本环节、供应链管理，以及相关的技术等内容。精心挑选的英文原文资料，内容涉及物流系统的各个方面。

全书包括四个方面专业内容：①以物流的术语定义作为起点，对物流的基本内容、运输、仓储、配送、包装、装卸搬运、流通加工等各环节的基本内容进行了讨论，在物流信息管理的基础上，探讨电子商务、B2B、B2C 等方面的内容。②介绍供应链管理的基本内容，探讨供应链管理技术的发展趋势、ERP 系统和 MRP 系统。③对第三方物流、第四方物流、国际物流、绿色物流等方面的内容展开介绍，并讨论在物流中应用比较广泛的技术RFID。④本书选择了两个案例——利盟国际的供应链评价和惠普的供应链管理风险分析，将理论的探讨与实际案例的分析结合起来，深化并活化理论知识。这四个方面内容体现在所选录的 52 篇文章中，它们相对独立而又相互关联，未作 4 个部分的硬性划分。

全书分 26 课，每课有 A、B 两篇，其中 A 篇为精读课文，B 篇为阅读课文。文中的生词、短语及部分句子均加以了注释，并在每一课的最后列出了若干讨论主题。此外，在书后附录中给出了物流及工业工程的专业术语与技术词汇的"英－汉"、"汉－英"对照表，以及物流常用缩略词与组合词表。为了方便教学，本书另配有电子教案，向采纳本书作为教材的教师免费提供（获取方式：登录电子工业出版社华信教育资源网 www.hxedu.com.cn 或电话联系010-88254537 获得）。

本书由武汉理工大学张庆英博士（教授）主编，李郁副教授任副主编，其他参编的老师有：武汉理工大学的张鹏、张艳伟、褚伯贵老师和岳卫宏博士，山东科技大学的刘海英老师。钱晨、程丹、巫宇南、张梦雅等同学为本书的资料整理提供了大力帮助，在此一并表示感谢。

在本书的编写过程中，参考和借鉴了很多专业书籍和网站的资料，编者已尽可能全面地列于参考文献中，但恐有疏漏，敬请谅解，并向各位作者致敬、致谢！

本书可作为物流及相关专业本科生的专业英语教材，也可供物流专业的研究者及工程技术人员学习参考。

编　　者

Contents

Unit 1 ·· (1)
  Introduction to Logistics ·· (1)
  Logistics Management ·· (6)
Unit 2 ·· (11)
  Definition of Logistics Terms ·· (11)
  The Role of Material Flow Systems ·· (18)
Unit 3 ·· (23)
  Freight Transportation Planning and Logistics（Ⅰ）···················· (23)
  Freight Transportation Planning and Logistics（Ⅱ）···················· (28)
Unit 4 ·· (35)
  Transportation ··· (35)
  Jeddah Bestrides East West Route ·· (41)
Unit 5 ·· (45)
  Container Transportation ·· (45)
  Optimizing Container Transfers At Multimodal Terminals ·············· (52)
Unit 6 ·· (57)
  Inventory Management ··· (57)
  Approaches to Inventory Management ······································ (63)
Unit 7 ·· (68)
  Warehouse Design ·· (68)
  Warehousing management ·· (75)
Unit 8 ·· (81)
  Distribution Management ·· (81)
  Planning Physical Distribution ·· (91)
Unit 9 ·· (98)
  Materials Handling ··· (98)
  Automated Guided Vehicle（AGV）·· (104)
Unit 10 ·· (109)
  Packing, Marking and Shipment ·· (109)
  Contract and Confirmation ·· (115)
Unit 11 ·· (118)

Distribution Processing ·· (118)

Client-Server System ··· (123)

Unit 12 ·· (130)

Information Engineering ·· (130)

Management Information System ··· (136)

Unit 13 ·· (143)

Electronic Commerce Definitions ·· (143)

Appropriate Research Methods for Electronic Commerce ···································· (149)

Unit 14 ·· (155)

B2B: The Real World ··· (155)

B2C Security: Be Just Security Enough ·· (163)

Unit 15 ·· (172)

Supply Chain Management ··· (172)

The Evolution of Supply Chain Technologies ·· (179)

Unit 16 ·· (185)

Top 10 Supply Chain Technology Trends (I) ·· (185)

Top 10 Supply Chain Technology Trends (II) ·· (190)

Unit 17 ·· (196)

Enterprise Resource Planning (ERP) Systems ·· (196)

How to Implement ERP ·· (204)

Unit 18 ·· (213)

Material Resource Planning ··· (213)

A Preliminary Definition for MRP III ·· (222)

Unit 19 ·· (229)

Third-party Logistics ·· (229)

International Logistics ··· (235)

Unit 20 ·· (243)

Global Trade Drives 3PL Provider's Expansion (I) ··· (243)

Global Trade Drives 3PL Provider's Expansion (II) ·· (249)

Unit 21 ·· (254)

Green Logistics ··· (254)

The Green Paradoxes of Logistics in Transport Systems ······································ (259)

Unit 22 ·· (265)

Reverse Logistics ··· (265)

Reverse Logistics in theUrban Environment ·· (270)

Unit 23 ·· (275)

What is a 4PL(I) ··· (275)

VI

    What is a 4PL(Ⅱ) ·· (280)

Unit 24 ·· (286)

    The Introduction to RFID ·· (286)

    Benefits and Applications of RFID ·· (291)

Unit 25 ·· (296)

    Case Study 1-1　The Best Way to Measure a Supply Chain：At Lexmark，

    Cash is King ··· (296)

    Case Study 1-2　The Best Way to Measure a Supply Chain：At Lexmark，

    Cash is King ··· (302)

Unit 26 ·· (308)

    Case Study 2-1　HP Invents New Framework for Managing Supply

    Chain Risk ·· (308)

    Case Study 2-2　HP Invents New Framework for Managing Supply

    Chain Risk ·· (314)

Appendixes ··· (318)

    附录 A　汉英物流术语解释 ·· (318)

    附录 B　英汉物流术语解释 ·· (322)

    附录 C　汉英物流常用词汇 ·· (325)

    附录 D　英汉物流常用词汇 ·· (330)

    附录 E　物流常用缩略词和组合词 ·· (336)

References ·· (345)

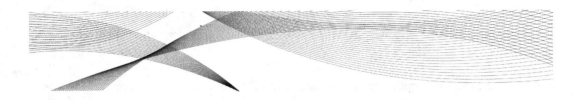

Unit 1

Passage A

Introduction to Logistics

1. Definition of Logistics

Logistics, the logistics center and its flow characteristics of materials, called logistics. Logistics originally formed in the United States Called "physical distribution (PD)","distribution in kind" or "goods delivery". Japan imported after the 1960s as "the link between the production and consumption of goods custodian, transportation, handling, packaging, processing functions and control such functions as a backup to the information role. It played a role as a bridge in sales material [1]. "

Logistics is a hot topic in China and the whole world. Although it is anything but a newborn baby, lots of people still have limited awareness of, and knowledge about logistics [2]-the subject matter of this textbook. People tend to refer logistics as the flow of goods, yes, it is partly right, but logistics is much more than that. So what logistics realty is?

When you look up the term "logistics", you might surprise to find out there are various definitions of different editions, each have slightly different meaning.

To avoid potential misunderstanding about the meaning of logistics this book adopts the current definition provided by the Council of Supply Chain Management Professionals (CSCMP) (known as "Council of logistics Management") — one of the world's most prominent organizations for logistics professionals[3].

According to CSCMP, logistics is the process of planning, implementing and controlling the efficient, effective flow and storage of goods, services and related

1

information from point of origin to point of consumption for the purpose of meeting customer requirements. It is quite a long definition, to understand it better, let's analyze it in closer details.

1.1 It is a process of "plan Implement and control"

First, logistics is a process of "plan, implement, and control". Of particular importance is the word "and", which suggest that logistics should be involved in all three activities planning, implementing, controlling — not just one or two. [4] Some suggest, however, that logistics is more involved in the implementation than in the planning of certain logistical policies.

1.2 Refer to "efficient and effective flow and storage"

Note that the definition also refers to "efficient and effective flow and storage". Broadly speaking, effectiveness can be thought of as "how well does a company do what they say they are going to do? " For example, if a company promises that all orders will be shipped within 24 hours of receipt, what percentage of orders are actually shipped within 24 hours of receipt? In contrast, efficiency can be thought of as how well (or poorly) company resources are used to achieve what a company promised it can do.

1.3 Involves "goods, services, and related information"

The definition also indicates that logistics involves the flow and storage of "goods, services, and related information". Indeed, in the contemporary business environment, logistics is as much about the flow and storage of information as it is about the flow and storage of goods. Advances in information technology make it increasingly easy — and less costly — for companies to obtain important information to make logistical decision.

1.4 Purpose of logistics is to meet customer requirements

Finally, the definition indicates that the purpose of logistics is to meet customer requirements. This implies that logistics strategies and plans should be based upon customer wants and needs. Therefore, management must first find out what those wants and needs are, and to meet their requirement.

Logistics starts with the provision of raw materials and semi-finished goods for the manufacturing process, and finishes up with the physical distribution and after sales service of the products.

Economically, this creates a new source of profit characterized by the development of mass distribution and attention to service quality. The two basis objectives in practicing business logistics, cost reduction and time saving have enabled companies to profit not only in performance and quality but also in customer satisfaction.

Operationally, companies realize that by regrouping the different aspects of logistics and instead of viewing them as separate processes, substantial savings can be made within their business' outgoing expenditure.

In a more practical sense, logistics refers to the systematic management of the various activities required to move benefits from their point of production to the customer. Often these benefits are in the form of a tangible product that must be manufactured and moved to the user; sometimes these benefits are intangible and are known as services. They too must be produced and made available to the final consumer. But logistics encompasses much more than just the transport of goods.

The concept of benefits is a multifaceted one that goes beyond the product or service itself to include issues regarding timing, quantity, supporting services, location, and cost. So a basic definition of logistics is the continuous process of meeting customer needs by ensuring the availability of the right benefits for the right customer. In the quantity and condition desired by that customer, at the time and place the customer wants them, all for a price the buyer is willing to pay. These concepts apply equally well to profit industries and non-profit organizations, as the earlier discussion on military requirements illustrated.

New Words and Expressions

1. logistics [lə'dʒistiks] *n.* 物流学,后勤学
2. tend to *vt.* 倾向于(有助于,易于,引起,造成,势必)
3. refer[ri'fə:]*vt.* 提交,谈及,归于,指点,把……提交;*vi.* 提到,涉及,查阅,咨询
4. adopt [ə'dɔpt]*vt.* 采用,收养,接受
5. various['vɛəriəs]*adj.* 不同的,各种各样的,多方面的,多样的
6. potential [pə'tenʃ(ə)l]*adj.* 潜在的,可能的;*n.* 潜能,潜力
7. council['kaunsil]*n.* 理事会,委员会,参议会,讨论会议,顾问班子,立法班子
8. prominent['prɔminənt] *adj.* 卓越的,显著的,突出的
9. implement['implimənt] *vt.* 贯彻,实现;*v.* 执行
10. consumption [kən'sʌmpʃən]*n.* 消费,消费(量)
11. involve [in'vɔlv]*vt.* 包括,笼罩,潜心于,使陷于
12. receipt[ri'si:t]*n.* 收条,收据,收到;*v.* 收到

13. indicate[ˈindikeit]*vt.* 指出，显示，象征

14. reception[riˈsepʃən]*n.* 接待，招待会，接收

Notes

1. Japan imported after the 1960s as "the link between the production and consumption of goods custodian, transportation, handling, packaging, processing functions and control such functions as a backup to the information role. It played a role as a bridge in sales material. "

在 20 世纪 60 年代后，日本引入了这样的概念，即：物流是实现产品和消费品之间的管理、运输、装卸搬运、包装等联系的过程，并且作为一种信息角色的支持来控制这类功能。在销售物料中它扮演桥梁角色。

2. Logistics is a hot topic in China and the whole world. Although it is anything but a newborn baby, lots of people still have limited awareness of, and knowledge about logistics.

物流是一个中国乃至全世界的热门话题。虽然它已经不是一个新生事物了。但是不少人对物流的认识仍然有限。

be aware of something:意识到

Example：John has been aware of having done something wrong. 约翰已意识到自己做错了事情。

3. To avoid potential misunderstanding about the meaning of logistics, this book adopts the current definition provided by the Council of Supply Chain Management Professionals (CSCMP)—one of the world's most prominent organizations for logistics professionals.

为了避免可能发生的对物流含义的误解，本书采用美国供应链管理专业协会（前身为美国物流管理协会）目前的定义，该协会是全世界物流专业领城中最著名的组织。

to avoid something(doing something)避免，避开

Example：She tried to avoid answering my questions. 她试图避而不答我的问题。

4. First, logistics is a process of "plan, implement, and control". Of particular importance is the word "and", which suggests that logistics should be involved in all three activities, planning, implementing, controlling—not just one or two.

首先，物流是"计划，执行与控制"。特别重要的是这个"与"字，它指出物流应该包括所有这三方面——计划，执行和控制——而不仅仅是其中一个或两个方面。

Topics for Discussion

1. Is logistics a new concept? If it is not, do you know anything about the origin and history of logistics? Please share the information you have with your group member.

2. How much do you know about the literal meaning of logistics?

3. Why do the advances in information technology make it increasingly easy—and less costly-for companies to obtain important information to make logistical decision?

Passage B

Logistics Management

1. New Logistics Management Paradigm

Logistics, as defined by the Council of Logistics Management, "is that part of the supply chain process that plans, implements and controls the efficient, effective flow and storage of goods, services and related information from the point of origin to the point of consumption in order to meet customers' requirements." To make this happen, transportation, distribution, warehousing, purchasing and order management organizations must execute together. This is no small task, especially in an environment that is becoming increasingly demanding, with customers expecting their products to be delivered as quickly as possible and according to their exact specifications.

Most experts talk about inventory and shipment visibility as the key to successful logistics execution. But, when asked to define visibility, those same experts give a fancy response that in plain English means knowing the status of "in-transit' shipments or inventory. Unfortunately, the reality is that knowing the status of something once it is already in-transit adds no value to the supply chain.

What many companies fail to realize and understand is that there are four conditions that are changing the way companies are thinking about visibility and the logistics operation as they struggle to meet the ever-increasing customer demands:

The Internet B2B Economy: A dramatic transformation in the use of the Internet for business transactions between companies.

Reverse Logistics: The management of returned products to distributors, manufacturers or retailers.

Real-time Logistics Event Management: The need for accurate and timely management of information in order to maintain on-time deliveries, reduce inventory levels and ensure that the right product is in the right place at the right time[1].

Technology Solutions Provide Visibility: New logistics event management technologies to gain real-time visibility into logistics operations; ensure a more accurate, efficient and effective flow of goods; reduce costs and increase customer satisfaction.

The four conditions outlined above have significantly changed the role and expectations of the logistician. Companies must radically adapt their logistics management strategy in order to compete in today's tumultuous marketplace, marked with ever-decreasing tumultuous times, increased competition and lower profit margins. This article focuses primarily on how these conditions are affecting logistics today, with a particular emphasis on the new technologies that are improving the flow of goods. There are numerous companies in the marketplace that offer technology solutions claiming real-time visibility into inventory levels and logistics; unfortunately, what most offer does not match up with what businesses really need to improve costs and customer satisfaction.

2. The Internet B2B Economy

There has been explosive growth in business-to-business (B2B) transactions via the Internet. According to Forrester Research, the B2B e-Commerce segment of the economy will grow to $2.7 trillion by the year 2004. AMR is even more optimistic, predicting that the market will reach $5.7 trillion during the same time period. Forrester predicts that as much as 20 percent of all transportation transactions will take place over the Internet by 2004. With this dramatic growth in Internet-based transactions, "E-logistics" has created new categories of logistics management providers including:

(1) Fourth Party Logistics (4PL) firms

Organizations that manage the full scope of logistics services for companies by aggregating and coordinating are the services of multiple logistics service providers.

(2) Logistics Exchanges (LX)

Internet-based marketplaces for the buying and selling of logistics services, management of logistics content, and the optimization of logistics activities.

(3) Logistics Visibility Providers (LVP)

Internet-based service providers that capture data from logistics service providers; cleanse, verify and analyze the data; and report on logistics activities to facilitate total supply chain visibility.

All of these providers rely on the Internet in some way to provide a service to a business organization. However, it is difficult to determine who participates in which category and who really delivers the functions they promise.

3. Reverse Logistics

Typically, a fifth of all purchased items are returned to the manufacturer, distributor or retailer in a process that can shed up to 85 percent off of their original retail value. In the year 2000, the total value of returned merchandise was estimated at $60 billion by IDC, while the cost of handling returns stood at $40 billion. With such a high price tag, companies must decide if managing product returns is part of their core competency. It was presented that the top five reasons for electronically-generated orders not meeting customer expectations are:

(1) Late delivery;

(2) Wrong product/quantity;

(3) Not shipped at all;

(4) Technical problems;

(5) Returns.

4. Real-time Logistics Event Management

Typical benefits from integrating the supply chain range from 28 percent to 60 percent improvement in delivery performance and inventory reduction, to 10 to 30 percent improvement in capacity realization and fill rates. Therefore, the potential money savings from real-time logistics visibility is staggering[2].

The combination of supply chain complexity and market conditions puts even more pressure on manufacturers to provide the right amount of products, at the right time, for the lowest possible price. A few factors have made this increasingly difficult. There have been many recent inventory debacles as a result of the inability of ERP systems to properly forecast demand and prevent inventory build-up. In addition, the lead times for producing products has shrunk dramatically. And finally, most organizations now outsource manufacturing of components to third-party organizations. Our current connected economy has drastically changed the role and operations of transportation. As a result, the logistics management departments must try to perform transportation "miracles" on a daily basis in order to meet these monumental goals. Transportation professionals can meet most of these demands, but at what cost? Every dollar spent at this point is a decrease in net profitability. That is a significant concern for companies. It becomes an even bigger concern if what was shipped was shipped out incorrectly and has to be returned or routed differently.

In this collaborative economy, enterprises have to acknowledge the increased role of transportation management and how to use technology to their best advantage. Table 1.1 compares "old school" logistics with the logistics of today.

Table 1.1 Comparison of "old school" logistics and logistics today

	"Old School" Logistics	Logistics Today
Orders：	Predictable Variable	Small Lots
Order Cycle Time：	Weekly	Short OTD/Daily or Hourly
Customer：	Strategic	Broader Base
Customer Service：	Reactive，Rigid	Responsive，Flexible
Replenishment：	Scheduled	Real-time
Distribution Model：	Supply-driven（Push）	Demand-driven（Pull）
Demand：	Stable，Consistent	More Cyclical
Shipment Type：	Bulk	Smaller Lots
Destinations：	Concentrated	Geographically Dispersed
Warehouse Reconfiguration：	Weekly/Monthly	Continual，Rules-based
International Trade Compliance：	Manual	Automated

One additional aspect of logistics that needs to be covered is that of in-transit inventory. If managed properly, in-transit inventory can reduce customer lead times and distribution network costs. The downside is, without appropriate technology and integration into TMS or OMS, The result is that the customer gets what they ordered, but at a significant cost to the enterprise. There is technology that exists today to manage customer requirements before the product is shipped. In logistics management, from the raw materials procurement to the customer destination, value or cost is added along the way. To correct a deviation from the original customer requirements as it approaches its destination is a very costly proposition not only in terms of dollars but in terms of time. There is a solution. It is real-time logistics event management using some of the leading edge technology solutions available today.

New Words and Expressions

1. council[ˈkaunsl]*n.* 政务会，理事会，委员会
2. execution [ˌeksiˈkjuːʃən]*n.* 实行，实施；执[履]行，完成
3. maintain [menˈtein]*vt.* 保持；维持；继续
4. outline[ˈautlain]*n.* 轮廓，外形
5. primarily[ˈpraimərili]*adv.* 最初，首先；原来
6. optimistic [ɔptiˈmistik]*adj.* 乐观的；有信心的
7. trillion[ˈtriljən]*n.* [美、法]万亿，兆；[英、德]百亿亿，百万兆；大量

8. verify['verifai]*vt.* 证实；查证，鉴定，验证

9. manufacturer [ˌmænjuˈfæktʃərə]*n.* 制造商，厂主；

10. technical['teknikəl]*adj.* 工艺[业，程]的，技术[能]的

11. complexity [kəmˈpleksiti]*n.* 复杂(性，度)，错综，复合状态

12. dramatically [drəˈmætikəli]*adv.* 戏剧地，引人注目地

13. profitability [ˌprɔfitəˈbiliti]*n.* 盈利能力，获利能力，有利性

Notes

1. Real-time Logistics Event Management：The need for accurate and timely management of Information in order to maintain on-time deliveries，reduce inventory levels and ensure that the right product is in the right place at the right time.

实时物流事件管理：对精确的信息和及时管理的需求以便维持准时交货、降低库存水平和确保正确的货物按时按地送到。

2. Typical benefits from integrating the supply chain range from 28 percent to 60 percent improvement in delivery performance and inventory reduction，to 10 percent to 30 percent improvement in capacity realization and fill rates. Therefore，the potential money savings from real-time logistics visibility is staggering.

整合供应链的典型好处包括递送速度增加 28%～60%、库存减少 28%～60%、仓库利用率增加 10%～30%，仓库补库率提高 10%～30%。因此，从实时物流可见性获得的潜在节约额是令人惊奇的。

Topics for Discussion

1. What are the four conditions that are changing the way companies are thinking about visibility and the logistics operation as they struggle to meet the ever-increasing customer demands?

2. What are the new categories of logistics management created by "E-logistics"?

3. What are the factors which make the management of real-time logistics event difficult?

4. What can be improved or eliminated by eliminating discrepancies between purchase order，sales order and shipping information?

5. Explain the process by which the technology helps enhance event management visibility.

6. What capabilities with which advanced technology will arm the logistician?

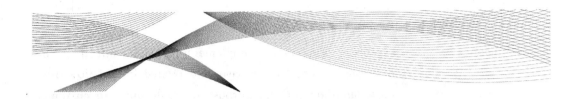

Unit 2

Passage A

Definition of Logistics Terms

Basically, Logistics means having the right thing, at the right place, at the right time.

1. What is logistics

Here are some definitions of logistics.

• **Logistics** — (*business definition*) Logistics is defined as a business planning framework for the management of material, service, information and capital flows. [1] It includes the increasingly complex information, communication and control systems required in today's business environment. — (Logistics Partners OY, Helsinki, FI, 1996)

• **Logistics** — (*military definition*) The science of planning and carrying out the movement and maintenance of forces... those aspects of military operations that deal with the design and development, acquisition, storage, movement, distribution, maintenance, evacuation and disposition of material; movement, evacuation, and hospitalization of personnel; acquisition of construction, maintenance, operation and disposition of facilities; and acquisition of furnishing of services. [2] — (JCS Pub 1-02 excerpt)

• **Logistics** — The procurement, maintenance, distribution, and replacement of personnel and materiel. — (Webster Dictionary)

• **Logistics** — The branch of military operations that deals with the procurement, distribution, maintenance, and replacement of materiel and personnel.

2. The management of the details of an operation.

- **Logistics** — ... the process of planning, implementing, and controlling the efficient, effective flow and storage of goods, services, and related information from point of origin to point of consumption for the purpose of conforming to customer requirements.[3] Note that this definition includes inbound, outbound, internal, and external movements, and return of materials for environmental purposes. — (Reference: Council of Logistics Management, http://www.clml.org/mission.html, 12 Feb 98)

- **Logistics** — The process of planning, implementing, and controlling the efficient, cost effective flow and storage of raw materials, in-process inventory, finished goods and related information from point of origin to point of consumption for the purpose of meeting customer requirements. — (Reference: Canadian Association of Logistics Management, http://www.calm.org/calm/AboutCALM/AboutCALM.html, 12 Feb, 1998)

- **Logistics** — The science of planning, organizing and managing activities that provide goods or services. — (MDC, Log Link / Logistics World, 1997)

- **Logistics**—Logistics is the science of planning and implementing the acquisition and use of the resources necessary to sustain the operation of a system. — (Reference: ECRC University of Scranton / Defense Logistics Agency Included with permission from: HUM — The Government Computer Magazine "Integrated Logistics" December 1993, Walter Cooke, Included with permission from: HUM — The Government Computer Magazine.)

- **Logistics Functions** — (*classical*) Planning, procurement, transportation, supply, and maintenance. — (United States Department of Defense DOD)

- **Logistics Processes** — (*classical*) Requirements determination, acquisition, distribution, and conservation. — (United States Department of Defense DOD)

- **Business Logistics** — The science of planning, design, and support of business operations of procurement, purchasing, inventory, warehousing, distribution, transportation, customer support, financial and human resources. — (MDC, Log Link / Logistics World, 1997)

- **Cradle-to-Grave** — Logistics planning, design, and support which take in to account logistics support throughout the entire system or product life cycle. — (MDC, Log Link/Logistics World, 1997)

- **Acquisition Logistics** — Acquisition Logistics is everything involved in acquiring logistics support equipment and personnel for a new weapons system. The formal

12

definition is "the process of systematically identifying, defining, designing, developing, producing, acquiring, delivering, installing, and upgrading logistics support capability requirements through the acquisition process for Air Force systems, subsystems, and equipment."

- **Integrated Logistics Support (ILS) (1)** — ILS is a management function that provides planning, funding, and functioning controls which help to assure that the system meets performance requirements, is developed at a reasonable price, and can be supported throughout its life cycle. (Reference: Air Force Institute of Technology, Graduate School of Acquisition and Logistics.)
- **Integrated Logistics Support (ILS) (2)** — Encompasses the unified management of the technical logistics elements that plan and develop the support requirements for a system. This can include hardware, software, and the provisioning of training and maintenance resources.
- **Logistics Support Analysis (LSA)** — Simply put, LSA is the iterative process of identifying support requirements for a new system, especially in the early stages of system design. The main goals of LSA are to ensure that the system will perform as intended and to influence the design for supportability and affordability.

3. Definition of Terms

Material flow is the linking of all processes for the acquiring, processing, matching and distribution of material goods within defined areas.

An important aspect of the definition of the term is its limitation to material goods, therefore excluding the transport of energy or of information. However, material goods are not restricted solely to materials forming part of the production process, i. e. raw materials, semi-finished and finished products, but also other materials such as, for instance, waste, pallets and packaging. [4]

Roughly speaking, differentiation is made in material flow between handling, conveying and transporting.

- **Handling** — Handling refers to all motion sequences used for the starting or ending of production processes and also of transporting and storage. This includes, for instance, the insertion of a work piece in a work piece retainer or the stacking of work pieces at a storage place. Handling therefore includes all material flow processes taking place at a workstation.
- **Conveying** — Conveying is the movement in horizontal or vertical direction via limited distances and is therefore generally restricted to in-plant processes. Examples

13

are: The supply of screws by means of a vibratory bowl feeder and the transporting of vehicle bodies by means of overhead conveyors.

• **Continuous conveyor** — These examples immediately highlight an important difference: in the first example, a continuous conveyor is used. Continuous conveyors operate continuously (at least over an extended time period). The second example involves an intermittent-flow conveyor. Each cabin of the overhead conveyor has its own timetable, to which it operates, with alternating travel operation, empty running and stops.

• **Steady-flow** — conveyors are generally more economical to operate than intermittent-flow conveyors. Being of identical dead weight, these have greater conveyor capacity whilst requiring less drive power. [5] This is partly due to the continuous operating mode, thereby eliminating the continuous starting and decelerating of the drive, handling equipment and material to be conveyed.

On the other hand, intermittent-flow conveyors are frequently more flexible in application. As shown by the example, these are predominantly used for heavy individual loads.

Conveyors often have yet a secondary function resulting from the dwell time of the material being conveyed. For example, in the case of a refrigerated conveyor, parts cool down to a point where they reach the temperature required for further processing. Conveyors are also used as buffers in order to harmonize the working cycle of several processing stations.

• **Transporting** — The term "transporting" describes the movement of goods across larger, generally horizontal distances. Transporting takes place on roads rail and more rarely on waterways. As such, transport mainly involves external, non-operational movement. Owing to its nature, transport is intermittent, since the use of vehicles is necessary for transporting.

• **Material to be conveyed** — Differentiation is made between material to be conveyed in so far as this has a significant effect on the method of conveying or transporting. [6]

• **Bulk materials** — Bulk material constitutes a load consisting of a large number of small items, and also plastics granular material or sand. Bulk materials always require an enclosing container although, occasionally, it is possible to convey these in pipelines, similar to fluids.

• **Fluid materials** — Fluid materials are generally transported in silo containers. However, to meet internal conveying requirements, pipelines are used.

14

• **Packaged goods** — Packaged goods are unit loads which can be established according to the number of items. Bulk materials may also be treated as packaged goods, if these are packed in boxes or sacks.

4. Analysis of material flow

The terms handling, conveying and transporting are contrasted in different stages of material flow. The first stage of material flow includes transport between the factory and its suppliers or customers. This stage of material flow involves location planning, which does not form part of MPS training and is therefore not discussed here. The second stage of material flow includes movement within the factory site between the various sectors of the operation, e. g. factory building. Factory planning again takes into account material flow and evolves an appropriate building plan. Again, this stage of material flow will not be dealt with at this point. The third stage of material flow includes the movement between the individual departments of an operational area and, within the departments, the movements between the various workstations, machine groups and storage areas, etc. This stage can be dealt with as part of MPS. The fourth stage of material flow involves movement on the workstation itself. This stage deals primarily with handling equipment for the automation of material flow on the workstation. This represents a major aspect of MPS.

In order to determine the optimum layout of equipment and the respective handling equipment involved, plus the possibly required storage and buffer stores, it is necessary to establish the material flow. The first step towards this involves the structure of the material flow.

New Words and Expressions

1. framework['freimwə:k]*n*. 构架,结构,组织
2. capital['kæpitəl]*n*. 资金
3. acquisition [,ækwi'ziʃən]*n*. 获得,获得物
4. evacuation [i,vækju'eiʃən]*n*. 撤退,走开
5. disposition [dispə'ziʃən]*n*. 部署
6. procurement [prə'kjuəmənt]*n*. 获得,取得
7. implement['implimənt]*vt*. 实现协议,诺言;履行
8. inbound['inbaund]*adj*. 内地的,归航的
9. outbound['autbaund]*adj*. 开往外地的,开往外国的

10. pertain [pə(ː)'tein]v. 适合，属于

11. encompass [in'kʌmpəs]v. 包围，环绕，包含或包括某事物

12. provision [prə'viʒn]vt. 供给食品及必需品

13. iterative['itərətiv]adj. 重复的，反复的

14. supportability [sə,pɔ:tə'biliti]n. 可支持，可忍受，可忍耐

15. affordability n. 供给能力

16. exclude [iks'klu:d]vt. 拒绝接纳，把……排除在外，排斥

17. solely['səu(1)li]adv. 独自地，单独地，唯一，只有

18. raw material 原材料

19. semi-finished adj. 半成品的

20. vibratory['vaibrətəri]adj. 振动的，振动性的

21. intermittent [,intə(ː)'mitənt]adj. 间歇的，断断续续的

22. steady['stedi]adj. 稳固的，稳定的，坚定的，扎实的，坚定不移的

23. dead weight 死沉沉的重物

24. decelerate [di:'seləreit]vt. & vi. 减速

25. dwelltime n. 停留时间

26. buffer['bʌfə]n. 缓冲器

27. harmonize['hɑ:mənaiz]vt. & vi. 调和，协调

28. differentiation [,difə,renʃi'eiʃən]n. 区别

29. rivet['rivit]n. 铆钉；v. 固定

30. granular['grænjulə]adj. 由小粒而成的，粒状的

31. sack [sæk]n. 大袋，大袋之量，麻布袋，短而松的袍装，布袋装，洗劫

32. optimum['ɔptiməm]n. 最适宜；adj. 最适宜的

33. layout['lei,aut]n. 规划，设计，（书刊等）编排，版面，配线，企划，设计图案，（工厂等的）布局图，版面设计

Notes

1. Logistics is defined as a business planning framework for the management of material, service, information and capital flows.

物流的定义是：管理物质流、服务流、信息流和资金流的商业计划构架。

2. those aspects of military operations that deal with the design and development, acquisition, storage, movement, distribution, maintenance, evacuation and disposition of material; movement, evacuation, and hospitalization of personnel; acquisition of construction, maintenance, operation and disposition of facilities; and acquisition of

furnishing of services.

军事行动的方面是处理物质的设计、发展、获得、储存、运送、传播、维修、撤退和部署；人员的活动、撤退及医疗服务；设备的安装、维修、操作和部署；以及配备服务。

3. ... the process of planning, implementing, and controlling the efficient, effective flowand storage of goods, services, and related information from point of origin to point of consumption for the purpose of conforming to customer requirements.

按照客户的要求计划、履行、控制从开始生产到消费环节的货物、服务和相关信息的有效快捷的流动和储存。

4. However, material goods are not restricted solely to materials forming part of the production process, i. e. raw materials, semi-finished and finished products, but also other materials such as, for instance, waste, pallets and packaging.

不过，物品不仅仅局限于形成生产过程的物质，即原材料、半成品、成品，还包括如废料、托盘及包裹之类的其他物质。

5. Being of identical dead weight, these have greater conveyor capacity whilst requiring less drive power.

在相同的自重下，这些输送机(恒定速度的输送机)拥有更大的输送能力而所需驱动力更小。

6. Differentiation is made between material to be conveyed in so far as this has a significant effect on the method of conveying or transporting.

对所输送材料的区分，应根据其对输送运输方式的重要影响而进行。(注：材料的物理性质对其所采用的运输传送方式有着重要影响。)

Topics for Discussion

1. What's your opinion of the integrated logistics? Please share the information you have with your group member.

2. In the text, how many parts can be included in the field of logistics? Do you know some other parts that not been mentioned above?

3. "Logistics means having the right thing, at the right place, at the right time." Could you give us your understanding about it?

4. What's the main goal of ILS and LSA?

5. What equipment is connected with what other equipment?

6. In what order is the equipment started?

7. What is the difference made in material flow between handling, conveying and transporting according to the text?

Passage B

The Role of Material Flow Systems

The objective of the industrial firm may be stated as the effective coordination of men, materials, machines and money to provide a product or service when and where needed at a price attractive to the customer, which will provide a profit to the firm and serve society [1]. In a product (as opposed to service) enterprise the satisfaction of this objective is largely accomplished by conversion of the form or shape of materials and the relocation or movement of these materials [2]. Men and machines are allocated to accomplish this conversion and movement. The requirements for monies result from decisions related to accomplishing the allocation of these other resources as well as the procurement and distribution of materials. Profits are directly related to the control of costs and costs, in the sense above, are to a large degree dependent upon the control of materials conversion and location. To control materials conversion requires control of material quantity at each stage of the conversion. If quantity and location are to be controlled most effectively, timely and accurate information must be available upon which to base the control decisions [3]. It is the interrelationship between material quantities at the various stages of conversion, the location and movement of these materials, and the information necessary for decisions related to conversion and location that is referred to as the material flow system.

The effectiveness of the production enterprise in the above context is largely, if not totally, related to the organization's ability to control quantity and location of materials. In turn, the potential effectiveness of this control is to a high degree dependent upon the quality of the decision information available to the decision maker at the time a quantity or location decision must be made [4]. A little reflection on the basic or primary objectives of various functional units of the organization will verify the above statement. Purchasing is concerned with procurement of materials and vender relations, inventory control with time and quantity schedules and accountability for materials, stores and warehousing for physical control, production control with quantity and location during processing, sales with customer satisfaction with material quality and time of material delivery, and physical distribution with satisfaction of the customer at minimum cost to the firm. Each function is restricted in satisfying its objectives by the ability to have accurate information available to secure effective movement of the

18

materials. These requirements for information and movement will not be totally under any single function's control but rather interlaced across facets of many functions. It may be concluded therefore, that to improve the effectiveness of the functional units, singularly and jointly, it is necessary to establish an integration of,

(1) materials: quantity control at all stages of conversion and distribution

(2) materials: movement to provide quantity allocations at desired locations, and

(3) information: necessary to arrive at proper decisions to maximize the effectiveness of quantity control and materials movement.

It is therefore necessary for the material flow system to provide means to improve the effectiveness of this integration.

The question might be raised, "So what's new?" The newness is in the integration of quantity control, material movement, and information processing as a single system, rather than three somewhat autonomous subsystems. Organizationally it is usually possible to identify a material handling function (movement) and a data processing function (information), which, although they may service the entire firm, nevertheless they have their individual identity and set of objectives. Quantity control is not this well identified functionally. True there is usually an inventory control or materials control group but too often their concern is restricted to stock levels planning and stock maintenance for process input materials. Procurement of quantities to satisfy these stock levels is a purchasing responsibility. In-process inventories are then controlled and assigned by production control or manufacturing. Warehouse material inventories and in transit shipments are controlled by groups reporting to purchasing or sales. The result is that the firm does not have a single materials quantity control subsystem but a set of subsystems, which may or may not be adequately coordinated. If coordinated, the coordination is likely to be accomplished by means of a computer information system which may have been designed by a data processing systems group concerned with data processing efficiency and not information in a form, and at a time of maximum value to the using function.

The recognition of the need to develop a computer based total information system implies recognition of the need for more effective material flow control. Difficulty in reaching full effectiveness arises due to:

(1) The imposition of the data system upon the existing organization and control system without changing the basic operating procedures, or

(2) The imposition of a generalized data system which conceptually appears adequate but does not give adequate consideration to the firm's operating environment and existing practices with their related effect on input data[5].

The first type installation fails because the existing organization's functional relationships, procedures, and communications are not compatible to necessary information system functional relationships for effective or efficient data processing. The second type of installation fails because of the failure to recognize that each firm has its own peculiar operational constraints and a good general concept must be altered to fit these peculiarities. The results to be attained are only as good as the information system and the information system is only as good as its input. The failure to recognize and adjust for either operation or data processing system constraints negates an effective system.

If the information system is only as good as its input it is important that the input be both accurate and timely. Furthermore, if the necessary information for decision and action is primarily related to material, or allocation of other resources to act on materials, the input must reflect completed action on material and its affect on desired results for the future. Decision is then concerned with getting from the present (completed) to the future in the most effective manner.

Disregarding for a moment the problem of accomplishing input, consider the required content of input. There are only four bits of knowledge or data required to fully define material flow information:

(1) Event—or what occurred to the individual material control unit.

(2) Quantity—of material in the control unit for which the event occurred.

(3) Time—at which the event occurred.

(4) Location—at which the event occurred.

Following procurement the events related to material can generally be classified as operation on, movement, or storage. Although quantity must be known in-process control is usually by a batch which should be identifiable from all other batches of similar material. This batch identity is often accomplished by lot number, production order number, or similar identity.

Having these four bits of information, evaluation of performance against prior plans and projection of data for future planning decisions can be accomplished. The failure to either provide the necessary bits of information, or errors or inadequacies in interpretation of results, increases requirements for men and facility resources in order to reduce the effect of these errors or inadequacies. Operational crisis then arise more frequently and management by exception becomes difficult since exceptions or deviations from plan is the rule. For example if location data is in error extra, manpower must be provided to search. In addition extra in-process inventory is usually generated which demands additional facilities as well as manpower.

The more effectively one can plan the flow of material, identify and measure the actual flow relative to plan, and reduce the frequency with which exceptions occur, the more effective is the entire business process. One cannot expect to eliminate problems of, or deviation from, plan but they can be reduced.

New Words and Expressions

1. coordination [kəuˌɔːdiˈneiʃən]n. 同等,调和
2. enterprise[ˈentəpraiz]n. 企业,事业,计划,事业心,进取心,干事业
3. procurement [prəˈkjuəmənt]n. 获得,得到
4. to a large degree 在很大程度上
5. interrelationship n. 相互关系[联系,影响],干扰
6. vender[ˈvendə]n. 卖主,售卖者
7. interlace [ˌintə(ː)ˈleis]v. 使交织,使交错;交错,交织
8. autonomous [ɔːˈtɔnəməs]adj.自治的
9. subsystem[ˈsʌbˌsistim]n. 次要系统,子系统
10. coordinate [kəuˈɔːdinit]n. 同等者;adj. 同等的,并列的;v. 调整,整理
11. imposition [ˌimpəˈziʃən] n. 强迫接受
12. generalized [ˈdenərəlaizd]adj.无显著特点的,不能适应特殊环境的
13. constraint [kənˈstreint] n. 约束,强制,局促
14. peculiar [piˈkjuːljə]adj.奇特的,罕见的,特殊的;n. 特有财产,特权
15. disregard [ˌdisriˈgɑːd] v. 不理,漠视;n. 漠视,忽视
16. projection [prəˈdʒekʃən] n. 发射
17. manpower[ˈmænpauə]n. 人力
18. deviation [ˌdiːviˈeiʃən]n. 背离

Notes

1. The objective of the industrial firm may be stated as the effective coordination of men, materials, machines and money to provide a product or service when and where needed at a price attractive to the customer, which will provide a profit to the firm and serve society.

工业公司的目标可以解释为人力、材料、设备和资金的有效整合,以便在合适的时间、地点(适时适地的)为用户提供具有价格优势的产品或服务,使公司盈利,为社会造福。

2. In a product (as opposed to service) enterprise the satisfaction of this objective

islargely accomplished by conversion of the form or shape of materials and the relocation or movement of these materials.

相对于服务业而言,生产企业目标的满足,很大程度上取决于材料形式或形状的转变及其位置的移动与改变。

3. If quantity and location are to be controlled most effectively, timely and accurate information must be available upon which to base the control decisions.

要使数量和场所得到有效、及时、准确的控制,就需要有及时而准确的信息,这种信息是做出控制决策的基础。

4. In turn, the potential effectiveness of this control is to a high degree dependent upon the quality of the decision information available to the decision maker at the time a quantity or location decision must be made.

反之,在必须对数量和场所加以确定时,决策者所依据的关键信息可靠与否,就在很大程度上决定了这种控制的潜在效力。

5. The imposition of a generalized data system which conceptually appears adequate but does not give adequate consideration to the firm's operating environment and existing practices with their related effect on input data.

强制推行一种不适应环境的数据系统,这种系统看上去很合理但并没有充分考虑企业的操作环境和有关的现状。

Topics for Discussion

1. After reading the materials above, what is the objective of material flow system?

2. In order to improve the effectiveness of the functional units singularly and jointly, what kind of integration will it be necessary to establish?

3. What should be the basis of controlling quantity and location more efficiently?

4. Is it necessary for the material flow system to provide means to improve the effectiveness of this integration?

5. What's the main role of material flow function? Please discuss it with your partner.

6. What's the difficulty in reaching full effectiveness?

7. What will increase the requirements for manpower and facility resources in order to reduce the effect of these errors or inadequacies?

8. What are the bits of knowledge or data required to fully define material flow information?

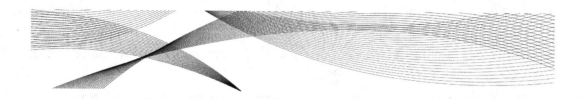

Unit 3

Passage A

Freight Transportation Planning and Logistics (I)

A well-functioning freight transportation system is an essential element in any successful economy. However, at the beginning of the new millennium, the prediction is that the demand for goods movement will outstrip the rate of improvements to the physical infrastructure. Marked growth in time-sensitive freight markets will tax demands on a system that already is operating near capacity in some areas.

Key issues and challenges that will affect freight planning and logistics in the future include the following:

(1) The demands for freight transportation and logistics services, and the ability of the physical and information infrastructure to meet these demands;

(2) The role of road pricing in urban freight transportation;

(3) The impact of information technology on goods movement; and

(4) New developments in logistics management.

1. Supply, Demand, and Pricing

In the new millennium, the freight transportation system will face challenges that will require the development of new paradigms of operations and planning. This situation will result from a combination of factors.

Firstly, domestic and international freight demand will continue to grow. Domestically, the consumption of goods will increase as new segments of the population enjoy more effective income. Internationally, the incorporation of the former socialist republics into the world trade system and the expansion of economic activities in developing countries will significantly augment the flow of goods and merchandise. Concurrently, pressure for enhanced economic competitiveness — a consequence of the economic unification of Europe and the resurgence of the Asian economies — will increase.

New freight-transport systems must be responsive to user needs and expectations. The trends in service differentiation that have characterized the late 1990s will shape the freight systems in the next century. Consumers will demand more control of the nature of the service they receive[1]. This trend will be accentuated by the availability of information systems and technologies that enable users to specify the kinds of service they require and to integrate their operations effectively with the freight transportation system.

In addition, freight planners will have to deal with significant constraints. Additional infrastructure will be increasingly difficult to obtain and possibly undesirable in some *Transportation in the New Millennium* 2 communities; therefore, more efficient use of existing infrastructure and careful development of new capacity will become increasingly important. Examples of this trend include the implementation of intelligent transportation systems (ITS) to manage traffic flow, the development of the Alameda Corridor in California, and assessments under way in the New York — New Jersey area for developing exclusive truck routes linking intermodal facilities, new maritime terminals, and a new rail freight tunnel.

2. Road Pricing

Differential road pricing — that is, using different toll rates for different classes of vehicles at different times of the day to manage traffic and reduce congestion — is being assessed in some metropolitan areas, and its role is likely to increase [2]. However, the demand — driven nature of freight movement today — customers can specify the precise time when freight is to be delivered — may make congestion pricing for freight less effective. Any implementation of road pricing must consider the impact on certain industry and commodity clusters. Some businesses must receive their goods during peak periods for reasons that include production schedules, community curfews, security, and labor considerations.

Finding appropriate solutions to these challenges will require new paradigms for cooperation between private industry and government. These new paradigms should revolve around three issues:

(1) Using public funds to finance freight infrastructure projects that would benefit

24

private industry,

(2) Incorporating private industry input into the planning process, and

(3) Streamlining of the environmental approval process and the resolution of disputes between regulatory agencies and the freight industry.

Freight issues must be elevated to a level commensurate with their importance in the transportation planning process. From an institutional standpoint, one of the major challenges will be to implement a planning process for freight transportation that is both responsive to and flexible enough to accommodate the needs and expectations of the different stakeholders. This goal must be accomplished while transforming the planning agencies into truly multimodal agencies. Public awareness of the importance of freight movement also must be improved. It should not take a crisis—for example, a strike by a major freight provider, threatened terminal closures, or freight traffic diversions that result from delays in port dredging—to make the public recognize the value of reliable freight service [3].

The planning process also will require the development of new modeling paradigms for freight demand. Regrettably, not enough progress has been made toward improving the state-of-the-practice for estimating freight demand. The lack of appropriate models, the inherent difficulty of obtaining reliable data on freight movements, and the lack of substantial research initiatives in this area—and the funds for them—pose significant obstacles to the proper and expedient incorporation of freight issues into transportation planning [4].

New Words and Expressions

1. millennium [mi'leniəm]n. 太平盛世，一千年

2. outstrip [aut'strip]v. 超过

3. infrastructure['infrə'strʌktʃə]n. 下部构造，基础下部组织

4. tax [tæks]n. 税，税款，税金；vt. 对……征税，使负重担，指控，责备

5. segment['seɡmənt]n. 段，节，片段；v. 分割

6. paradigm['pærədaim,-dim]n. 范例

7. augment [ɔːɡ'ment]v. 增加，增大；n. 增加

8. concurrent [kən'kʌrənt]n. 同时发生的事件；adj. 并发的，协作的，一致的

9. merchandise['məːtʃəndaiz]n. 商品，货物

10. implementation [ˌimplimen'teiʃən] n. 执行

11. resurgence[ri'səːdʒəns]n. 苏醒

12. accentuate [æk'sentjueit]v. 重读，强调，着重强调

13. constraint [kən'streint]vt. 强迫，抑制，拘束

14. route[ruːt]n. 路线，路程，通道；v. 发送

15. intermodal[ˌintə(ː)'məudl]adj.互调的

16. maritime['mæritaim]adj. 海上的，海事的，海运的，海员的

17. toll [təul]n. 通行税(费)，费，代价，钟声；vt. 征收，敲钟，引诱；vi. 征税，鸣钟

18. congestion[kən'dʒestʃən]n. 拥塞，充血

19. assess [ə'ses]vt. 估定，评定

20. metropolitan [metrə'pɔlit(ə)n] adj. 首都的，主要都市的，大城市

21. commodity [kə'mɔditi]n. 日用品

22. cluster['klʌstə]n. 串，丛；vi. 丛生，成

23. peak [piːk]n. 山顶，顶点，帽舌，（记录的）最高峰；
    adj. 最高的；vi. 到达最高点，消瘦，缩小

24. curfew['kəːfjuː]n. (中世纪规定人们熄灯安睡的)晚钟声，打晚钟时刻，
    宵禁令(时间)

25. revolve[ri'vɔlv]v. (使)旋转,考虑,循环出现

26. streamline['striːmlain]adj.流线型的

27. commensurate [kə'menʃərit]adj. 相称的，相当的

28. stakeholder['steikhəuldə(r)] n. 挖泥，捕捞

29. obstacle['ɔbstəkl]n. 障碍，妨碍物

30. initiative [i'niʃətiv]v. 主动

Notes

1. Consumers will demand more control of the nature of the service they receive. nature 在句中的意义为"种类"或"特性"。

2. Differential road pricing—that is, using different toll rates for different classes of vehicles at different times of the day to manage traffic and reduce congestion—is being assessed in some metropolitan areas, and its role is likely to increase.

采用不同的公路定价，即在一天中的不同时段对于不同类型的车辆制定不同的税率，以缓解交通堵塞，在一些大的城市，就是这么做的。而且这种趋势似乎日渐明显。

3. It should not take a crisis—for example, a strike by a major freight provider, threatened terminal closures, or freight traffic diversions that result from delays in port dredging—to make the public recognize the value of reliable freight service.

不必用此冒险的方式让公众认识到货运业务可靠性的价值——例如，主要货运供应

商罢工来威胁至终点站的关闭或者在港口推迟来转移货运。

4. The lack of appropriate models, the inherent difficulty of obtaining reliable data on freight movements, and the lack of substantial research initiatives in this area—and the funds for them—pose significant obstacles to the proper and expedient incorporation of freight issues into transportation planning.

适当的模型的缺乏、货物运转的可靠数据的内在矛盾以及区域中实质调查的主动性的不足——以及为之付出的资金——对货物合适有利的输送与运输计划的协调一致设置了巨大的障碍。

Topics for Discussion

1. What are the key issues and challenges that will affect freight planning and logistics in the future? Share your ideas with your group.

2. What are the basic issues for the cooperation between private industry and government?

3. What will be the obstacles to the proper and expedient incorporation of freight issues into transportation planning?

Passage B

Freight Transportation Planning and Logistics (II)

1. Information Technology

The impact of information technology on the freight transportation system has been significant and likely will increase sharply. The steadily declining prices of new technology, coupled with an increased awareness among freight operators of the technology's potential benefits, will encourage the freight industry to increase its use of information technology. The industry already has implemented cutting-edge technologies to improve customer service and to reduce expenditures.

Information technology also will have varying effects on the different modes of transportation. Carriers in all modes increasingly will rely on continuous updates on the location and status of the vehicles and containers in their system. Additional growth in the intermodal freight market requires an increase in information sharing across companies. The productivity of integrated freight transportation providers such as Federal Express and United Parcel Service will improve with increased use of information technology. Nonintegrated intermodal users may achieve even greater gains as electronic waybills replace the paper trail that follows freight movements and as shipper service and status requests take place via electronic data interchange [1]. Electronic commerce (e-commerce) probably will bring about changes in both the configuration and profitability of a portion of the freight sector. It also might lead to reductions in average shipment size, corresponding increases in shipment frequency, and an emphasis on time-definite delivery.

Recent technological advances include but are not limited to electronic data interchange (EDI) technologies, automatic vehicle and container identification systems, location and navigational systems, mobile communication technologies, mobile computers, database management and value-added data manipulation systems (e. g., data mining), container status information systems, and advanced traffic information and management systems. The result of these developments is that freight transport is moving toward operational integration, both within and between companies.

28

Information technology will make nonintegrated transport providers more competitive with integrated ones. Appropriate sharing and integration of information will substitute for full-scale control.

The information revolution is responsible for changes that originate both inside and outside the freight transportation system. Information technology available to manufacturing and retail firms affects their distribution strategy in many ways. Just-in-time manufacturing and distribution systems rely on a continuous and reliable stream of information on the current and near-term status of every link in the supply chain. Manufacturers and distributors leverage information to reduce their inventories significantly.and to shift inventories from warehouses and distribution centers to rolling stock in the transportation network. This shift increases the burden of responsibility on the carriers as well as the need for shippers and carriers to cooperate. Information sharing by shippers and consignees will reduce inventory further, if the providers of freight transportation are integrated into the information stream.

2. Logistics

Logistics is concerned with the efficient flow of raw materials, of work in process inventory, and of finished goods from supplier to customer. In addition to transportation, logistics entails inventory control, warehousing, materials handling, order processing, and related information activities involved in the flow of products. How these activities are managed and organized determines the quantity and quality of transportation demanded and the nature of the commercial relationships between shippers and transportation service providers [2].

The globalization of business has increased the need for global supply chains that are longer, more complex, and inherently costlier. Businesses will seek logistics service suppliers who can meet their global logistics needs [3]. This development will spur the growth of global third-party logistics (3PL) providers who provide a full portfolio of logistics services, including transportation. It also will encourage the development of modern and efficient transport ˙infrastructures to minimize the cost of transport operations on major trade routes. These infrastructures include right of way, intermodal facilities, and communications links for all modes.

The need to reduce inventory investment by reducing cycle time has led away from these *push* systems, which are driven by the supply of materials and goods, to *pull* systems, in which actual demand for goods triggers product flow [4]. Just-in-time and quick-response are some of the names given to these logistics systems. Production or ordering is postponed until products are sold or consumed. The product is produced and transported in smaller quantities. Because the product demand is known with great accuracy, products bypass the traditional storage and holding processes in warehouses and distribution centers. Instead, they are delivered directly to customers or are mixed with other freight for immediate delivery in cross-dock facilities.

Pull processes require fast, frequently, and reliable transportation systems with shipment visibility. This requirement has fueled the growth of time-sensitive transport alternatives such as air freight and priority ground transport. Full-load transport is not inappropriate for the frequent delivery of small quantities of a particular product, because full loads can comprise multiple products from multiple sources. At the same time, direct delivery of small, individual shipments via parcel carriers to consumers is becoming the rule rather than the exception, as speed is built into the logistics system rather than being reserved for emergencies. Transport suppliers must be able to provide shipment visibility by adopting mobile communication, e-commerce, vehicle status, and other technologies.

Outsourcing activities previously involved a single logistics service, such as transportation. Today, 3PL providers offer an array of bundled logistics services, including strategic planning and control of the logistics process. The attractiveness of outsourcing is evidenced by the rapid growth of the 3PL industry from $ 10 billion in gross revenue in 1992 to $ 40 billion in 1998, and annual growth forecast between 15 and 20 percent through 2003. Some of the leading suppliers are subsidiaries of transportation companies, and most large transportation companies offer comprehensive logistics services through subsidiaries or affiliates.

Shippers traditionally purchased transportation from asset-based carriers that could provide service at less cost because of economies of scale, utilization, and specialization. However, non-asset-based logistics suppliers are increasingly important as information technology plays an ever-greater role in supply chain integration and as operations research models become more sophisticated. Increasingly, economies of scope, or the benefits arising from being able to manage and integrate complementary logistics services, have become the source of reduced cost or improved service and therefore are prime criteria for choosing a logistics service provider.

Traditional transport firms face the dilemma of expanding their capabilities and becoming 3PLs or becoming suppliers to 3PL providers that represent the end customer. The competitive boundaries between transport companies and 3PL providers are blurred because both are competitors and partners in meeting the demand for transportation and logistics services. Similarly, regional or domestic providers must decide how to provide the seamless, one-stop service demanded by global customers. Direct expansion was considered the most effective means to achieve broader coverage in the past, but alliances and partnerships rapidly are becoming an effective alternative for extending logistics services and geographic areas.

Partnerships between firms and logistics suppliers are growing and taking on more importance with the outsourcing trend. The traditional transaction-based relationship will continue, but more companies will seek the benefits of coordination and collaboration through partnerships. Successful alliances often involve concentrating business to fewer suppliers to leverage the customer's buying power and make the process economical.

The ability to build partnerships will be a critical advantage for a transportation company or 3PL. Partnerships with customers and suppliers will be important, but so will alliances with other transportation and logistics suppliers. These alliances provide the strategic advantages of multiple partners to meet the demand for one-stop, seamless, global, and comprehensive logistics services. Although the adoption of interim communications technology will be important in implementing partnerships, the ability to build and sustain relationships with other firms will be the key to success.

3. Conclusion

Freight movement uses local, regional, national, and international systems. Cooperation between private and public sectors — requiring changes in both — will be needed to ensure a transportation system that meets the freight needs of businesses and consumers. Because customers will require one-stop shopping, freight movement increasingly will be intermodal and multimodal. This trend will accelerate cooperation and coordination between modes and transportation companies. Successful freight transportation providers will offer an increasingly wide array of logistics services or they will partner with well-equipped logistics management firms. In short, the roles are changing for freight transport users, transport providers, and policy makers interested in ensuring the swift and efficient movement of goods, which is vital to the strength of our economy and the prosperity of our communities. Although increased coordination and involvement has started in some regions, a greater effort is needed to achieve a shared vision for freight movement.

New Words and Expressions

1. expedient [iks'pi:diənt] adj. 有利的; n. 权宜之计
2. waybill ['weibil] n. 乘客名单
3. configuration [kən,figju'reiʃən] n. 结构, 构造, 配置, 外形
4. expenditure [iks'penditʃə, eks-] n. 支出, 花费
5. profitability [,prɔfitə'biliti] n. 收益性, 利益率
6. database ['deitəbeis] n. [机] 数据库
7. manipulation [mə,nipju'leiʃən] n. 处理, 操作, 操纵, 被操纵
8. mining ['mainiŋ] n. 采矿, 矿业
9. retail ['ri:teil] n. 零售; adj. 零售的; vt. 零售, 转售; vi. 零售; adv. 以零售方式
10. strategy ['strætidʒi] n. 策略, 军略
11. leverage ['li:vəridʒ] n. 杠杆作用
12. inventory ['invəntri] n. 详细目录, 存货, 财产清册, 总量
13. rolling stock n. 全部车辆
14. consignee [kɔnsai'ni:] n. 受托者, 收件人, 代销人
15. entail [in'teil] vt. 使必需, 使蒙受, 使承担, 遗传给; n. [建] 限定继承权
16. costly ['kɔstli] adj. 昂贵的, 贵重的
17. portfolio [pɔ:t'fəuliəu] n. 文件夹; 公事包; 纸夹; 绘图纸; 文件; 部长职务
18. trigger ['trigə] vt. 引发, 引起, 触发; n. 扳机
19. bypass ['baipɑ:s] n. 旁路; vt. 设旁路, 迂回
20. outsourcing ['aut,sɔ:siŋ] vt. [商] 外部采办, 外购
21. bundle ['bʌndl] n. 捆, 束, 包; v. 捆扎
22. subsidiary [səb'sidjəri] adj. 辅助的, 补充的
23. affiliate [ə'filieit] v. (使……) 加入, 接纳为会员
24. asset ['æset] n. 资产, 有用的东西
25. sophisticate [sə'fistikeit] n. 久经世故的人; v. 篡改, 曲解, 使变得世故, 掺合
26. criteria [krai'tiəriə] n. pl. 标准
27. dilemma [di'lemə, dai-] n. 进退两难的局面, 困难的选择
28. blur [blə:] v. 涂污, 污损(名誉等), 把(界线, 视线等)弄得模糊不清, 弄污
29. seamless ['si:mlis] adj. 无缝合线的, 无伤痕的
30. alliance [ə'laiəns] n. 联盟, 联合
31. collaboration [kə,læbə'reiʃən] n. 协作, 通敌
32. Implement ['implimənt] n. [常 pl.] 工具, 器具; vt. 贯彻, 实现; v. 执行

33. multimode[ˈmʌltiməud] *n.* 多模式

34. swift [swift] *adj.* 迅速的，快的，敏捷的，立刻的；*adv.* 迅速地，敏捷地

35. intermodal [ˌintə(ː)ˈməudl] *adj.* 联合运输的

36. warehouse[ˈwɛəhaus] *n.* 仓库；*vt.* 存入仓库

37. inherently [inˈhiərəntli]*adj.* 固有的，内在的，与生俱来的

38. priority [praiˈɔriti]*n.* 先，前，优先，优先权

39. prosperity[prɔsˈperiti]*n.* 繁荣

Notes

1. Nonintegrated intermodal users may achieve even greater gains as electronic waybills replace the paper trail that follows freight movements and as shipper service and status requests take place via electronic data interchange.

两个 as 分别引导出两个状语从句。

2. How these activities are managed and organized determines the quantity and quality of transportation demanded and the nature of the commercial relationships between shippers and transportation service providers.

How 引出的是主语从句，谓语动词为 determines，宾语有两部分，一是 the quantity and quality of transportation，（demanded 是过去分词作定语），二是 the nature of the commercial relationships between shippers and transportation service providers.

3. Businesses will seek logistics service suppliers who can meet their global logistics needs.

句中 who 引导的是定语从句，修饰 suppliers。

4. The need to reduce inventory investment by reducing cycle time has led away from these *push* systems, which are driven by the supply of materials and goods, to *pull* systems, in which actual demand for goods triggers product flow.

主句为 The need has led away from *push* systems to *pull* systems。

which are driven... 和 in which... 是两个定语从句，分别修饰 *push* systems 和 *pull* system。

Topics for Discussion

1. From the text, what is the impact of information technology on the freight transportation system? You could also add some other aspects you know.

2. How to ensure a transportation system that meets the freight needs of businesses

and consumers?

3. Why will the information technology so important in many aspects of transportation?

4. Why the cooperation between private and public sectors — requiring changes in both — will be needed to ensure a transportation system that meets the freight needs of businesses and consumers?

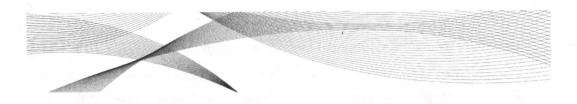

Unit 4

Passage A

Transportation

1. What is Transportation

As one of the important contents of logistics, transportation is ordinarily defined as a means of conveyance or travel from one place to another, or, it is a public conveyance of passengers or goods especially as a commercial enterprise. The importance of transportation in world development is multidimensional[1]. For example, one of the basic functions of transportation is to link residence with employment and producers of goods with their users. From a wider viewpoint, transportation facilities provide the options for work, shopping, and recreation, and give access to health, education, and other amenities. Nearly every day, items in the news remind us of transportation's vital role in our economy and its significant relationship to our quality of life. Mobility is important to the whole community. An exploration of the realm of transportation, with emphasis on key aspects of its engineering and its close relationship to our social and economic lives is focused in this course, which is likely to be helpful to lead to transportation engineering solutions in the real world.

2. Definitions of Transportation

What is transportation? How do you define your relationship to transportation? Is it only the trips that you make? Or is it the car that you drive? Whether we are considering people or goods, each trip begins at an origin and ends at a destination. Transportation is everything involved in moving either the person or goods from the origin to the

35

destination [2].

3. Contents of Transportation and Transportation System

Transportation is simply thought as the physical movement of people and goods between points. It represents one of the most important human activities worldwide. It is a multidimensional service that affects many aspects of our daily lives. While transportation is complex and multifaceted, one might also view transportation as simply the movement between two or more points.

Transportation includes infrastructure, administration, vehicles, and users and can be viewed from various aspects, including engineering, economics, and societal issues. A transportation system can be defined narrowly as a single driver/vehicle with its second-by-second interactions with the road and other vehicles. The system can also be defined broadly as a regional transportation infrastructure with its year-by-year interactions with the regional economy, the community of transportation users and owners, and its control components such as transportation administration and legislature. These two extremes exemplify the range of transportation systems, with various intermediate scenarios possible.

Transportation systems engineering is customarily considered as a discipline aimed at the functional design of physical and/or organizational actions on transportation systems.

4. Transportation System Matters

Five basic transportation modes are considered as highways, railways, waterways, flight, and pipelines.

The transportation system in a developed nation consists of a network of modes. The system consists of vehicles, guide ways, terminal facilities, and control systems; these operate according to established procedures and schedules in the air, on land, and on water. The system also requires interaction with the user, the operator, and the environment. The systems that are in place reflect the multitude of decisions made by shippers, carriers, government, individual travelers, and affected nonusers concerning the investment in or the use of transportation. The transportation system that has evolved has produced a variety of modes that complement each other. Intercity passenger travel often involves rail, auto and air modes; intercity freight travel involves pipeline, water, rail, and trucking. Urban passenger travel involves auto or public transit; urban freight is primarily by truck.

5. Basic Requirement of Transportation Systems

Mobility and accessibility are two of the basic requirements of transportation system. Besides, productivity is also the main demand of it.

Ubiquity refers to the amount of accessibility to the system, directness of routing between access points, and the system's flexibility to handle a variety of traffic conditions. Highways are very ubiquitous compared to railroads, the latter having limited ubiquity as a result of their large investments and inflexibility. However, within the highway mode, freeways are far less ubiquitous than local roads and streets.

Mobility is the quantity of travel that can be handled. The capacity of a system to handle traffic and speed are two variables connected with mobility. Here again, a freeway has high mobility, whereas a local road has low mobility. Water transport may have comparatively low speed, but the capacity per vehicle is high. On the other hand, a rail system could possibly have high speed and high capacity.

Efficiency is thought as the relationship between the cost of transportation and the productivity of the system. Direct costs of a system are composed of capital and operating costs, and indirect costs comprise adverse impacts and unquantifiable costs, such as safety. Each mode is efficient in some aspects and inefficient in others.

6. Historical Development of Transportation

Some of the most outstanding technological developments in transportation have occurred in the preceding 200 years:

- The first pipelines in the United States were introduced in 1861.
- First railroad opened in 1825.
- The internal-combustion engine was invented in 1866.
- The first automobile was produced in 1886 (by Daimler and Benz).
- The Wright brothers flew the first heavier-than-air machine in 1903.
- The first diesel electric locomotive was introduced in 1921.
- Lindbergh flew over the Atlantic Ocean to Europe in 1927.
- The first diesel engine buses were used in 1938.
- The first limited-access highway in the United States (the Pennsylvania Turnpike) opened in 1940.
- The Interstate Highway system was initiated in 1950.
- The first commercial jet appeared in 1958.
- Astronauts landed on the moon in 1969.

- The use of computers and automation in transportation grew dramatically through the 1960s and 1970s and continues to grow unabated.

- Microcomputers have revolutionized our capabilities to run programs since the 1980s and such capabilities have helped us to examine alternatives quickly and efficiently.

The fantastic spur in technology promotes the world on the upgrade, and expedites the evolution of transportation. The acceleration of technology itself is frequently dramatized by a brief account of the progress in transportation. It has been pointed out, for example, that in 6000 BC, when the clarion was invented that the maximum speed was raised to roughly twenty miles per hour.

So impressive was this invention, so difficult was it to exceed this speed limit, that nearly 3,500 years later, when the first mail couch began operating in England in 1754, it averaged a mere ten mph. The first steam locomotive, introduced in 1825 could have a top speed of only thirteen mph and the great sailing ship of the time labored along at less than half that speed. It was probably not until the 1880's that man, with the help of a more advanced steam locomotive, managed to reach a speed of one hundred mph. It took the human race millions of years to attain that record.

It took only fifty-eighty years, however, to go four times that fast, so that by 1938 men in airplanes were traveling at better that 400 mph. It took a mere twenty-year flick of time to double that limit again. And by the 1960's rocket planes approached speeds of 4,000 mph, and men in space capsules were circling the earth at 1,800 mph.

Thousands of years go by, and then, in our own times, a sudden bursting of the limits, a fantastic spurt forward. Whether we examine distance traveled, or the speed transported, the role of technology is not to be sneezed. It is absolutely clear and unmistakable that the advancement of transportation relies basically on technology.

7. Development of Transportation Technologies

Multifarious advanced technologies are gaining ground. Transportation engineering increasingly involves the applications of advanced technologies known collectively as intelligent transportation systems (ITS), which has a broad spectrum of advanced technology, ranging from in-vehicle components to advanced traffic management systems, and have come forth during the last decades. The urgency for using ITS technology stems from the fact that in the past 10 years, there has been a 30% increase in traffic. It is envisaged that ITS technology will reduce the congestion problem considerably.

New Words and Expressions

1. ordinarily [ˈɔːdinərili] *adv.* 正常地，规律地
2. conveyance [kənˈveiəns] *n.* 运送，运输，搬运
3. access [ˈækses] *n.* 接近；达到；进入；入口，通路，引桥[道]，调整孔；舱口
4. significant [sigˈnifikənt] *adj.* 有意义的；意味深长的
5. mobility [məuˈbiliti] *n.* 可动性，流动性；能动性
6. destination [ˌdestiˈneiʃən] *n.* 预定的目的，目标
7. multifaceted [ˌmʌltiˈfæsitid] 有许多不同块
8. year-by-year *adj.* 一年又一年的，每年的
9. organizational [ˌɔgənaiˈzeiʃənəl] *adj.* 组织(上)的；编制的；机构的
10. terminal [ˈtəːminl] *n.* 终端，终点；极限
11. freight [freit] *n.* 货运
12. ubiquitous [juːˈbikwitəs] *adj.* 无所不在的；普遍存在的；
   [谑](人)到处看见其踪影的
13. productivity [ˌprɔdʌkˈtiviti] *n.* 生产力
14. preceding [pri(ː)ˈsiːdiŋ] *adj.* 在前[先]的，前面的；上述的
15. locomotive [ˌləukəˈməutiv] *n.* 火车头，机车
16. multifarious [ˌmʌltiˈfɛəriəs] *adj.* 多种多样的，千差万别的，五花八门的

Notes

1. As one of the important contents of logistics, transportation is ordinarily defined as a means of conveyance or travel from one place to another, or, it is a public conveyance of passengers or goods especially as a commercial enterprise. The importance of transportation in world development is multidimensional.

作为物流中的一个重要环节，运输通常被定义为从一个地方到另个地方的运输或者特别是作为商业企业中顾客或者物品的公共运输。运输在世界发展中的重要性是多面性的。

2. What is transportation? How do you define your relationship to transportation? Is it only the trips that you make? Or is it the car that you drive? Whether we are considering people or goods, each trip begins at an origin and ends at a destination. Transportation is everything involved in moving either the person or goods from the origin to the destination.

什么是运输呢？你如何定义运输和你的关系呢？它仅仅是你的一次远足吗，或者是你开的车？无论我们是否考虑人或者物品，每次旅行都在一个起点开始在一个目的地结束。运输是包括将人或者物品从起点搬运到终点的一切事物。

Topics for Discussion

1. According to the definition above, what's your own opinion on the meaning of transportation? And how is the relationship with your life usually?

2. What's the difference between the transportation and transportation system?

3. How many basic transportation modes are considered in the text? And what is their special function?

4. What about the development of transportation technologies?

Passage B

Jeddah Bestrides East West Route

Jeddah Islamic Port is located on Saudi Arabia's Red Sea coast, placing it squarely in the middle of the major international shipping route between east and west.

It is the country's most important port, handling 59% of seaborne imports. Thanks to its proximity to the holy cities of Mecca and Medina, it is also a major passenger port, with hundreds of thousands of pilgrims passing through every year.

Most of its expansion has come in recent decades, since the formation of the kingdom's Seaport Authority in 1976.

Over the past 26 years, facilities have been expanded from a modest ten berths to the 58 in operation today, with an overall length of 11.2 km.

These include seven at the south container terminal and four at the north container terminal; ten at the ro-ro and passenger terminal; seven at the bulk grain terminal; two at the bulk edible oil and sugar terminal; twelve at the south general cargo terminal and ten at the north general cargo terminal; four at the chilled and frozen cargo terminal; and two at the livestock terminal.

The south container terminal is operated by Siyanco DPA, a joint venture between local company Siyanco and Dubai Port Authority, which concluded a 20 year lease to develop, manage and operate the facility in 1999. Some Dollars 25m has since been invested in replacing ageing equipment.

Productivity is reportedly at record levels since the new equipment came on stream, with berth productivity often exceeding 50 gross moves an hour.

Meanwhile, the north container terminal—which opened for business in 2000 after conversion from a bulk and general cargo facility, and which has a capacity of around is managed by Gulf Stevedoring Contracting.

The new operator, which previously ran the south terminal, is a sister company of Kuwait Gulf Links.

Clients include Pacific International Lines, Iranian Shipping Co., Uniglory's Red Sea service operated with Cosco, and the P&O Nedlloyd/Cont ship Anzac service.

Productivity is said to be pretty good, with vessels averaging between 70 and 90 moves an hour, depending on the number of cranes deployed.

Together, the two terminals give Jeddah a nominal container capacity of around 2.5m TEU per annum. They are also part of an "internal market" arrangement, designed to bring the forces of competition to bear within the port.

Britain's Drewry Shipping Consultants last year estimated that actual container throughput at the port topped 1m TEU in 2000, representing the absolute majority of the Red Sea market of 1.7m, and an average annual growth rate of 6% since 1996.

Most of that volume is import/export traffic, with domestic traffic is growing at around 10% a year, according to the Saudi Ports Authority.

Again using figures from Drewry, transshipment traffic amounted to 208,000 TEU, making up some 4.7% of total transshipment traffic in the Red Sea and Persian Gulf markets.

However, potential for further transshipment growth is restricted by the country's adherence to Islamic law, which means that alcohol and pork products, for instance, are banned [1].

However, the port realizes the situation and is doing what it can to ameliorate the situation. Interestingly, Jeddah was the first port in the country to establish a bonded and re-export zone, covering an area of 900,000 square meters next to the north terminal.

Jeddah Islamic Port — which claims to be largely free of congestion problems — occupies 10.5 sq km, and can take ships with draughts of up to 16 m, allowing calls from even 6,500 TEU box ships.

The port has a large fleet of marine craft such as salvage tugboats, firefighting boats, buoy laying vessels and workboats equipped to tackle pollution, pilot age, mooring and garbage collection [2]. A floating crane of 200 tons capacity is also available.

A marine tower controls traffic and is equipped with wireless communications to serve navigation.

Cargo handling equipment includes quay container gantry cranes, straddle carriers, rubber-tired gantry cranes and yard cranes.

Four super ship-shore gantry cranes were installed in December 2001. The first vessel to use them was P&O Nedlloyd's Nedlloyd America.

There are also various types of low and high trailer forklifts with different load capacities, and ample provision of reefer points.

Purpose-built workshops are located throughout the port area to facilitate equipment maintenance.

There is 2. 1 sq km of open storage area and a covered storage area of 0. 4 sq km, which consists of 59 warehouses and transit sheds.

In addition, there are silos for the storage of grain and tanks for the storage of edible oil.

One of the most important facilities in Jeddah Islamic Port is King Fahad Ship Repair Yard, fully equipped for the repair and maintenance of vessels and the building of small crafts.

The yard has two floating docks. The Nedlloyd America was the first vessel to use the new super ship-shore gantry cranes at South Container Terminal.

New Words and Expressions

1. squarely ['skwɛəli]*adv.* 方形地，直角地，四角地
2. seaborne['si:bɔ:n]*adj.* 海上运输的，漂流的
3. proximity [prɔk'simiti]*n.* 接近，亲近
4. berth [bə:θ]*n.* 停泊处，卧铺（口语）职业;*v.* 使停泊
5. chilled [tʃild] *adj.* 已冷的，冷硬了的，冷冻的
6. livestock['laivstɔk]*n.* 家畜，牲畜
7. ageing[eidʒiŋ]*n.* 成熟，变老
8. throughput['θru:put]*n.* 生产量，生产能力，吞吐量
9. nominal['nɔminl]*adj.* 名义上的，有名无实的，名字的，[语]名词性的;*n.* 名词性词
10. traffic['træfik] *n.* 交通，通行，运输，贸易，交通量，交易，交往，通信量
11. domestic [də'mestik]*adj.* 家庭的，国内的，与人共处的，驯服的
12. adherence[əd'hiərəns]*n.* 粘着，忠诚，坚持
13. ameliorate [ə'mi:ljəreit]*v.* 改善，改进
14. congestion [kən'dʒestʃən]*n.* 拥塞，充血
15. draught [drɑ:ft]*n.* 拖，拉，一网（鱼），气流
16. salvage['sælvidʒ]*n.* 抢救财货，获救的财货，救难的奖金，海上救助，抢救，打捞
17. tugboat['tʌgbəut]*n.* 拖船，拖轮
18. buoy [bɔi]*n.* （湖，河等中的）浮标，浮筒，救生圈;*vt.* 使浮起，支撑，鼓励
19. tackle['tækl]*n.* 工具，复滑车，滑车，辘轳，用具，装备;*vt.* 扭倒
20. pilotage['pailətidʒ] *n.* 领航,驾驶,领航费
21. mooring['muəriŋ]*n.* （U）系船，停泊;(C)[常 ~s] 系船 [停泊] 设备 [装置]
22. navigation [ˌnævi'geiʃən]*n.* 航海，航空，导航，领航，航行
23. quay [ki:]*n.* 码头

24. Trailer[ˈtreilə]n. 追踪者，拖车；vi. 乘拖车式活动房屋旅行；vt. 用拖车载运

Notes

1. However, potential for further transshipment growth is restricted by the country's adherence to Islamic law, which means that alcohol and pork products, for instance, are banned.

不过，更进一步的船运增长由于该国对伊斯兰教教义的坚持而受到限制，例如，其对酒产品和牛肉产品的禁令。

2. The port has a large fleet of marine craft such as salvage tugboats, firefighting boats, buoy laying vessels and workboats equipped to tackle pollution, pilot age, mooring and garbage collection.

该港口拥有大量海上船队，如海上打捞拖船、救火船、救生船、配备有固定污染物设备及领航设备、停泊设备和垃圾收集设备的工作船。

Topics for Discussion

1. After reading the text, could you give us some main features of JEDDAH Islamic Port?

2. What's the container capacity of this port and how about its development these years?

3. When the port realizes the situation, what can it do to ameliorate the situation?

4. What does Cargo handling equipment include? Please list them.

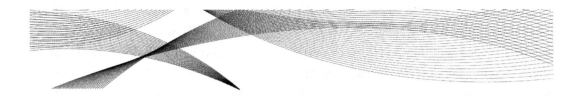

Unit 5

Container Transportation

A container is a large reusable receptacle that can accommodate smaller cartons or cases in a single shipment, designed for efficient handling of cargo.

1. The Increasing Role of Containers

It is not surprising that the maritime sector should have been the first mode to pursue containerization. It was the mode most constrained by loading and unloading time. A conventional break-bulk cargo ship could spend as much time in a port as it did at sea. Containerization permits the mechanized handling of cargoes of diverse types and dimensions that are placed into boxes of standard dimensions. In this way goods that might have taken days to be loaded or unloaded from a ship can now be handled in a much shorter time period as a modern container crane can handle about one movement in two minutes.

Transportation of containerized cargoes is the most expedient way of transportation when it is necessary to deliver cargoes over long distances combining various modes of transportation. Containerized cargo transportation is carried out by sea, by railway and by truck; however, sea transportation much predominates [1]. In fact, standard cargo containers were first designed in the mid-20th century specially to transport cargo along sea lines of transportation.

In recent years, the world economy has become more integrated internationally and container transportation has become increasingly more important as the proportion of all trade using containers is continuously growing.

45

Standard ISO containers fit well on all the various modes of transportation and are easily lifted by common handling equipment from a ship, railcar, or truck. Containers can be stored several high and can be sealed with their contents unknown to discourage theft. Intermodal yards that handle the transfer of containers from rail to truck (or vice versa) have sprung up in most major cities. In many places, they have replaced rail classification yards.

The container movement began with railcars carrying truck trailers on flat cars, called TOFC. The trailers were moved from the railcar at a rail yard near the destination, hooked to a truck tractor, and hauled the remainder of the journey over the road. The advantage was that the rail movement for a long haul was more efficient than the truck and did not require a driver. The disadvantage to the railroad was the air spaces around the bottom of the container increased the aerodynamic drag, requiring considerable added power to attain the speeds necessary to be a competitive freight mode.

Gradually, railroads realized that containers on flat cars (COFC) did not have the aerodynamic drag disadvantages but that they required the added capital equipment of a full truck chassis at the terminal to go the remainder of the trip by truck. Containers going into a marine terminal by rail did not require the added chassis.

2. Container and Its objects

In order to adapt to the increasing containerization trend, it is essential to plan and construct adequate ports and facilities to cope with this development.

2.1 What Is a Container

A container is a large standard size metal box conferred flexibility and hardiness which is either made of steel (the most common for maritime containers) or aluminum (particularly for domestic) into which cargo is packed for shipment aboard specially configured oceangoing vessels and designed to be moved with common handling equipment enabling high-speed intermodal transfers in economically large units between, ships, railcars, trucks, chassis, and barges using a minimum of labor. The container, therefore, serves as the load unit rather than the cargo contained therein, making it the foremost expression on intermodal transportation. The usage of containers shows the complementarily between freight transportation modes by offering a higher fluidity to movements and a standardization of loads.

A Container is an object that stores other objects (its elements), and that has methods for accessing its elements. In particular, every type that is a model of Container has an associated type that can be used to iterate through the Container's elements. There is no guarantee that the elements of a Container are stored in any definite order; the order might, in fact, be different in each one through the Container. Nor is there a guarantee that more than one into a Container may be active at any one time. (Specific types of Containers, such as , do provide such guarantees.) A Container "owns" its elements: the lifetime of an element stored in a container cannot exceed that of the Container itself.

One popular method of shipment is to use containers obtained from carriers. These containers vary in size, material, and construction and accommodate most cargo, but they are best suited for standard package sizes and shapes. Also, refrigerated and liquid bulk containers are usually readily available. Some containers are no more than semi-truck trailers lifted off their wheels, placed on a vessel at the port of export and then transferred to another set of wheels at the port of import.

2.2 Carrying Capacity of Containers (in cubic feet)

A wide variety of container sizes have been put in use. The most prevalent container size is however the 40 foot box, which in its 2,400 cubic feet has the capacity to carry the equivalent of 22 tons of cargo. The initial container sizes were the "20-foot" and the "40-foot" agreed upon in the 1960s and became an ISO standard. Initially, the "20-foot" was the most widely used container. However, as containerization became widely adopted in the 1990s, shippers switched to larger container sizes, notably the "40-foot". Larger sizes confer economies of scale in loading, handling and unloading, which are preferred for long distance shipping as well as by customers shipping large batches of containerized commodities. The same ship capacity would take in theory twice as much time to load or unload if 20-foot where used instead of 40-foot. There is thus an evident rationale to use the largest container size possible. Consequently, the 20-foot is gradually been phased out. "Hi-cube" containers have also been put in use, notably since they do not require different handling equipment or road clearance. They are one feet higher (9'6") than the standard 8'6" height and a 40-foot hi-cube container provides about 12% more carrying capacity than its standard counterpart. Most North American double stack rail corridors can handle two stacked hi-cube containers, creating an additional multiplying effect in terms of total capacity per rail car.

2.3 Generation of Container Ship

The first containerships were modified bulk vessels or tankers that could transport up 1,000 TEU. Indeed, the container was at the beginning of the 1960s an experimental transport technology and modifying existing ships proved out to be the least expensive solution. These ships were carrying onboard cranes. Once the container was massively adopted at the beginning of the 1970s, the construction of the first containerships (second generation) entirely dedicated for handling containers started. They carry the cellular denomination since they are composed of cells lodging containers up to stacks of 12. Cranes were removed from the ship design so more containers could be carried. Six generation of container ship is shown in Table 5.1.

Table 5.1 Generation of container ship

Container ship generation	year	Load age
First generation	1956—1970	700—1,000TEU
Second generation	1970—1980	1,800—2,000TEU
Third generation	1980—1986	2,500—3,000TEU
Fourth generation	1986—1993	3,000—4,500TEU
Fifth generation	1993—2000	4,500—6,000TEU
Sixth generation	2000 till now	Above 8,000 TEU

3. Advantages of Container Transport

Containers have shown a high capability to use standard transport modes, notably maritime. Containerized cargo transportation has important advantages. First of all, you don't have to unload and load your goods in the process of transportation. Your goods will be once loaded into containers at supplier and will be unloaded already at your destination warehouse. This makes it possible to save considerably on funds and to combine effectively and flexibly various modes of transportation. And, of course, containerized cargo transportation is remarkable for its high level of safety and security. Modern cargo containers have a strong design and are hermitically sealed.

It is universally recognized that among the numerous advantages related to the success of containers in international transport, following five aspects are the main predominance of container, they are:

(1) Standard transport product

48

A container can be manipulated anywhere in the world as its dimensions are an ISO standard. Indeed, transfer infrastructures allow all elements (vehicles) of a transport chain to handle it with relative ease.

(2) Flexibility of usage

It can transport a wide variety of goods ranging from raw materials (coal, wheat), manufactured goods, and cars to frozen products. There are specialized containers for transporting liquids (oil and chemical products) and perishable food items in refrigerated containers (called "reefers" which now account for 50% of all refrigerated cargo being transported).

(3) Management

The container, as an indivisible unit, carries a unique identification number and a size type code enabling transport management not in terms of loads, but in terms of unit. Computerized management enables to reduce waiting times considerably and to know the location of containers (or batches of containers) at any time. It enables to assign containers according to the priority, the destination and the available transport capacities.

(4) Costs

Relatively to bulk, container transportation reduces transport costs considerably, about 20 times less than bulk transport. While before containerization maritime transport costs could account between 5% and 10% of the retail price, this share has been reduced to about 1.5%. The main factors behind costs reductions reside in the speed and flexibility incurred by containerization.

(5) Speed

Transshipment operations are minimal and rapid. This is notably attributable to gains in transshipment time as a crane can handle more movements (loading or unloading). With less time in ports, containerships can spend more time at sea, thus be more profitable to operators. Further, containerships are on average 35% faster than regular freighter ships.

(6) Warehousing

The container limits the risks for goods it transports because it is resistant to shocks and weather conditions. The packaging of goods it contains is therefore simpler and less expensive. Besides, containers fit together permitting stacking on ships, trains (doublestacking) and .

(7) Security

The contents of the container are unknown to shippers as it can only be opened at the origin, at customs and at the destination. Spoilage and losses, especially those of valued commodities, are therefore considerably reduced.

In spite of numerous advantages in the usage of containers, some drawbacks are evident, which are mainly: consumption of space; infrastructure costs; stacking; management logistics; empty travel, and illicit trade.

Containers offer a fast, safe and cost effective means of transportation in exporting and importing commodities; they are easily transferred from one mode of transport to another; they enable operators to offer door-to-door, land-sea through services, with predictable delivery times; and they reduce pilferage en route. For these reasons, world-wide, 80 percent of general cargo, measured in terms of value, and 50 percent in terms of weight, now move by containers. Thus, they effectively shrink economic distances between coastal ports and inland production centers, and can stimulate import and export industries in the hinterland. Many companies in developed countries are now unwilling to place orders with factories located in areas where there are no container services.

Over the last decade, China's international container shipping has grown rapidly with port. Indeed, most are stripped in ports and their cargoes are carried in break-bulk to inland destinations. As a result, the benefits of container transport, as a means for door-to-door or dock-to-dock transport, have to be realized by the government and more and more people.

Recognizing the critical importance of developing an inland distribution system for seaborne containers, Chinese Government encouraged and supported the study and development of container conveying to improve intermodal container links along selected corridors between gateway ports and inland destinations [2].

New Words and Expressions

1. maritime['mæritaim]adj. 海上的；海运的；沿海的；生在沿海地带的
2. cargo['kɑːgəu]n. 船（装）货，货物；载运的货物
3. diverse [dai'vəːs]adj. 不同的；多变化的
4. crane[krein]n. 吊车，起重机，升降架，升降设备
5. chassis['ʃæsi]n. 底盘，底架，底板[座]
6. oceangoing['əuʃənˌgəuiŋ]adj. 远洋航行的
7. equivalent [i'kwivələnt]adj. 相等的，相当的，相同的
8. switch[switʃ]n. 开关，电闸，电键

9. clearance['kliərəns]*n.* 清理，清除，空隙，排除障碍

10. containership[kən'teinəʃip]*n.* 货柜船

11. commodity [kə'mɔditi]*n.* 产品；有用的东西

12. vessel['vesl]*n.* 器皿，容器

13. intermodal [ˌintə(ə)'məudl]*adj.* 联合运输的

14. gateway['geitwei]*n.* 入口；门口；通道

Notes

1. Transportation of containerized cargoes is the most expedient way of transportation when it is necessary to deliver cargoes over long distances combining various modes of transportation. Containerized cargo transportation is carried out by sea, by railway and by truck; however, sea transportation much predominates.

当所运货物须历经长距离且结合多种运输方式时，集装箱货物的运输将是其运输中最适宜的方法。集装箱货物可以走海路运输、铁路运输、卡车运输，然而海路运输比较占优势。

2. Recognizing the critical importance of developing an inland distribution system for seaborne containers, Chinese Government encouraged and supported the study and development of container conveying to improve intermodal container links along selected corridors between gateway ports and inland destinations.

当认识到为海轮运输集装箱发展内陆配送系统的关键性时，中国政府鼓励和支持针对于集装箱的研究和发展，这些能增强在入港口和内陆目的地之间被选择通路间的联合运输集装箱的联系。

Topics for Discussion

1. From the content, what is the increasing role of containers?

2. What's your understanding of the container? And how is the carrying capacity?

3. It is universally recognized that among the numerous advantages related to the success of containers in international transport, what aspects are the main predominance of container?

4. Could you imagine the future of the container transportation? Please discuss it with your classmates.

Optimizing Container Transfers
At Multimodal Terminals

The seaport terminals have changed dramatically after the introduction of containerization. These changes include alterations to the storage area, the introduction of specialized container handling equipment and storage methods (stacking abilities). The role of a multimodal container terminal (MCT) is to ensure a smooth transfer of freight between the two modes. Such freight may be in containers, flat trays, piggyback (trailer on flat wagon), or road trailers (trailers capable of road and rail movement without requiring rail wagons). The main factors influencing terminal operating performance are as follows: operating strategies, physical layout, ship and train plans, management/work practice, and ship and train reliability, pick-up-delivery cycle times, lifting equipment and customer requirements, etc. Some of these factors are going to be discussed below.

Two main operating philosophies for the loading and unloading of containers are the random access system and the use of skeletal trailers. Under the random access system, customers' deliver/pickup containers directly to/from a train or to/from ground storage. This is the method commonly used in Australian and European intermodal freight terminals. The skeletal trailer system is mainly used in North America and is based on the use of a dedicated fleet of skeletal trailers which are used to pick-up containers directly from trains [1]. Those trailers are then moved to a trailer storage area ready to be picked up by individual customers. The reverse process is followed when loading on to the train. This study uses the random access system operating philosophy.

The equipment available to handle containers in the intermodal terminal is of three main types: gantry cranes (rail mounted or rubber tyre); side loaders (forklifts and reach stackers) and straddle carriers (rubber tyre). The choice of equipment will depend on container throughput, operating strategy, physical operating space, track layout and degree of standardization in container sizes and types [2]. Each type of equipment has different capital cost, land requirements for operating purposes and pavement strength requirements.

Overall transit times, reliability of delivery times and costs are the main factors influencing mode choice in the freight transport sector. Users of intermodal terminals have as their main requirements: reliability of delivery times, container pick-up and delivery cycles which are delay free, and the ability to monitor the progress of their consignments (i. e. , real time information regarding container location and estimated arrival times)[3].

Whichever technology is applied, it has to be taken into consideration that the "container transport" system consists of a number of sub-systems, the capacities of which need to be well harmonized in order to prevent bottle-necks within the transport chain[4]. It is absolutely essential to meet this demand, not only with regard to investment in facilities, but also with regard to the operational management. The ideal situation is for containers to be transferred to the berth before the arrival of the ships to reduce the port time, and then to be stowed on the ships by the shore cranes. If the import containers are not on the top of the ship then the other containers should be unloaded and rest owed. Thus, many containers on the dock will cause delays.

When a container vessel calls to port, the containers on board must be unloaded and stored at the port until they are transported further by rail or road. The containers must be stored in a manner so as to minimize the amount of handling needed to place a container in the storage area and to remove it when needed. Therefore, the problem being investigated is the minimization of the total throughput time which is the handling time for all the containers from ships at berth and the transferring time of the containers to the MCT. When dealing with export containers, the problem would be reversed; that is, the minimization of the handling time of the containers from first arrival at the port until the ship carrying the containers departs from the port. When a vessel arrives and its cargo is unloaded, the stevedoring company will receive information about where some of the containers are to be transported.

The containers that are remaining must be placed in storage areas until they are needed. The company does not know when or in what order the containers will be called for loading or unloading. Therefore, they must stack the containers in a manner, so as to minimize the time taken to retrieve a container by considering the storage area constraints. In the case of exports, the stevedoring company usually knows when a container will depart as it arrives. The stevedoring company charges a fee for containers that are delivered too early in respect to the departure time and after cut-off times no containers are received [5].

The Brisbane Multimodal Terminal (BMT) works by removing import containers from the marine container terminals by trucks and then transferring them on to container wagons at the BMT. Export containers arriving by rail are transferred to the marine container terminals by BMT trucks. Empty container wagons are prepared for the next trip and stored at container parks which are adjacent to the Brisbane Multimodal Terminal . Reach stackers and forklifts can handle 20 feet or 40 feet containers at the terminal to load and unload the rail wagons and transport containers between the wagons and the BMT trucks.

The Brisbane Multimodal Terminal eliminates costly shunting, and thus, saves time and money for importers and exporters in the base of operation. There are currently two container terminals at the Port of Brisbane, with a total length of 1,300m. The terminals are owned by the Port of Brisbane Corporation but are leased to two stevedore companies. One container terminal (Berths 2 and 3) is leased and operated by Australian Stevedores and the other container terminal (Berths 4 and 5) is leased and operated by Conaust Ltd. .

Shore cranes are used to lift the containers on and off container vessels. The containers are unloaded into the marshalling area where they wait until forklifts or high stackers move them to the storage areas or to awaiting trucks for transportation to the Brisbane Multimodal Terminal[6]. Each container terminal has storage areas but remote storage areas are also located on Fisherman Islands and at other locations around Brisbane, which include Murrarie, Acacia Ridge, and Nudgee.

The trial data set used for the solution and subsequent sensitivity analysis is detailed below. It takes an average of 2.7 minutes for each crane to unload one container. From the marshalling area, an average of 15% of containers are transferred to the BMT trucks, an average of 5% of containers are transferred to the empty container storage area and the remaining 80% of containers are transferred to stored in the two storage areas. It takes ten minutes per container to move from the marshalling area to the empty container storage area.

When using Berth 1, the containers to be stored are moved to Storage Areas 1, 2 and empty storage area. Each of the storage areas is divided into four sections, and each section has a different traveling time but all sections have a capacity of 500 containers/ stack. The maximum level of stack is three. The distribution of handling time of shore crane is normal. The traveling times are normally distributed. Mean traveling times from the marshalling area to Section 1 takes 3 minutes, to Section 2 takes 3.5 minutes, to Section 3 takes 4 minutes and to Section 4 takes 6 minutes per container. To move a container from the marshalling area to the BMT trucks takes an average of 3 minutes per container. The containers moved to the BMT tracks are transported to the BMT and each container takes an average of 6 minutes. Eventually, all the containers in storage will be moved to the BMT to be distributed by road or rail. From the total of containers that were unloaded from ships, an average of 73.2% will be distributed by rail and the other 26.8% by road.

At the present container terminal, the number of shore cranes available for use is two, the number of high stackers (include forklifts) is ten and the number of trucks is six. The problem was solved by using GAMS for different time periods. Sensitivity analysis was performed with the same information but changing the number of shore cranes high stackers, and trucks available for use.

New Words and Expressions

1. wagon['wægən] *n.* (an open railway freight car) 铁路货车, 一种无篷铁路运货车
2. layout['lei‚aut] *n.* 规划, 设计, 布局
3. delivery[di'livəri] *n.* 运送, 输送
4. skeletal['skelitl] *adj.* 骨骼的; 骨干的, 轮廓的
5. marshal['mɑ:ʃəl] *vt.* 整理(编组, 引导), 整顿, 配置, 汇集
6. rubber['rʌbə] *n.* 橡皮, 橡胶
7. tyre['taiə] *n.* 轮胎 (AmE. = tire)
8. forklift['fɔ:klift] *n.* 叉车; 铲车;
9. reach stacker *n.* 外伸式堆积[码垛]机
10. straddle carrier 跨车 (铁路与公路间装卸集装箱用), 跨式搬运设备
11. consignment [kən'sainmənt] *n.* (货物的) 交托, 交货, 发货, 运送,
12. container vessel *n.* 集装箱船
13. stevedore['sti:vidɔ:] *vt.*, *vi.* 装(卸)货; *vt.* 装货上船
14. retrieve[ri'tri:v] *vt.* 补救, 补偿, 弥补(损失等)
15. cut-off *n.* 定点; 取舍点; 分离点; 切断, 截止, 切去

Notes

1. The skeletal trailer system is mainly used in North America and is based on the use of a dedicated fleet of skeletal trailers which are used to pick-up containers directly from trains.

这种架式托车系统主要用于北美, 并且只使用一个专用的架式托车队, 用于直接从火车上分拣集装箱。

2. The choice of equipment will depend on container throughput, operating strategy, physical operating space, track layout and degree of standardization in

container sizes and types.

设备的选择是基于集装箱的吞吐量,作业方式,自然作业场所,轨道配置及集装箱尺寸和类型的标准化程度。

3. Users of intermodal terminals have as their main requirements: reliability of delivery times, container pick-up and delivery cycles which are delay free, and the ability to monitor the progress of their consignments (i. e., real time information regarding container location and estimated arrival times).

联合运输的码头用户的主要需求是:运输时间的可靠性,无延迟的集装箱的分拣和运输周期,以及具备监控它们交货过程的能力(例如,关于集装箱位置的实时信息报告和估计到港次数)。

4. Whichever technology is applied, it has to be taken into consideration that the "container transport" system consists of a number of sub-systems, the capacities of which need to be well harmonized in order to prevent bottle-necks within the transport chain.

无论采用哪种技术,都必须考虑包含多子系统的"集装箱运输"系统,为避免运输连锁线中的瓶颈情况的出现,系统的容量需要很好地协调和控制。

5. The stevedoring company charges a fee for containers that are delivered too early in respect to the departure time and after cut-off times no containers are received.

对于集装箱交货时间太早于离港时间,以及过了截止时间没有收到集装箱,搬运公司就要收额外的费用。

6. The containers are unloaded into the marshalling area where they wait until forklifts or high stackers move them to the storage areas or to awaiting trucks for transportation to the Brisbane Multimodal Terminal.

集装箱被卸到指定的场所安放着,直到叉车或大型集装箱码垛机将它们运送到这个存放地或者等着运输卡车把它们运到布里斯班多功能码头。

Topics for Discussion

1. The seaport terminals have changed dramatically after the introduction of containerization . So what are those changes?

2. What are the two main operating philosophies for the loading and unloading of containers?

3. At the present container terminal, how many shore cranes is available for use? What about the number of high stackers (include forklifts) and the number of trucks?

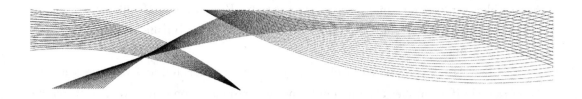

Unit 6

Passage A

Inventory Management

1. Introduction to Inventory

1.1　What Is Inventory

Inventory refers to stocks of good that are maintained for a variety of purposes, such as for resale to others, as well as to support manufacturing or assembling processes. Inventory is the key issue to supply chain management success. Customers demand that their orders be shipped complete, accurate and on-time. That means having the right inventory at the right place at the right time.

Inventory applied to finished goods, raw materials, parts and components, MRO (maintenance/repair/operating) and WIP (work-in-process). It includes new products and existing products. It covers all types of businesses-manufacturers, distributors, wholesalers, retailers and others in about every industry.

1.2　Reasons for Holding Inventory

Some major reasons of keeping inventory are as follow.

(1) Meet demand

For example, a retailer must have the products on hand when the customer wants them. Hence, if a good is not in inventory, it can result in lost of sale.

(2) Keep operations on

A manufacturer must have certain purchased items (raw materials, components, or subassemblies) in order to manufacture its product. Running out of only one item can prevent a manufacturer from completing the production of its finished goods.

(3) Lead time

Lead time is the time between placing a, purchase order and actually receiving the goods ordered. If a supplier cannot supply the required goods on demand, then the client fin must keep an inventory of the needed goods. The longer the lead time, the larger quantity of goods the fin must carry in inventory.

(4) Quantity discounts

Often firms are given a price discount when purchasing large quantities of goods. This also frequently results in inventory in excess of what is currently needed to meet demand.

1.3 Inventory's Classifications

It is important to know the key classifications of inventory because the classification influences the way the inventory is managed. Inventory is most frequently classified as cycle (base) stock, safety (buffer) stock, in-transit (pipeline) stock, speculative stock and dead stock (See Figure 6. 1).

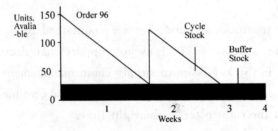

Figure 6. 1 Inventory's classification

(1) Cycle (base) stock

Cycle, or base stock refers to inventory that is needed to satisfy normal demand during the course of an order cycle. If demand and lead time is constant, only cycle stock is necessary [1].

(2) Safety (buffer) inventory

Safety or buffer inventory referred to inventory that is held in addition to cycle stock to guard against uncertainty in demand and/or lead time [2]. Generally, the higher the level of buffer inventory, the better the fin's customer service. This occurs because the farm suffers fewer "stock-outs". Obviously, the better the customer service the greater the likelihood of customer satisfaction.

58

(3) Transit inventory

Transit inventories result from the need to transport items or material from one location to another. Goods shipped by truck or rail can sometimes take days or even weeks to go from a regional warehouse to a retail facility. The increase of transit time for these inventories would lead to an increase in the size of the transit inventory.

(4) Speculative inventory

Oftentimes, providers will purchase and hold inventory that is in excess of their current need for a possible future event. Such events may include a price increase, a seasonal increase in demand. This tactic is commonly used by retailers, who always build up inventory months before the demand for their products will be unusually high (i. e. , at Halloween, Christmas)[3].

(5) Dead inventory

Dead inventory refer to product for which there is no demand m at least under current marketing practices. Because dead inventory increases inventory carrying cost, reduces inventory turnover and takes up space in warehousing facility, companies should minimize the size of dead inventory [4].

2. Inventory management

Inventory management is the active control program which allows the management of sales, purchases and payments.

Inventory Management and Inventory Control must be designed to meet the dictates of the marketplace and support the company's strategic plan. The many changes in market demand, new opportunities due to worldwide marketing, global sourcing of materials, and new manufacturing technology, means many companies need to change their Inventory Management approach and change the process for Inventory Control.

Despite the many changes that companies go through, the basic principles of Inventory Management and Inventory Control remain the same. Some of the new approaches and techniques are wrapped in new terminology, but the underlying principles for accomplishing good Inventory Management and Inventory activities have not changed.

The Inventory Management system and the Inventory Control Process provides information to efficiently manage the flow of materials, effectively utilize people and equipment, coordinate internal activities, and communicate with customers. Inventory Management and the activities of Inventory Control do not make decisions or manage operations; they provide the information to Managers who make more accurate and timely decisions to manage their operations.

The basic building blocks for the Inventory Management system and Inventory Control activities are:

- Sales Forecasting or Demand Management
- Sales and Operations Planning
- Production Planning
- Material Requirements Planning
- Inventory Reduction

The emphases on each area will vary depending on the company and how it operates, and what requirements are placed on it due to market demands. Each of the areas above will need to be addressed in some form or another to have a successful program of Inventory Management and Inventory Control.

3. Inventory Optimization for the Supply Chain

Learn about what inventory best practices reduce inventory costs across the supply chain. ABC analysis, systems contracting & stockless buying, vendor-managed inventory and Efficient Consumer Response (ECR) strategies have reduced inventory investments in leading organizations.

3.1 Logistics solutions

Reduce Inventory with these 3 Supplier Partnership Strategies. Here are three inventory reduction strategies that are a result of supplier partnerships. Each strategy requires closer relationships with suppliers in addition to web-enabled information systems to track and monitor product movement and create better forecasts. Issues to consider when considering these strategies include confidentiality and inventory ownership.

3.2 Sustainable inventory reduction strategies

Can you remember the last time you went to the grocery store to buy ketchup for your weekend barbecue? How many different brands, flavors, packages, sizes, etc. did you find? Can you imagine no less than 15? Here are four long-term inventory reduction strategies that will help reduce inventory while maintaining customer service.

Managing inventory in the supply chain is critical to ensure high customer service levels. However, it is also a very costly asset to maintain. Having the right amount of inventory to meet customer requirements is critical. Find out what inventory best practices reduce inventory costs across the supply chain.

New Words and Expressions

1. Inventory[ˈinvəntri]*n.* 库存
2. finish goods 产成品
3. raw material 原材料
4. part and component 零部件
5. work-in-process（WIP） 在制品库存
6. safety (buffer)inventory 安全库存
7. in-transit inventory 在途库存
8. speculative inventory 投机库存
9. dead inventory 呆滞库存
10. assemble [əˈsembl]*vt.* 集合，聚集，装配吐集合
11. distributor [disˈtribjutə]*n.* 分销商
12. wholesaler[ˈhəulseilə]*n.* 批发商
13. retailer[riːˈteilə]*n.* 零售商
14. transit[ˈtrænsit]*n.* 经过，通行，搬运，转变；*vt.* 横越，通过，经过
15. speculative[ˈspekjulətiv,-leit-]*adj.* 投机的
16. subassembly *n.* 组件；局部装配
17. lead time 提前期，前置期
18. uncertainty [ʌnˈsəːtnti]*n.* 变化无常，不确定
19. likelihood[ˈlaiklihud] *n.* 可能，可能性
20. in excess of 超过
21. tactic[ˈtæktik]*n.* 策略，战略
22. inventory carrying cost 库存持有成本
23. turnover[ˈtəːnˌəuvə]*n.* 流通量，周转

Notes

1. Cycle,or base stock refers to inventory that is needed to satisfy normal demand during the course of an order cycle. If demand and lead time is constant,only cycle stock is necessary.

周转库存是指那些用于满足一个订货周期内正常需求的库存。如果需求和提前期是不变的，那么只有周转库存是必需的。

2. Safety or buffer inventory referred to inventory that is held in addition to cycle

61

stock to guard against uncertainty in demand and/or lead time.

安全(缓冲库存)是指周转库存之外的额外存货,以应对需求和提前期的不稳定性。

3. This tactic is commonly used by retailers, who always build up inventory months before the demand for their products will be unusually high (i. e. at Halloween, Christmas).

零售商们常使用这种策略,他们总是提前几个月就储备库存以应对产品需求量的提高(例如万圣节,圣诞节)。

4. Because dead inventory increases inventory carrying cost, reduces inventory turnover and takes up space in ware housing facility, companies should minimize the size of dead inventory.

因为呆滞库存会增加库存持有成本,减慢库存周转,并且占用仓储空间,所以企业应该将呆滞库存减到最低。

Topics for Discussion

1. Some people believe inventory only refers to the stock that a company is holding inside its warehouse, do you agree? If not, what else can also be called the company's inventory?

2. Why companies have to keep inventory? Do you think it is possible for a company to keep zero inventories and still maintain normal operation?

3. Can you find out what inventory best practices reduce inventory costs across the supply chain?

4. How can companies minimize the size of dead inventory?

Passage B

Approaches to Inventory Management

There are various contemporary approaches to inventory management. ABC analysis, Just-In-Time, and Vendor-Managed Inventory are the main ones.

1. ABC Analysis of Inventory

Firms that carry hundreds or even thousands of different parts can be faced with the impossible task of monitoring the inventory levels of every single part. To solve this problem, many firm's use an ABC analysis of inventory, which is also called Pareto's law. A small percentage of the product lines may account for a very large share of the total inventory budget (they are called class a items, or sometimes the vital few). Aside from the class A items, and in the opposite direction, there exists a large percentage of product lines which tend to constitute a much smaller portion of the budget (they are called class C items). The remaining 20% to 30% of the items in the middle are called class B items.

This approach recognizes that inventories are not of equal value to a firm and that, as a result, all inventory should not be managed in the same way [1]. According to ABC analysis, 20 percent of all inventory items represent 80 percent of inventory costs. Therefore, a fin can control 80 percent of its inventory costs by monitoring and controlling 20 percent of its inventory. But, it has to be the correct 20 percent.

The top 20 percent of the firm's most costly items are termed "A" items (this should approximately represent 80 percent of total inventory costs). Items that are extremely inexpensive or have low demand are termed "C" items, with "B" items falling in between A and C items. B items usually represent about 30 percent of the total inventory items and 15 percent of the costs. C items generally consist 50 percent of all inventory items but only around 5 percent of the costs (See Figure 6.1 and Table 6.1).

By classifying each inventory item as an A, B or C, it can determine the resources (time, effort and money) to assign to each item. Usually this means that the firm monitors A items very closely but can check on B and C items on a periodic basis (for example, monthly for B items and quarterly for C items).

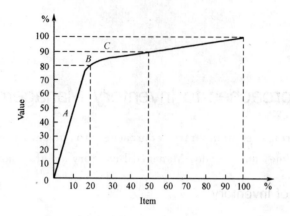

Figure 6.1   ABC analysis

Table 6.1   ABC Analysis

	A	B	C
Item	5%~10%	15%~25%	25%~85%
Value	70%~85%	10%~20%	5%~10%
Inventory control	tight	nomnal	minimal
Data accuracy	high	reasonable	low
Review of usage rate and demand	frequent	occasional	waived sometimes
Cycle counting	frequent	less frequent but regular	minimal

2. Kanban and Just-In-Time (JIT)

While Material Requirements Planning systems were being developed in the United States, some Japanese manufacturers achieved widely acclaimed success with a different system. By producing components "just-in-time" to be used in the next step of the production process, and by extending this concept throughout the production line so that even the finished goods are delivered just-in-time to be sold, they obtained substantial reductions in inventories. One of the key factors for establishing just-in-time is altering the manufacturing process to drastically reduce the setup times and simplifying the ordering and procurement process so that ordering costs are cut down. The idea is to enable the producer to operate with small lot sizes, which get produced when the need arises (and not before).

Once just-in-time is established, an information system is used to determine the timing and quantities of production. Card signals—that is, visible records (in Japanese, Kanban) — are used to specify withdrawals from preceding production stages, and to

64

order for production the number and type of items required. Because small batches of production have become economical, the production orders can be filled just in time. Advocates of Kanban characterize it as a pull process and criticize Material Requirements Planning as a push system. Though Kanban is a simple idea and yields an adaptive-flexible production system, its appropriateness hinges on whether setup and ordering costs have been drastically reduced so as to allow small production batches.

Because of the system's emphasis on low (no) safety inventory, the supplier must deliver high-quality materials to the production line on time. Defective materials may result in a production line shutdown and cause big lose for the producer[2].

3. Vendor-Managed Inventory (VMI)

In traditional inventory management, placing replenishment orders is the responsibility of the party using inventory, such as a distributor or retailer. Under vendor-managed inventory (VMI), by contrast, the vendor (can be manufacturer or other kind of supplier) is responsible for maintaining the distributor's inventory levels. The vendor has access to the distributor's inventory data and is responsible for generating purchase orders. This access is accomplished electronically by Electronic Data Interchange (EDI) and / or Internet.

The adoption of VMI helps distributor and retailer to reduced stock-out and achieve higher inventory turnover, and at the same time, vendor benefit from better demand forecasting because of early access to data of its customer [3].

4. Ordering Policies

Continuous-review and fixed-interval are two different modes of operation of inventory control systems. The former means the records are updated every time items are withdrawn from stock. When the inventory level drops to a critical level called reorder point (s), a replenishment order is issued. Under fixed-interval policies, the status of the inventory at each point in time does not have to be known. The review is done periodically (every t periods).

Many policies for determining the quantity of replenishment use either fixed-order quantities or maximum-order levels. Under fixed-order quantities for a given product, the size of the replenishment lot is always the same (Q). Under maximum-order levels, the lot size is equal to a pre-specified order level (S) minus the number of items (of that product) already in the system. Different combinations of the alternatives for timing and lot sizes yield different policies known by abbreviations such as (s, Q), (s, S), (s, t,

S), and (t, S). Other variations of the form of inventory control policies include coordination of timing of replenishments to achieve joint orders, and adjustment of lot sizes to the medium of transportation.

5. Simulation

Computer simulation is also used for such purposes. By simulating inventory systems and by analyzing or comparing the performance of different decision policies, further insights can be acquired into the specific problem on hand and a more cost-and service-effective inventory control system can be developed.

New Words and Expressions

1. approach [əˈprəutʃ]n. 方法,途径,接近,走进,步骤
2. classify[ˈklæsifai]vt. 分类,分等(常用同根词:classification)
3. periodic [ˌpiəriˈɔdik]adj. 周期的,定期的
4. quarterly[ˈkwɔːtəli]adj. 每季的;adv. 每季地
5. defective [diˈfektiv]adj. 有缺陷的
6. shutdown[ˈʃʌtdaun]n.(工厂等由于纠纷、假日、修理或没有订货而)停工,歇业
7. vendor[ˈvendɔː]n. 卖主
8. replenishment[riˈpleniʃmənt]n. 补货,补给,补充
9. electronically:[ilekˈtrɔnikəli]adv. 电子地
10. Electronic Data Interchange(EDI) 电子数据交换
11. adoption n. 采用,收养

Notes

1. This approach recognizes that inventories are not of equal value to a firm and that, as a result, all inventory should not be managed in the same way.

ABC存货分析方法认为不同的存货对企业的价值是不一样的,因而,不能对所有的存货用同一种方法进行管理。

2. Because of the system's emphasis on low(no)safety inventory, the supplier must deliver high-quality materials to the production line on time. Defective materials may result in a production line shut down and cause big lose for the producer.

因为这一系统强调低甚至零安全库存,所以供应商必须准时将高质量的材料送达生产线。有缺陷的材料可能会导致生产线停顿,对生产企业造成重大损失。

3. The adoption of VMI helps distributor and retailer to reduced stock-out and achieve higher inventory turnover, and at the same time, vendor benefit from better demand forecasting because of early access to data of its customer.

采用供应商管理库存的方法帮助分销商和零售商减少缺货并且提高了库存周转率。同时,供应商也从中得到好处,因为他们可以更早地得到顾客的数据信息,这样他们就能做出更好的需求预测。

Topics for Discussion

1. After reading the text, what are the Contemporary Approaches to Inventory Management? Please list them with your mates and try to find some other ways.

2. What are the features of ABC Analysis of Inventory, JIT approach and VMI? Could you give the typical strengths and weakness when apply them in different situations.

3. So after reading the text, what are the contemporary approaches to inventory management?

4. What's the advantage of adoption of VMI and JIT respectively? How can you differentiate them?

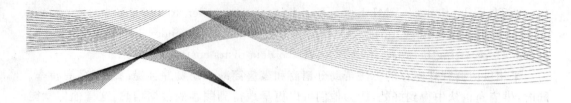

Unit 7

Warehouse Design

The design of a warehouse and handling system is not only the production of a drawing showing the position and size of rack or other storage areas, and the aisle runs, handling area, offices and truck charging points. It is that, but it is also the specification of the unit load, equipment types and quantities, operating system and methods including ancillary and service activities, information and communication system, staff levels and organizational structure, and the capital and capital operating costs. It should also indicate the external layout and space requirements for vehicle access, maneuver and parking, and for car parking, site security and other external activities.

1. Design Procedure

The design of a warehouse and handling system involves a number of stages, starting with the definition of system requirements and constraints, and finishing with an evaluated preferred design[1]. Although set out sequentially below, the design process is developed, and assessing the interactions that necessarily occur throughout the process. Any design process uses a range of skills and disciplines . As well as warehouse design expertise, it is appropriate to draw on the operational experience of managers and staff to incorporate their perspective and help produce a design that is technically, financially and operationally.

The design process includes the following steps:

1.1 Define system requirements and design constrains

The design requirements for a warehouse or distribution depot operation, taking account of future growth forecasts and other likely business developments are likely to include:

- Required capacities, both storage and throughput;
- Service level to be achieved;
- Relevant constraints can include;
- Time limit;
- Financial limit;
- Technical limit.

1.2 Define and obtain data

The accuracy and completeness of the data on which any designed is based will affect how well the final design meets the specified requirements. It is most unlikely that any design will be based on current levels of business, and it is important to establish anticipated growth and other changes to the business that the warehouse is to be designed to satisfy [2]. However, there are often gaps in the available data, and on occasions assumptions have to be made based on informed opinion and experience, and they should be clearly highlighted and justified in the final design document. Depending on circumstances, it may be appropriate to draw up a data report, including any assumptions, for all interested parties to see and agree before the full design is carried out.

The data required for warehouse design includes:

(1) Goods handled

- Handling and other relevant characteristics, size, weight, temperature or other constraints
- Packaging and unit loads
- Inventory levels—maxima, average minimum and seasonal variations
- Throughput levels—maxima, average minimum and seasonal variations
- Forecast growth trends.

(2) Order characteristics—influence order picking system

- Service levels for time and for completeness of order fill
- Size distribution
- Order frequency

- Special or priority order requirements.

(3) Goods arrivals and dispatch patterns

- Vehicle sizes, types, frequencies and times
- Unit load to be handled
- Consignment sizes
- Own vehicles or third party.

(4) Warehouse operations

- Basic operations to be carried out
- Ancillary activities, e. g. packing and packaging store, returns, quality control, battery charging, offices.

(5) Site and building details

- Location, size, gradients, access
- Adjacent activities and scope for expansion, constraints or obstructions services available.

(6) Any existing facilities or equipment that may be used size, condition, numbers.

1.3 Analyze data

The purpose of data analysis is to provide the foundation for the designer's proposals for appropriate operating methods and system, equipment, layouts, staffing levels and costs.

Data may be analyzed and presented in various ways, including graphs and charts, table, drawings, statistical analyses, drawings and networks.

1.4 Establish what unit loads will be used

Examples of unit loads Include pallets stillage, roll cage pallets, skid sheets, tote boxes and hanging garment rails.

Unit loads to handle and stored in a warehouse, which may change as material moves through the warehouse, will influence the choice of equipment required and the ability to utilize space effectively, and should therefore be established early in the design process. Suppliers may specify dispatch unit loads, but the warehouse designer should use whatever freedom of choice exists to ensure the most appropriate unit loads for the processes being carried out.

The benefits of using unit loads include equipment standardization, minimization of movement, material security, and facilitating and minimizing the time for loading and unloading vehicles.

70

1.5 Postulate basic operations and methods

The basic operations that will take place in a warehouse, and how they will be carried out, must be determined before it is possible to specify the equipment, space or staffing levels required for them. These will include vehicle unloading and goods receipt, storage, picking operations, order collation and packing, vehicle loading for dispatch and all associated handling.

The information and communication requirements for the operations must also be established, and this will build up into a specification for the warehouse management systems will be used, or " paperless " system, which can include radio data communication, picking by lights and the use of bar codes.

In addition to these fundamental considerations, however, there will be ancillary activities required to support the basic operations, they can include:

- packing operations and associated packaging material storage;
- Pallet repair;
- returned goods area;
- waste disposal;
- warehouse cleaning and cleaning equipment;
- battery;
- maintenance workshop;
- services—heating, ventilation, fire prevention;
- offices;
- amenities—changing and locker room, toilets, rest-room, restaurant, first aid;
- security facilities including gatehouse;
- car parking;
- vehicle wash.

1.6 Consider possible equipment types for storage and handling

It should be able to specify the appropriate equipment for a particular application which clearly requires an awareness of what is available and an understanding of the basic operating characteristics of the different equipment types.

1.7 Calculate equipment quantities

The amount of equipment required is calculated from the basic design data and equipment operational characteristics. Typically the stock-holding requirements will dictate how much storage capacity to incorporate into a design, and the type of storage will also influence the final numbers.

Handling equipment requirements will be based on material movements in the warehouse, including seasonal variations and short-term peak loads, and operational data on equipment capacities, typically manufacturers' technical data plus operation experience. Shift working patterns will affect these calculations.

The number of order picking trucks will depend not only on total warehouse throughput, but also on order sizes and frequencies.

Using stock and through figures, and equipment operating characteristics, the calculations of basic equipment are generally straightforward. What is not easy to calculate however are the effect of all the mobile equipment and operating staff, working together, and interacting and interfacing, and sometimes getting in the way of one another, and causing queues and delays. This dynamic situation is nearer the real operational situation. For this reason, computer-based dynamic simulation techniques are used, to validate the static calculations and to take account of potential interference between activities when running simultaneously.

1.8 Calculate staffing levels

The requirements for operating staff are closely linked to the mobile equipment requirements, and in many cases will fall out of the equipment calculations. Quite clearly, staffing levels have to be established as part of the design, and to enable a full costing of the warehouse to be made.

1.9 Prepare possible building and site layouts

The layout brings together all the components of the warehouse operation inside the building, and also the external site features.
- the general principles for internal layout include;
- good access to stock;
- minimizing the amount of movement required for people and for handling equipment;
- making the best use of building volume;
- safe systems of work.

2. External Layouts

The relevant factors that affect the site layout include:

- vehicle access to the site;
- security including harriers, gatehouses and separate access for cars and commercial vehicles;
- internal roads and directions of movement, one-way or two-way circuits;
- car parking;
- access for fire appliances;

The original design objectives and constraints will have defined the commercial, financial and technical requirements to be met by the new warehouse and these form the principal criteria for assessing the design. The basic requirements for storage capacity, building size and layout, site layout and building position, and staffing levels can all be fairly readily validated. Capital cost (land, building, equipment, system, etc.) and operating costs (staff, equipment operating, maintenance, building insurance and rates, depreciation, etc.) can also be obtained. As suggested earlier in the chapter, the use of components are working together and interacting with one another, and the use of dynamic simulation is a powerful final arbiter of the feasibility of a warehouse.

3. Identify the Preferred Design

As a design progresses, there will inevitably be a process of iteration, of checking back to the design requirements, and partial evaluation of ideas to assist the process of homing in on the final preferred design. The preferred design should then present the proposed operating processes and methods, service requirement, equipment specifications and requirements, staffing levels, capital and operating costs, and layout drawings.

Finally, the aim of a design should always be to get the right design and technology to meet the given requirements. Whatever level of technology is used, whether fairly basic or a very sophistically automated or robotic system, effective information and communication system, probably computer-based, should always be incorporated into the operational design.

New Words and Expressions

1. expertise [ˌekspəˈtiːz]n. 专门技术
2. chill store 冷藏库
3. maxima maximum 的复数
4. queue [kjuː]v. 排队等待
5. stillage[ˈstilidʒ]n. 滑板输送器架

6. appropriate [ə'prəupriit] *adj.* 适合的；适当的；相称的

7. skid [skid] *n.* 叉车

8. depreciation [diˌpriːʃi'eiʃən] *n.* 折旧

9. unloading [ˈʌn'ləudiŋ] *n.* 卸载

10. arbiter [ˈɑːbitə] *n.* 仲裁者

11. paperless [ˈpeipəlis] *adj.* 无纸传输信息的

12. operational [ˌɔpə'reiʃənl] *adj.* 操作[工作]上的；用于操作的；运转的

Notes

1. The design of a warehouse and handling system involves a number of stages, starting with the definition of system requirements and constraints, and finishing with an evaluated preferred design.

仓库和搬运系统的设计包括了许多不同阶段，从最初定义的系统要求和约束，到最后对所选择的设计进行评价。

2. The accuracy and completeness of the data on which any designed is based will affect how well the final design meets the specified requirements. It is most unlikely that any design will be based on current levels of business, and it is important to establish anticipated growth and other changes to the business that the warehouse is to be designed to satisfy.

任何数据的精确性和完整性将影响最终的设计是否能符合所规定的要求。不太可能苛求任何设计都能满足现行水平的事物，但建立符合业务发展和变化的设计是很重要的，仓库往往可以满足这一需求。

Topics for Discussion

1. How many steps does design procedure include?

2. In which aspects will the data be required for warehouse design consider?

3. What are the relevant factors that affect the site layout? Please read the text carefully; draw your own conclusions and share them with whole class.

Passage B

Warehousing management

1. General Introduction of Warehousing

Warehousing has been defined as the part of logistics systems that store products (raw materials, parts goods-in-process, finished goods...) at and between points of origin to points of consumption. Warehousing can be provided by either warehouses or distribution centers. Warehouse emphasizes the storage of product and their primary purpose is to maximize usage of available storage space [1]. In contrast, distribution centers emphasize the rapid movement of products through a facility, and thus attempt to maximize throughput (the amount of product entering and leaving a facility in a given time period).

Modern warehouses employ a wide range of handling equipment. The type of equipment most used is forklift trucks, towlines, tractor-trailer devices, conveyors, and carousels. They are described as following.

1.1 Forklift trucks

Forklift trucks can move loads of master cartons both horizontally and vertically. A pallet or slip sheet forms a platform upon which master cartons are stacked. A slip sheet consists of a thin sheet of material such as solid fiber or corrugated paper. Slip sheets are an inexpensive alternative to pallets and are ideal for situations which product is handled only a few times. A forklift truck normally transports a maximum of two unit loads (two pallets) at a time. However, forklift trucks are not limited to unit-loads handling. Skids or boxes may also be transported depending on the nature of the product.

Many types of forklift trucks are available. High stacking trucks capable of up to 40 feet of vertical movement, pallet less side-clamp versions, and trucks capable of operating in aisles as narrow as 56 inches can be found in logistical warehouses. Particular attention to narrow aisle trucks has increased in recent years, as warehouses seek to increase rack storage density and overall storage capacity. The forklift truck is not economical for long distance horizontal movement because of the high ratio of labor per unit of transfer. Therefore, forklifts are most effectively utilized in shipping and receiving, and to place merchandise in high cube storage. The two most common power sources for forklifts are propane gas and electricity.

1.2 Walk-rider pallet trucks

Walk-ride pallet trucks provide a low-cost, effective method material handing utility. Typical applications include loading and unloading, order selection and accumulation, and shuttling loads over longer transportation distances throughout the warehouse.

1.3 Towlines

Towlines consist of either in floor or overhead mounted drag devices. They are utilized in combination with four wheel trailers on a continuous power basis.

The main advantage of a towline is continuous movement. However, such handling devices do not have the flexibility of forklift trucks. The most common application of towlines is for order selection within the warehouse. Order selectors place merchandise on a four wheel trailer, which is then towed to the shipping dock. A number of automated decoupling devices have been perfected that route trailers from the main line to selected shipping docks.

1.4 Tow tractor with trailers

A tow tractor with trailer consists of a drive-guided power unit towing a number of individual four wheel "trailers" that hold several palletized loads. The typical size of the trailers is 4 by 8 feet. The tow tractor with trailer like the towline is typically used to support order selection. The main advantage of tow tractor with trailers is flexibility. It is not as economical as the towline because it requires greater labor participation and is often idle. Considerable advancements have been made in automated guided vehicle systems (AGVS).

1.5 Conveyors

Conveyors are used widely in shipping and receiving operations and form the basic handling device for a number of order selection systems. Conveyors are classified according to (1) power, (2) gravity, or (3) roller or belt movement. In power systems, the conveyor uses a drive chain from either above or below. Considerable conveyor flexibility is sacrificed in such power configuration installations. Gravity and roller or

76

belt systems permit the basic installations be modified with minimum difficulty. Portable gravity-style roller conveyors are often used at the warehouse for loading and unloading.

1.6 Carousels

A carousel operates on a different concept than most other mechanized handling equipment. It delivers the desired item to the order selector by using a series of bins mounted on an oval track. The entire carousel rotates and brings the desired bin to the operator. A wide variety of carousels are available.

The typical application involves selection of individual packages in pack-and-repack and service parts operations. The rationale behind carousel systems is to shrink order selection labor requirements by reducing walking length /paths and time. Carousels, particularly modern stackable or multitier systems, also significantly reduce storage floor requirement.

1.7 Pick-to-light systems

Technology has also been applied to carousel systems in an application known as "pick-to-light". In these systems, order selectors pick designated items and put them directly into cartons from carousel bins or conveyors. A series of light or a "light tree" in front of each pick location indicates the number of items to pick from each location. The light system may also be used to indicate when a carton is ready to move on. In systems where an item is picked to fill multiple orders, "soft bars" show the order selector how many items are needed in a carton, since each carton typically represents a separate order. Some carousel systems also utilize computer-generated pick lists and computer-directed carousel rotation to further increase selection productivity. These systems are referred to as "paperless picking" because no paperwork exists to slow down employee efforts.

2. Types of Warehouses

2.1 Private warehouse

Private warehouses provide more control since the enterprises has absolute decision-making authority over all activities in the warehouse. The control facilitates the ability to integrate warehouse operations with the rest of the firm's internal logistics process. But private warehousing is also characterized by some drawbacks, including high fixed cost of private storage and the necessity of having high and steady demand volumes[2]. The largest users of private warehousing are retail chain stores; they handle large volumes of products on a regular basis. Manufacturing firms also utilize private warehousing.

2.2 Public warehouse

The public warehouse is essentially space that can be leased to solve short-term distribution needs. Using public warehouses offer more flexibility for the users since it require no capital investment on the user's part. Retailers that operate their own private warehouses may occasionally seek additional storage space if their facilities have reached capacity limit, or if they are making a special, large purchase of products. Public warehouses may also provide a number of specialize services that aren't available from other sources, such as value-added services as repackaging larger shipments into retail-size package, product assembly and product testing [3].

2.3 Contract warehousing

For many years, organizations had two choices with respect to warehousing-public and private. But more recently, contract warehousing (also referred to as third-party warehousing) has emerged as another warehousing alternative. Contract warehousing is a long term. Mutually beneficial arrangement which provides unique and spacious tailored warehousing and logistics services for one customer [4]. Contract warehousing is becoming a preferred choice for many organizations because it allow a company to focus on its core competencies (what it does best), with warehousing provided by experts. Contract warehousing also tends to be more Cost-effective than private warehousing with almost the same degree of control, because key specifications can be included in the contract [5].

2.4 Distribution center

There are some warehouses where product storage is considered a very temporary activity. There warehouses serve as points in the distribution system at which products are received from many suppliers and quickly shipped out many customers. In some cases, such as with distribution centers handling perishable food (e. g. , produce), most of the product enters in the early morning and is distributed by the end of the day.

New Words and Expressions

1. distribution [ˌdistri'bjuːʃən] *n.* 分发，分配，配送
2. retail['riːteil] *n.* 零售；*adj.* 零售；*vt.* 零售；*vi.* 零售
3. chain store 连锁店铺
4. distribution center 配送中心
5. goods-in-process 在制品
6. value-added 增值的
7. storage['stɔridʒ] *n.* 储存，储藏
8. facilitate [fə'siliteit] *vt.* （不以人作主语的）使容易
9. tailor['teilə] *n.* 裁缝，工具，装置；*vt.* 剪裁，缝制（衣服）
10. drawback['drɔːˌbæk] *n.* 不利点
11. solid fiber 致密纤维板
12. slip sheet 薄衬板
13. conveyor [kʌn'veiə(r)] *n.* 输送机
14. corrugated paper 瓦楞纸
15. configuration [kənˌfigə'reiʃən] *n.* 结构
16. skid [skid] *n.* 低平台（有时有轮子）
17. sacrifice['sækrifais] *vi.* 献出
18. carousel [ˌkærə'zel] *n.* 回转运输机
19. towline [ˌtəulain] *n.* 拖缆
20. oval track *n.* 椭圆形轨道

Notes

1. Warehousing can be provided by either warehouses or distribution centers. Warehouse emphasizes the storage of product and their primary purpose is to maximize usage of available storage space.

仓储可以由仓库或配送中心提供。仓库强调产品的存储，其主要目标是存储空间的最大化使用。

2. But private warehousing also characterized by some drawbacks, including high fixed cost of private storage and the necessity of having high and steady demand volumes.

但私人仓库也有一些缺点，包括私人仓储的固定成本高，并且只有在需求量高且稳定

的情况下才有利可图。

3. Public warehouses may also provide a number of specialize services that aren't available from other sources, such as value-added services as repackaging larger shipments into retail-size package, product assembly and produce testing.

公共仓库可能提供许多其他地方不能提供的专业服务，比如提供将较大宗货物重新进行零售包装，产品组装和产品测试等增值服务。

4. Contract warehousing is a long term, mutually beneficial arrangement which the operators of warehouse facility provide unique and specially tailored warehousing and logistics services for one customer.

合同仓储是一个长期的双方互惠协定，仓储设施的经营人对其客户提供独特的，专门的仓储和物流服务。

5. Contract warehousing also tends to be more cost-effective than private warehousing with almost the same degree of control, because key specifications can be included in the contract.

合同仓储往往比私人仓储更经济，却能达到和私人仓储相近的控制度，因为企业的重要要求都可以在合同中详细列明。

Topics for Discussion

1. What makes a distribution center different from a warehouse?

2. What type of handling equipment is most used?

3. What are the functions of the light systems of pick-to-light systems?

4. How many pallets can a forklift truck normally transport at a time?

5. What is the characteristic of forklift trucks?

6. What are the typical applications of walk-rider pallet trucks?

7. What is the main advantage of tow tractor with trailers?

8. What does the debate about towlines involve?

9. What are often used at the warehouse for loading and unloading?

10. How does a carousel operate?

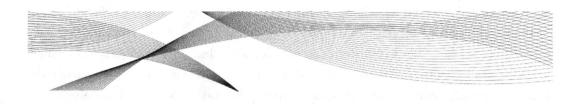

Unit 8

Distribution Management

Logistics is defined as the obtaining, producing, and distributing of goods in the proper order and the proper place. In the industrial world, the emphasis placed on logistics is the distribution function. The distribution channel is the route a product travels from raw material to the customer. It is composed of logistics channel and marketing channel. The former performs physical movement of products from suppliers to customers, members of this kind of channel involve carriers that transport products, and warehouses that store them; the latter, with channel members acting as intermediaries such as wholesalers and retailers, helps to transfer the ownership of the goods.

1. Distribution Networks

Along the route, inventory must be managed from point of manufacturer to the final customer. This management may include several layers of inventory when the product is stocked at distribution centers, wholesalers and retailers. The distribution network structure defines the channel and therefore the relationship between various levels of inventory.

The distribution structure will include the manufacturing site or a central supply center if the network does not include a manufacturing concern. Regional and area (branch) warehouses, distributor outlets, and retail outlets, may be part of the total network. The entire network may be controlled by a single entity such as a manufacturer, who not only manufactures the product, but also owns the network of

81

warehouses and retail outlets. This arrangement is known as a functional channel, in an institutional channel, the structure consists of vertically aligned companies where the ownership of the product is transferred at each level [1]. In many situations, the channel is a mixture of both functional and institutional. A manufacturer may market the product through company owned retail outlets and may also distribute through a network of separately owned distribution and retail outlets [2].

In the past, many major appliances such as refrigerators, washing machines, and television sets were distributed through a functional channel with the manufacturer controlling all inventory levels through company owned retail outlets. Sears, although not a manufacturer, was also an example of a functional channel in that the appliance would be manufactured under the Sears' brand name and distributed through Sears' stores [3]. In the past 10 to 15 years, functional channeling has given way to institutional channeling as it has become evident that the customer often prefers a choice of brand name products at one retail location. Some products, such as flashlight batteries, have always been distributed through institutional channeling.

The primary goals of the distribution network are to maximize the service to the customer while minimizing the cost of distribution. Customer service means timely delivery with availability of all products in the line. A Seattle warehouse will shorten the lead time to the customer. If the anticipated demand is uncertain, safety stock stored in the Seattle warehouse will increase the chances of product availability.

The presence of a Seattle warehouse may allow for transportation cost efficiencies for products shipped from Boston. The transportation cost advantage must be balanced with the additional costs of maintaining the warehouse as well as the cost of carrying additional inventory.

There are a number of decisions required in the determination of a distribution network structure. They are:

(1) How many stocking levels will there be in the structure?

The cost of regional warehouses may be justified by consolidated freight saving and reduced inventory requirements for branch warehouses.

(2) Where should the warehouses be located?

Geographical locations of customer demand and freight consolidations must be considered.

(3) What stock should be stored at what location?

Fast moving items may be stored at the branch warehouses, slower moving items at the regional warehouses, and other slow moving or questionable items at the central

82

supply center. A decision as to where to store safety stock is also required.

(4) Are the stocking locations in the structure owned by the manufacturer, sub-contracted to an independent company, or owned by the retail outlet?

The nature of the product and the market are often the determining factor.

(5) How is the system to be managed?

Proper inventory control and transportation decisions are required. The determination of a distribution network requires a complete understanding of the product, the market, the customer needs, and the complicated costs of maintaining the distribution system.

2. Cost of Distribution

The real costs of distribution must be identified when management deals with a company's cost structure. Distribution is an important aspect of a company's marketing and production effort and the costs of distribution bear on the final delivered cost of any product. In one sense, any major distribution decision can affect every cost center in the business because all costs are related to other costs. Experience indicates that the following cost elements and interrelationships are the ones that are most likely to prove critical in evaluation of alternative distribution strategies and the effect on total costs and overall profits [4].

Transportation costs. Both inbound and outbound transportation costs must be considered. The most used mode of transportation is highway motor transport. It may be by over-the-road equipment or specialized short-haul equipment. The advantages of motor transport are flexibility, short-haul capability, and the ability to handle variable capacities. Rail transport can be less costly than motor, but large volumes are required and there is a loss of flexibility. Water carriers are cost effective, but are slow and limited by geographic location. Air transport is expensive, but is the fastest mode over medium to long distances. Pipeline transport, which has a high initial cost and low operating costs, is limited by application and geography.

Storage costs. To provide customer service through the company's chosen channels of distribution, some warehousing is required. This requirement can range from one factory-based warehouse used to supply all customers, to a network of warehouses dispersed geographically for regional distribution. Service to the customer is usually higher as the number of warehouses increases. However, as the number of warehouses increases, the average size tends to decrease. Costs per item handled/stored tend to rise and customer service levels can be affected by space limitations. Any change in the number, type and location of storage points will have effects on customer service levels and distribution costs.

The keeping of stocks gives rise to costs which are not directly attributable to distribution but which must nevertheless be borne by that function. These costs include the capital tied up in stocks, insurance costs, warehousing costs, losses through pilferage or deterioration and in many cases stock taxes. Customer service levels improve when stocks are held close to the customer's premises but this usually increases the total of stocks held. This in turn increases the costs of stockholding. These costs are closely connected to warehouse location strategies and the desired level of customer service.

The greater the total level of stocks held by a company, the greater the risk of the products stored becoming obsolete. This will involve capital write-off. This is a particularly important factor in those industries whose products have a short shelf life, such as fashion goods and perishables.

Costs of production vary between locations, with the level of investment and with the volume of output. Production decisions must take account of distribution costs if the overall cost profile of the company is to be minimized.

Communications and data processing costs vary with the complexity of the distribution function and operation. This includes the level of customer service provided, order processing, inventory control and transport documentation.

Stock-outs (the fact that orders are unfulfilled because there are no stock, of a product in a warehouse), excess delivery times or unreliability of delivery can all lead to lost sales. For the company this can be far more serious than the direct losing of one sale. Stock-outs, excess delivery times or unreliability of delivery can lead to a loss of goodwill and affect repeat orders and brand loyalty. Any change in the distribution system which affects these factors, especially if it results in loss of goodwill, must be counted as a cost set against the distribution function.

3. Reducing the Distribution Cost

Once the individual cost elements have been identified, the whole system can be investigated to ascertain what improvements can be made. Savings in distribution costs can be made from a number of sources, the following factors are important:

(1) Simplification of the system.

Physical distribution combines the management of both the movement and the storage of goods. The more streamlined the system, the lower the cost and the easier the planning task. After the initial planning and implementation of a distribution system, additions can be made without careful consideration of their impact on the whole system. With careful planning as an on-going tool, the system can be kept as simple as possible with any changes being carefully implemented and monitored to make sure that the whole system is still effective after the changes.

(2) Reduction of stocks.

This can be achieved by rationalizing stock-holding such that the shelf life of the products is determined and the stocks held for optimum periods. The consolidation of stocks in fewer locations serving more customers can drastically reduce the level of stocks held though this can only be undertaken after an analysis of the effect this will have on other distribution costs [5].

(3) Improvements in packaging.

This is a case of each area of a product's cycle from design through production to distribution being seen in isolation. Packaging serves two purposes. It is needed to enhance the appeal of the product to the consumer—the packaging designer, marketing people and product designer working closely together. Packaging is also protection, covering the product during transit to ensure that the product arrives in good order in the market place. Uniform and regular packaging sizes present greater efficiency in transport and storage but may be unattractive to marketing personnel. It is vital that each section understands the needs of the other and that packaging of products fulfils these needs.

(4) A constant quest must be followed to find more efficient methods of transport, better equipped warehouses, the most cost-effective materials handling systems and documentation. Changes of methods are always occurring in these areas and efforts must be made to keep abreast of developments, implementing those that reduce costs and increase efficiency.

(5) As technology changes, distribution systems must be adapted to these changes. Recently there has been a growth in the use of containers, the impact of desk-top computers and the greater use of electronic data transmission aids.

4. Role of Intermediaries

When mentioning the distribution channel, we can not neglect intermediaries, who play an important role in transferring the title to goods to the customers. If producers do not use intermediaries, and market their products directly to the users, they are carrying out direct marketing. Direct marketing calls for a great deal of financial resources that many producers lack greatly. It also requires many producers to become intermediaries for the products of other producers in order to achieve mass distribution economies, because many producers find it unpractical to set up small shops that sell only their own products. They will sell their own products along with many other things. The firms find it easier to work through a network of privately-owned distributors; even those who can afford to set up their own channels can often earn a greater return by increasing their investment in their core business.

The use of intermediaries largely boils down to their greater efficiency in making goods available to target markets. Through their contacts, experience, specialization and scale of operation, intermediaries usually offer the firm more than it can achieve on its own.

From the economic system's point of view, the role of intermediaries is to transform the assortments of products into the assortments wanted by consumers. Producers make narrow assortments of products in large quantities. But consumers want broad assortments of products in small quantities. In the distribution channel, intermediaries buy large quantities from many producers and break them down into the smaller quantities and broader assortments wanted by consumers. Thus, intermediaries play an important role in matching supply and demand.

5. Considerations for Channel Design Decisions

Firms have several alternatives to choose when designing distribution channels. A new firm, usually with limited capital, uses only a few existing intermediaries in each market — a few manufacturers ~ sales agents, a few wholesalers, some existing retailers, a few trucking companies and a few warehouses. If the new firm is successful, it might branch out to new markets. Again, the manufacturer will tend to work through the existing intermediaries, although this strategy might mean using different types of channels in different areas. In smaller markets the firm might sell directly to retailers; in larger markets it might sell through distributors. In one part of the country it might grant exclusive franchises because the merchants normally work this way; in another it might sell through all outlets willing to handle the merchandise. The manufacturer's channel system thus evolves to meet local opportunities and conditions.

Like most logistics decisions, designing a channel starts with the customer. Each member in the channel adds customer value for the customer. The success of one company depends not just on its own action, but on how well its entire channel competes with the channels of other companies. Thus, designing distribution channels begins

86

with finding out what values consumers want from the channel. For example, do consumers want to buy from nearby locations or are they willing to travel to more distant centralized locations? Would they rather buy over the phone or through the mail? Do they want immediate delivery or are they willing to wait? Do consumers value breadth of assortment or do they prefer specialization? Do consumers want many add-on services (delivery, credit, repairs, installation) or will they obtain this elsewhere? The more decentralized the channel, the faster the delivery, the greater the assortment provided and the more add-on services supplied, the greater the channel's service level.

But providing the faster delivery, the greater assortment and the more serve ices might not be possible or practical. The company and its channel members might not have the resources or skills needed to provide all the desired services. The company must balance consumer service needs against not only the feasibility and costs of meeting these needs but against consumer price preferences. [6] The success of off-price and discount retailing shows that consumers are often willing to accept lower service level if this means lower price.

If the manufacturer tends to sell products abroad, it involves international channel designing, which brings many additional complexities. Each country has its own unique distribution systems that have evolved over time and change very slowly. These channel systems can vary from country to country. Thus manufacturers must adapt their channel strategies to the existing structures within each country. In some markets, for example, in Japan, many layers and large numbers of intermediaries unify as a closely knit, tradition-bound distribution network, the distribution system is complex and hard to penetrate. At the other extreme, distribution systems in developing countries may be scattered and inefficient, or lacking. Markets in these countries are much smaller than the population. Because the distribution systems are inadequate, most companies can profitably access only a small portion of the population located in each country's most affluent cities.

6. Relationship between Manufacturer and Intermediaries

When the product changes ownership in an institutional network, the manufacturer of the product tray continues to maintain a degree of control. The control may be defined in a legal document, such as a licensing agreement. The manufacturer may also informally maintain some control by supplying advertising dollars which work to the advantage of both parties. The question of who has the control may depend on the clout or strength of the two parties. Retail operations, like Sears or Wal-Mart, deal from a position of strength when dealing with their suppliers. The small dealer does not have this strength when dealing with General Motors. Manufacturers may choose to use a wholesaler who is placed between the manufacturer and the retailer. The wholesaler offers not only knowledge of the marketplace, but also assumes the inventory management responsibility that goes with product ownership. The disadvantage to the manufacturer may be loss of control of price and promotion.

7. New Trend in Distribution Channel

Customers are placing orders on the Internet at an increasing rate. This mode, in some situations, may eliminate the retail level of the network, but the Product must still be delivered in a timely manner and a treasonable freight cost. The network may just consist of the manufacturer and the customer as is the distribution channel used by Dell Computer. The Internet may also be an ordering device used by a retailer like Barnes and Noble which not only markets books through their retail outlets. An automobile purchaser may search the net for a specific car and then pick an available dealer with the most favorable price. Internet technology creates a new set of distribution possibilities and challenges.

New Words and Expressions

1. outlet[ˌautlet,-lit]*n.* 经销店
2. entity['entiti]*n.* 实体
3. align [ə'lain]*v.* 与……结盟
4. appliance [ə'plaiəns]*n.* 用具,器具
5. supplier[sə'plaiə]*n.* 供应者,补充者;供应货物等的人或商店
6. disperse [dis'pəːs]*v.* (使某人[某物])散开,消散;驱散
7. pilferage['pilfəridʒ]*n.* 偷窃
8. deterioration [diˌtiəriə'reiʃən]*n.* 变质,恶化
9. obsolete['ɔbsəliːt]*adj.* 不再使用的,过失的
10. ascertain [ˌæsə'tein]*v.* 查明,弄清,确定
11. streamline['striːmlain]*v.* 使……效率更高,作用更大
12. rationalize['ræʃənəlaiz]*v.* 使……合理
13. drastically['dræstikəli]*adv.* 激烈地,猛烈地
14. appeal [ə'piːl]*n.* 吸引力
15. title['taitl]*n.* 所有权

16. penetrate['penitreit] *v.* 进入

17. affluent['æfluənt]*adj.* 丰富的,富裕的

18. clout [klaut]*n.* 权力,影响力

19. functional channel 功能性渠道

20. institutional channel 机构性渠道

21. give way to 被某事物取代

22. bear on 与某事物有关,对某事物有影响

23. short-haul 短途运输

24. write-off 严重损坏而值得修理的东西,报废的车

25. brand loyalty 品牌忠诚度

26. keep abreast of 跟上某事物

27. core business 核心业务

Notes

1. … in an institutional channel, the structure consists of vertically aligned companies where the ownership of the product is transferred at each level.

机构性渠道结构由纵向结盟的公司构成,在结构的每个层面上都进行产品所有权的转移。

2. A manufacturer may market the product through company owned retail outlets and may also distribute through a network of separately owned distribution and retail outlets.

制造商可能通过自己的零售店来销售产品,也可能通过由自主所有的经销商和零售店构成的网络来分销产品。

3. Sears,although not a manufacturer,was also an example of a functional channel in that the appliance would be manufactured under the Sears' brand name and distributed through Sears' stores.

西尔斯虽然不是制造商,但它却是功能性分销渠道的一个样例,因为其销售的电器、器具是以西尔斯为品名生产的,并通过西尔斯的商店来分销。

4. Experience indicates that the following cost elements and interrelationships are the ones that are most likely to prove critical in evaluation of alternative distribution strategies and the effect on total costs and overall profits.

经验表明下面的各成本项目及其相互关系对各可选分销战略的评估及总成本和总利润都很可能是非常关键的。

5. The consolidation of stocks in fewer locations serving more customers can

drastically reduce the level of stocks held though this can only be undertaken after an analysis of the effect this will have on other distribution costs.

通过整合将存货储存在更少的地点并为更多的顾客提供服务可以大量减少库存,但这只有在分析了其对其他分销成本的影响后才能达到。

6. The company must balance consumer service needs against not only the feasibility and costs of meeting these needs but against consumer price preferences.

公司不仅要对顾客服务水平和满足顾客需求的灵活性和成本进行权衡,还要考虑消费者的价格偏好。

Topics for Discussion

1. What is distribution channel?

2. What are the two types of distribution channel?

3. What should be considered when we determine the structure of distribution networks?

4. Tell the elements of distribution cost?

5. How can we reduce the distribution cost?

6. Are the intermediaries important? Why?

7. Why is international channel design so complex?

8. What's the relationship between manufacturer and intermediaries?

9. What are the new trends in channel development?

Passage B

Planning Physical Distribution

In this chapter a particular approach to the planning of physical distribution strategy is developed and described.

The question of the number, size and location of facilities in a company's distribution system is a complex one. There are many different elements that go to make up the distribution mix, and it is necessary to take into account all of these when considering the question of physical distribution structure or facilities location [1]. Prior to the depot location decision a lot of wok must be undertaken. This is necessary to help to understand the key requirements of the company and to collect and collate sufficient data that represents a numerical picture of the distribution structure so that appropriate analysis can be carried out to test potential options for improvement.

Before trying to determine the most appropriate number and location of depots, it is also necessary to ensure that there is an efficient flow of products from source to final destination. This assessment of the different patterns of product flows is known as sourcing analysis.

It is worthwhile to begin the discussion by concentrating on the most practical aspects of importance to an individual company. Generally, it is necessary for a compromise to be reached between what is "best" and what is currently in existence. The very high cost of depots and vehicle fleets is the main for this, as well as the high cost and great disruption involved in making any changes to existing systems.

Despite this it is very important for companies to know how their distribution networks might be improved. Although some networks are planned from the beginning of a company's operation, this is a rare occurrence. The majority of systems are unplanned; it well be evolve with companies evolving. This may be a steady growth (or decline), or may be in short steps or large leaps as mergers and take-over occur.

1. The Role of Depots and Warehouses

There are a number of reasons why depots and warehouses are required. These vary in importance depending on the nature of a company's business. In general, the main reasons are:

- To keep down production costs by allowing long production runs, thus minimizing the time spent for machine set up;
- To help link demand requirements with production capabilities, to smooth the flow and assist in operational efficiency;
- To enable large seasonal demands to be catered for more economically;
- To provide a good customer service;
- To allow cost trade-offs with the transport system (bulk delivery etc.);
- To facilitate order assembly.

These reasons emphasize the importance of the facilities location decision, and also given an indication of the complex nature of that decision. It is possible to summarize the main rear for developing a physical distribution network as "the need to provide an effective service to the customer, whilst minimizing the cost of that service". Service and cost factors are thus of paramount importance when determining facilities number, size and location.

For the best possible customer service, a depot would have to be provided right next to the customer and it would have to hold adequate stocks to all the goods the customer might require. This would obviously be a very expensive solution.

At the other extreme, the cheapest solution would be to have just one depot (or central warehouse) and to send out a large lorry to each customer whenever his or her orders were sufficient to fill the vehicle so that an economic full load could be delivered. This would be a cheap alternative for the supplier, but as deliveries might then only be made to a customer once or maybe twice a year, the supplier might soon find himself losing the customer's business.

There is obviously a suitable compromise somewhere between these extremes. This will usually consist of the provision of a number of depots on a regional or area basis, the use of lame trunk vehicles to service these, with smaller delivery vehicles to run the orders to customers. For certain operators of course, even these simple relationships will vary because of the need for very high levels of customer service or the high value of products.

In addition, it should be noted that there are a number of different types of depot, each of which might be considered in the planning of a suitable physical distribution structure. These might include:

Finished goods depots/warehouses—they hold the stock fm factories;

Distribution centers, which might be central, regional (are), and national (NDC) or local depots—all of these will hold stock to a greater or lesser extent;

Transshipment depots or stockless, transit or cross—docking depots-by and large, they do not hold stock, but act as intermediate points in the distribution operation for the transfer of goods and picked orders to customers;

Seasonal stock—holding depots;

Distribution network and depot location strategies are aimed at establishing the mot appropriate blend of storage and transport at a given customer service level.

2. Cost Relationships

To plan an efficient logistics structure it is necessary to be aware of the interaction between the different distribution costs, specifically as to how they vary with respect to the different depot alternative (number, size, type and location), and what the overall logistics cost will be [2].

Portance of storage and warehousing costs will be dependent on such factors as the size of the depot and the number of depots with the distribution network as a whole. Thus, as the number of depots in a distribution network increases, then the total storage (depot) cost will also increase.

The two most important categories of transport costs are trucking and final delivery. These are affected differently according to the number of depots in a distribution network. Delivery transport is concerned with the delivering of orders from the depot to the customer. The trucking of primary transport element is the supply of products in bulk (i. e. in full pallet loads) to the depots from the central finished goods warehouse or production point. The effect is greatest where there are a smaller number of depots.

If the cost for both delivery and trucking are taken as a combined transport cost then the total transport costs can be related to the different number of depots in a distribution network. The overall effect of combining the two transport costs is that total transport costs will reduce when increases the number of depots in the system.

Another important cost that needs to be included is the cost of holding inventory. The key costs can be broken down into four main areas:

- Capital cost—the cost of the physical stock...
- Storage costs—which were considered earlier with warehousing costs.
- Risk costs—which occur through pilferage, deterioration of stock, damage and stock obsolescence.
- The final cost element for consideration is that of information system costs. These costs may represent a variety of information or communication requirements

ranging from order processing to load assembly lists.

It has been shown that any change in one of the major element within a logistics system is likely to have a significant effect on the costs of both the total system and the other elements. By the same token, it is often possible to create total cost savings by making savings in one element that creates additional costs in another but produces an overall cost benefit.

3. Matching Logistics Strategy to Business Strategy

Having modeled the logistics options, and selected one or more that perform well when measured against service and cost, then the impact for these on the total business strategy must be assessed. Three main areas where this will impact are:

(1) Capital cost

If increased factory storage, new depots, new equipment or new vehicles are required, then capital or leasing arrangements will be needed. In certain situations capital constraints can exclude otherwise attractive options. In other case an increase in working capital (e. g. stock-holding) may exclude an option.

(2) Operating costs

He minimum operating cost is frequently the main criterion for selection between options. In some situations increased operating costs can be accepted in the light of future flexibility.

(3) Customer service

Although options should have been developed against customer service targets, the selected short list must be examined for the customer service level achieved. The balance of the mix might have change in an effort to reduce costs. Stock held close to the customer might need to be in creased to improve service reliability.

4. Depot Site Considerations

After a suitable series of depot locations has been determined, there are various factors that should be taken into account when deciding on a particular site in a preferred general area:

- Size and configuration of site;
- Site, access;
- Local authority plans;
- Site details;
- Financial considerations;

- Legislation and local regulations;
- Building factors;
- Availability of skilled labor;
- Availability of suitable sites;
- Proximity to transport infrastructure;
- Government grants.

These can have an influence on the overall effectiveness and operation of a depot, and on the scope of any projected future expansion.

The size and configuration of the site have to be sufficient to accommodate the proposed depot building and any ancillary or other building facilities (e. g. vehicle workshops, vehicle wash, separate office, canteen or amenity blocks, waste deposal facilities, security office, etc.).

The amount of space required for vehicle movement on site, for vehicle parking, maneuver and access to the depot building, is often underestimated. This can lead to congestion and time being wasted on vehicle movement, as well as potential inconvenience to customers and suppliers vehicles. Estimates of space required, of course, necessitate knowledge of the number and type of vehicles using the site. Any future plans for development of the road network in the vicinity of the site that could possibly affect the ease of site access should be explored generally; goods will arrive and leave by road transport so that local links to the motorway network or other major roads are of significance.

Without initially having the benefit of detailed layout plans, some assessment should be made about the general shape and configuration of the site, and big consequent ability to enable a sensible layout of the depot building and other ancillary structures and site roads. Finally, consideration should be given to the extent to which the site should also be able to accommodate future anticipated expansion.

Certain site details relating to the features of a potential site should be considered. These can influence any proposed depot building, and also influence such aspects as construction costs, site security and depot operation. In general the site should be suitable in term of soil conditions (load-bearing), slope and drainage. Such factors may exert a significant influence on construction costs in terms of piling excavation, backfilling and similar civil engineering factors. The necessary services should be available, or planned, and accessible-power, water, sewage, and telephone links.

Financial considerations are also important. When occupying a site by either putting up new buildings or taking over existing buildings or facilities, there will be legislation and local replications and planning requirements to be considered and met.

When considering the site, some typical constraints are the requirement for a minimum number of employee car parking spaces, an upper limit on the height of any building to be put up on the site and limits to the type of building to be constructed. It is not unusual for a warehouse or depot operation to be set up in an existing applied building not specifically designed for the operation it is to accommodate. This applies typically on industrial and trading estates where the buildings have been put up by a developer.

New Words and Expressions

1. merger['mə:dʒə]*n.* 合并
2. dual['dju(:)əl]*adj.* 双重的
3. lorry['lɔri]*n.* 铁路货车
4. criterion[krai'tiəriən]*n.* 标准
5. dock [dɔk]*n.* 码头，船坞
6. company image　公司形象
7. intermediate [ˌintə'mi:djət]*adj.* 中间的
8. site[sait]*n.* 地点
9. seasonal['si:zənl]*adj.* 季节性的
10. proximity [prɔk'simiti] *n.* 邻近
11. overflow['əuvə'fləu]*n.* 过剩
12. infrastructure['infrə'strʌktʃə]*n.* 基础结构
13. network['netwə:k] *n.* 网络
14. maneuver [mə'nu:və]*n.* 机动
15. mileage['mailidʒ]*n.* 英里数
16. congestion [kən'dʒestʃən]*n.* 拥塞
17. bulk [bʌlk]*n.* 散装

Notes

1. The question of the number, size and location of facilities in a company's distribution system is a complex one. There are many different elements that go to make up the distribution mix, and it is necessary to take into account all of these when considering the question of physical distribution structure or facilities location.

在企业配送系统中,如何确定设备的数量、尺寸和位置是一个复杂的问题。有许多不同方式来处理配送的复杂性,当考虑配送结构或者设施位置时很有必要考虑所有的这些情况。

2. To plan an efficient logistics structure it is necessary to be aware of the interaction between the different distribution costs, specifically as to how they vary with respect to the different depot alternative (number, size, type and location), and what the overall logistics cost will be.

为了计划一个有效的物流结构,有必要意识到在不同配送成本间的相互作用,特别是怎样使他们在不同的仓库(数量、尺寸、种类、位置)选择中适应变化,并且考虑到整体的物流成本。

Topics for Discussion

1. Why depots and warehouse are required?

2. What is the relationship between number of depots and total storage cost?

3. What is an approach to logistics and distribution strategy planning?

4. What are the factors that should be taken into account when deciding on a particular site?

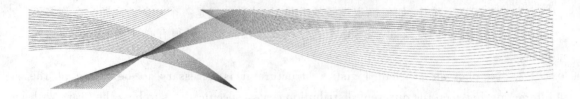

Unit 9

Passage A

Materials Handling

Materials handling is concerned with moving, storing, and controlling material. It covers a wide range of applications, such as luggage handling at an airport or parcel handling by an overnight delivery service. However, it is especially associated with parts flow in manufacturing systems or warehousing/distribution systems, where controlling the material flow and ensuring that parts (or unit loads) are available is a critical task [1]. In some cases, it can be maintained that manufacturing and distribution are predominantly materials-handling activities (interrupted by processing of materials or parts/loads).

1. Automated systems

Much of the progress made in materials-handling systems engineering has occurred in fully automated or semi-automated, computer-controlled equipment used for parts storage/retrieval or movement in manufacturing and distribution. There has also been considerable improvement in manual systems, such as industrial lift trucks. However, such improvements are aimed primarily at the ergonomics and safety associated with materials handling.

2. Storage/retrieval systems

Developments continue in automated storage/retrieval systems, which can store and retrieve loads under complete computer control. A typical automated system consists of a storage/retrieval machine (which is often aisle captive) and a rectangular storage rack located on either side of the aisle. The storage/retrieval machine is fully automated; load movement in and out of the rack is accomplished through a telescoping shuttle mechanism. The storage/retrieval machine has three separate drives: a horizontal motor to move the mast up and down the aisle, a vertical motor to move the shuttle mechanism up and down the mast, and a shuttle drive to move the load in and out of the rack on either side. The horizontal and vertical drives are activated concurrently to position the shuttle mechanism in front of the appropriate rack opening. Once the storage/retrieval machine is positioned, the shuttle mechanism is activated to store or retrieve a load. An on-board, dedicated computer controls the storage/retrieval machine movements and communicates with a central computer, which keeps track of the activities of all the storage/retrieval machines and also maintains an inventory map (that is, the status and contents of all the rack openings).

Well-known examples of automated storage/retrieval systems include unit load (for palletized loads), miniload (for small to medium parts stored in special trays), micro-load (for small to medium parts stored in tote boxes), person-on-board (which allows an operator to ride the machine and have direct access to individual rack openings), and deep lane (where each rack opening is two or more loads deep). For example, in unit-load automated storage/retrieval systems, palletized drums are stored and a roller conveyor is used to bring loads to or from the system.

3. Input/output

Loads to be stored in or retrieved from the automated storage/retrieval system are brought to or taken away from the system typically via either conveyors or automated guided vehicles. The interface point between the automated storage/retrieval system and conveyors or automated guided vehicles is the input/output point, which is located typically at the lower left corner of the storage rack. Each aisle has its own input/output point, which often consists of a short segment of chain conveyor or roller conveyor that can hold a load while it is transferred to or from the storage/retrieval machine.

4. Work-in-progress

Engineering developments concerned with automated storage/retrieval systems have occurred in both the application domain and system hardware. For the former, the primary trend has been toward building smaller systems (that is, smaller number of rack openings and fewer aisles) and at the same time moving the automated storage/retrieval system for raw-material or finished-goods storage to work-in-process (or work-in-progress) storage. In other words, rather than building large automated storage/retrieval systems at the front or back end of manufacturing plants, the trend is to build smaller systems, sometimes at multiple locations, to store unfinished parts/loads (work-in-progress) within a factory. Such a trend is a natural consequence of the just-in-time operation principle, which drives inventory levels down throughout the system but also requires tighter control of work-in-progress (i. e. knowing the exact quantity and status of all the parts, loads, or jobs on the factory floor)[2]. Since automated storage/retrieval systems run under computer control, they provide the right work-in-progress visibility required to implement just-in-time effectively.

When an automated storage/retrieval system is used for work-in-progress storage, it is also important to size the system correctly (that is, the number of rack openings to be provided). Certain analytical models (based on queuing theory) may be used to estimate the total expected work-in-progress in the system so the automated storage/retrieval system is sized properly. Furthermore, with work-in-progress storage, the storage and retrieval requests from the work centers will, generally speaking, arrive randomly. Providing the right number of aisles (and storage/retrieval machines) to meet the storage and retrieval requests is crucial. Although simulation has been the primary tool used for automated storage/retrieval system design and analysis, there are some analytical models which can quickly narrow down the alternatives.

5. Parts movement

In parts movement, while industrial lift trucks continue to play a significant role, shrinking load sizes (that is, smaller quantities of parts being moved from one work center or machine to the next) has led to an increased emphasis on one-piece-flow automated conveyors, automated electrified monorails, and unit-load (or multi-load) automated guided-vehicle systems. Even if the same production rate is maintained, moving the parts in smaller quantities increases the frequency with which loads are transferred between the work centers or machines. In fact, the highest frequency is reached when parts are transferred one at a time, resulting in the highest demand placed on the handling system.

One notable development in parts movement is three-dimensional handling systems based on monorails, which have been used successfully in Japan. A typical monorail is positioned overhead, and it moves the loads in a horizontal (x, y) plane. By modifying the carrier (that is, the self-powered unit that moves the load on the monorail), vendors are able to move the load vertically (in the z dimension) as well. With such an approach, loads can be transferred more readily to floor-bound entities (such as machines or automated guided vehicles), and vertical handling in multi-floor buildings is facilitated.

6. Vehicle dispatch

Advances in automated guided-vehicle systems include more sophisticated dispatching rules (that is, deciding which load is to be moved by which vehicle), guide wire-free vehicles, and remote diagnostics. Vehicle dispatching is important in automated guided-vehicle systems in that it reduces empty-vehicle travel and improves the response time of the system. A new dispatching concept based on bidding was shown to improve the system response time considerably. Each time a load that needs to be transferred (that is, a move request) arrives at the system, each vehicle places a bid for that load based on the vehicle's current workload and status. The load either is assigned to the lowest-bidding automated guided vehicle or is offered for bidding again shortly thereafter. While previous dispatching rules assigned a load only when a vehicle became empty, with the bidding approach the status of all vehicles is considered and it is not necessary to wait until a vehicle becomes empty.

Guide wire-free automated guided vehicles have been available for some time and are inherently more flexible and adaptable as flow patterns in the facility change. Remote diagnostics allows the vendor to log into the client's computer and monitor the automated guided-vehicle system as if the engineer were on-site. Problems associated with the control system or bottlenecks can often be diagnosed and fixed without having the engineer travel to the client site.

7. New developments

As for system hardware, a notable development is preengineered automated storage/retrieval systems. Although such systems allow very little or no tailor to meet exact specifications, they can considerably shorten the lead time (primarily the time required to engineer, install, and test the system) while reducing overall system cost[3]. Preengineered systems come in user-selectable modules that offer specific storage and throughput capacities.

Another development is the enhancement of the storage/retrieval machine itself, including the use of faster and lighter-weight drive motors and twin-shuttle (or multi-shuttle) machines which can handle more than one load at the same time. Typical speeds for unit-load storage/retrieval machines is $450 \sim 550$ ft/min ($137 \sim 168$ m/min) horizontally and $80 \sim 120$ ft/min ($24 \sim 37$ m/min) vertically. The acceleration/deceleration rate in both directions is approximately 1.5 ft/s2 (0.46m/s2). Some twin-shuttle storage/retrieval machines are now commercially available, and there is ongoing work on storage/retrieval machines with multiple shuttles. These shuttles are installed vertically between the twin masts of the machine; and an entire column of loads is moved in and out of the aisle as opposed to moving the loads one at a time. Also under development are even smaller, low-cost automated storage/retrieval systems which resemble vertical enclosures (or towers) that are located at multiple points throughout the factory.

New Words and Expressions

1. retrieval[ri'tri:vəl]*n.* 取回，恢复，修补，重获，挽救，拯救

2. ergonomics [ˌə:gəu'nɔmiks]*n.* 人类工程学，生物工程学，工效学

3. aisle [ail]*n.* 走廊，过道

4. captive['kæptiv]*n.* 俘虏，被美色或爱情迷住的人；*adj.* 被俘的，被迷住的

5. palletize['pæliˌtaiz]*vt.* 把……放在货盘上，码垛堆集，用货盘装运

6. mini-load   *n.* 中小型装载设备

7. tray[trei] *n.* 盘，碟，盘子

8. tote [təut]*vt.* 手提，背负，携带；*n.* 手提，拖，拉

9. lane [lein]*n.* (乡间)小路，巷，里弄，狭窄的通道，航线

10. segment['segmənt]*n.* 段，节，片断；*v.* 分割

11. domain [dəu'mein]*n.* 领土，领地，(活动、学问等的)范围，领域

12. analytical [ænə'litik(ə)l]*adj.* 分析的，解析的

13. shrink[ʃriŋk]*v.* 收缩，(使)皱缩，缩短

14. electrify [i'lektrifai]*vt.* 使充电，使通电，使电气化；*v.* 电气化

15. monorail['mɔnəureil]*n.* 单轨铁路

16. dispatch [dis'pætʃ]*vt.* 分派，派遣；*n.* 派遣，急件

17. diagnostics[ˌdaiəg'nɔstiks]*n.* 诊断学

18. bid[bid] *vt.* 出价，投标，祝愿，命令，吩咐；*n.* 出价，投标；*v.* 支付

19. preengineered[pri:'endʒiniəd] *adj.* 预制标准间的

20. tailor['teilə] *n.* 裁缝；*vt.* 剪裁，缝制(衣服)，适应，适合；*v.* 制做

21. throughput['θru:put]*n.* 生产量，生产能力，吞吐量

22. approximately [əprɔksi'mətli]*adv.* 近似地，大约

23. ongoing['ɔngəuiŋ]*adj.* 正在进行的

24. resemble [ri'zembl] *vt.* 像，类似

Notes

1. However，it is especially associated with parts flow in manufacturing systems or warehousing/distribution systems，where controlling the material flow and ensuring that parts (or unit loads) are available is a critical task.

然而，它（指前句中的 material handling）基本上是与生产系统或仓储/配送系统中的工件流动结合起来的，在这些系统中，物资流动的控制，以及确保这些工件（或单元载荷）的及时到位，是很关键的任务。

2. Such a trend is a natural consequence of the just-in-time operation principle，which drives inventory levels down throughout the system but also requires tighter control of work-in-progress (i. e. knowing the exact quantity and status of all the parts，loads，or jobs on the factory floor).

这样一种趋势，是准时生产制原则的必然结果，准时生产制使整个系统的库存水平得以下降，但与此同时，也就需要对在制品进行更加严格的控制，（即了解所有工件的准确数量及位置，以及工厂范围内装载及工作的情况）。

3. Although such systems allow very little or no tailoring to meet exact specifications，they can considerably shorten the lead time (primarily the time required to engineer，install，and test the system) while reducing overall system cost.

although 引出的是状语从句，尽管……，主句为：they can considerably shorten the lead time，他们可以显著地缩短交付时间，while reducing overall system cost，状语：从而降低整个系统的成本。lead time 为前置时间，也叫交付周期，即产品从订货到交货的时间。

Topics for Discussion

1. What's the main difference between the automated systems and the storage/retrieval systems? Please list the respective advantages and disadvantages about them.

2. How many parts in logistics are associated with the materials handling?

3. Please choose any of the materials-handling activities mentioned in the text above；describe it in details to your classmates.

Passage B

Automated Guided Vehicle (AGV)

An AGV is a computer-controlled, driverless vehicle used for transporting materials from point to point in a manufacturing setting [1]. They represent a major category of automated materials handling devices. An AGV can be used for any and all materials handling tasks from bringing in raw materials to moving finished products to the shipping dock [2].

In any discussion of AGVs, three key terms are heard frequently:

(1) guide path

(2) routing

(3) traffic management

The term guide path refers to the actual path the AGV follows in making its rounds through a manufacturing plant. The guide path can be one of two types. The first and oldest type is the embedded wire guide path. With this type, which has been in existence for over 20 years, the AGV follows a path dictated by a wire that is contained within a path that runs under the shop floor. This is why the earliest AGVs were sometimes referred to as wire-guided vehicles. The more modern AGVs are guided by optical devices.

The term routing is also used frequently in association with AGVs. Routing has to do with the AGVs ability to make decisions that allow it to select the appropriate route as it moves across the shop floor. The final term, traffic management, means exactly the same thing on the shop floor that it means on the highway. Traffic management devices such as stop signs, yield signs, caution lights, and stop lights are used to control traffic in such a way as to prevent collisions and to optimize traffic flow and traffic patterns. This is also what traffic management means when used in the context of AGVs.

1. Rationale for using AGVs

Some manufacturing plants still use traditional materials handling systems. Some use automated storage and retrieval systems. Others use AGVs. Many use all of these together. Manufacturing technology students should understand why manufacturing

104

firms use AGVs. Five of the most frequently stated reasons are as follows:

- Because they can be computer controlled, AGVs represent a flexible approach to materials handling.
- AGVs decrease labor costs by decreasing the amount of human involvement in materials handling.
  - AGVs are compatible with production and storage equipment.
  - AGVs can operate in hazardous environments.
  - AGVs can handle and transport hazardous materials safely.

Of the various reasons frequently given for using AGVs, perhaps the two that are the most important to the future of manufacturing are flexibility and compatibility. Because they are so versatile, they can be adapted to be compatible with most production and storage equipment that might exist in a typical manufacturing setting. Their flexibility and compatibility allow AGVs to fit in with trends in the world of manufacturing, including automation and integration of manufacturing processes [3].

2. Types of AGVs

Automated guided vehicles are called on for use in a variety of different manufacturing settings. Consequently, there is no one type that will meet the needs of every setting. Fig10.3 and 10.4 show typical AGVs. In the current state of development, there are six different types of AGVs:

- towing vehicles
- unit load vehicles
- pallet trucks
- fork trucks
- light load vehicles
- assembly line vehicles

These AGVs are the work horses. Towing vehicles are the most widely used type of AGVs. Their most common use is in transporting large amounts of bulky and heavy materials from the warehouse to various locations in the manufacturing plant. A popular approach is to arrange a series of vehicles into a train configuration. In such a configuration, each vehicle can be loaded with material for a specified location and the train can be programmed to move throughout the manufacturing facility, stopping at each location [4].

2.1 Unit Load Vehicles

Unit load vehicles represent the opposite extreme from towing vehicles. Whereas towing vehicles are used in settings requiring the movement of large amounts of material to a variety of different locations, unit load vehicles are used in settings with short guide paths, high volume, and a need for independent movement and versatility [5]. Warehouses and distribution centers are the most likely settings for unit load vehicles. An advantage of unit load vehicles is that they can operate in an environment where there is not much room and movement is restricted.

2.2 Pallet Trucks

The pallet truck is different from other AGVs in that it can be operated manually. Pallet trucks are used most frequently for materials handling and distribution systems. They are driven along a guide path from location to location and are unloaded as they go. Because they can be operated manually pallet trucks represent a very flexible approach to materials handling.

2.3 Fork Trucks

The fork truck type AGV is to the automated manufacturing plant what the fork lift is to a traditional materials handling setting. Fork trucks are designed for use in highly automated manufacturing plants. They are used when it is necessary to pick material up at the shop floor level and move it to a location at a higher level or to pick up material at a higher level and move it down to the shop floor level. Unlike the traditional fork lift, however, fork truck type AGVs travel along a guide path.

2.4 Light Load Vehicles

Light load vehicle technology is simply the miniaturization of unit load vehicle technology. Light load vehicles, as the name suggests, are used in manufacturing settings where the material to be moved is neither heavy nor bulky.

2.5 Assembly Line Vehicles

As the name implies, assembly line vehicle type AGVs are used in conjunction with an assembly line process. Their most common use is in the assembly of automobiles. Assembly line vehicles can be used to transport major subassemblies such as automobile engines transmissions, doors, and other associated subassemblies to the proper location on an assembly line. Using such vehicles can enhance the flexibility of an automobile assembly line.

New words and Expressions

1. AGV(Automated Guided Vechicle)　自动导引小车
2. dock[dɔk]n. 原义是指船底在低潮时拖出的泥沟。船坞,码头
3. embedded [em'bedid]adj.植入的,深入的,内含的,[修]嵌入;n.装入,压入
4. dictate [dik'teit] v.命令,支配;指定
5. optical['ɔptikəl]adj.源自希腊语 optikos 光的,光学的
6. routing['ru:tiŋ]n.发送(指令);程序安排;路线选择,道路定线
7. rationale [ˌræʃə'nɑːli]n.基本理论,理论基础;原理的说明或解释;合逻辑的论据
8. retrieval[ri'tri:vəl] n.检索;[取还]
9. hazardous['hæzədəs]adj.危险的,冒险的,危害的
10. compatibility [kəmˌpæti'biliti]n.兼[相]容性;[适用性]
11. fork truck　叉车,叉式运货车
12. material handling　物料输送;原材料处理
13. unit load vehicle　组合运货车
14. towing vehicle　拖曳车,牵引车
15. pallet truck　码垛车
16. fork lift　叉形起重机,驻式升降机,叉架起货机,叉式起货机,叉式升降机,叉车
17. light load vehicle　轻载运货车
18. assembly line　装配作业线,流水作业装配线
19. warehouse['wɛəhaus] n.仓库,货栈,大商店
20. bulk [bʌlk]n.散装,正货,船上的货物
21. versatility [ˌvɜːsə'tiləti]n.通用性,多功能性,易变性;多功能性,多面性

Notes

1. An AGV is a computer-controlled，driverless vehicle used for transporting materials from point to point in a manufacturing setting.

AGV 是一个有计算机控制的在生产场所中点到点无人驾驶的运载工具。

2. An AGV can be used for any and all materials handling tasks from bringing in raw materials to moving finished products to the shipping dock.

从运进原始材料到将完成好的产品运输到船码头,AGV 可用于所有的物料搬运作

业。

3. Their flexibility and compatibility allow AGVs to fit in with trends in the world of manufacturing, including automation and integration of manufacturing processes.

AGV 的灵活性和兼容性使得它们适应于制造业市场，包括生产过程的自动化和一体化。

4. In such a configuration, each vehicle can be loaded with material for a specified location and the train can be programmed to move throughout the manufacturing facility, stopping at each location.

在这一配置中，每一辆 AGV 都能用于特殊场所的装货作业，并且该牵引车可以被程控运输生产设备的通货量，在每个地点停顿的通货量。

5. Whereas towing vehicles are used in settings requiring the movement of large amounts of material to a variety of different locations, unit load vehicles are used in settings with short guide paths, high volume, and a need for independent movement and versatility.

但是牵引车适用于需要将大量物料运往各种不同地点的场所，组合运货车适用于短途、高量且需要独立运转和多功能的场所。

Topics for Discussion

1. When discuss about AGV, what key terms should we pay attention to?

2. Can you compare the uses in different types of AGVs?

3. Please try your best to differentiate the main features of AGV mentioned in the text. You can turn to your classmates.

4. What's the trend for the development of AGVs?

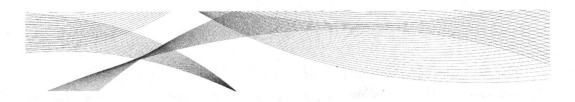

Unit 10

Packing, Marking and Shipment

It is clear that transportation costs are determined by volume and weight, specially reinforced and lightweight packing materials have been developed for exporting. Packing goods to minimize volume and weight while reinforcing them may save money, as well as ensure that the goods are properly packed. It is recommended that a professional firm be hired to pack the products if the supplier is not equipped to do so. This service is usually provided at a moderate cost.

Exporters should be aware of the demands that international shipping puts on packaged goods. Exporters should keep four potential problems in mind when designing an export shipping crate: breakage, moisture, pilferage and excess weight.

Generally, cargo is carried in containers, but sometimes it is still shipped as break bulk cargo. Besides the normal handling encountered in domestic transportation, a break bulk shipment transported by ocean freight may be loaded aboard vessels in a net or by a sling, conveyor, or chute that puts an added strain on the package. During the voyage, goods may be stacked on top of or come into violent contact with other goods. Overseas, handling facilities may be less sophisticated than in the United States and the cargo could be dragged, pushed, rolled, or dropped during unloading, while moving through customs, or in transit to the final destination. Except for the cargo in bulk, such as coal, oil, etc., and the nude cargo, such as steel bar, iron, etc., most export goods need packing for the purpose of transport and sales.

1. Outer Packing and Inner Packing

Packing can be generally divided into two types, outer packing and inner packing.

109

Outer packing is used for the convenience of protecting and transporting goods. Inner packing, also known as small packing or immediate packing, is designed for the promotion of sales [1].

The goods should be packed in a way according to the importer's instructions or the trade custom, without violating the import country's regulations on outer packing material, length and weight, or gong against the import country's social customs and national preference for inner packing colors and designs, etc.

2. Marks on the Outer Packing

To facilitate the identification of goods, the outer packing must be marked clearly with identifying symbols and numbers which should be the same as indicated in the commercial invoice, the consular invoice, the bill of lading and the other shipping documents [2].

The marks can be generally divided into two kinds: shipping mark or simply known as mark, and indicative and warning mark.

Shipping mark is usually a symbol consisting of the name or initials of the consignee or shipper, destination and packaging number, etc. Indicative and warning mark gives handling instructions in words or by internationally recognized symbols, such as "This Side Up", "Keep Dry", "Handle with Care" and so on. Apart from these two kinds of marks, there may be some other marks to indicate dimensions and weight.

3. Shipping Advice

Outer packing and marking serve for the shipment of goods, which is of utmost importance in international trade.

Generally speaking, shipment refers to the process of loading the export goods on board a carrier. However, in international trade, as it is neither necessary nor convenient for the exporter to deliver the goods directly to the importer, the delivery under such price terms as FOB, CFR and CIF are symbolically made when the exporter finishes the shipment and obtains a clean bill of lading. In the sense, therefore, the term shipment is customarily used to replace delivery.

Contrary to the symbolic delivery is the physical or actual delivery, which means the actual transfer of the goods from the seller directly to the buyer or his agent at the agreed time and place under such terms as Ex Works, Ex Factory, Ex Ship or Ex Quay.

In sea transport, there are two types of ocean shipping services: liners and tramps.

Liners sail on scheduled dates/times between groups of ports. But tramps, also called general trader, usually trades in various ports in search of cargo transportation business.

Once the goods are loaded on board a ship or placed under the control of the shipping company, the shipping company or its agent issues a bill of lading (B/L) to the shipper, usually the exporter, as a receipt for goods and evidence of contract of carriage between the shipping company and the shipper. The bill of lading is also an important document of title to the goods.

When the exporter finds it necessary to have a whole ship at his disposal for the carriage of goods, he charters a ship, that is to say, to hire a ship from the ship owner. The chartering of a ship can be on the basis of voyage, time or demise.

The contract between the ship-owner and charterer, one who hires the ship, is known as the Charter Party.

Either a charter party or a bill of lading is a contract between the ship-owner and the consignor (one who sends the goods).

In customary practice, the exporter should send a shipping advice to the importer as soon as the shipment is made, so that the importer may insure the shipment against risks for FOB and CFR transactions unless otherwise specified in the contract or L/C. But for FOB transaction, the importer is supposed to inform the exporter of the name of the carrying vessel before the shipment.

As time of shipment is very important, it should be appropriately decided. In writing, there are usually three ways to express the time of shipmen:

(1) The shipment is stated with a fixed date, for examples, shipment during January (or January shipment), shipment at or before the end of March, shipment on or before May 15th, shipment during April/May (or April/ May shipment).

(2) An indefinite date of shipment is stipulated depending on certain conditions such as shipment within 30 days after receipt of L/C, shipment subject to shipping space available, shipment by first available steamer.

(3) The shipment is indicated with a date in the near future usually in such terms as immediate shipment, prompt shipment, and shipment as soon as possible, but without unified interpretation as to their definite time limit. It is advisable, therefore, to avoid using these ambiguous terms.

4. Labeling and Marking the Shipment

Specific marking and labeling is used on export shipping cartons and containers to:
- Meet shipping regulations;

- Ensure proper handling;
- Conceal the identity of the contents;
- Help receivers identify shipments; and
- Insure compliance with environmental and safety standards.

If packages are labeled in accordance with their guidelines and labeling regulations, you will most likely prevent misunderstandings and delays in shipping. Following additional information must be provided on the outside of the shipment containers:

- Name of the person sending the shipment (the shipper);
- Shipper's business name and address;
- Country of origin (for example, "U. S. A. "), prominently displayed.
- Weight markings (in pounds and kilograms);
- Size markings of shipping containers (in both inches and centimeters);
- Handling markings (always use international pictorial symbols);
- Handling instructions (in your country's language and the language of the country of destination);
- Cautionary markings (such as "This Side Up" or "Use No Hooks");
- Number of packages that are part of the shipment (for example, "1 of 6", "2 of 6", "3 of 6", and so on);
- Markings unique to hazardous materials (use universal symbols adapted by the International Air Transport Association and the International Maritime Organization); and
- Ingredients (if applicable, also included in the language of the destination country).

Letters marked on the packing are generally stenciled onto packages and containers in waterproof ink. Markings should appear on three faces of the container, preferably on the top and on the two ends or the two sides. Any old markings must be completely removed from previously used packaging.

5. Cautionary Markings

Cautionary Markings are also called care marks, safety marks, or protective marks, including two types, i. e. pictorial cargo handling marks, which are the symbols usually international understandable and cautionary words.

Some pictorial marks or symbols often seen on packaging are shown followed. Each has a specific meaning. The symbols are normally very simple and easy to understand.

For example, the first symbol, two hands holding or protecting the package is another reminder that the contents should be handled with care. An umbrella is a symbol reminding those handling the package to keep out of the rain and not to store it in damp conditions. It is normally found on card based packages which would be damaged if placed in contact with water. A broken wine glass suggests that the product inside the packaging could be easily damaged if dropped or handled without care and attention. The contents are fragile. The symbol with thermometer and two temperatures in it is found mainly on packages containing food and drink. The symbol clearly shows that the contents should be stored at a temperature between 10 and 20 degrees (centigrade).

Widely known cautionary words are laid out as follows:

"Handle With Care/With Care/Treat Care", "This Side Up/This End Up", "Use No Hooks/Do Not Use Dog Hooks/No Hooks", "Don't Turn Over", "Don't Drop/ Not To Be Dropped", "Keep Dry/Guard Against Wet/Guard Against Damp", "Keep Flat/Stow Level", "Never Lay Flat", "Stand On End/To Be Kept Upright/Keep Upright", "Perishable Goods", "Stow In A Cool Place/Keep Cool/Keep From Heat/ Stow Cool", "Keep Away From Boiler/Stow Away From Boiler", "Not To Be Laid Flat/Never Lay Flat", "Not To Be Thrown Down", "Not To Be Packed Under Heavy Cargo/Not To Be Stowed Below Another Cargo", "Fragile-With Care", "Flexible", "Away From Boilers And Engines", "Liquid", "No Smoking", "Inflammable", "Explosives", "Glass With Care/Glass", "Poison", "Heave Here", "Open Here", and "Maximum Stack", etc.

There are also many pictorial marks, which are not listed here because of the length limitation.

Words and Expressions

1. volume['vɔljuːm;(US)-jəm] *n.* 卷，册
2. reinforce [ˌriːin'fɔːs]*vt.* 加强，加固；补充
3. lightweight['laitweit]*adj.* 平均重量以下的(人或物)
4. breakage['breikidʒ]*n.* 破坏，裂口，破损处
5. moisture['mɔistʃə]*n.* 湿气，水分，潮湿；(空气中的)水蒸气；泪水；降雨
6. facilitate [fə'siliteit]*vt.* 使容易，使不费力
7. consular['kɔnsjulə]*adj.* 领事的；执政官的
8. initial [i'niʃəl]*adj.* 最初的，开始的，初期的
9. indicative [in'dikətiv]*adj.* 指示的；表示的；象征的；预示的

10. disposal [dis'pəuzəl]*n.* 布置，安排；陈列

11. demise [di'maiz]*v.* (不动产的)转让；遗赠

12. consignor [kən'sainə(r), kɔnsai'nɔ:(r)]*n.* 委托者，发货人，寄件人，交付人

13. customary['kʌstəməri]*adj.* 通常的，(合乎)习惯的，(根据)惯例的

14. cautionary['kɔ:ʃənəri] *adj.* 劝告的；注意的；警戒的

15. package['pækidʒ]*n.* 包裹，包；捆，束，件头

16. pictorial [pik'tɔ:riəl]*adj.* 绘画的

Notes

1. Outer packing is used for the convenience of protecting and transporting goods. Inner packing, also known as small packing or immediate packing, is designed for the promotion of sales.

外包装用于保护和运输物品。内包装，也称为小包装或者立即包装，是为了促销而设计的。

2. To facilitate the identification of goods, the outer packing must be marked clearly with identifying symbols and numbers which should be the same as indicated in the commercial invoice, the consular invoice, the bill of lading and the other shipping documents.

为了便于商品的辨认，外包装必需清晰地标记上可以识别的记号，并且显示和商业发票、领事发票、提单以及其他发送单据里相同的数据。

Topics for Discussion

1. How many types of marks can be generally divided? And what are they?

2. As time of shipment is very important, it should be appropriately decided. So how many ways can express the time of shipmen usually?

3. What kind of additional information must be provided on the outside of the shipment containers?

Passage B

Contract and Confirmation

As any other business, logistics service is also unable to do without a contract.

A contract is an agreement that is enforceable by law. It can be long or short, formal or informal, simple or complicated, and verbal or written (only written form is accepted by China law). Without a contract or agreement to bind the contracting parties, any international business or transaction would be impossible.

A contract is the only document between the parties to which they may refer for clarification of mutual responsibilities. It must be drafted with an awareness of the background of the law in which the transaction takes place. It is proper to obtain legal advice as to the best set of contractual terms appropriate to the product and type of business [1].

Before a transaction can be made, the two parties involved reaching an agreement over the goods to be bought or sold as well as the terms and conditions of the deal [2]. A contract is concluded when such an agreement is reached. In a typical business transaction, this occurs when the other party finally and unconditionally accepts an offer made by one party. Once the concerned parties officially sign a contract, it creates legal obligations in the sense of law. In other words, the contract will come into force as soon as it is signed by two parties.

Though most of the contracts have many provisions in common, each is different from the others owing to the nature of the goods. Whether we are dealing with a long or pre-printed form of the contract, there are certain key provisions that every contract should contain to avoid ambiguity and possible future conflicts. These key provisions are divided into three parts:

1. Effects Part

• The contract number, names of the contract parties and their principal place of business or residence addresses, date and place of signature of the contract. This is normally in the opening, i. e. the heading of the contract.

• Languages to be used in the contract and their effectiveness, the number of original and the signatures. This is normally in the closing of the contract.

2. Rights and Obligation Part

• Subject matter/commodity clause: name of commodity, specifications, quality, quantity, packing, etc.

• Price clause: unit price, total value, etc.

• Transportation clause: time of shipment, port of shipment/destination, etc.

• Insurance clause

• Payment clause

• Inspection clause

• Force Majeure clause

• Law applying clause

3. Claim and Disputes Settlements Parts

• Compensation and other liabilities for breach of the contract.

• Arbitration, i. e. ways for settlement of disputes in case of disputes arising from the contract. Whether to include other specific provisions depends on the type of goods, shipping and insurance complexities, and degree of trust and mutual confidence existing between the buyer and the seller [3]. All these clauses are normally in the text of the contract.

New Words and Expressions

1. verbal['vəːbəl]*adj.* 口头的

2. transaction[træn'zækʃən] *n.* 办理,处理,会报,学报,交易,事务,处理

3. obligation [ˌɔbli'geiʃən]*n.* 义务,职责

4. provision[prə'viʒən] *n.* 供应,预备

5. conflict['kɔnflikt] *n.* 斗争,冲突;*vi.* 抵触,冲突

6. residence['rezidəns]*n.* 居住,住处

7. inspection [in'spekʃən]*n.* 检查,视察

8. liability [ˌlaiə'biliti] *n.* 责任,义务,倾向

Notes

1. It is proper to obtain legal advice as to the best set of contractual terms appropriate to the product and type of business.

116

应当建立有关产品和商业类型的契约条款。

2. Before a transaction can be made, the two parties involved reaching an agreement over the goods to be bought or sold as well as the terms and conditions of the deal.

交易之前,有关双方应就买卖的货物以及交易条款与条件达成协议。

3. Whether to include other specific provisions depends on the type of goods, shipping and insurance complexities, and degree of trust and mutual confidence existing between the buyer and the seller.

是否包含其他特殊供应品将取决于货物类型、船只和保险的复杂性以及信赖的程度和买卖双方的现有的相互信任度。

4. to sign a contract   签合同

to enter into a contract   订合同

to draw up a contract   拟订合同

to cancel the contract   撤销合同

to be stipulated in the contract   在合同中予以规定

to be laid down in the contract   在合同中列明

to carry out the contract   执行合同

non-execution of the contract   不履行合同

non-payment   拒不付款

to come into effect   生效

to go (enter)into force   生效

to cease to be in effect/force   失效

in duplicate   一式两份

Topics for Discussion

1. What's the common definition of contract in life, and how about its definition by law?

2. There are certain key provisions that every contract should contain to avoid ambiguity and possible future conflicts. So how many parts should these key provisions include?

3. Once the concerned parties officially sign a contract, it creates legal obligations in the sense of law. What's your understanding towards the sentence above?

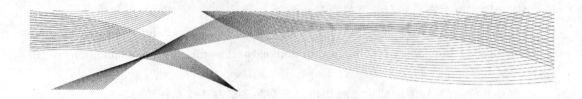

Unit 11

Passage A

Distribution Processing

1. What is distribution processing

Distribution processing is the general term of operations during the process of moving the goods from manufacturing area to the destination, which contains packing, dividing, measuring, sorting, marking, labeling and assembling [1].

The aim of distribution processing is to increase the speed of logistics and the utilization of goods. After entering the circulation area, the goods are going to be treated according to requirements from customers. That is to treat the goods to some extent during the process of moving it from producers to consumers, at the purpose of promoting sales, maintaining quality and improving logistics efficiency.

Distribution processing achieves the role of "bridge and link" by changing and improving the circulation of commodities, consequently, distribution processing is a special form of circulation. With the growth of economic, the increase of national income and the diversification demands of customers, the area of circulation carried out distribution processing. At present, logistics centers or warehouses in many countries and areas have service of distribution processing, in Japan, the United States and other logistics developed countries, service of distribution processing is even more common.

2. The types of distribution processing

There are different types of distribution processing, according to the occasions they applied for various purposes.

(1) Used for satisfying diversification

To get a high efficiency and high production, mass production is considered a common way, which produces lots of identical products. In order to meet different requirements of separate customers, transformation to the selfsame products, the first kind of distribution processing, is evidently necessary, e. g. stretching, and cutting to the steel Coil, hacking the glass plate into needed size, dicing the round log to make crosstie and plank.

(2) For the convenience and labor-saving

The goods are treated into the available state according to the requirement of downstream production by means of distribution processing. For example, the steel is treated into given shape and length, and the cement is made to be mixing and stirring concrete.

(3) Protecting goods

In order to protect the commodities during the process of logistics, some additional treatments are taken, such as modifying, preserving, refrigerating and lubricating. Freezing treatment to marine products, meats, and eggs, disposal route to the silk, flax, and woven cotton fabrics to guard against moth and damp, decaling and spraying paint on the surface of metals, are some examples of this kind of distribution processing.

(4) Eking out the completeness of production

Fabricating in the field of manufacturing is usually done to certain extent rather than truly accomplished. Some further processing has to be made at the distribution center. For example, wood is usually tooled in the workshop into some regular size and shape, such as cylindrical, slabby, and quadrangular.

(5) Promoting sales

Distribution processing plays a significant role in sales promotion. For instance, the huge goods and goods in bulk are treated into small packages qualified to sale; vegetables and meat are cut and washed to meet the needs of customers.

(6) Improving efficiency

The inefficiency of treatment in some original manufacturing enterprises is due to the limited number of primary parts. Distribution processing solves this problem by completing similar treatments of the products gathered from various manufacturers centralized at the distribution center.

(7) Loss reduction

The forms of some goods make it difficult to carry out logistics operations, and goods are possibly damaged during the process of transporting, loading and moving. Some special distribution processing is capable of figuring it out. For example, bits of woods used for paper making are ground into the wooden meal, so the security and efficiency of transportation is obviously guaranteed.

(8) Joining different transportation modes

Distribution processing is helpful to execute intermodal transportation commendably, e. g., it is quite convenient and smooth to accomplish the transportation when bulk cement is packed in small bags, especially when the modes have to be changed from one to another.

(9) Integrating production and circulation

An integration of production and circulation registered as a new form of distribution processing tends to improve and adjust the structure of product and industry, which is available to boost a reasonable organization of production and circulation, and give full scope to the advantages of the enterprises.

(10) Processing for distribution

This form of distribution processing is carried out to realize distribution activities and to meet the needs of customers. Putting sand, cement, gravel and water into the rotating tank proportionally, and rolling them when the agitating lorry is driving, is viewed as a typical example.

3. Distribution 2008 Executive Summary

Distribution centers and warehouses are critical partners to many sectors of the economy. Manufacturers depend on them to efficiently house their parts and accurately execute just-in-time delivery. Retailers and distributors — including those with firmly entrenched online operations—use them for similar reasons, as well as customer-service offerings like handling product returns. Indeed, warehouse/distribution facilities are crucial leverage points for the supply chain in our global economy; any mistake during the distribution process spells loss of profits and friction with customers. Savvy warehouse/distribution managers are benchmarking key metrics and adopting best practices to make sure they stay one step ahead of the competition.

Distribution 2008 examines the survey responses of distribution managers around the United States and defines the practices and performances that correlate with success—and stronger supply chains — as well as offering benchmark metrics for key areas of operation. Data from this year's survey are presented in easy-to-understand tables and charts. Highlights of Distribution 2008 include:

(1) Warehouse employment levels continue to grow, but so does annual labor turnover as job openings spur employee searches for greener pastures.

(2) the most widely adopted best practices in the distribution industry are continuous improvement programs, benchmarking, and lean/lean-material management.

(3) The top value-added activities performed for customers continue to be relabeling/repackaging, product returns, kitting, and light manufacturing/assembly.

(4) International business is growing. A median 25% of respondents' materials came from overseas (average 36.7%).

(5) About a quarter of facilities import 60% of their goods and 84% import at least some percentage of goods.

(6) Information-technology (IT) and capital-equipment spending is expected to continue rising. About 10% of managers said their IT spending would increase by more than 20%, and 11% reported that their capital-equipment expenditures would see a similar rise.

(7) The three most common capital-equipment investments are lift trucks and related vehicles, facility remodeling/expansion, and storage equipment.

(8) Healthcare costs continue to rise — 85% of Census of Distribution facilities reported an increase in the past 12 months.

But managers say the top three threats to profitability are finding skilled labor, energy/fuel costs, and health of the economy [2]. These and many other research insights wait inside Distribution 2008.

New Words and Expressions

1. link [liŋk]n. 环，链环，滑环
2. purpose['pə:pəs]n. 目的，意图，宗旨
3. efficiency [i'fiʃənsi]n. 效率；效能；实力
4. selfsame['selfseim]adj. 同一的；同样的
5. refrigerate[ri'fridʒəreit]vt. 使冷，制冷，致冷
6. disposal [dis'pəuzəl]n. 布置，安排；陈列
7. fabric['fæbrik] n. 布；(毛，丝)织物
8. qualify['kwɔlifai] vt. 使具有资格，使符合要求
9. enterprise['entəpraiz]n. 工作，事业；企业
10. guarantee [ˌgærən'ti:] n. 保证，担保，保证书
11. respondent[ris'pɔndənt] adj. 回答的；有反应的

12. bulk [bʌlk] *n.* 容积，体积；厚度

13. facility [fə'siliti] *n.* 便利，设备，器材

14. capital-equipment   资本设备

Notes

1. Distribution processing is the general term of operations during the process of moving the goods from manufacturing area to the destination, which contains packing, dividing, measuring, sorting, marking, labeling and assembling.

流通加工的过程是一个在将物品从生产区间转移到目的地的过程中，进行包装、拆分、测量、分类、标签和收集等作业。

2. But managers say the top three threats to profitability are finding skilled labor, energy/fuel costs, and health of the economy.

但经理认为影响效益的三个最重要的威胁分别是：找到技术劳动者、能量消耗成本以及经济健康。

Topics for Discussion

1. What is distribution processing? And what are the types of distribution processing? Could you list them and give some more explanation?

2. Data from this year's survey are presented in easy-to-understand tables and charts. What will the highlights of Distribution 2008 include?

3. What are the top three threats to profitability by the manager?

4. Could you tell us more information about your idea of the distribution processing?

Passage B

Client-Server System

A client-server system is a computing system that is composed of two logical parts: a server, which provides services, and a client, which requests them. The two parts can run on separate machines on a network, allowing users to access powerful server resources from their personal computers. From Figure 11.1, we can see that clients request services of the server independently but use the same interface.

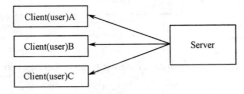

Figure 11.1　Client-server system

Client-server systems are not limited to traditional computers. An example is an automated teller machine (ATM) network. Customers typically use ATMs as clients to interface to a server that manages all of the accounts for a bank. This server may in turn work with servers of other banks (such as when withdrawing money at a bank at which the user does not have an account). The ATMs provide a user interface and the servers provide services, such as checking on account balances and transferring money between accounts.

To provide access to servers not running on the same machine as the client, middleware is usually used. Middleware serves as the networking between the components of a client-server system; it must be run on both the client and the server[1]. It provides everything required to get a request from a client to a server and to get the server's response back to the client. Middleware often facilitates communication between different types of computer systems. This communication provides cross-platform client-server computing and allows many types of clients to access the same data.

The server portion almost always holds the data, and the client is nearly always responsible for the user interface. The application logic, which determines how the data should be acted on, can be distributed between the client and the server (Figure 11.2).

123

The part of a system with a disproportionately large amount of application logic is termed "fat"; a "thin" portion of a system is a part with less responsibility delegated to it. Fat server systems, such as groupware systems and web servers, delegate more responsibility for the application logic to the server, whereas fat client systems, such as most database systems, place more responsibility on the client.

Since the distribution of the user interface and data is fixed, the distribution of the application logic distinguishes fat client systems from fat server systems, as shown in Figure 11. 2.

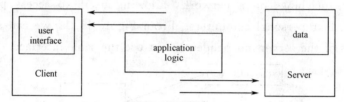

Figure 11. 2   Distribution of elements of a client-server system

1. Multitiered systems

The canonical client-server model assumes two participants in the system [2]. This is called a two-tiered system; the application logic must be in the client or the server, or shared between the two[3]. It is also possible to have the application logic reside in a third layer separate from the user interface and the data, turning the system into a three-tier system. Complete separation is rare in actual systems; usually the bulk of the application logic is in the middle tier, but select portions of it are the responsibility of the client or the server.

The three-tier model is more flexible than the two-tier model because the separation of the application logic from the client and the server gives application logic processes a new level of autonomy. The processes become more robust since they can operate independently of the clients and servers. Furthermore, decoupling the application logic from the data allows data from multiple sources to be used in a single transaction without a breakdown in the client-server model. This advancement in client-server architecture is largely responsible for the notion of distributed data.

Standard Web applications are the most common examples of three-tier systems. The first tier is the user interface, provided via interpretation of Hyper Text Markup Language (HTML) by a web browser. The embedded components being displayed by the browser reside in the middle tier, and provide the application logic pertinent to the system. The final tier is the data from a web server. Quite often this is a database-style system, but it could be a data-warehousing or groupware system.

2. Software components

The desire to distribute servers across a network and have clients find them on demand has led to the development of component technologies [4]. Components are the smallest self-managing, independent, and useful parts of a system that can work with other components to provide useful services. Each component provides an interface, which is a contract to do certain things asked of it. Therefore, systems can be quickly assembled by reusing existing components. For example, a program that needs to sort a list may ask a sorting component to do this so the programmer writing the new application need not write the sorting code [5]. Components that provide the same interfaces can be interchanged for one another; For example, a user could purchase and install a faster sorting component, and programs using the old sorting component would automatically use the improved version.

3. Middleware packages

The use of components requires additions to the traditional middleware package that can coordinate components and help components locate one another. The two primary middleware packages providing these services are the Common Object Request Broker Architecture (CORBA) and the Distributed Component Object Model (DCOM).

4. CORBA

An industry-wide consortium created and advocates the standard known as CORBA. CORBA objects can exist anywhere on a network; their location is completely transparent (Figure 11.3). Details such as an object's language or its operating system are also hidden from clients. Thus, the implementation of an object is of no concern to an invoking object; the interface is the only entity that a client needs to consider when selecting a serving object.

Communication between components (denoted by arrows) is facilitated by object request brokers (ORBs), which have been omitted for clarity. The remote method invocation system allows an object on one host to cause a method of an object that resides on another host to be executed on that remote host.

The most important part of a CORBA system is the object request broker (ORB). CORBA uses the object request broker to establish a client-server relationship between

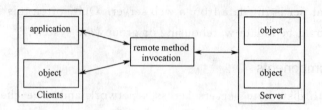

Figure 11.3 Client-server computing using distributed objects

components. The object request broker intercepts service requests from the client objects and routes them to an appropriate server. CORBA uses an interface file written in an interface definition language (IDL) to specify the services that an object can provide, but programmers write code in their language of choice.

When clients request services, the requests are routed to the remote server using a local "stub" object and the object request broker. The stub relieves the application programmer from the burden of routing the message.

CORBA specifies two means by which an object can locate another object in a system. The first is the Naming Service. This service is analogous to the white pages in a phone book: An object looks up another object by the name under which the object registered itself with the object request broker when it was initialized. The second service is the Trading Service, which is like the yellow pages: Objects can ask the Trading Service which objects have registered with certain service characteristics. The trading repository then returns references to salient objects and gives the client information regarding the properties of the services.

5. DCOM

Like CORBA, DCOM separates interface from functionality by using an interface definition language. The client-server contract is fulfilled by using object interfaces that make the implementation language and the location of objects transparent. When a DCOM client needs a server, it issues a request for an object supporting the required interface instantiated so that the interface becomes available.

Using interface pointers to mask stub-like objects, DCOM supports transparent communication between clients and remote server objects. DCOM uses a model quite similar to the mechanism employed by CORBA to provide location-independent access to objects. Since DCOM provides access to interfaces only (and not objects), there is no means by which to locate specific objects.

6. Java

Java is a programming language that allows programs to run on a variety of computing platforms without being modified; such a system is referred to as a mobile code system. Mobile code is distinguished from traditional application code in that it is dynamically executed by an application that provides the run-time environment. For code to be considered mobile, it must be portable, meaning the code can be run on a variety of platforms. Java uses byte codes to provide portability and security. The bytecode system calls for programs to be "compiled" to the point where they can be run on a Java virtual machine, which translates the byte codes into actual machine instructions in real time. Java virtual machines must adhere to a standard; this ensures that a Java program executes in the same manner on any machine. To provide security, the Java Verifier checks all code scheduled to be executed for malicious code.

Java's promise of "write once, run anywhere" makes it an appealing language in which to author pieces of a client-server system [6]. Java also provides core classes that are a part of standard Java implementations. These core classes provide basic services that many programs require, and can decrease application development times by reducing the amount of code a programmer needs to write and debug.

When coupled with distributed object technology, Java forms a strong basis for the development of a robust system that supports client-server computing. A platform for universal network computing can be created by using Java as a programming language and mobile code system and CORBA or DCOM as an integration technology. Using DCOM or CORBA allows Java components to be split into client- and server-side components in many cases, providing the system with enhanced flexibility in distributing web-based applications.

New Words and Expressions

1. request[ri'kwest]*vt.* 请求，要求；*n.* 请求，要求，邀请
2. interface['intə(:)ˌfeis]*n.* [地质] 分界面，接触面，[物、化] 界面
3. withdraw [wið'drɔ:]*vt.* 收回，撤销；*vi.* 缩回，退出；*v.* 撤退
4. access['ækses]*n.* 通路，访问，入门；*vt.* 存取，接近
5. middleware['midlweə(r)]*n.* [计]中间设备，中间件
6. facilitate [fə'siliteit]*vt.*（不以人作主语的）使容易，使便利，推动，帮助
7. cross-platform　交叉平台

8. salient ['seiljənt]*adj.* 易见的，显著的，突出的，跳跃的

9. delegate['deligit]*n.* 代表；*vt.* 委派……为代表

10. groupware [计] 组件，群件

11. canonical [kə'nɔnik(ə)l]*adj.* 规范的

12. reside[ri'zaid]*vi.* 居住

13. decoupling [di'kʌpliŋ]退耦（装置）

14. browser [brauzə(r)]*n.* 浏览器，吃嫩叶的动物，浏览书本的人

15. embed [im'bed]*vt.* 使插入，使嵌入，深留，嵌入，[医] 包埋

16. pertinent['pəːtinənt]*adj.* 有关的，相干的，中肯的

17. invoke [in'vəuk]*v.* 调用

18. denote[di'nəut]*vt.* 指示，表示

19. clarity['klæriti]*n.* 清楚，透明

20. invocation [ˌinvəu'keiʃən]*n.* 祈祷，符咒

21. host [həust]*n.* 主人，旅馆招待 许多；*vt.* 当主人招待

22. intercept [ˌintə'sept]*vt.* 中途阻止，截取

23. stub [stʌb]*n.* 树桩，残余，断株，烟蒂，用突了的笔，存根

24. analogous [ə'næləgəs]*adj.* 类似的，相似的，可比拟的

25. initialize [i'niʃəlaiz]*vt.* 初始化

26. repository[ri'pɔzitəri]*n.* 储藏室，智囊团，知识库，仓库

Notes

1. Middleware serves as the networking between the components of a client-server system; it must be run on both the client and the server.

中间件就像客户方与服务方之间的连接网络，它必须在客户和服务者两边都能运行。

2. The canonical client-server model assumes two participants in the system.

规范的客户——服务模型设定系统有两个成员。

3. This is called a two-tiered system; the application logic must be in the client or the server, or shared between the two.

这叫做双排系统，应用逻辑必须在客户方或服务方，或者二者共享。

4. The desire to distribute servers across a network and have clients find them on demand has led to the development of component technologies.

服务应当遍及整个网络，客户可根据需要选择服务，这样的需求导致了结构技术的发展。

5. For example, a program that needs to sort a list may ask a sorting component to

do this so the programmer writing the new application need not write the sorting code.

例如,一个程序需要用到分类列表时,可要求分类模块来做这件事,因此,新的应用程序的编写就不必包含分类的指令代码。

6. Java's promise of "write once, run anywhere" makes it an appealing language in which to author pieces of a client-server system.

"一次编写,各处可用",Java 的这一承诺使它在创建客户－服务系统的过程中成为一种很受欢迎的语言工具。

Topics for Discussion

1. From Figure 11. 1 and Figure 11. 2, what information can you get? What aspects do they show in the text above? Please discuss it with your mates.

2. What additions will the use of components require?

3. What's Java and what function will it make in a system?

4. Can you give us your general understanding of client-server system? Please share it with your classmates.

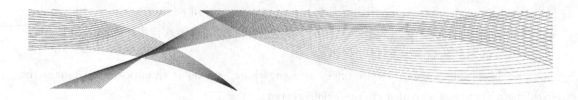

Unit 12

Passage A

Information Engineering

In the next few years, an increasing number of companies separated by distance, function, and ownership will join to deliver products and solutions for the global marketplace. The trends toward virtual corporations and increasing global networking of economics will accelerate. Information systems, with the Internet as the primary communication and integration platform, will play an increasingly critical role in providing a competitive edge for organizations in the networked economy. Information engineering is the process of networking, collecting, analyzing, and reporting information, as well as controlling business, manufacturing, or service operations. The ongoing developments of information engineering in industrial operations address e-commerce concepts and software applications as well as business process and engineering technology in an integrated framework.

1. Intelligent manufacturing

Virtual enterprise systems such as (distributed) computer-integrated manufacturing, e-design, e-logistics, and e-business systems are typically large and complex. Fluctuations in market demands, technology evolution, and changing regulations require very flexible enterprise operations for reacting to changes. These reactions must be based on relevant and up-to-date information synthesized by decision support technology. Information engineering encompasses a wide range of ways for getting the needed information to decision-makers and improving business efficiency and effectiveness.

130

Production and manufacturing practices are undergoing revolutionary changes due to the acceptance of customer-centric business models that address global competition and Internet commerce. Products have shorter life cycles and are subject to frequent design changes. Processes have smaller lot sizes and limited in-process inventories. Many companies have used computer-aided design (CAD) and computer-aided manufacturing (CAM) to handle these challenges. Computer-integrated manufacturing (CIM) is now realizing the potential it offered many years ago as software systems have become widely available for product data management (PDM), manufacturing resource planning (MRP), and manufacturing execution systems (MES)[1]. Computer-integrated manufacturing systems promise to make production more agile and flexible in meeting customer demands and raw material and regulation restrictions.

To shorten product and process development cycles, designers and manufacturers are starting to use forms of groupware for coordinating design activities over the Internet with customers and suppliers. Some groupware supports virtual conferences for sharing CAD plans, material costs, and manufacturing schedules in real-time, and makes changes for exploring "what-if" scenarios. These e-design tools are connected to e-logistics and e-business systems for supporting the design-to-manufacturing and design-to-delivery activities.

Because of the popularity of e-commerce practices and the trend of outsourcing enterprise operations to alliance partners, efficient logistics support becomes more demanding and complicated. "Personalization" trends in business amplify these pressures. Thus, the logistics operations require an intelligent information management system (IIMS) to meet customer demands. The data warehouse (a database specifically structured for information access and reporting) plays a central role in the intelligent information management system. By networking data warehouse application to the logistics planning system (LPS), warehouse management system (WMS), and enterprise backbone systems, the intelligent information management system can manage limited resources effectively. For example, an intelligent transportation-planning module can facilitate resource allocation and execution to ensure that materials and finished goods are delivered at the right time, to the right place, according to schedule, and at minimal cost.

Due to dynamic changes and outsourcing trends in the business environment, many companies are building their e-business operations to meet customer demands and create competitive edges. Typically, e-business operations are supported by a collection of software, such as customer relationship management (CRM), supply chain management

(SCM), Enterprise Resource Planning (ERP), data warehousing, and decision support systems (DSS). For example, the supply chain management system (software) fulfils customer-specific needs for goods and value-added services in a timely, efficient, and cost-effective manner. The supply chain management software is composed of several modules for order planning, production, replenishment, and distribution management. For instance, the order-planning module generates and consolidates demand forecasts from all business units in large corporations. The order commitment module allows vendors to accurately quote delivery dates to customers by providing real-time, detailed visibility into the entire fulfilment cycle from the availability of raw materials and inventory to production status and prioritization rules [2]. Advanced scheduling and manufacturing planning modules provide detailed coordination of all manufacturing and supply efforts based on individual customer orders. Scheduling is based on real-time analysis of changing constraints throughout the process from equipment outages to supply interruptions. These software modules can be equipped with a range of statistical and forecasting tools to formulate the needed business intelligence.

2. Information systems

In terms of quality, information systems should be accurate (for example, no information distortion among preceding supply chains), secure, easy to use and access, scalable to handle more users and business functions, and reliable for meeting dynamic customer demands and information technology support service. It is very challenging to meet many of these requirements, considering the complexity of information technology infrastructure. Typical information technology infrastructure includes interface and communication devices [such as E-mail, electronic data interchange (EDI), groupware collaboration, and location tracking tools], databases (for example, legacy databases, relational databases, object databases, data marts, groupware databases, and data warehouses located at various systems owned by different trading partners), and system architecture.

To make the enterprise information system useful to support decision-making activities, the design of information technology architecture should align well with the business vision and process, and consider people and technology issues. The computer-integrated manufacturing open-system architecture (CIMOSA) is commonly used in enterprise engineering to describe business, service, or manufacturing process functionality and behaviour.

When designing intelligent information management system architecture in an e-

132

business operation, the heart of the design is the data warehouse. The data warehouse uses various tools such as data mining, online analytical processing, multidimensional data visualization, statistical analysis, metadata, Internet browsers, and report-generating systems to extract needed knowledge from the stored data. This warehouse is connected to customer relationship management and sales chain management systems to support marketing, sales, and customer service operations. The warehouse is also networked to the Enterprise Resource Planning, manufacturing execution systems, supply chain management, logistics planning system, and other application software to support activities in material procurement, production, logistics, and partner alliance. The data warehouse also supports the financial, accounting, auditing, and human resource management systems to meet the expectations of stakeholders and employees. The Internet becomes the information and market exchange platform, and the Extensible Mark-up Language (XML) is the integration enabler. The selection of architecture, application software systems, integration platforms, and security software agents is the key challenge in e-business integration and e-collaborative operations (such as e-design, e-buying, and e-auction) for sharing information and resources with third parties seamlessly and securely.

In building the data warehouse, structuring a set of well-defined principles will assist an organization in adapting to changes in business operations and technology development. Such principles should strive to ensure consistent data models; data cleaning and restructuring processes to guarantee that the information supports queries, reports, and analyses; as well as metadata, scalability, and warehouse management standards [3].

Information synthesis tools, such as data and text mining procedures, support the data warehouse. Commonly used data mining algorithms include association rules, decision trees, classification and regression procedures, artificial neural networks, instance-based learning, and many statistical methods. There are also various data segmentation, aggregation, and visualization tools available for helping users to search relationship, trend, or hidden patterns for solving problems. Many vendors provide data mining software and consulting support. Very often, in practice, decision-makers face the problem of "information overload". A challenge in data mining is processing large amounts of information in a short time window. One solution is to split the data intelligently into many pieces, process the data using parallel computing techniques, and then integrate all synthesized results in a coherent manner. Text mining is needed to extract useful knowledge from operational reports, business transaction documents, or research and development publications. Ultimately, the data and text mining tools will provide users business and manufacturing intelligence at different hierarchical levels of details.

3. Outlook

Society is moving from the industrial age to the information age. Information systems and decision-making technologies will play a central role in daily life and business activities. There are many opportunities for improving the quality and efficiency of the information systems, the underlying concepts of building the system, and the implementation process.

New Words and Expressions

1. virtual corporation　虚拟企业
2. e-commerce　电子商务
3. intelligent manufacturing　智能制造
4. synthesize[ˈsinθisaiz]v. 综合，合成
5. encompass [inˈkʌmpəs]v. 包围，环绕，包含或包括某事物
6. computer-aided design (CAD)　计算机辅助设计
7. computer-aided manufacturing (CAM)　计算机辅助制造
8. computer-integrated manufacturing (CIM)　计算机集成制造
9. potential [pəˈtenʃ(ə)l]adj. 潜在的，可能的，势的，位的
10. product data management (PDM)　产品数据管理
11. manufacturing resource planning (MRP)　制造资源计划
12. manufacturing execution systems (MES)　制造执行系统
13. groupware　[计] 组件，群件
14. intelligent information management system (IIMS)　智能信息管理系统
15. logistics planning system (LPS)　物流计划系统
16. warehouse management system (WMS)　仓储管理系统
17. customer relationship management (CRM)　顾客关系管理
18. supply chain management (SCM)　供应链管理
19. Enterprise Resource Planning (ERP)　企业资源计划
20. decision support systems (DSS)　决策支持系统
21. visibility [ˌviziˈbiliti]n. 可见度，可见性，显著，明显度，能见度
22. infrastructure [ˈinfrəˈstrʌktʃə]n. 下部构造，基础下部组织
23. electronic data interchange (EDI)　电子数据交换

24. computer-integrated manufacturing open-system architecture (CIMOSA)
计算机集成制造开放式架构
25. multidimensional [ˌmʌltidiˈmenʃənl]*adj.* 多面的，多维的
26. scalability [ˌskeiləˈbiliti]*n.* 可量测性
27. hierarchical [ˌhaiəˈrɑːkik(ə)l]*adj.* 分等级的

Notes

1. Computer-integrated manufacturing (CIM) is now realizing the potential it offered many years ago as software systems have become widely available for product data management (PDM), manufacturing resource planning (MRP), and manufacturing execution systems (MES).

计算机综合制造正在不断发掘出其在多年以前就以表现出来的潜力，因为软件系统在很多方面得到广泛的应用，比如产品信息管理，制造物料管理，制造执行系统。

2. The order commitment module allows vendors to accurately quote delivery dates to customers by providing real-time, detailed visibility into the entire fulfilment cycle from the availability of raw materials and inventory to production status and prioritization rules.

定购服务模块通过实时监测，以及通过原材料、产品状况和优先规则而得到的对整个实行情况的详细了解，能让货主精确估算出给顾客的送货时间。

3. Such principles should strive to ensure consistent data models; data cleaning and restructuring processes to guarantee that the information supports queries, reports, and analyses; as well as metadata, scalability, and warehouse management standards.

这些法则应该尽量去保证数据库模式的一致；数据库的整理和重构过程也应该保证信息的可询问性、可报告性和可分析性，就像元数据一样，具有可量测性，并符合数据库管理标准。

Topics for Discussion

1. To shorten product and process development cycles, what will the designers and manufacturers do?

2. To make the enterprise information system useful to support decision-making activities, what point should the designer of information technology architecture pay attention to?

3. What's the outlook of information engineering in this chapter, and what's your own opinion about it?

Passage B

Management Information System

The terms management information system (MIS), information system (IS), and information management (IM) are synonyms. They refer both to an organization system that employs information technology in providing information and communication services and the organization function that plans, develops, and manages the system.

1. The Structure of an MIS

The structure of an information system may be visualized as infrastructures plus applications. The applications have a conceptual structure based on the purposes or needs being met and the functions of the organization that employ them. The three infrastructures that provide the general capacity and capabilities for information access and processing are technology, data, and personnel. The infrastructures enable specific applications and activities [1].

(1) The technology infrastructure

It consists of computer and communication hardware, system software, and general purpose software systems. The computer hardware consists of computers and related storage, input, and output devices. The communications hardware contains devices to control the flow of communications within internal networks and with external network providers. Computer hardware is made operational through system software that provides generalized functions necessary for applications. "Computer operation systems", communications software, and network software are examples. Generalized software is not specific to a single application but provides facilities for many different applications. An example is a database management system to manage databases and perform access and retrieval functions for a variety of applications and users.

(2) The databases form a data infrastructure

They provide for storage of data needed by one or more organizational functions and one or more activities. There will be a number of databases based on organization activities. Planning of the database infrastructure involves determining what should be stored, what relationships should be maintained among stored data, and what restrictions should be placed on access. The result of database planning and implementation with database management systems is a capacity to provide data both for applications and ad hoc needs. Comprehensive databases designed for ad hoc use may be termed "data warehouses".

(3) The information systems personnel

It can be viewed as a third infrastructure, which includes all personnel required to establish and maintain the technology and database infrastructures and the capacity to perform user support, development, implementation, operation, and maintenance activities. The personnel may be divided between an MIS function and functional areas. There may be, for example, general purpose user's support personnel in the MIS function and functional information management support personnel in the functional areas of the organization.

The application portfolio provides the specific processing and problem-solving support for an organization. It consists of the application "software" and related model bases and "knowledge" bases. The application software consists of applications that cross functional boundaries and applications identified with a single function. Although there is significant integration of applications because of the use of common databases and use of the same application by more than one function, the application portfolio reflects a federation of systems rather than a totally integrated system. A single, integrated system is too complex; the selective integration by interconnection, among the federation of systems is more manageable and robust. A visualization of the MIS based on the application portfolio consists of applications in direct support of each business function (marketing, production, logistics, human resources, finance and accounting, information systems, and top management) plus general-purpose applications and facilities. Although the database management system provides general-purpose support, it also supports databases common to many functions and databases unique to a function. The applications can also be classed as being associated with transaction processing, products and services and management. The management applications can be classified as related to operational control, management control, and strategic planning.

The transaction processing and goods and services applications tend to support lower-level management and operating personnel. The applications tend to incorporate programmed decision processes based on decision rules and algorithms. Applications supporting higher-level management processes are less structured and require human interaction to specify the decision process and data to be used. Because of these differences, the application structure of a management information system is often described as a pyramid.

2. Information System Support for Management Activities

In addition to its use to transaction processing, business processes, and within products and services, information systems support management processes such as planning, control, and decision making. This use of information technology can provide significant value to the organization [2]. The Anthony framework is used by both academic researchers and business practitioners to model and classify the information system support for management. The three levels of the Anthony hierarchy define the nature of the management support applications.

(1) Operational control ensures that operational activities are conducted efficiently and effectively according to plans and schedules. Examples of applications in support of operational management are scheduling, purchasing, and inquiry processing for operations. The decisions and actions cover short time periods such as a day or a week. An example of processing in support of operational control is the sequence of operations to authorize an inventory withdrawal. The balance on hand and an order is examined to determine the need for a replenishment order. The size of the replenishment order is based on reorder quantity algorithms to control inventory levels. An order document is prepared automatically for review and acceptance or modification by a purchasing analyst before it is released.

(2) Management control focuses on a medium-term time period such as a month, quarter, or year. It includes acquisition and organization of resources, structuring of work, and acquisition and training of personnel. Budget reports, variance analysis, and staffing plans are typical of management control applications.

(3) Strategic management applications were designed to assist management in doing long range strategic planning. The requirements include both internal and external data. The emphasis is on customer trends and patterns and competitor behavior. Market-share trends, customer perceptions of the organization and its products and services, along with similar perceptions for competitors, and forecasts of technology changes, are examples of information useful in strategic management.

A set of applications and retrieval/report facilities within an MIS designed especially for senior executives has been termed an "executive information system (EIS)". It focuses on the unique needs of senior management. These include an ability to formulate executive-level inquiries, construct special information requests, explore, various alternative analyses, and so forth. The databases used for an EIS include portions of the corporate transactions databases, selected summary and comparative data, and relevant external data.

3. Information System Support for Decision-making

The decision-making support provided to an organization by its information system can be described to terms of Simon's three phases of the decision-making process: intelligence, design, and choice. The support for the intelligence phase of discovering problems and opportunities consists of database search and retrieval facilities. For example, an analyst investigating collections policy can use retrieval software to obtain data on customers, sales, and collections for a representative period. The decision design phase to which decision alternatives are generated is supported by statistical, analytical, and modeling software. In the collections example, the decision design might involve correlation of collection times with customer characteristic, and order characteristics. The support for the choice phase includes decision models, sensitivity analysis, and choice procedures. A choice procedure for a collections policy might involve the use of models to compare collection policies on various dimensions and rank order the policies.

"Expert systems" support decision-making by rule-based or knowledge-based systems. The most commonly used rule-based systems incorporate decision procedures and rules derived from the decision making processes of domain experts. Data items presented to the rule based system are analyzed by the expert system and a solution is suggested based on the rule, derived from experts. The decision may be supported by an explanation facility that details the rules and logic employed in arriving at the decision. Unlike expert systems based on rules, "neural networks" are a decision-support procedure based on the data available for a decision. The neural network is established (or recalibrated) by deriving the factors and weights that will achieve a specified outcome using an existing set of data. The factors and weights are applied to new data to suggest decisions. An example of neural network use is decision-making relative to credit worthiness for a loan or credit approval for a transaction.

The term "Design support system (DSS)" refers to a set of applications within an MIS devoted to decision support. Although some writers distinguish between MIS and DSS, the MIS concept is typically defined to include a DSS. The concept of a DSS incorporates the Anthony framework and the decision-making categories of Herbert Simon (1977). The classic description of the concept is by Ciorry and Scott Morton (1971). Their framework for a DSS classifies decisions as structured, semi-structured, and unstructured within the three levels of management. Structured decisions can be incorporated in the programmed procedures of computer software, but unstructured (and many semi-structured) decisions are best supported by analytical and decision models and analytical and modeling tools. These facilities aid human decision-makers to deal with difficult problems that cannot be solved with algorithms. The concept of a DSS incorporates human-system interaction as the human decision-maker formulates scenarios, models alternatives, and applies analytical procedures in order to explore alternative solutions and evaluate consequences.

4. The Future of Information Systems and Function

Systems based on information technology have become an integral part of organization processes, products, and services, the data available for analysis and decision-making has increased with the capabilities for computer-based storage and retrieval. The infrastructures have become more complex as more information technology is distributed to individuals and departments. The planning, design, implementation, and management of information resources have become more complex and more vital to organizations. The need for a specialized MIS function has increased. Although some routine functions may be outsourced, the critical functions that affect competitive advantage are likely to remain part of an MIS function in the organization.

Information technology is still changing rapidly, and new opportunities for business use continue to emerge. The rate of innovation and change and the investment implications also underlines the minced for an MIS function to support organizational use of information technology for information access, processing, and communication [3].

New Words and Expressions

1. conceptual [kən'septʃuəl,-tjuəl] *adj.* 概念的
2. output ['autput] *n.* 产量;产品
3. restriction [ris'trikʃən] *n.* 限制,限定,束缚,自制
4. comprehensive [ˌkɔmpri'hensiv] *adj.* 广泛的,全面的,综合的;综合教育的
5. lower-level   *n.* 低级别
6. framework ['freimwəːk] *n.* 骨架,结构框
7. hierarchy ['haiərɑːki] *n.* 僧侣统治集团,僧侣统治
8. sequence ['siːkwəns] *n.* 继[连]续;一连串
9. authorize ['ɔːθəraiz] *vt.* 批准;认可

10. determine [di'tə:min]*vt.* 决心，决意

11. personnel [ˌpə:sə'nel]*n.* 全体人员，职员，班底

12. dimension [di'menʃən] *n.* 尺寸(长，宽，高)，尺度，线度

13. neural['njuərəl] *adj.* 神经(系统)的；神经中枢的

14. semi-structured　　板结构方式的

15. specialized['speʃəlaizd]*adj.*专用的；专门的(也作：specialised)

16. mince [mins] *vt.* 切 [剁，绞]碎；斩细(肉等)

Notes

1. The structure of an information system may be visualized as infrastructures plus applications. The applications have a conceptual structure based on the purposes or needs being met and the functions of the organization that employ them. The three infrastructures that provide the general capacity and capabilities for information access and processing are technology, data, and personnel. The infrastructures enable specific applications and activities.

信息系统的结构可以被视作基础设施加上应用。这个应用有个基于目的或者需求的概念性结构以及组织功能。其中，为信息获取及运行提供总容量和总能力的三个基础是技术、数据和人员。基础设备可以实现特殊应用及活动。

2. In addition to its use to transaction processing, business processes, and within products and services, information systems support management processes such as planning, control, and decision making. This use of information technology can provide significant value to the organization.

除了在交易过程、买卖过程中使用外，也同时应用在产品、服务和信息系统支持管理过程，例如：计划、控制和决策。这样信息技术的应用能为组织提供重要的价值。

3. Information technology is still changing rapidly, and new opportunities for business use continue to emerge. The rate of innovation and change and the investment implications also underlines the minced for an MIS function to support organizational use of information technology for information access, processing, and communication.

信息技术仍然发展迅速，并且商业应用的机会正持续出现。革新的速度、变化以及投资倾向也都突出了 MIS 系统支持针对信息获取、处理和沟通等信息技术的组织使用。

Topics for Discussion

1. The infrastructure of MIS enables specific applications and activities; so could

you give a brief introduction about their basic functions?

2. Can you imagine the future of Information Systems and Function? Please give us some reasonable explanation.

3. What's the future of information systems and what about its function?

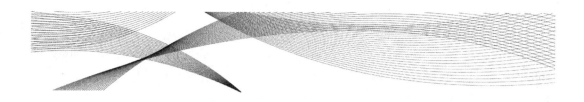

Unit 13

Electronic Commerce Definitions

1. A Classification Scheme for Traded Items

I use "traded items" as a collective term for the entities that are purchased and sold. The characteristics of traded items are a major determinant of the form of the trading mechanism. I find it useful to classify those characteristics across the following three dimensions.

(1) Goods and Services

Two groups can be readily distinguished, which are conventionally referred to as "goods" and "services". A good is an identifiable physical entity, which is "delivered", whereas a service is an act, which is "performed".

(2) Physical and Digital Traded Items

It is also valuable to distinguish physical from digital traded items. A "digital item" is one that may be delivered or performed entirely through a telecommunications network. This is further discussed below, under Digital Goods and Services. On the other hand, the delivery or performance of a "physical item" involves logistical activities such as the transportation of goods, or of the person and/or facilities whereby the service will be performed [1].

This is a separate dimension from the previous one, because both goods and services may be either physical or digital; for example, an audio-CD is a physical good, whereas an audio-file downloaded over the Internet is a digital good; and a haircut is a physical service, whereas the display of an animated graphic on a purchaser's screen is a digital service.

(3) The Degree of Productisation of Traded Items

A product is a normal offering by a supplier, which can be ordered simply by nominating a product-identifier.

2. Digital Goods and Services

Electronic commerce can support most of the processes involved in the purchasing of physical goods and services, with the exception of the Logistics phase of the Deliberative model, and the Get phase of the Spontaneous model [2].

Digital goods and services are those that can be delivered using the information infrastructure. Hence, for digital goods and services, the market space provides a context sufficient for the entire procurement process [3].

Digital goods and services include:

- documents, including articles and books;
- data, including statistics;
- reference information, including dictionaries and encyclopedias;
- news;
- weather forecasts;
- projected sound, such as speeches and musical performances;
- projected video and video-with-sound, including television, video-conferencing and video-clips; and
- interactive voice, such as telephone conversations and teleconferencing;
- interactive video and video-with-sound, such as video-conferencing;
- images, including structured graphics such as diagrams and musical scores, and photographs;
- entertainment, infotainment, edutainment and education via multi-media;
- bookings and tickets for live events;
- software, quite generally;
- commerce in insurance;
- commerce in money, including foreign currencies;
- commerce in securities, and financial derivatives such as stock-based, interest-rate-based and index-based options; and
- Commerce in commodities, and commodities derivatives such as futures.

3. Market Spaces

The concept of "market space" is used to distinguish the "location" in which electronic commerce is conducted, from conventional, physical marketplaces.

It refers to a virtual context in which buyers and sellers discover one another, and transact business. It is a working environment that arises from the complex of increasingly rich and mature telecommunications-based services and tools, and the underlying information infrastructure.

4. Categorization of Market spaces

A convention has arisen that analyses market spaces into categories, depending on the nature of the buyer and of the seller. Some fairly silly things are said in the popular literature. This section provides a taxonomy that uses the conventional terms, but defines them in meaningful ways.

(1) B2B (Business to Business)

This kind of market space involves one business enterprise selling to another. In practice, even-handed markets are uncommon, and instead the seller (s) seek to structure the process in their own favor, and the buyer(s) seek to do the same. Which achieves how much depends on the degree to which market power exists or can be contrived, whether the available technology fits the needs of one side more than the other, and how the arm-wrestling works out.

Many observers have failed to allow for the fact that business enterprises differ vastly in terms of their size, their capacity to invest in technology, and their adaptability to new threats and opportunities [4]. The conventional distinction between "SMEs" (small and medium-sized enterprises) and large enterprises is useless. It's advisable to distinguish the following strata of business enterprises:

- Micro-enterprises (with c. 0-3 employees);
- SEs (Small Business Enterprises, with c. 3-100 employees);
- MEs (Medium-Sized Business Enterprises, with c. 100-200/500 employees);
- LEs (Large Business Enterprises, with c. 200/500-5,000 employees);
- VLEs (Very Large Business Enterprises, with more employees than that);
- Conglomerates (i. e. large corporations with multiple, relatively independent business units); and
- Multinational corporations (MNCs)

It's becoming increasingly important to recognize an additional category, orthogonal to the size dimension, for Virtual Business Enterprises (or "dynamic networks")[5].

(2) B2G / G2B (Business to Government / Government to Business)

Some authors identify a separate category of B2G. In some cases, it is used to refer to sales by business enterprises to government. There are some differences between this and other variants of B2B (e. g. more formality in RFT/RFP/RFQ processes, more emphasis on probity, and contracts entered into with the relevant body politic rather than with the purchasing organization itself); but there are not necessarily enough differences to warrant significantly different treatment from B2B generally.

In other cases, B2G refers to service delivery by government to business enterprises (for which "G2B" would make more sense), or is concerned with regulation by government of business enterprises. This may be a more worthwhile distinction from B2B, because it commonly involves different goods and services, different approaches to the transaction, and different requirements of technology (e. g. payment systems, and aspects of security).

(3) B2C (Business to Consumer)

The term B2C is commonly used to refer to sale by a business enterprise to a person (or "consumer"). The term is misleading, in that a business enterprise may also be a consumer.

As argued in greater detail in relation to the poor performance of net-marketers, and in relation to the privacy aspects of direct marketing, the use of the "2" involves a misunderstanding of the dynamics of Internet commerce that is both fundamental and very significant. Until sellers discover that, on the net, buyers are not inert targets of a mass broadcast medium, consumer e-commerce will continue to develop very slowly.

(4) C2C (Consumer to Consumer)

An often overlooked category of marketspaces is the use of electronic tools to support transactions between individuals.

Some of these are conventionally economic in nature, as in "classified ads" and auctions of personal possessions. Others involve 'indirect or deferred reciprocity'. Still others involve gifts. All of these various categories of market are capable of being supported by electronic tools.

5. Supra-Organizational Systems

Information systems are complexes of human and machine-performed activities which together assist an organization in the performance of its functions. Intra-

146

organisational systems are those that are substantially internal to one organization.

Electronic commerce involves interaction among the information systems of two or more organizations. As these interactions have matured, it has become increasingly sensible to conceive of a single system that extends beyond the boundaries of a single organization. I coined the term "supra-organizational systems" in 1988 as the collective term for all of the various forms that such information systems can take.

New Words and Expressions

1. entity['entiti]*n.* 实体
2. referred to as   把……称为……
3. whereas [(h)wɛər'æz]*conj.* 然而，反之，鉴于，尽管，但是
4. logistic [ləu'dʒistik]*adj.*后勤学的，后勤的
5. whereby [(h)wɛə'bai]*adv.* 凭什么，为何
6. animated graphic   动画
7. productisation   *n.* 生产
9. infrastructure['infrə'strʌktʃə]*n.* 下部构造，基础下部组织
10. statistics [stə'tistiks]*n.* 统计学，统计表
11. conglomerate [kɔn'glɔmərit]*vt.* 使凝聚成团
12. projected sound   立体声
13. clip [klip]*n.* 夹子，回形针，子弹夹；*vt.* 夹住，剪短，修剪
14. interactive [ˌintər'æktiv]*adj.*交互的，相互影响的
15. musical score   乐谱
16. edutainment   *n.*教育娱乐（合成词）
17. securities   *n.* 有价证券
18. transact [træn'zækt,-'sækt] *vt.* 办理，处理，执行；*vi.* 做交易，谈判

Notes

1. On the other hand, the delivery or performance of a "physical item" involves logistical activities such as the transportation of goods, or of the person and/or facilities whereby the service will be performed.

另一方面，物资的输送包括各种物流活动，如货物、人和/或设备的运输，后者使得服务过程得以完成。

2. Electronic commerce can support most of the processes involved in the

purchasing of physical goods and services, with the exception of the Logistics phase of the Deliberative model, and the Get phase of the Spontaneous model.

电子商务可以支持大多数包括产品和服务的购买过程,除了协商模拟物流阶段和自然模拟的获取阶段。其中,with the exception of the Logistics······是状语从句,起补充说明的作用。

3. Hence, for digital goods and services, the market space provides a context sufficient for the entire procurement process.

所以,对于数字产品和服务而言,市场为整个进货过程提供足够的衔接。

4. Many observers have failed to allow for the fact that business enterprises differ vastly in terms of their size, their capacity to invest in technology, and their adaptability to new threats and opportunities.

很多观察者都不能考虑到企业规模,以及他们的科技投资能力和面临危险和机遇时的适应能力间的巨大差别这一事实。

5. It's becoming increasingly important to recognize an additional category, orthogonal to the size dimension, for Virtual Business Enterprises (or "dynamic networks").

对于虚拟商务企业(或动态网络)而言,认清其种类与规模大小的关系已变得愈加重要。

Topics for Discussion

1. What are the common classification schemes for traded items?

2. Could you give us some example of the digital goods or services and try your best to find them as possible as you can.

3. Can you have a clear recognition about this categorization of market spaces? If so, please describe each in your own word.

4. In the last part, what does "supra-organizational systems" mean?

Passage B

Appropriate Research Methods
for Electronic Commerce

The research domain of electronic commerce is particularly challenging, because of the lack of established definitions, and the high volatility of the phenomena. The urgent need for quality information presents a classic case of the need for instrumentalist research, which pursues outcomes of relevance to practitioners of the discipline, subject to the constraint of achieving sufficient rigor.

Research techniques can be distinguished firstly on the basis of whether or not they are empirical, that is to say, they involve observation of the "real world".

Among the empirical techniques, "scientific" techniques are distinguishable from "interpretive" techniques on the basis that science claims to be able to achieve a high degree of "objectivity", in some sense such as the reliability of experiments, whereas interpretivists question whether objectivity is attainable, or even meaningful[1].

This section categorizes research techniques into the following groups:
- non-empirical techniques;
- scientific research techniques;
- interpretive research techniques;
- research techniques at the scientific/interpretive boundary; and
- engineering research techniques

1. Non-Empirical Techniques

The following techniques are detached from real-world data. This is not to say that they are necessarily totally remote or irrelevant, but rather that they are once-removed, depending on synthetic data, or on conceptual thinking about abstractions [2]. The primary techniques are:
- Conceptual research

This is based on opinion and speculation, and comprises philosophical or "armchair" analysis, and argumentative/dialectic analysis;
- Theorem proof

This applies formal methods to mathematical abstractions, in order to demonstrate that, within a tightly defined model, a specific relationship exists among elements of that model; [3]

- Simulation

This is the study of a simplified, formal model of a complex environment, in order to perform experimentation not possible in a real-world setting;

- Futures research, scenario-building, and game- or role-playing;

Individuals interact in order to generate new ideas or gather new insights into relationships among variables. A specific instance that is often applied in the information systems discipline is the Delphi technique;

- Review of existing literature, or "meta-analysis"

The literature examined in such research may include the opinions and speculations of theorists, the research methods adopted by empirical researchers, the reports of the outcomes of empirical research, and materials prepared for purposes other than research.

2. Scientific Research Techniques

The following are common techniques that can be applied by information systems researchers to the electronic commerce research domain, within the scientific tradition:

- Forecasting

This technique involves the application of regression and time-series techniques, in order to extrapolate trends from past data;

- Field experimentation and quasi-experimental designs

Opportunities are sought in the real-world which enable many factors, which would otherwise confound the results, to be isolated, or controlled for [4];

- Laboratory experimentation

This involves the creation of an artificial environment, in order to isolate and control for potentially confounding variables.

A number of additional techniques may be applied within either a scientific or an interpretive context. They are listed below.

3. Interpretive Research Techniques

The following are techniques which are unequivocally interpretive in their style:

- Descriptive/interpretive research

In these techniques, empirical observation is subjected to limited formal rigor.

150

Controls over the researcher's intuition include self-examination of the researcher's own pre suppositions and biases, cycles of additional data collection and analysis, and peer review;

- Focus group research

This involves the gathering of a group of people, commonly members of the public affected by a technology or application, to discuss a topic. Its purpose is to surface aspects, impacts and implications that are of concern.

- Action research

The researcher plays an active role in the object of study, e. g. by acting as a change-agent in relation to the process being researched.

- Ethnographic research

This technique applies insights from social and cultural anthropology to the direct observation of behavior.

- Grounded theory

This is a specific technique that it is claimed enables the disciplined extraction of a theory-based description of behavior, based on empirical observations. Additional techniques, which may be applied within either a scientific or an interpretive context, are listed below.

4. Research Techniques at the Scientific/Interpretive Boundary

Several research techniques can be applied within either a scientific or an interpretive context. In each case, there are differences in the detailed application of the technique, because work undertaken within the scientific tradition requires careful attention to the rigor with which the instrument is designed and validated, and the data is captured and analyzed; whereas, in the interpretive tradition, the focus is on openness to alternative perspectives and on the identification of ambiguities in the data and the setting. The techniques include:

- Field study

The object of study is subjected to direct observation by the researcher.

- Questionnaire-based survey

This involves the collection of written data from interviewees, or the collection of verbal responses to relatively structured questions.

- Interview-based survey

This involves the recording of verbal data from interviewees, which arises in relatively unstructured interviews or meetings;

- Case study

This involves the collection of considerable detail, from multiple sources, about a particular, contemporary phenomenon within its real-world setting.

- Secondary research

Rather than producing new data, this technique analyses the contents of existing documents. Commonly, this is data gathered by one or more prior researchers, and it is re-examined in the light of a different theoretical framework from that previously used. The documents may also include materials prepared for purposes other than scientific research.

5. Engineering Research Techniques

Information systems research conducted within the computer science and engineering context uses two categories of research technique:

- Construction

This approach involves the conception, design and creation (or "prototyping") of an information technology artifact and/or technique (most commonly a computer program, but sometimes a physical device or a method). The new technology is designed to intervene in some setting, or to enable some function to be performed, or some aim to be realized. The design is usually based upon a body of theory, and the technology is usually subjected to some form of testing, in order to establish the extent to which it (and, by implication, the class of technologies to which it belongs) achieves its aims;

- Destruction

In this case, new information is generated concerning the characteristics of an existing class of technologies. This is typically achieved through testing the technology, or applying it in new ways. The design is usually based upon a body of theory.

New Words and Expressions

1. volatility[ˌvɔləˈtiliti]*n.* 挥发性；挥发度,轻快,易变,短暂
2. phenomena [fiˈnɔminə] *n.* 现象(phenomenon 的复数)
3. instrumentalist [instrəˈmentəlist] *n.* 乐器演奏家,乐器家,工具主义者
4. practitioner[prækˈtiʃənə]*n.* 从业者,开业者,实践者,练习者
5. subject to　*v.* 使服从,使遭受
6. constraint[kənˈstreint] *n.* 约束,强制,局促

7. rigour['rigə] *n.* 严格

8. on the basis of 基于……,在……基础上

9. empirical [em'pirikəl] *adj.* 完全根据经验的,经验主义的,[化]实验式

10. replicability [ˌreplikə'biləti] *n.* 可复制性,复现性

11. detach [di'tætʃ] *vt.* 拆开,分离

12. synthetic [sin'θetic] *adj.* 合成的,人造的,综合的;*n.* 合成物质

13. argumentative[ɑːgju'mentətiv] *adj.* 好辩论的,争论的

14. dialectic [ˌdaiə'lektik]*adj.* 辩证的,辩证法的,方言的

15. speculation [ˌspekju'leiʃən]*n.* 思考,投机,作买卖

16. philosophical [filə'sɔfik(ə)l]*adj.* 哲学的,冷静的,哲学上的

17. theorem['θiərəm] *n.* [数]定理,法则

18. elements *n.* 基本原理

19. scenario [si'nɑːriəu] *n.* 方案,情节,剧本

20. regression[ri'greʃən]*n.* 回归;复原,逆行,退步

21. extrapolate [eks'træpəleit] *v.* 推断,[数]外推 *n.* 推断,外推

Notes

1. Among the empirical techniques,"scientific" techniques are distinguishable from "interpretivist" techniques on the basis that science claims to be able to achieve a high degree of "objectivity",in some sense such as the repeatability of experiments,whereas interpretivists question whether objectivity is attainable,or even meaningful.

在各种经验式的工艺方法中,"科学"方法与"主观解释"的区别在于,科学主张能够达到"客观"的高度,在某种意义上好比实验的复现性,反之主观解释质疑客观可否能够达到或有意义。

2. This is not to say that they are necessarily totally remote or irrelevant,but rather that they are once-removed,depending on synthetic data,or on conceptual thinking about abstractions.

这并不意味着它们必须完全隔开或不相关,而是说它们应当在综合数据或其要点的概念性思考的基础上进行一次性去除。

3. This applies formal methods to mathematical abstractions,in order to demonstrate that,within a tightly defined model,a specific relationship exists among elements of that model;

这是应用正规的数学方法,去证明在严格定义的模型中各个因素之间特定的关系。

4. Opportunities are sought in the real-world which enable many factors,which

would otherwise confound the results, to be isolated, or controlled for;

本句结构为：Opportunities are sought to be isolated, or controlled for。which 引导的从句作定语修饰 real-world，后一个 which 作先行词引导主语从句。

Topics for Discussion

1. What are the common techniques that can be applied by information systems researchers to the electronic commerce research domain?

2. Can you describe the two categories of research technique in details? If so, you can discuss it with your classmates in class.

3. What are the techniques which are unequivocally interpretivist in their style?

4. What are the two categories of research technique conducted within the computer science and engineering? Please discuss them with your mates.

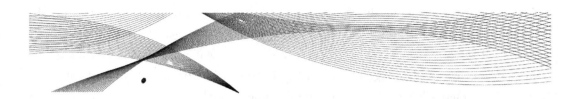

Unit 14

B2B: The Real World

A clear technology strategy is pivotal to your B2B projects and initiatives, from integrating with legacy ERP order-entry systems to implementing newer technologies such as Internet-based supplier collaboration systems. If you do not align these initiatives with a clear B2B strategy, your firm risks having a series of complex, disparate, stand alone but closely related projects, with none leveraging the other [1]. Most firms want the final plan to be a phased series of projects and technologies, prioritized by *value*. But in defining your B2B roadmaps, how do you measure the value of these initiatives?

Measuring a B2B initiative's value is not simple. In some cases it depends on the financial management techniques employed by your organization when it builds its business cases. Assessing the value of an entire B2B technology strategy adds even more complexity—typically crossing many functions within a firm's value chain, from purchasing and suppliers to selling and customers, requiring the attainment of new operational efficiencies and new revenue opportunities. Combine this with the complexity and range of systems that you can use, from those that execute transactions (such as e-procurement) to those used to make better decisions (such as collaborative sourcing), and the exercise may appear futile.

To begin addressing these complex issues, you should start by assessing the value of your B2B technology strategy in two ways: qualitatively and quantitatively[2].

1. Qualitative Assessment

Since B2B projects typically cross many functions throughout the value chain, it makes sense that they should be strongly aligned with your firm's business strategy. In other words, from a qualitative standpoint, how effectively does a specific B2B project support and reinforce your business strategy? Does it provide your company support for a unique competitive advantage that other companies cannot or do not want to copy? Or is it a "best practice", which is important for operational efficiency, but by definition replicates industry leaders' business practices and does not distinguish your organization with a unique advantage?

Keep in mind that best practices are not a mistake—in fact, they are incredibly important to business success. When you need to reduce cost, and "wasteful" systems or procedures exist within an organization, established best practices can make certain activities more efficient, such as procurement and inventory planning. If you don't adopt best practices, and thus face higher cost structures or longer cycle times, you are giving your competitors an advantage based strictly on known and replicable operational efficiencies. Best practices are particularly critical in addressing supporting functions or activities that aren't part of a company's high-level strategy or core business, such as accounts payable and accounts receivable. Best practices by definition imitate more efficient competitors. In some cases, doing something unique means not following best practices.

For example, I was the IT director at a hospitality company that maintained remote offices in hotels catering to business meetings. These hotels had to procure goods and services to sell or rent to their guests for use in meetings, from flipcharts and markers to screens and projectors. The execution of these buying and receiving transactions had to be extremely quick and flexible in order to make customers happy and ensure their continued business and loyalty. As a result, the e-procurement system the hotel employees used to buy these goods and services was actually a highly strategic business system and a driver of competitive advantage that let the firm more widely source, buy, receive, and pay better than the competition.

To achieve this differentiation from competitors, industry best practices such as national vendor contracts or commodity-based approval rules were purposefully not adopted. In this specific firm, the best practice would have limited the flexibility in satisfying a demanding client. Instead, we established a unique way of running a highly demand-driven, decentralized buying process while still maintaining a centralized procurement organization built to serve the needs of field offices in hotels.

Our implementation of the B2B purchasing applications required a highly tailored configuration of the e-procurement system, including how it was integrated with other systems not typically associated with purchasing, such as the sales quotation and customer billing systems. While competing hotels could replicate this process, they didn't want to, because doing so would have meant abandoning their own rules of how to run field office operations and procurement. That uniquely tailored demand-driven e-procurement system helped support and reinforce sustainable competitive advantage through being highly flexible with business clients. The company chose to implement its B2B system in this manner because it qualitatively supported the company's strategic positioning.

On the other hand, enhancements to the general ledger system, which reduced costs and time and improved performance, were not a core business driver and didn't provide any substantial competitive advantage. Therefore, we configured the general ledger system with best practices in mind. The system's processing of tasks such as journal entries and monthly reporting were not extensively customized, as the basic "vanilla" configuration[3] delivered by the ERP vendor was sufficient. In this case, while having a good general ledger system was important, it wasn't actually strategic; it didn't differentiate us from the competition. While best practices are a required cost of doing business, they are not a source of sustainable competitive advantage because by definition, competitors can, and will, adopt them.

When you build a business case for B2B initiatives, the first tool to prioritize and analyze these projects should be a qualitative assessment of how well technologies support and reinforce the overall business strategy. How critical is the set of activities and B2B technologies that supports you in achieving competitive advantage? Are you trying to replicate industry best practices or trying to achieve unique strategic positioning? Neither is "right" or "wrong", but without a qualitative assessment, your business case can become weak, if only because you don't have clear reasons for evaluating B2B systems for implementation[4].

2. Quantitative Assessment

A variety of benefit models are available for B2B initiatives that measure value quantitatively, but the most common strategies address lowering operational costs [5]. These strategies include:

• **Improved productivity**. This strategy is usually measured in process cost savings through time studies, which are most apparent when automating a paper-based manual process, such as requisitioning.

• **Improved policy compliance.** This strategy also improves quality and timeliness—

157

whether you are forcing specific general ledger codes that eliminate manual corrections later or forcing buys from only approved vendors.

- **Better data for more informed decisions**. Often, B2B systems provide a repository of information to generate more useful information in the future, such as identification of vendor issues.

- **Higher employee satisfaction**. When users have easier access to information and automated processes, they have higher job satisfaction, so retention and productivity can indirectly increase.

Many recent B2B initiatives focus on extending legacy ERP systems, such as purchasing and order entry, to wider audiences inside the enterprise (such as e-procurement) or outside the enterprise (such as digital storefronts). These technologies are a natural evolution of ERP solutions (purchasing and order entry) and much of the value in these B2B systems lies in unlocking and extending the value in existing ERP implementations.

Here's one way to illustrate how extending ERP with B2B solutions can be valuable: think of a bank teller vs. an automated teller machine (ATM). If you've ever glanced at the system a bank teller uses when recording your transaction, you've probably noticed that it's very complex. The teller's system can, of course, perform every transaction, no matter how complicated, that the teller requires. As a result, tellers usually have to fill in many dense screens with a lot of information and remember many commands, for which they may even need self-reminder notes[6].

You can think of the bank teller's system as part of an ERP system targeted to a very small audience of users (bank tellers) who have to service the transactions of a much larger audience.

However, when these same processes were exposed to a larger audience (customers), banks needed a new kind of system. These new systems were meant to let banks place the power of their core systems into the hands of a much larger audience: the customers (you and me). In many cases, the vendors who were very good at developing the core banking transaction systems, targeting bank departments with small groups of users, were not nearly as adept at developing systems that had to be simple and easy-to-use so they could interact with a huge number of users.

As a result, new companies evolved to create systems that began putting a "pretty face" on the banks' core systems with ATMs, letting anyone perform basic bank transactions quickly and with minimal training. So you have the following analogy: ATMs add value to bank teller's systems in similar ways that certain B2B systems add

158

value to ERP systems. They unlock the power of the core ERP systems and put it directly into the hands of the users—inside or outside the enterprise—reducing costs and improving user satisfaction. The value of B2B systems can extend well beyond a user-friendly interface. They can allow coordination and collaboration between firms that was never before possible. Even so, the operational cost savings of extending the reach of ERP is frequently the starting point in B2B initiatives.

Nevertheless, these operational cost-saving methods are only part of the equation. Sometimes if subject matter experts in supply chain management or procurement develop the technology business case, the B2B system will only focus on cost-saving benefits. These operationally focused solutions are usually on the buy-side of the value chain, with systems and processes that interact with suppliers.

On the sell-side of the value chain, working with channels and customers, B2B technology strategy makes revenue-enhancing benefits possible.

These benefits include:

- **New channels**. Establishing new channels such as a trading exchange, a new distribution network, or direct selling, can provide revenue opportunities that you are not currently capturing. For example, what new revenue opportunities result from establishing a trading exchange to leverage the sale of your products and services as a new channel?

- **New customers**. Often a side effect of establishing a new channel is the ability to reach alternative customers that you are not currently serving effectively. Can you reach other geographies or other customer types through B2B technologies? For example, if you extend EDI systems to XML or interactive Web sites, will you gain new desirable customers not currently being serviced?

- **New information products**. B2B technologies may capture data previously not available, and the packaging of this data may provide another product to sell. Is the data you already have valuable, or can you make it more valuable—such as through supplier, channel, product, or customer information that you can sell?

- **New services**. When extending a process, opportunities exist to supplement the parties involved with new services. What other value-added services make sense in your industry such as dispute resolution, financial settlement, logistics, or authentication?

- **Higher customer satisfaction**. By having a better and deeper relationship with customers, you can have happier and more loyal customers who spend more money and return more often. If you are the easiest and simplest channel to buy from and offer rich customer value (most variety, best information on availability, highest quality, and so on), then you have a competitive advantage.

Assessing the value of your B2B technology strategy is critical to its success. A key success factor is ensuring that you don't overlook either the buy-side or the sell-side of the value chain—consider benefits and opportunities from both operational efficiency and new revenue potential. And, don't focus only on quantitative measures without first qualitatively aligning your B2B technology strategy to your business strategy. By addressing all of these considerations, you will have the opportunity to create sustainable competitive advantage for your firm with advanced B2B technologies [7].

New Words and Expressions

1. B2B　企业与企业之间的贸易往来等（Business to Business 的缩写）
2. pivotal['pivətəl]*adj.*枢轴的，关键的
3. legacy['legəsi]*n.* 遗赠（物），遗产（祖先传下来）
4. ERP　企业资源计划（Enterprise Resource Planning 的缩写）
5. qualitatively['kwɔlitətivli] *adv.* 从质量方面看,定性地
6. quantitatively['kwɔntitətivli] adv. 数量上,定量地
7. sustainable [sə'steinəbl]*adj.*可以忍受的，足可支撑的，养得起的
8. enhancement [in'hɑːnsmənt]*n.* 增进，增加
9. make sense　有意义;意思清楚;有道理
10. best practice　最优方法,优质方法
11. procurement [prə'kjuəmənt]*n.* 收买;采购,物资技术供应;供货合同,调拨,调配
12. field office　外地办事处
13. tailored['teiləd]*adj.*简明的,简洁的,特制的;量身定做的
14. industry['indəstri]*n.* 工业，产业，行业，勤奋
15. business strategy　经营战略,经营策略,企业经营战略,商务策略
16. authentication[ɔːˌθenti'keiʃən]*n.* 经营策略
17. if only　若是……那该多好啊;真希望……;只要,只要……就好
18. ATM　自动出纳[柜员]机（Automated Teller Machine 的缩写）
19. EDI　（Electronic Data Interchange 的缩写）电子数据交换

Notes

1. If you do not align these initiatives with a clear B2B strategy, your firm risks

having a series of complex, disparate, stand alone but closely related projects, with none leveraging the other.

如果一开始就没有一个清晰的 B2B 策略,那么你的公司(或企业)将承担一系列的风险,去开发这些复杂的、迥异的、彼此孤立而又密切相关的计划,而且相互之间又缺乏有力的支持和补充。

2. To begin addressing these complex issues, you should start by assessing the value of your B2B technology strategy in two ways: qualitatively and quantitatively.

在开始处理这些复杂的问题之前,应该首先从定性和定量两个方面评估你的 B2B 技术策略的价值。

3. The system's processing of tasks such as journal entries and monthly reporting were not extensively customized, as the basic "vanilla" configuration…

此句中的"vanilla",本意是"香草",通常用来指那些随软件附送的小的实用功能程序。

4. Neither is "right" or "wrong," but without a qualitative assessment, your business case can become weak, if only because you don't have clear reasons for evaluating B2B systems for implementation.

当然,这无所谓"正确"与"错误"之分;但是,如果没有定性的评估,你就不可能清晰地评测要实现的 B2B 系统,你的经营状况也可能会变得"疲软"。

5. A variety of benefit models are available for B2B initiatives that measure value quantitatively, but the most common strategies address lowering operational costs.

虽然存在众多的效益模型可以用来定量地评测 B2B 的价值,但是最常用的策略仍是如何降低运营成本。

6. As a result, tellers usually have to fill in many dense screens with a lot of information and remember many commands, for which they may even need self-reminder notes.

结果,银行出纳员通常不得不用大量信息和命令填充密集的屏幕,为此,他们甚至还可能需要自我提醒的便条。…for which they may even need self-reminder notes 是结果状语从句。

7. By addressing all of these considerations, you will have the opportunity to create sustainable competitive advantage for your firm with advanced B2B technologies.

从以上这些方面去考虑,借助先进的 B2B 科技,你将会有机会为你的公司获得创造足够的竞争优势。

Topics for Discussion

1. What's the qualitative assessment?

2. What are the basic strategies for the quantitative assessment?

3. How to assess the value of B2B technology strategy in two ways which have been mentioned above?

4. When these same processes were exposed to a larger audience (customers), why will banks need a new kind of system? And what kind of system will they need? You could discuss it with your classmates.

Passage B

B2C Security: Be Just Security Enough

1. Introduction

For the Internet a sufficiently secure facility is required in order to make Business to Consumer (B2C) transactions work. The large number of transactions that is expected to take place in the years to come require being secure. Security experts' today talk about a 100% solution. We think you should be able to conduct transactions securely up to a certain level. In this article a new scenario for transaction securely is described that does not need a Trusted Third Party (TTP) but will provide easy to use and sufficient security in every day transactions. The type of transactions we will conduct in the near future, using the abundant Web-shops available.

There is an evident need for a simple and cheap way to secure simple transactions. Money is trusted, to a certain degree, because forging it is not easy. It is not impossible either, but most of the time you'll be safe when you trust it.

The simple way to secure your electronic transactions is using the public/private key pair. In this scheme you publish your public key but you keep your private key secret. Any information you encrypt with your private key, your signature for example, can be decrypted only using your public key. So, anyone having your public key, and when certain that it is in fact yours can verify you are actually you. This works two ways: anyone encrypting something with your public key knows only you can make sense out of it, as your private key is required to decrypt. By challenging each other using each other's public key, both ends of the transaction can ascertain identities. But, you need to be sure the public key you got is the right public key for the person you expect to be on the other side.

2. Security Expert View

The security community came up with the Public Key Infrastructure (PKI) idea, to store the public key in a certified way, in such a secure way that anyone may ask a Validation Authority (VA) to produce the certificate with your public key in it. The Validation Authority is able to request which Certification Authority (CA) stores your

163

key and if they trust the search path (as all need to trust all in this approach), a certificate with your public key is produced.

As you may have a different Certification Authority than the other person in the transaction, all CAs need to be able to validate each other in order to be trustworthy. This inter-CA trust is not something you have any control over. At best, your CA is liable if they certified someone unreliable, through a path along CAs that did not prove to be as good as they thought.

For most people the whole PKI scheme is okay, as long as the Certification Authority will pay up when things go wrong. Some will even accept a small personal risk, similar to what you now have using a credit card. Unfortunately, it is almost certain that CAs will not be in business for a long time if they accept liability on providing someone's public key through a chain of CAs. Even if they trust each other, the liability would ultimately lie with the CA providing the wrong key. And this is an entity you may never get in touch with, even if you wanted to. Imagine a failing CA in Japan, providing you with the wrong public key, leaving you with a transaction that you paid for but you will never receive the ordered goods.

The PKI scheme works fine for business partners (they have negotiated liability anyway), but we think it is not feasible on a B2C or Consumer to Consumer (C2C) scale. The large amount of low value transactions do not allow for costly security verification. That is why we thought up another idea to obtain someone's public key. It will complement PKI, is doesn't challenge it. It uses the chaotic properties of the Internet to make it difficult to impersonate someone, thus ensuring who is who in a transaction.

3. The Lack of Electronic Money

The need for a way to conduct safe business on the Internet is evident. The one who is provding the goods or services requires certainty that you will pay, you on the other hand want certainty of delivery. It would be extremely useful to have a facility in which each transaction can be viewed as a micro-contract.

In the Internet arena electronic money is not widely available yet. You may use your credit card, but the permanent stream of concerns about impersonating someone else and abusing their credit card clearly points out fundamental difficulties here. An easy way around the lack of e-money is making sure that you know exactly whom you are dealing with. If a business can be prove—in court if needed—that it was you who ordered the goods or services, you will have to pay up. So, if the business part of the

164

B2C transaction is able to identify you for certain, things become very easy. They know you, they can find you, and they can sue you. On the other hand, if you, the consumer part of the B2C transaction, can identify the business party for sure, then you know who is going to provide you with the goods or services. You would be able to prove you ordered and paid for them. Moreover, you would be able to prove the business party confirmed their consent to conduct the transaction, in court if you need to. In short, by being able to identify yourself and others in a transaction, you can negotiate terms, order goods, and make payments. Creating a legal trail is key here.

Security experts say that the most promising technique to create secure transactions is using the Public Key Infrastructure (PKI). Using the public and private key pair that forms the core of the PKI mechanism, it is possible to verify the identity of the person or entity at the other side of the transaction. It will be impossible to impersonate anyone; hence, you are able to prove a valid transaction took place. The consumer will be able to insist on delivery, the business is able to insist on payment. The current thoughts on this PKI issue suggests that you (a person) will need to trust some legal entity to keep the correct and certified version of your public key. Furthermore, this legal entity will need to verify that it is in fact you that they store the key for. Such a legal entity is the Certification Authority (CA). You may have to visit the office of this certification authority to get your public key stored, so they can see you, look at your eyes, take your fingerprints or obtain some DNA from you. Then they know you are you.

From that moment Validation Authorities (VAs) may inquire for a certificate with your public key in it at your CA.

When you are acquainted with the entity, for you it is not a problem to trust an entity as a CA. For instance, it may be your employer. Now, the fundamental problem in using PKI, especially within the realm of the Internet, is that you have to trust a chain of entities you do not know to provide you with the right public key of someone you wish to transact with. And you may in fact never physically meet this person with whom you transact. Again, the PKI mechanism with a CA hierarchy that is to be trusted by individuals will work in several contexts, like B2B, employer and employee and within communities that know each other or meet each other (e. g. a club or other Consumers to Consumer transactions). It will not work on the Net.

4. What We Need on The Internet

For the Internet we propose a virtual Verification Authority (vVA), consisting of

165

all VAs you're able to reach within a limited amount of time and effort, to check someone's identity. So, you are not asking a specific entity you then have to trust, you just ask a lot of entities for the same thing. If you require the key of say, a guy named Douwe, you would get his key somewhere (e. g. ask Douwe) and verify this key through as many VA-parties you can reach (or know). As long as they all provide you with the same public key as an answer, you are sufficiently certain you are communicating with Douwe. Instead of needing to trust a complicated set of procedures of multiple CAs and VAs, you just trust nothing but chance and the law of big numbers[1].

How Douwe's key gets published to all these VA-parties is another subject, which in essence is the solution, suggested in this article and the main deviation from the PKI principle. Instead of being stored only at one Certification Authority, the public key is stored on a number of Public Key Systen (PKS) servers, comparable to the Dynamics Name System (DNS) servers. In fact, it máy be stored on as many servers as a person is happy with. When you request any of the Public Key System servers for a public key of someone, you would get the public key back that is stored on the server. If you do this for a large number of servers the key is stored on, it will confirm to you that this is the key of the person you thought it was. For this to work properly, the public key that will stem from only one single CA source, must be distributed over the net slowly. It may take up to three months for your public key to have been propagated sufficiently for you to be considered a trustworthy person.

The more servers you can challenge, the more confident you can be that you are really in the possession the key of the right person [2]. After you are confident, you can use the public key to check if the person is who the person is claiming to be, by sending a message encrypted with the public key and requiring a reply (only someone with the right private key can provide this reply).

Now what are the advantages of working with the PKS's concept? Obviously, when you have the key distributed at several places, it becomes more difficult to have your key messed up. An impersonator has to find out where your key is located all over the globe and change them all to prevent detection of the impersonator. This will not be impossible, but the more places that have to be changed the better will be the chance of catching up with the attempted impersonating before any damage is done. Furthermore the best message from the extensive, global, PKS mechanism is discouragement: as it is so difficult to fool it completely, the intruder will probably give up before actually having started.

166

5. Variable Security (Be Just Secure Enough)

Another advantage is that you, as a person requiring security, can vary the security level you desire. When it is not so important to know if you are dealing with the person you want to deal with, you just ask one or two person you want to deal with, you just ask one or two servers, and your public key verification transaction will be quick. You should consult the servers in a random way, to make it difficult for intruders to delude you. If you want to be very sure you are talking to the right person, there is the option but to randomly consult a lot of servers. If all the servers confirm, then you consult the more time your security validation transaction will take.

Storing the keys on a server like the DNS servers in the Internet is in fact not a big issue. Within the Internet specifications key storage is already provided for. Propagating your key to other servers is something that needs to be created, and this process can use the current IP network to do so.

The Propagating process itself must not be very quick. It should take several months before your key is spread out to all servers. This makes it very difficult for anyone to pull a fast one by deleting your key and replacing it by another. To decrease the changes of quickly setting up a person, conducting some fraudulent transactions and disappearing, a key will propagate through the Internets known vVA-parties (PKS servers) at a slow rate. If it takes ten weeks for a new key to spread sufficiently to be considered trustworthy, quick scams are virtually impossible.

6. Multiple Keys Are Required

All the examples up until now have been about one single key pair, one public and one private key. As a person you will have multiple keys for separate types of use: signing, encrypting, paying, personal information, medical information, credentials, etc. This set of multiple keys allows you to discern between use types. If you wish to give colleagues access to your files on your PC, you would like to have a key that is specially meant for file access only. The key is then associated with a particular use. Losing the private key of the pair (by mistake or by a criminal act) will impair only the type of transactions the key is meant for. You will have to revoke that public key of course, but you will not be completely helpless because of it.

There will be one key that is "you" and this is provided to you at birth. Maybe verified by something like an iris-photo or, a bit more drastic, a DNA marking. Suggestions were made to us to store the private key of the pair on a clip somewhere implanted behind your ear. Difficult to steal, easy for you to remember, if a link to your brain is invented with it, that is!

7. Technical Aspects

We suggested a DNS look-alike in technical infrastructure for the PKS idea for two reasons. Firstly, it is a mechanism that exists and can be understood easily. Secondly, the storing and providing of keys is already an Internet facility called DNS Security Extensions, described in several papers. However, the PKS does not work the same as a DNS; it works in a similar environment and is based on the same approach.

This implies that little infrastructure changes are needed to make the PKS idea work. In fact, it would be a very natural service for Internet Service Providers (ISPs) to provide.

Obviously, you need a client application, one that can run on your PC or mobile device that you are using the initiate the transaction. The development of this software is exactly in line with what needed for PKI to work. Hence, no new facilities are required, while providing you with a cheap and easy way to secure transactions (using PKS) and an expensive but potentially 100% proof way (using PKI).

8. Summing It All Up

Instead of trusting a difficult to verify mechanism of Certification Authorities that certify each other, we suggest to trust no one in particular and ask around a lot before trusting anyone for just the single transaction you are considering to initiate. In fact, the suggested PKS solution does not require you to put your trust in anyone or anything; it helps to find out how confident you can be in trusting some particular party.

In practice, both solutions are viable. The PKI solution will be extensively used for business to business situations, the PKS solution for business to consumer and consumer to consumer (person to person) transactions.

PKI will require a fee, PKS can be for free.

9. Other Issues

• Business to Consumer (B2C) Security

Businesses to Consumer (B2C) transactions require security that is related to the importance or value of the transaction. Just like in real life today, you will trust money to be genuine straight way when used for small transactions. For instance to pay for the book you selected at the bookstore. For larger transaction you'd rather use a credit card or the bank, which requires a signature from you and leaves a transaction trail that can be followed.

As small amount B2C transactions will grow to a massive number in the next decade, there is an evident need for an easy, quick and, most importantly cheap confirmation that the payment is valid.

The security need in this type of transactions is not the same for both sides. The business side wishes to be secure about payment. The consumer side wishes to secure delivery and establish a legal transaction that will provide services like maintenance and back up guarantees on quality and durability when required.

- Consumer to Consumer (C2C) Security

Consumer to Consumer (C2C) transactions are small, personal transactions. They may involve second-hand products that are sold or small services provided, like gardening or house-keeping. These transactions may in fact also include elements such as, as security in these areas is also required. As these transactions tend to have an individual aspect, Person to Person (P2P) security may describe it better.

- Public Key Infrastructure

The Public Key Infrastructure (PKI) is based on a mechanism in which you, as a person, have two encryption keys. One key is public; you give that to anyone that is asking for it. Any message encrypted with your public key can only be decrypted (made readable) by you, as you need to keep your private key that is needed in this process. So, you need to keep your private key secret, and you need your public key published. For you this will do, as you are able to read any messages in a secure way. For the other side of the transaction this is not sufficient, as they wish to know for sure the public key they use is yours. Because then they know for sure they are conducting a transaction with you (and that you cannot deny that later). The Public Key Infrastructure resolves this issue by instating a Trusted Third Party (TTP), an entity that checked you and can vouch for the public key they provide being yours. The TTP can certify the public key being yours; they act as a certification authority for your key.

The problem is that the trust issue is now moved from trusting you to provide the correct public key to the TTP. In the context of an organization, a company or some other legal entity this may not pose a problem. For the Internet it will be impossible to find a third party that everybody on the Net will trust.

New Words and Expressions

1. forging[ˈfɔːdʒiŋ]n. 锻炼，伪造
2. public key 公共密钥
3. private key 私人密钥
4. encrypt [inˈkript]v. [计] 加密，将……译成密码
5. decrypt [diːˈkript]v. 译(电文)，解释明白，译码，解码，解密
6. identity[aiˈdentiti]n. 同一性，身份，一致，特性，恒等式
7. Public Key Infrastructure (PKI) 公共密钥基础
8. Validation Authority (VA) 有效性管理，合法性管理，确认机构
9. Certification Authority (CA) 认证管理，认证权限，认证机构
10. Businesses to Consumer (B2C) 企业与消费者之间的商业关系
11. Consumer to Consumer (C2C) 消费者与消费者之间的商业关系
12. credit card 信用卡
13. legal entity 企业法人，法律实体，法人实体，法人
14. fingerprint[ˈfiŋgəprint]n. 指纹，手印；vt. 采指纹
15. DNA Deoxyribonucleic Acid 脱氧核糖核酸
16. realm[relm]n. 王国，国土；区 [领] 域；界；类；门；范围
17. Public Key Systen (PKS) 公共密钥系统
18. Dynamics Name System (DNS) 动态命名系统
19. IP abbr. Internet Protocol 网际协议
20. iris[ˈaiəris]n. [解] 虹膜，鸢尾属植物，[希神] 彩虹之女神，虹，虹彩
21. Internet Service Provider (ISP) 因特网服务提供商
22. in line with 符合，和……一致
23. Trusted Third Party (TTP) 可信赖的第三方，委托方

Notes

1. Instead of needing to trust a complicated set of procedures of multiple CAs and VAs, you just trust nothing but chance and the law of big numbers.

the law of big numbers 数学中的"大数定律"，一种用于生成密钥的算法。

2. The more servers you can challenge, the more confident you can be that you are really in the possession the key of the right person.

你所访问的服务器越多，你对是否真正拥有该当事人的密钥也就越有信心。

170

Topics for Discussion

1. From the introduction, what's the security experts' view about the B2C security?

2. What's the main difference between the B2C security and C2C security?

3. Can you compare the other security ways with them? Please give us more things in details.

4. In the security experts' mind, what is the most promising technique to create secure transactions? You could analyze this point and share your own perspective in class.

5. In technical aspects, what is the DNS look-alike in technical infrastructure used for and how to make it functional?

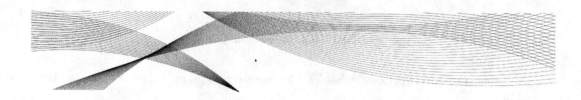

Unit 15

Supply Chain Management

Beginning with the work of Ford W. Harris in 1915 on the economic order quantity (EOQ) model, many researchers developed a variety of mathematical models for minimizing the costs associated with holding inventories (raw materials, components, subassemblies, work in process, and finished goods) in industries and businesses [1]. The subject dealing with these problems was initially called inventory control. These models were essentially single-decision-maker models involving one item. In those days, several reasons for holding sizable inventories were given, including economies of scale; uncertainties in demand, supply, delivery lead times, and prices; and a desire to hold buffer stocks as a cushion against unexpected swings in demand and to assure smooth production flow.

Starting in the 1950s, Japanese manufacturers (in particular Toyota) initiated the just-in-time (JIT) philosophy to reduce work-in-process inventories to a minimum, and implemented it using a simple Kanban (which means card or ticket in Japanese) system to track the flow of in-process materials through the various operations. In the late 1960s, Toyota extended the JIT philosophy to reduce all inventories to a minimum by developing collaborative working relationships with its component suppliers and distributors with the aim of encouraging them to make and accept small and frequent JIT deliveries; providing for careful monitoring of quality and workflow; and ensuring that products were produced or received only as they were needed.

In today's world of rapid technological developments, frequent design changes, and shorter product cycles, carrying as little stock as possible is crucial. The more one relies

172

on stock, the more difficult it will be to accommodate design changes. That's why the JIT philosophy is now being integrated into the overall business strategy worldwide, changing the nature of manufacturing and business dramatically. It has expanded beyond the walls of a factory or shop to include the capabilities, skills, and cooperation of its suppliers and the insights of its customers. This new expanded system is now referred to as the supply chain. Supply chain management comprises planning and processing orders; handling, transporting, and storing all materials purchased, processed, or distributed; and managing inventories in a harmonious, coordinated, and synchronized manner among all the players on the chain to build to order (to fulfil customer orders as they arise) rather than build to stock (to build up stock level to fulfil anticipated future demand).

1. Strategic Partnering

As part of the collaboration with their suppliers, many companies are adopting the practice of vendor managed inventories in which the company provides warehouse space to its suppliers for storing their components, to be delivered to the company as demand arises (demand pull basis). With such an arrangement, the process of ordering components usually takes the following form:

• Before each quarter the company informs the supplier of the aggregate quantity of the component that they expect to order during that quarter. This is to let the supplier know how much of their production capacity to dedicate to the manufacture of the buyer's components.

• Before the beginning of each week the company provides the supplier with a revised estimate of the quantity of the component to be ordered that week. This is to help the supplier plan shipments of the component from its manufacturing facilities, which may be far away, to the warehouse space in the company, and be ready to deliver according to orders placed each day.

• Each workday morning the company puts in an order for the quantity of the component to be delivered that day. This quantity is usually delivered within approximately 4 hours.

Instead of ordering once daily, some companies order once in every planning period (maybe a shift or half-a-shift)[2]. For the purpose of this discussion, a day will be used as the planning period.

In this mode of operation, it is critical to maintain good databases on demand, production, quality, and inventory levels, and to develop Web-based interfaces containing relevant information to which all players on the supply chain have access [3].

2. Demand Distribution

The key to making this whole process run smoothly is accurate forecasting of the component demand each day (or whatever planning period is used).

The actual demand is usually a random variable with a probability distribution that can be estimated from past data. The range of variation of daily demand is divided into a convenient number of demand intervals (in practice about 10-25) of equal length, and the relative frequency of each interval is defined to be the proportion of days during which the observed demand lies in that interval. The chart, obtained by marking the demand intervals on the horizontal axis and erecting a rectangle on each interval with its height along the vertical axis equal to the relative frequency, is known as the relative frequency histogram of daily demand or its empirical distribution The relative frequency in each demand interval I_i is an estimate of the probability p_i that the daily demand lies in that interval (Figure 15. 1).

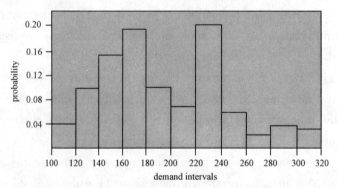

Figure 15. 1   Relative frequency histogram for daily demand for a major component at a plant

Let $I_1, \ldots, I_n$ be the demand intervals with $u_1, \ldots, u_n$ as their midpoints; and $p = (p_1, \ldots, p_n)T$, the probability vector in the empirical distribution of daily demand. Let Eqs. (1) apply.

$$\mu_D = \sum_{i=1}^{n} u_i p_i$$

$$\sigma_D = \sqrt{\sum_{i=1}^{n} p_i (u_i - \mu_D)^2} \tag{1}$$

Then μ_D is an estimate of the expected (or average or mean) daily demand, and σ_D is an estimate of the standard deviation of daily demand (which is a measure of the variability) of the component.

In inventory control, the demand distribution is usually approximated by the normal distribution, a continuous distribution that is symmetric around its mean. The normal distribution (Figure 15. 2) is completely specified by two parameters—the mean μ and the standard deviation σ.

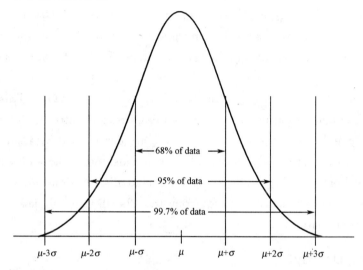

Figure 15. 2　Normal distribution with mean μ and standard deviation σ

The interval of $\mu \pm 3\sigma$ is associated with a probability of 0. 997 in the normal distribution.

One of the theoretical advantages that the normality assumption confers is that when the demand distribution changes (as might arise after a product promotion), one has to change only the values of the mean and the standard deviation in the models. In practice, almost always it is only the value of the mean that is changed; the standard deviation is usually assumed to remain unchanged [4].

3. Determining The Daily Order Quantity

The distribution of daily demand is used to determine the order quantity Q for a day, to balance the expected cost of overage (ordering too much) and underage (ordering too little). The quantity Q left over at the end of this day has to support production the next morning until the delivery ordered on that day arrives. If Q is too small, the company may be forced to shut down the production line until delivery of the order occurs. So, the company sets a safety level D_1 for Q and a penalty of $cs representing the shortage penalty incurred if $Q \leqslant D_1$.

If Q is too large, it may exceed the amount of convenient storage space near the production line that is allocated for this component. So, the company sets up a desired upper limit D_2 for Q, and an excess stock penalty of \$ ce per unit that Q is over D_2. The total expected penalty as a function of the order quantity Q is expressed in Eq. (2),

$$g(Q) = c_s[\text{probability}(Q \leqslant D_1] +$$

$$c_e[\text{expected value of excess of } Q \text{ over } D_2] \qquad (2)$$

which can be computed very easily for any given value of Q using the distribution of daily demand. To determine the optimal Q, the values of $g(Q)$ for various values of Q in a range around the mean demand are computed, and the optimum value of Q is considered to be the one that gives the smallest value for $g(Q)$. This is the most commonly used single period model for determining order quantities.

The weekly and the quarterly order amounts are determined by a similar procedure using the distributions of weekly and quarterly demands. Since there may not be enough past data to estimate weekly and quarterly demand distributions directly from data, these distributions are usually derived from the distribution of daily demand using convolutions or simulation.

4. Forecasting Demand

Successful inventory management systems depend heavily on good demand forecasts. History shows many examples of firms benefiting from accurate forecasts and paying the price for poor forecasting.

The purpose of forecasting is commonly misunderstood to be that of generating a single number. This misunderstanding is created because all existing demand forecasting methods output only an estimate of the expectation of future demand. So, these methods are useful only when changes in the probability distribution of demand can be captured by the value of a single parameter, the expectation. All these methods that forecast only the expected value seem very inadequate to capture all the dynamic changes occurring in the shapes of probability distributions of demand.

Another important factor today is the highly competitive environment and the rapid rate of technological change that is shortening product life cycles. When a new product is introduced in the market, it enjoys growing demand due to gradual market penetration for some time, followed by a short stable period, and finally a period of declining demand. Because of this constant change, multiperiod stochastic (probabilistic) inventory models based on a stable demand distribution do not seem to be appropriate for application. Single period models of the type discussed above, combined with

176

frequent updating of the demand distribution based on the most recent data, offer the most practical value.

Considering these arguments, it has been suggested that a better strategy is to approximate the probability distribution of demand by its empirical distribution obtained from past data, which in this context is called the discretized distribution of demand. This is the initial distribution at the time it is computed. This distribution is periodically updated using recent data.

New Words and Expressions

1. cushion['kuʃən]n. 垫子，软垫，衬垫;v. 加衬垫

2. swing [swiŋ]v. 摇摆，摆动，回转，旋转;n. 秋千，摇摆，摆动

3. track [træk]n. 轨迹，车辙，跟踪，航迹，足迹，路，磁轨，途径

4. collaborative [kə'læbəreitiv]adj. 合作的，协作的，协力完成的

5. dramatically[drə'mætikəli]adv. 戏剧地，引人注目地

6. harmonious [hɑː'məunjəs]adj. 和谐的，协调的，和睦的，悦耳的

7. synchronize['siŋkrənaiz]v. 同步

8. aggregate ['ægrigeit]n. 合计，总计，集合体;adj. 合计的，集合的；聚合的

9. erect [i'rekt]adj. 直立的，竖立的，笔直的

10. histogram['histəugræm]n. 柱状图

11. symmetric [si'metrik]adj. 相称性的，均衡的

12. overage['əuvəridʒ]adj. 过老的;n.（商品）过剩，过多

13. underage['ʌndəridʒ]n. 缺乏，久缺;adj. 未成年的,未到法定年龄的

14. penalty['penlti]n. 处罚，罚款

15. convolution [ˌkɔnvə'ljuːʃən]n. 回旋，盘旋，卷绕

16. forecast['fɔːkɑːst]n. 先见，预见，预测，预报;vt. 预想，预测，预报，预兆

17. penetration [peni'treiʃən]n. 穿过，渗透，突破

18. stochastic [stəu'kæstik]adj. 随机的

19. discretize['diskriːtaiz]v. 使离散

20. vector['vektə]n. [数] 向量，矢量，带菌者;vt. 无线电导引

Notes

1. Beginning with the work of Ford W. Harris in 1915 on the economic order quantity (EOQ) model, many researchers developed a variety of mathematical models

for minimizing the costs associated with holding inventories (raw materials, components, subassemblies, work in process, and finished goods) in industries and businesses.

从 1915 年 Ford W. Harris 研究出经济顺序量模型开始,许多的研究者建立了大量的数学模型,在工业及商业领域内,通过(原材料、零件、部件、在制品和成品等的)库存控制,将成本降到最低。

2. Instead of ordering once daily, some companies order once in every planning period (maybe a shift or half-a-shift).

有些公司变每天一次的下订单为每个计划周期下一张订单(一个计划周期可能为一个班次,或者半个班)。

3. In this mode of operation, it is critical to maintain good databases on demand, production, quality, and inventory levels, and to develop Web-based interfaces containing relevant information to which all players on the supply chain have access.

在这种运行模式中,很关键的一点,是要根据需求、生产、数量和库存水平等内容建立完善的数据库,并且开发出包含相关信息的网络界面以方便供应链各个成员的访问。

4. In practice, almost always it is only the value of the mean that is changed; the standard deviation is usually assumed to remain unchanged.

在实际中,几乎总是只有平均值发生变化,而标准差通常会保持不变。

Topics for Discussion

1. What form does the process of ordering components usually take?

2. Why is the JIT philosophy being integrated into the overall business strategy worldwide, changing the nature of manufacturing and business dramatically?

3. From Part two. What's the key to make this whole process run smoothly?

4. How to balance the expected cost of overage (ordering too much) and underage (ordering too little)?

5. What is the successful inventory management systems depending on?

Passage B

The Evolution of Supply Chain Technologies

The aftermath of the Sept. 11[1] terrorist attacks[1] has had a grave impact on companies and their supply chains (locally and globally). In addition to just-in-time inventory, a new term has become popular: just-in-case inventory, which accounts for supply chain disruptions. To address these issues, this column will cover the evolution of supply chain management (SCM) technologies prior to Sept. 11[1], and the second installment will discuss the impact of Sept. 11[1] on their continued evolution.

1. Less is More—The Trend Toward Modularization

Increasingly, the SCM trend is to move away from tightly integrated technologies that provide a wide range of functionality and features to modular application with a narrow focus. The aim here is two-fold: to reduce the implementation risk and increase the customer base that can afford the lower-priced modules. SCM technology vendors listened to their customers and learned that a major factor that inhibited successful implementation of prior technologies was the complexity involved in installing a fully integrated system [2].

Increasingly, SCM technology modules are priced to attract companies that couldn't previously afford fully integrated packages. Similarly, CRM suites force automation functionality; CRM requires integration with processes and features in the supply chain. Conversely, certain supply chain practices need access to functionality provided in the CRM modules. These needs point to an evolutionary path where various categories of application software like SCM and CRM as we know them today will blend and cross categories.

Especially in touch economic times, enterprises will assemble their own customer service and supply chain processes, supported by modular technologies. Portal technology will continue to evolve and provide an incremental technology infrastructure to glue these modules together. Portal technology infrastructure will also increasingly become the gateway to virtually integrate (not outsource) companies providing services that aren't part of the manufacturing process.

2. From Supply Chains to Virtual Integration

To distinguish between virtual integration (VI) and outsourcing, it's necessary to understand vertical integration. Vertical integration came into vogue at the start of the industrial revolution. In the past, the parent company owned activities across the supply chain to ensure reliability of raw materials and resources. Consider the example of tire manufacturers. They not only owned rubber plantations but also the shipping companies and intermediate sap processors to ensure a steady supply of raw materials. Manufacturer-owned tire stores were the norm. Vertically integrating the activities from the rubber plantation to the tire showroom ensured control and predictability in operating the manufacturing plant at an optimum level. Vertical integration, however, inhibited the competitive flexibility of the enterprise and increased its capital costs. These problems led to the natural evolution of the enterprise divesting itself of vertically integrated upstream and downstream functions.

The modern enterprise still has vertically integrated functions. However, these functions come at the cost of reduced competitive flexibility. Virtual integrating these functions is one way to improve competitive flexibility without loosing the benefits of vertical integration.

3. Outsourcing Different

Outsourcing differs from VI because it's typically an arms-length transaction, involving a commodity, product, or service with standard features. Consider outsourced payroll processing—the interaction with internal systems within the company. Business processes of the virtually integrated supplier would appear to be customized to the company and would perform as an employee of the company. As a company moves from vertical to VI, a department that previously belonged to the company can become a supplier linked by an integration infrastructure.

Traditionally, SCM technologies have been associated with the source, make, and delivery of manufactured products. The traditional role of SCM systems has been expanded to cover procurement of products and services of that aren't directly utilized to manufacture the company's finished products [3]. Examples of these products and services are categories such as office supplies, marketing services, maintenance resources, and healthcare services. Technologies with intelligent workflow engines support the procurement of these non-strategic products to reduce the total landed cost of using them. Most enterprises have to use a combination of push and pull SCM

180

technologies for strategic raw materials — those raw materials companies directly use to manufacture the finished product. The portal is the technology infrastructure that's emerging as a critical integration mechanism within the company and among its suppliers, distributors, and VI partners.

Portal technologies are at a relatively early stage compared to traditional SCM technologies. The compelling feature of portals as an integration platform is the incremental nature in which they can be implemented. Previously, the toughest thing for an IT person to do was justify the technology infrastructure to support cross-functional initiatives that required a common enabling technology platform. The common technology platform would cost more than the application development costs to support the cross-functional initiative within the enterprise. This fact made getting funding for technology infrastructure very tough.

The typical company may have up to four categories of portals. Portals to support traditional SCM practices will develop for the buy-side, in-side, and sell-side integration. The buy-side integration portal would support the procurement of strategic and non-strategic raw materials, products, and services from a number of sources. These could range from e-marketplaces to the established supply chain partners. The compelling value provided by the buy-side integration portal is the aggregation and management of all supplier integration points through one point of contact. This reality is especially relevant when managing the security aspects of integrating with members of a global supply chain. Similarly, the in-side integration platform is important for supporting the many specialized technologies within the company: functions such as finance, manufacturing, and inventory management [4]. Sell-side integration serves a similar purpose in providing a single point of contact for integrating with all direct and indirect distribution channels for the company's product.

A new breed of SCM technologies is evolving to support products with extremely short life cycles with out-side integration portals. Consider the area of consumer electronics. Whether it's video game device or the convergence of handheld devices with cell technology, the pace of change is very rapid. Many companies in this arena are relative newcomers, without much experience in areas such as customer service, logistics, and manufacturing. These companies will develop and launch new products with the ability to scale rapid using the VI infrastructure. Customer service, logistics, and manufacturing can be virtually integrated with specialists in those areas, leaving the company to focus on marketing its innovative product. Out-side integration portals will increasingly shape the evolution of the company over the next few years. SCM and CRM technologies will evolve to support the virtually integrated enterprise[5].

4. Economic drivers for this technology blueprint

The current economic climate, in addition to disillusionment with technology in general, is going to make funding very difficult for multimillion-dollar and multiyear IT projects. Currently, most companies have little control on sales revenue. However, cost of goods sold and general administrative expenses are completely within the company's internal control. The technology blueprint discussed in this column is geared toward improved efficiencies in the areas that a company controls in this harsh economic environment. It will be much easier to get backing for, and implement, the incremental technologies where the payback can be achieved quickly and, most importantly, measured. To borrow a phrase, now more than ever companies will be demanding, "Show me the money".

New Words and Expressions

1. supply chain　供应链
2. aftermath['ɑːftəmæθ]n. 结果,后果
3. just-in-time　准时制
4. just-in-case　预防制
5. inventory ['invəntri]n. 详细目录,存货,财产清册,总量,库存量
6. accounts for　　v. 说明,占,解决,得分
7. disruption [dis'rʌpʃən]n. 中断,分裂,瓦解,破坏
8. term [təːm]n. 学期,期限,期间,条款,条件,术语
9. supply chain management (SCM)　供应链管理
10. module['mɔdjuːl]n. 模数,模块,登月舱,指令舱,组件
11. vendor['vendɔː]n. 卖主
12. norm [nɔːm]n. 标准,规范
13. access to　有权使用
14. CRM (Customer Relationship Management)　客户关系管理
15. blend [blend]vt. 混和;n. 混和
16. evolve [i'vɔlv]v. (使)发展,(使)进展,(使) 进化
17. incremental [inkri'mentəl]adj.增加的
18. infrastructure['infrə'strʌktʃə]n. 下部构造,基础下部组织
19. virtual integration (VI)　虚拟集成

20. vertical integration　竖向集成

21. come into vogue　开始流行,流行起来

22. showroom[ˈʃəurum]*n.*（商品样品的）陈列室

23. optimum [ˈɔptiməm]*n.* 最适宜;*adj.* 最适宜的

24. inhibited [inˈhibitid] *adj.* 羞怯的,内向的

25. upstream [ˈʌpˈstriəːm] *adv.* 向上游,溯流,逆流地;*adj.* 溯流而上的

Notes

1. The Sept. 11ᵗʰ terrorist attacks

指"9.11"恐怖分子袭击事件。本文阐述了"9.11"事件发生之前,供应链管理（SCM）技术的演变。在 Part Ⅱ,描述了"9.11"事件对 SCM 技术的持续发展所产生的冲击。

2. SCM technology vendors listened to their customers and learned that a major factor that inhibited successful implementation of prior technologies was the complexity involved in installing a fully integrated system.

SCM 技术的供应商听取顾客的意见,了解到决定这些前沿技术成功实现的因素在于这样一个高度集成系统的安装的复杂性。本句的谓语是 listened to their customers and learned that…,learned 后面是一个宾语从句,主干是 a major facto was the complexity。

3. The traditional role of SCM systems have been expanded to cover procurement of products and services of that aren't directly utilized to manufacture the company's finished products.

供应链关系管理系统的传统任务已经被拓展成覆盖产品和不能直接利用加工公司成品的服务输入。本句采用被动语态的完成时态。of that aren't directly utilized to manufacture the company's finished products 用来修饰限定 services。

4. Similarly, the in-side integration platform is important for supporting the many specialized technologies within the company: functions such as finance, manufacturing, and inventory management.

同样,内部集中平台对于支持很多公司内部的特殊技术有着重要的作用,如财政、制造和存货管理等功能。

5. Out-side integration portals will increasingly shape the evolution of the company over the next few years. SCM and CRM technologies will evolve to support the virtually integrated enterprise.

本句中 virtually integrated enterprise 虚拟（集成）企业,这是一种新型的企业模式,构建于计算机网络、硬件和软件的基础之上,可以根据实际的生产和加工需要,建立一种动态的企业联盟。因此,SCM 和 CRM 技术最终应该演变为支持虚拟企业的构建。

Topics for Discussion

1. Can you tell something about the evolution of Supply Chain Management (SCM)? Please discuss it in your group.

2. Could you give us some differences in the evolution of supply chain technologies?

3. Why will the outsourcing differ from VI? Could you give us some example about it?

4. What will be the economic drivers for this technology blueprint?

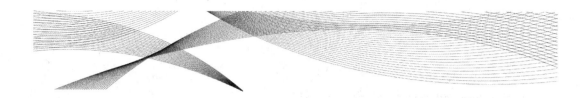

Unit 16

Passage A

Top 10 Supply Chain Technology Trends (I)

It is easy to name "mobility" and "wireless" as trends, but it is less clear exactly what direction these developments are taking and how they can be used to improve business. One can hardly pick up a business or IT magazine without seeing multiple articles about the growth of mobile and wireless technologies. And it seems people cannot put down their PDAs, smart phones and other mobile computing and communications devices, at least when judging by the adoption rates and future growth projections.

But what is missing in all this attention is context, particularly regarding how adoption of these technologies is creating improvements in enterprise and supply chain operations [1]. For example, identifying mobile computing, printing and GPS as growth technologies doesn't explain how one field service provider combined them to save at least 40 minutes per crew per day, and up to $2.1 million in overtime. This paper does.

Here are the top 10 trends and technologies impacting supply chain operations spanning production, distribution, retail and remote service.

• Comprehensive connectivity—from 802.11 wireless LAN technologies, cellular networks, Bluetooth

  • Voice and GPS communication integrated into rugged computers

  • Digital imaging

  • Portable printing

  • Speech recognition

- 2D & other bar coding advances
- RFID
- RTLS
- Remote management
- Wireless and device security

You are probably familiar with the technologies listed above, but perhaps not with the latest developments and trends. For example, did you know that practically any application can be easily modified to accept speech input because of the recent development of terminal emulation-based speech recognition technology? Did you know that Bluetooth, 802.11b/g, cellular and GPS communication are all available in a single handheld device? Read on to learn more about how these and other developments are helping make production, distribution, service and other supply chain operations more efficient.

1. Connectivity

The various forms of wireless connectivity — Bluetooth for personal area networking, 802.11 wireless local area networking, and cellular wide area wireless networks for voice and data communication — are all highly visible and provide compelling business cases for many specific operations. Although innovation and adoption is continuing at a strong pace, these trends aren't new. What is new and significant is how these technologies are being combined into single devices that provide multiple forms of wireless functionality, bringing convenience to both users and to IT staff responsible for managing mobile devices.

Smart phones have strong appeal because they provide convenient voice and data access. However they are extremely limited for delivery, field service and other mobile supply chain operations because the computer screens and interfaces aren't optimized for enterprise applications, and the devices themselves aren't rugged enough for everyday use in these environments. For operations with intensive data collection or transaction volume, companies have traditionally used ruggedized handheld computers to gain the reliability and performance they need, but these devices lacked cell phone capability.

2. Advanced Wireless: Voice & GPS

Now leading cellular carriers have certified rugged handheld computers for voice communication, enabling data collection, data communication and cell phone functionality to be converged into one device [2]. Users don't need to worry about

186

keeping separate cell phones and computers charged and maintained, nor do they need to switch back and forth between devices to complete routine tasks. Converging data and voice onto an integrated piece of equipment can cut the number of devices system administrators need to support in half, which provides sustainable operating cost savings. Bluetooth is also frequently integrated with these devices to interface peripherals and further reduce total cost of ownership by eliminating the costs of repairing and replacing cables.

Connectivity convergence continues with the integration of GPS communication into mobile computers. For example, Intermec's CN3 includes wide-area wireless voice and data, 802.11, Bluetooth and GPS connectivity in a handheld computer small enough to fit in a shirt pocket. Together with the falling costs of wide area wireless coverage (including GPRS, GSM, CDMA and other technologies) and more generous data plans, computing innovations like these make it affordable and practical for many companies to implement real-time data access systems for their delivery drivers, sales and service staff, inspectors and other personnel.

3. Digital Imaging

Like cellular voice, digital imaging is another technology consumers are familiar with that has now found a place in enterprise mobile computing equipment and applications [3]. Transportation and distribution companies are using digital cameras integrated into the mobile computers so their drivers can capture proof of delivery, store stamped invoices, and detail conditions that prevent delivery. Technicians use the technology for proof of service. Other applications include capturing shelf displays and monitoring trade promotion compliance, collecting competitive information, documentation by inspectors, collecting evidence for accident reports, and recording damage and usage conditions for warranty claims.

4. Portable Printing

Rugged portable printers are routinely used for output when documentation is required. Common applications include providing signed delivery receipts, purchase orders, work orders and inspection reports. Using mobile printers and computers together lets sales, service and delivery personnel give customers the documentation they desire, while creating an electronic record that frees the enterprise from having to process paperwork. Mobile printers remain one of the fastest-growing segments of the entire printing industry. Traditional applications are in field service and distribution, but adoption is growing quickly in warehouses and factories for forklift-based printing for picking, put-away, shipment labeling and other activities. Mobile printing provides proven labor savings in industrial environments by saving workers from having to make an unproductive trip to a central location to pick up labels, pick tickets, manifests and other output.

New Words and Expressions

1. millennium [mi'leniəm]n. 太平盛世，一千年
2. outstrip [aut'strip] v. 超过
3. infrastructure['infrə'strʌktʃə]n. 下部构造，基础下部组织
4. tax [tæks]n. 税，税款，税金；vt. 对……征税，使负重担，指控，责备
5. segment ['segmənt]n. 段，节，片段；v. 分割
6. paradigm['pærədaim,-dim]n. 范例
7. augment [ɔːg'ment]v. 增加，增大；n. 增加
8. concurrent [kən'kʌrənt] n. 同时发生的事件；adj. 并发的，协作的，一致的
9. merchandise['məːtʃəndaiz]n. 商品，货物
10. implementation [,implimen'teiʃən]n. 执行
11. resurgence[ri'səːdʒəns]n. 苏醒
12. assess [ə'ses]vt. 估定，评定
13. metropolitan [metrə'pɔlit(ə)n]adj.首都的，主要都市的，大城市
14. commodity [kə'mɔditi]n. 日用品
15. cluster['klʌstə]n. 串，丛 vi. 丛生，成
16. peak [piːk]n. 山顶，顶点，帽舌，(记录的)最高峰；adj. 最高的
17. curfew ['kəːfjuː]n. (中世纪规定人们熄灯安睡的)晚钟声
18. revolve [ri'vɔlv]v. (使)旋转，考虑，循环出现
19. streamline['striːmlain]adj.流线型的
20. commensurate [kə'menʃərit]adj. 相称的，相当的
21. stakeholder['steikhəuldə(r)]n. 赌金保管者
22. dredging['dredʒiŋ] n. 挖泥，捕捞
23. obstacle['ɔbstəkl]n. 障碍，妨碍物
24. initiative [i'niʃiətiv]v. 主动
25. expedient [iks'piːdiənt]adj.有利的；n. 权宜之计

Notes

1. But what is missing in all this attention is context，particularly regarding how adoption of these technologies is creating improvements in enterprise and supply chain operations.

但是，对于这一问题的关注中人们遗漏了环境方面的因素，尤其是关于由于采用了这些技术，企业和供应链运营如何得以推动进步这一方面。how adoption …supply chain operations 做介词 regarding 的宾语从句。

2. Now leading cellular carriers have certified rugged handheld computers for voice communication，enabling data collection，data communication and cell phone functionality to be converged into one device.

现在，领先的移动运营商已经通过使用便携式掌上电脑来实现声音传输，这种电脑能够将数据采集、数据交换以及手机功能融于一身。enabling data collection … to be converged into one device 作定语修饰前面的 rugged handheld computers。

3. Like cellular voice，digital imaging is another technology consumers are familiar with that has now found a place in enterprise mobile computing equipment and applications.

句中 another technology 有两个定语从句，即（that）consumers are familiar with；that has now found a place in enterprise mobile computing equipment and applications.

Topics for Discussion

1. After reading，what are the top 10 trends and technologies impacting supply chain operations spanning production，distribution，retail and remote service?

2. How many various forms of wireless connectivity do you know，and can you give us their applied fields?

3. What fields will the digital imaging be commonly used in? And what about portable printing?

Passage B

Top 10 Supply Chain Technology Trends (II)

1. Speech Recognition

The "other" voice technology for supply chain operations — speech recognition for hands-free data entry — is also undergoing a new wave of innovation and adoption. Speech recognition helps productivity by reducing the need for users to look at a computer display. Following the larger IT trends of open systems and interoperability, speech synthesis/recognition capability can now be easily embedded into numerous legacy software packages, including warehouse management, picking and put-away, inventory, inspection, quality control and other applications.

This simplified integration has been made possible by the recent development of terminal emulation TE-based speech recognition technology, which eliminates the need for a separate speech server and a proprietary interface between the speech system and the application software. TE enables speech synthesis to reduce the need to look at the display, and speech recognition to function as a true input technology, not as a separate application that has to be managed and integrated. By using terminal emulation to format and process speech input/output, data flows from and into existing software applications as if it had been entered by bar code scanning, key entry, or whatever method was previously used. TE-based speech recognition systems can work with warehouse management systems in real-time, which is another important innovation from traditional speech recognition technology.

Traditional speech recognition was often implemented for high-throughput operations where system planners valued speed and productivity over accuracy, especially for picking. Bar code data entry is considered more accurate, and speech input is generally acknowledged as enabling superior productivity because workers keep their hands and eyes on the picking operations and aren't interrupted by using the computer screen and keyboard or scanner to initiate and complete operations. One analysis for a high-volume distribution center concluded bar code data entry was four percent more accurate than traditional speech (99 percent compared to 95 percent), but bar coding would require 26 more full-time equivalent (FTE) workers to handle the same

190

transaction.

2. 2D Bar Code

Two-dimensional bar codes have long been a proven and popular technology for operations where it is desirable to present a lot of information in a limited space. However, 2D has remained a niche technology, in large part because symbols can be difficult to read in many usage environments. The recent emergence of auto-focus imaging technology will help bring 2D bar codes into the mainstream for item management, traceability, MRO and other operations.

Most organizations have needs for multiple bar code applications with different symbiosis, symbol sizes and encoded data. For example, large-format linear symbiosis are ideal for warehouse shelf location labeling, four-inch labels with a bar code field are common for shipment labeling, and 2D bar codes are ideal for work-in-process tracking plus lifetime part identification and traceability. A traditional reader couldn't recognize both a linear shelf label from 50 feet away and a 2D symbol on a part. Carrying two separate readers is impractical, so organizations have often foregone the use of 2D symbols in favor of more common linear bar code applications.

Now users no longer have to make a tradeoff. For example, Intermec's EX25 auto-focus scan engine is the first bar code reader that can read linear and 2D bar codes alike from 50 feet away and as close as six inches. Complementary developments in illumination technology enable bar codes to be successfully read in dark environments where they couldn't be read before. These developments make bar coding available in environments previously thought to require RFID, or where automated data capture was considered impractical. The use of Data Matrix and other 2D symbiosis is already growing strongly for permanent item identification, product genealogy and traceability. With a scanning infrastructure in place to process all types of codes at multiple distances, companies can start building advanced visibility and traceability features into their legacy production, inventory and distribution operations.

3. RFID

RFID is also more practical than ever before, with clear business cases being demonstrated for asset management and supply chain operations alike. For example, the U. S. Navy used RFID data entry to reduce the time for one mission-critical inventory process by 98 percent. TNT Logistics reduced its truck load verification time 24 percent by using RFID to automatically record goods loaded onto its trailers. Hundreds of other companies around the world are also implementing RFID-based shipping, receiving and inventory visibility applications.

A sub-trend behind RFID adoption for inventory, warehouse and distribution operations is the use of vehicle-mounted and other mobile RFID readers to enhance or replace stationary models. With a mobile infrastructure, companies don't need to purchase, install and maintain a separate RFID reader for each dock door. Forklift-mounted and handheld readers can cover multiple docks, and be used in warehouse aisles and elsewhere throughout the facility, further reducing the required RFID investment. Plus, they put information directly in the user's hands, so they can prevent errors, rather than just record them after they occur.

The flexibility of a mobile RFID infrastructure is helping many companies who implemented EPC Gen 2 systems to meet customer requirements to make internal use of the technology. Shipment verification and inventory update systems are most common, but advanced track-and-trace applications are emerging. For example, several pharmaceutical electronic pedigree (e-pedigree) systems have been developed to take advantage of EPC technology, and pending FDA regulations favor its use for supply chain traceability.

4. RTLS

Real Time Location Systems (RTLS) allow you to expand your wireless local area network into an asset tracking system. An important market driver is the Wireless Location Appliance from Cisco Systems, which enables asset tracking through a Cisco wireless LAN. Any device connected to the wireless LAN can be tracked and located. One application is to track forklifts via their vehicle-mounted computer's radio. The Wireless Location Appliance and supporting software can track the radio's location in real time to support efficient dynamic storage, routing, monitor dwell time, and gather data for productivity and asset utilization analysis. Many other expensive products and assets can be equipped with an RTLS device for real-time monitoring.

5. Remote Management

Using wireless LANs to track warehouse and factory assets is an example of how a mainstream IT resource has been adapted to benefit industrial environments. Another example, powerful remote management systems have been developed specifically to configure, monitor and troubleshoot bar code readers and printers, RFID equipment, ruggedized computers and other industrial data collection and communications

192

equipment. Network administrators have typically had little visibility or control over these remote devices because enterprise IT asset and network management systems are made for common PCs, servers, and network equipment and don't address the configurations and usage conditions specific to data collection and computing in industrial environments .

Here are a few examples of why general-purpose management systems have limited effectiveness for preserving uptime and managing equipment used in supply chain operations. Ruggedized computers are like their office cousins in that they periodically require software updates and security patches, and should be monitored to ensure consistency in configurations and software versions. Bar code and RFID smart label printers periodically need to be updated with new label templates and bar code formats, and use thermal print technology, which sometimes requires heat setting adjustments. Bar code printers have specialized command languages, so they are largely incompatible with print monitors and other applications made for office laser and inkjet printers. RFID readers can be optimized for their immediate environment by changing power output and making other tuning adjustments.

Device management software is available to meet all these needs providing real-time monitoring and notification if devices go offline, and if implemented with open systems standards, it can be accessed through your enterprise network management solution (e. g. Tivoli). Companies use such software to improve reliability and uptime in mission-critical production, distribution and service operations. Such software is also extremely valuable during rollouts and upgrades, because system administrators can use it to set configurations and install software remotely and across groups of devices, instead of having to handle each device individually. These features take a lot of the time and cost out of managing devices, making it much more cost efficient to keep systems up-to-date with new software and security enhancements.

6. Security

Stronger security is another mainstream business trend and requirement that is supported in supply chain technology. Mobile computers can be locked down so customer information and other data can't be accessed if the device is lost or stolen. Rugged wireless computers and data collection equipment also support many of the leading securities used to protect enterprise wireless networks, including 802.11i, 802. 1x, WPA, WPA2, LEAP, FIPS-140, RADIUS servers, VPNs and more. Wireless data collection devices that support Cisco Compatible Extensions (CCX) can be fully included in a Cisco Unified Wireless Network and take advantage of all the associated management, reliability and security features, including hacker and rogue access point detection, authentication and encryption, integrated firewalls and more.

7. Conclusion

Business needs for security, real-time visibility, and up-to-date information don't stop at the office door. These needs extend throughout supply chain operations, so reliable information systems must extend just as far. Developments in mobile computing, wireless communication, RFID, bar code and other data collection and communications technologies are helping businesses extend visibility and control over more areas of their operations [2].

New Words and Expressions

1. configuration [kən,figju'reiʃən]n. 结构,构造,配置,外行
2. inventory['invəntri]n. 详细目录,存货,财产清册,总量
3. recognition [,rekəg'niʃən]n. 认识;识别;认得
4. previously['pri:vju:sli]adv. 以前,先前;预先
5. productivity [,prədʌk'tiviti]n. 生产力
6. niche [nitʃ]n. 壁龛(放雕像、花瓶等的墙壁凹处)
7. encode [in'kəud]vt. 译成密码[电码];编[译]码
8. work-in-process   阶段产品;在制品
9. matrix['meitriks]n. 矩阵;基体
10. adoption [ə'dɔpʃən]n. 采纳,采用
11. verification [,verifi'keiʃən]n. 证实[明,据];验证,核对;确认;确定
12. appliance [ə'plaiəns]n. 器[用,工]具,设备,装置,仪表,器械,附件
13. configure [kən'figə]vt. 配置,使成形,使具形体
14. thermal['θə:məl]adj. 热(量)的,由热造成的
15. rollout['rəul,aut]n. 首次展示
16. authentication[ɔ:,θenti'keiʃən]n. 证明,鉴定
17. encryption [in'kripʃən]n. 编密码

Notes

1. Network administrators have typically had little visibility or control over these

remote devices…

little 在这里是否定的意思,因此这句话意思是:网络管理员对于远程设备既看不到也无法控制。

2. Business needs for security, real-time visibility, and up-to-date information don't stop at the office door. These needs extend throughout supply chain operations, so reliable information systems must extend just as far. Developments in mobile computing, wireless communication. RFID, bar code and other data collection and communications technologies are helping businesses extend visibility and control over more areas of their operations.

商业活动需要具备可靠性、实时可见性并且最新的信息是不会停止在办公室门口的。这些需求贯穿整个供应链操作,因此可靠信息系统必须能扩展得足够广。在移动计算、无线通信、RFID、条码技术和其他数据收集以及通信技术等领域的发展正在帮助商业活动扩展可见性且有助于控制它们操作的更多领域。

Topics for Discussion

1. Why it is said that the bar code data entry is considered more accurate, and speech input is generally acknowledged as enabling superior productivity?

2. What are the main advantages of using RFID data entry?

3. Why will the general-purpose management systems have limited effectiveness for preserving uptime and managing equipment used in supply chain operations? Can you explain it with practical examples?

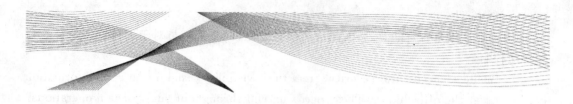

Unit 17

Passage A

Enterprise Resource Planning (ERP) Systems

1. What is ERP

ERP is a popular term, widely used yet probably not well understood. It is an acronym for Enterprise Resource Planning, a concept developed for the next generation Manufacturing Resource Planning systems (MRP II) by the Gartner Group in the early 1990's [1]. The concept posits integration of software applications of manufacturing beyond MRP II to other functions such as finance and human resources. Russell and Taylor (1995) define ERP as an updated MRP II with relational database management, graphical user interface, and client-server architecture. The initial definition of ERP was targeted at manufacturing companies. However, the concept of Enterprise Resource Planning has been adopted by other sectors also. ERP systems are now being configured for organizations in many different sectors such as services and government. Today, the term ERP encompasses all integrated information systems that can be used across any organization.

Watson and Schneider (1999) describe Enterprise Resource Planning (ERP) as a generic term for an integrated enterprise computing system. They defined it as an integrated, customized, packaged software-based system that handles the majority of an enterprise's system requirements in all functional areas such as finance, human resources, manufacturing, sales, and marketing. It has a software architecture that facilitates the flow of information among all functions within an enterprise. It sits on a common database and is supported by a single development environment.

Organizations configure ERP systems in three distinct ways:
- Integrated Standard Application Packages
- Integrating Systems In-house
- Joint Venture Systems

Standard application packages refer to integrated packaged applications developed by vendors to satisfy generic industry-wide business requirements. Many firms configure ERP by integrating best of breed functional applications by means of the shelf or specially developed middle-wares. In many cases standard integrated application packages and best of breed applications are integrated to meet ERP requirements. This combination of standard application packages and best of breed functional applications has been termed as joint venture systems by Dahlen and Elfsson (1999).

2. Evolution of ERP

The ERP applications we see today can be traced back to and have evolved from Materials Requirement Planning (MRP) and Manufacturing Resource Planning (MRP II) systems [2]. In the 1970s the focus in information systems shifted to the use of MRP (Materials Requirement Planning) systems in manufacturing, which translated the master schedule built for the end items into time-phased net requirements for subassemblies, components and raw material planning and procurement. In the 1980's the concept of MRP II (Manufacturing Resources Planning) evolved, which was an extension of MRP to shop floor and distribution management activities. In the early 1990's, MRP II was extended to cover areas like engineering, finance, human resources, and project management; i. e., the complete gamut of activities within an enterprise. Hence the term ERP (Enterprise Resource Planning) was coined. The evolutionary characteristics of ERP systems also include various added technical features like graphical user interface, relational database, client server architecture, open systems, portability, use of computer aided software engineering tools in development and use of fourth generation language.

ERP systems were mainly transaction processing systems and the primary development objective of these systems was to provide operational process support and control. Originally, ERP systems did not provide an environment for decision support activities such as analyzing historical trends, drawing conclusions, scenario building and planning. However, these systems have evolved with the growing needs of organizations and electronic business requirements. They have been extended to include World Wide Web capability and many advanced non-transactional, primarily data-analysis, and decision support applications. Enterprise applications such as business intelligence, data warehousing and mining, supply chain optimization, advance planning and scheduling, and customer relationship management can be integrated with ERP systems. These applications are identified individually as complimentary systems which often work with data generated by ERP systems and are supplied by specialized vendors. However, major ERP system developers such as SAP, Oracle, Baan, PeopleSoft, and J. D. Edwards have also developed many of these applications and provide them as an integral component of their ERP systems. When provided by ERP vendors as integrated components of the ERP systems they are identified as part of ERP systems in the adopting organization. The ERP systems continue to evolve with the organizational and market needs. The latest developments include functionality to support inter-organizational processes and transactions.

3. How Does an ERP System Work

ERP systems are comprehensive packaged software solutions that automate and integrate organizational processes. The core of an ERP system is a single relational database. The database is shared by inter-linked functional applications, which have a unified interface.

The system thus not only unifies enterprise-wide information, but also provides a seamless information flow making real time and updated information available to all the applications. Unified applications ensure tight integration of all functions and units. For example, in an ERP system, a purchase order entered by a sales person triggers necessary action at the production, inventory management, accounting, and distribution levels of the organization at the same time. If the systems are also interfaced with the supplier's systems, the same order also provides information to the suppliers for activating necessary actions required at their end to fulfill the order.

The integrative design of ERP systems enables an organization to achieve operational efficiencies and even extend the systems' reach beyond the organizational boundaries, encircling supply chain partners, and customers through various front end and e-commerce interfaces. With ERP systems interfaced with those of its suppliers and customers, an organization can have access to and visibility of real time information across the value chain. By integrating this information from partner systems into production schedules and inventory levels, organizations can further lower operation costs, improve forecasting, reduce cycle times, better relationships with suppliers, and increase customer satisfaction.

4. Benefits of an ERP System

(1) Easier access to reliable information

Traditionally, companies have utilized incompatible systems, like CAD and MRP systems, which had important data stored in them, with no easy way to find the data or transfer it between systems. ERP uses a common database management system. Thus, decisions on cost accounting or optimal sourcing, for example, can be run across the enterprise rather than looking at separate operational units and then trying to coordinate the information manually or reconciling data across multiple interfaces with some other application. An integrated system provides an opportunity to improve data reporting and to ensure accurate, consistent, and comparable data.

(2) Elimination of redundant data and operations

Driven by business processes re-engineering, the implementation of ERP systems reduces redundancy within an organization. With functional business units utilizing integrated applications and sharing a common database, there is no need for repetition of tasks such as inputting data from one application to another. In non-integrated systems, a piece of data might reside in six different places. ERP can help the company eliminate the redundant processes. The CIO of Steelcase Inc., a $3 billion maker of office furniture, remarked that we can achieve an $80 million reduction in operating expenses just by getting rid of redundant processes and cleaning up our data.

(3) Reduction of cycle times

ERP systems recognize that time is a critical constraint variable, the driving variable for both business and information technology. Time reductions are achieved by minimizing delays and by retrieving or disseminating information. Stevens (1997) noted how Colgate Palmolive dealt with and tracked customer orders before and after ERP implementation.

(4) Increased efficiency, hence reducing costs

ERP allows business decisions to be analyzed enterprise-wide. This results in timesaving, improved control and elimination of superfluous operations. Appleton (1997) noted that, a year after implementing ERP, Par Industries in Moline, Illinois, reduced lead time to customers from six to two weeks, delivery performance increased from 60% on time to more than 95%, work-in-progress inventory dropped almost 60%, and the life of a shop floor order went from weeks to hours.

(5) Easily adaptable in a changing business environment

Recognizing companies' need to reduce the time it takes to bring goods and services to market, ERP systems are designed to respond quickly to new business demands and can be easily changed or expanded without disrupting the course of business. The time required to deploy and continuously improve business processes will be greatly reduce. The companies are always finding new ways to go to market.

5. Today's Market Leaders

Five providers control nearly two-thirds of the ERP software market. The top ERP vendors include SAP AG, People-Soft, Baan, J. D. Edwards, and Oracle. These companies, which account for 64% of the ERP market revenue, have grown over the past year at the swift pace of 61%, according to an ERP software report by AMR Research Inc.. Several vendors have entered the ERP market with complete enterprise solutions, whereas some have tried to focus on the market by offering more industry-specific applications. However, five companies dominate the ERP market.

(1) SAP AG

SAP is the dominant leader in ERP, commanding 31% of the 56 market. In fact, in most business circles, the Walldorf, Germany, company's name has become synonymous with ERP, like Scotch tape or Q-tip has for certain consumer products. SAP's R/3 software package is a favorite among big user, and the company has been selling manufacturing software for 25 years. SAP was unknown before it introduced its R/3 product in 1993, the first Enterprise Resource Planning software suite to hit the market. This new technological development put SAP in the number-one spot in terms of ERP; other vendors have been playing catch-up ever since. Even with zero growth at SAP, it would take any competitor a couple of years of triple-digit growth to overtake this German powerhouse.

SAP may not provide complete solutions for everyone. Despite its successes with SAP R/3, Steelcase's CIO Greiner says, we found SAP was weak with scheduling plant operations, and focuses on make-to-stock but we make-to-order.

(2) Oracle Corp

Oracle, the leading provider of relational database management systems, is a distant second in the ERP race, commanding 14% of the market. Its complete package, known as Oracle Applications, is also available.

Oracle Corp. introduced its first application modules approximately in 1997. With original software roots in financial applications, Oracle now has more than 35 modules covering every facet of enterprise computing, from manufacturing and production control to human resources and sales force automation. Recently, Oracle has focused more attention on its applications business as a growth engine and seems to be reaching aggressively into the territory targeted by middle-market accounting players. General Electric is one of the companies standardizing its business units on Oracle's applications.

(3) J. D. Edwards

J. D. Edwards, established in 1977 to develop software for small and medium-size computers, has quickly advanced in the ERP ranks. The Denver-based company offers users a total ERP solution in World (AS400 based) and One World (client-server based) or a process-based solution with modules for areas such as finance, manufacturing, and logistics/distribution. The company distributes, implements, and supports its products worldwide through a network of direct offices and over 190 third-party business partners. Its products are available in 18 languages and are supported around the globe through a worldwide network of support 24 hours a day, 7 days a week. The company's greatest vulnerability is its current reliance on the momentum of IBM's AS/400 platform. J. D. Edwards needs to transition to new product lines and new platforms to maintain its market-leading position.

(4) PeopleSoft

Founded in 1987 as a provider of human resources software, PeopleSoft Inc. has expanded its offerings to become a leading ERP provider. Controlling 7% of the ERP market, the Pleasanton, a California company, offers Enterprise Solutions for finance, materials management, distribution, and manufacturing. PeopleSoft is one of the newer players in the ERP market. Barely 10 years old has the company experienced annual growth rates during the past 5 years exceeding 100%. One of its biggest advantages was being first to offer human resources and payroll applications for client/server model systems. PeopleSoft then expanded into the financial software arena, and in the fall of 1996, it offered its first integrated ERP system.

PeopleSoft's nine industry-specific ERP definitions cover most possible industries. We have every one of our target markets into one of those nine definitions, says Albert Duffield, PeopleSoft's senior vice-president of operations. The nine units are service industries, financial services, communications, transportation and utilities, health care, public sector, higher education, retail, and manufacturing.

(5) Baan Co.

Baan Co. has two corporate headquarters, one in the Netherlands and one in Menlo Park, California. In 1997 while there have not been any grand pronouncements from either site, Baan's actions over the past three years are a clear indication of a desire to be the dominant force in worldwide enterprise resource markets. Baan entered the North American market in 1994 with its Baan IV ERP suite and promptly sold major companies like Boeing on its ability to support complex, multi-national manufacturing operations. In 1995, it expanded further, establishing sales and distribution centers in over 40 countries. Moreover, Baan also announced this spring that it signed on 27 new distributors in Europe and North America that will concentrate on securing small and mid-sized companies.

New Words and Expressions

1. graphical['græfikəl] *adj.* 图形(像)的，绘成图画似的，绘画的
2. interface['intə(:)ˌfeis]*vt.* 接口，使连接，使协调
3. venture['ventʃə]*n.* 冒险；冒险事业[行动]；(商业)投机
4. account [ə'kaunt]*n.* 户头，账目
5. component [kəm'pəunənt]*adj.* 组件，组成的，合成的，成分的，分量的
6. evolutionary [ˌi:və'lu:ʃənəri]*adj.* 展开的，进化论的，进化的，发展的
7. historical [his'tɔrikəl]*adj.* 历史的；历史上的；过去的
8. complimentary [ˌkɔmpli'ment(ə)ri]*adj.* 问候的，祝贺的；称赞的
9. functionality [ˌfʌŋkəʃə'næliti]*n.* 功能性，泛函性
10. unify['ju:nifai]*vt.* 使成一体，统一；使一致，使一元化
11. seamless ['si:mlis]*adj.* 无缝的，无伤痕的
12. integrate['intigreit]*vt.* 使结合(with)；使并入(into)；

使一体化，使完全，使成一整体

13. timesaving['taimseiviŋ]*n.* 省时省力的；事半功倍的
14. superfluous [ˌsju:'pə:fluəs]*adj.* 过多的，多余的
15. approximately [əprɔksi'mitli]*adv.* 约，近似地
16. automation [ɔ:tə'meiʃən]*n.* 自动化，自动操作
17. target['tɑ:git]*n.* 目标，靶子

Notes

1. ERP is a popular term, widely used yet probably not well understood. It is an acronym for Enterprise Resource Planning, a concept developed for the next generation Manufacturing Resource Planning systems (MRP II) by the Gartner Group in the early

1990's.

ERP 是一个流行的词汇,被广泛使用但却不一定能很好理解。它是企业资源计划的缩写,一个由 Gartner 集团在 20 世纪 90 年代初专门针对下一代制造资源计划系统(MRP II)而发展的概念。

2. The ERP applications we see today can be traced back to and have evolved from Materials Requirement Planning（MRP）and Manufacturing Resource Planning（MRP II）systems.

我们今天所见到的 ERP 应用可以追溯到并演变自 MRP 物料需求计划和制造资源计划(MRP II)。

Topics for Discussion

1. What's the ERP system used for?

2. Generally speaking, can you tell us the differences between MRP and MRP II? And also their relationship with the ERP system.

3. How does an ERP System work? Please explain your own idea about it.

Passage B

How to Implement ERP

1. Significance of ERP Implementation

Companies have to clearly know what enterprise resource is planning before thinking of implementing them. The catch word of ERP implementation is speed. The faster it is implemented, the quicker and better are the advantages and delivery in terms of results [1]. This early process has another hold. The returns are sought at a shorter period. This deviation from the conventional practice has become the order of the day as far as many companies are concerned. Formerly business process reengineering played a vital role with respect to implementation. It is important to know the components of Enterprise Resource Planning. Merely defining Enterprise Resource Planning will not help in this.

This naturally paved way to development of gaps between the actual results and the one derived during the process of foreseeing. Tuning ERP as per the whims and fancies of the practices followed in the company became a routine affair. This led to slogging and dragging beyond the time limits permitted. It was monetarily pinching and played havoc in the customer's trust. It is also necessary to understand that mere ERP planning does not guarantee the benefit of ERP. It has to be implemented as planned after understanding the components of Enterprise Resource Planning.

In spite of having improved the implementation issues what remains static and unfettered is the manner in which companies go ahead with ERP implementation. They do it for the heck of it and without following systematic procedures. In fact they don't even check the desirability of going into ERP. Some issues that an organization has to address after defining Enterprise Resource Planning are:

- Popular information systems
- Likelihood of fluctuations in the choice of technology
- The ability of market players to stay in tune with it
- The ways and means to implement a business applications like ERP
- To benefit from the same so as to gain a competitive edge
- Their usage and services

- The necessity for innovating software applications

If an organization is able to answer these questions without any ambiguity and substantiate the results then it can be said that it has a path or up focus in taking ERP. The questions mentioned above are crucial and will even decide the business model of the company. ERP implementation is a vital in the whole process of ERP. They can take place only if one understands "What is Enterprise Resource Planning" and defining Enterprise Resource Planning in their organization.

It is essential to have an overview of the current approach. The current approach is claimed to be relatively successful. The current approach has two underlying principles:

(1) The idea which concentrates on molding the business

This category is prominent when the organizational unit calls for a radical process by all means. This process will be carried in all aspects of the business. Some of them include strategic maneuvered, operation of trade and the circumstances that call for change and adaptability. Defining Enterprise Resource Planning in context to the concerned organization will help to decide on this issue.

(2) The plan which lays more emphasis on technical parameters

Here business takes the back seat. The thrust lies on technical dimensions. This does not ignore the commercial viability as such but they occupy seat only in the due course of time more so when operations are triggered in full stream and not at the initial stage it. The advantage with this type is that it does not call for an immediate modification of the business structure. However it is essential to know the components of Enterprise Resource Planning.

2. ERP Implementation Guideline

Research on Enterprise Resource Planning has shown that the flaws in ERP implementation have resulted in the vast majority of companies failing to unleash the benefits of ERP software. This has led to lot of problems right from litigations to misinterpretations in business media. The vendor is always taken aback because the entire community blames him and the products. Enterprise Resource Planning phases are very important in this regard.

2.1 Probable reasons behind Failure

The actual problems lie in choosing the right software for your company. If this is either taken for granted or done hastily then the chances of ERP success are rare. Some of the reason for failure could be exorbitant costs, inadequate training, longer time, and failure of strategy and the lack of attitudinal change on the part of employees to accept and manage change. They have to analyze "What companies use Enterprise Resource Planning?"

2.2 Guidelines

(1) Very few companies succeed in the first instance after implementing ERP. ERP is not a fortune but a technology that delivers results only after effective execution of the laid down procedures. Therefore to merely bank on it will not suffice to obtain any results. What is more important is the implementation of the necessary changes in the organization so as to combat ERP.

(2) ERP is not an answer to the errors in business plans and tactics. In fact ERP consultants are reluctant to attend to it because they don't want it to disturb the purpose of ERP. It should therefore be understood that ERP is an IT tool that assists and facilitates the business process by being a part of it. On the contrary it is misunderstood that ERP can rejuvenate the business. The answer to the popular question "What companies use Enterprise Resource Planning?" will help in clearing this trouble.

(3) ERP gap analysis and business process reengineering should be performed properly. This will ensure that other steps are followed systematically and in accordance to the company's need. They are otherwise referred as Enterprise Resource Planning phases.

(4) IT facilities in the organization should be at par with market standards and international reputation. This will enable the operation people to constantly modify and update as and when it is necessary in order to stay in tune with the competition. Research on Enterprise Resource Planning will reveal this.

(5) The process of ERP implementation should be carried on by a team of competent personnel so as to ensure perfection, accountability and transparency.

ERP should become a part of the daily routine. If that does not happen then the company cannot expect any fruitful results in spite of having followed the above mentioned steps meticulously in order to ensure the successful implementation of ERP.

An organization needs to answer the following questions while thinking of taking up ERP:

- Perception of the business problems.
- The visualization of solving them.
- How is ERP going to solve the same and how worth is it and how effective are

the measures taken to implement it.

- How and who will coordinate the operation of ERP and is it justified in terms of costs, time taken and efforts?

- What is the accountability and transparency of ERP operations and how far it will affect issues like piracy, IPR and their impact on the organizations performance and image and the possible measures to curb any unnecessary elements?

3. ERP Implementation Life Cycle

The process of ERP implementation is referred to as "ERP Implementation Life Cycle". The following are the steps involved in completing the lifecycle.

(1) Shortlist on the basis of observation

Selecting an ERP package for the company can nevertheless be compared with the process of "Selecting the right Person for the Right Job". This exercise will involve choosing few applications suitable for the company from the whole many.

(2) Assessing the chosen packages

A team of Experts with specialized knowledge in their respective field will be asked to make the study on the basis of various parameters. Each expert will not only test and certify if the package is apt for the range of application in their field but also confirm the level of coordination that the software will help to achieve in working with other departments. In simple terms they will verify if the synergy of the various departments due to the advent of ERP will lead to an increased output. A choice is to be made from ERP implementation models.

(3) Preparing for the venture

This stage is aimed at defining the implementation of ERP in all measures. It will lay down the stipulations and criteria to be met. A team of officers will take care of this, who will report to the person of the highest hierarchy in the organization.

(4) GAP analysis

This stage helps the company to identify the gaps that has to be bridged, so that the companies practice becomes akin to ERP environment. This has been reported as an expensive procedure but it is inevitable. The conglomerate will decide to restructure the business or make any other alterations as suggested by GAP analysis in order to make ERP user friendly.

(5) Business process reengineering

Changes in employee rolls, business process and technical details find place in this phase of restructuring most popularly referred as business process engineering.

(6) Designing the System

This step requires lot of meticulous planning and deliberate action. This step helps to decide and conclude the areas where have to be carried on. A choice is to be made from ERP implementation models.

(7) In-house Guidance

This is regarded as a very important step in ERP implementation. The employees in the company are trained to face crisis and make minor corrections as well because the company can neither be at liberty nor afford the bounty to avail the services of an ERP vendor at all times.

(8) Checking

This stage observes and tests the authenticity of the use. The system is subjected to the wildest tests possible so that it ensures proper usage and justifies the costs incurred. This is seen as a test for ERP implementation.

(9) The real test

At this stage the replacement takes place in the new mechanism of operation and administration takes over the older one.

(10) Preparing the employees to use ERP

The employees in the organization will be taught to make use of the system in the day to day and regular basis so as to make sure that it becomes a part of the system in the organization.

(11) Post Implementation

The process of implementation will find meaning only when there is regular follow up and proper instruction flow thereafter and through the lifetime of ERP. This will include all efforts and steps taken to update and attain better benefits once the system is implemented. Hence an organization has to perform ERP implementation safely and correctly.

4. What Are The Different Methods in Implementing ERP

ERP implementation support includes all the services of the vendor. Companies spend a lot of time in discussing about the need to go for ERP. They make all sorts of assessments and bring the necessary resources to work on ERP. They even carry the exercises suggested in restructuring. When the stage is all set to take ERP the next million dollar question that comes to them is the appropriate method of implementation due to the risk for ERP implementation.

Some popular methods for implementation are as follows:

(1) Joint ventures with the Respective Industry

The company need not necessarily implement ERP all on its own. They can as well share it with leading players in the same industry. This will ensure that the risks will not be heavy in the case of loss. This practice is assuming greater significance in the current scenario. The sharing allows them to have an interface with the systems on the basis of a common platform. This is catching up in the market with the only trouble being reluctance of competitive firms to come together on a mutual agreement for fear of losing business tactics. It is also seen as ERP implementation problem solution.

Though the companies are at liberty to create security for their respective information there will not be any protection for the (pool of) records in the common database. However this has helped largely in many aspects [2]. For e. g. the medical history of a patient brought in an emergency condition can be immediately accessed though ERP. This particular fact has itself saved many lives. On the contrary they would have to go through the rigorous process of finding the patient's identity and the steps aftermath which brings down the chances of the patient's survival are very minimal, in the absence of ERP. This is one of ERP implementation support. Perhaps there are many risks for ERP implementation.

(2) Doing it all alone

This is in fact one of the primitive methods and is no doubt followed till date. This method takes a lot of risks in this method. But if they are calculated properly then the regime would be inscribed as a golden period in the company's history. The simple formula behind this phenomenon is that the company should go for it subject to its financial potential, requirements, technical acumen management policy and similar facts. All these will help them to arrive at ERP implementation problem solution.

(3) Full/Partial Implementation

It has always been said that ERP products and services are purely based on the needs and resources of the company. This is not a risk for ERP implementation. Hence the companies can choose to go for a full fledged ERP system and implement it thought the organization and thereby interlink the whole process and the people concerned. Otherwise they may prefer to go for an ERP system that performs a particular function of the company. This is an important step in choosing the appropriate ERP software but at the same time it also adds more value to the implementation process. It is also an important ERP problem solution.

5. Errors in ERP Implementation

ERP implementation failure is a major concern for companies. ERP implementation needs to be done without allowing any scope for limitations and mistakes. If it is not done perfectly then the success of ERP system will remain a question mark.

The first and foremost factor that discourages ERP in an organization is the exorbitant costs and investment. The second one is the drafting of an ERP implementation plan to ensure ERP implementation success.

Some more issues that arise during and after the course of ERP implementation is discussed below:

(1) Enhancement of ERP's functions

ERP's scope gets wider as it is implemented in an organization. There is a call for including many tasks under the purview. This dilutes the ERP Existing system after modifying it a couple of times. Repeated change in configurations and systems will only add to the confusions. When the functions are operated by a machine it becomes increasingly difficult to make the necessary changes. These troubles arise when they are not foreseen and addressed in the implementation stage. They have to be given a place in ERP implementation plan.

(2) Organizational reaction to change

Changes do happen quickly and immediately in the organization after ERP is implemented. But if there is no proper understanding of the process or mishandling of information, it will result in questioning the ERP process. If updating is not done in the machine it will only affect the business process and create unnecessary confusions. The changes don't happen all on a sudden in an organization and expecting it immediately will only cause needless disappointments. In spite of all this expecting every member in the organization to respond proactively will not happen. If that happens the chances of ERP implementation success are great.

(3) Inflating resources for ERP implementation

The implementation time and money always exceeds the promises and stipulated deadline and amount. This makes companies to lose faith on ERP and ERP vendors. They think that ERP vendors overplay on the costs and time required but it is not so. In fact they are aware of it in the very beginning stage itself but have a different reason for concealing. They don't disclose it in the beginning because it would look like exaggerating. In fact no one would like to lose a prospective business and vendors are equally aware of the fact that "Truths are always bitter"! However many people mistake

210

this to be the cause for ERP implementation failure.

(4) Organizations non adherence to the stated principles

Organizations largely experience a wide gap between practices and preaching. In fact this has a negative effect on the entire business scenario itself. The voracity and impact of loss could be greater and more devastating when this turns out to be true even in the case of ERP. Since ERP successful functioning is purely based on following the laid down procedures the lag could throw a serious challenge on ERP's potential right from the stage of its implementation.

(5) Problem of Transformation due to ERP

Employees find it hard to digest the transformations that place in an organization all on a sudden due to ERP implementation. In fact employees exhibit positive signs as everything goes right in the first place. But as one progresses he finds difficult to work as it gets more complex. The initial interest and expectation turns into apprehensiveness in due course of time. There is another category of people who did not encourage ERP right from the conceptualization stage. Their state of mind during these circumstances deserves no special mention.

New Words and Expressions

1. whim [(h)wim]*n.* 忽起的念头，一时的兴致；怪念头；任性

2. systematic [sistə'mætik]*adj.* 系统的；规划的；有计划的

3. vital['vaitl]*adj.* 生命的，生机的；维持生命所必需的

4. restrict[ris'trikt]*vt.* 限制；约束；制[禁]止

5. manoeuvre [mə'nuːvə] *n.* 花招，伎俩，手法

6. initial [i'niʃəl]*adj.* 最初的，开始的，初期的

7. modification [ˌmɔdifi'keiʃən] *n.* 变更，修正；改进；缓和；限制；修改；减轻

8. exorbitant [ig'zɔːbitənt]*adj.* 过高的，过度的，过分的；荒唐的

9. implementation [ˌimplimen'teiʃən] *n.* 执行，履行；落实

10. accountability [əˌkauntə'biliti] *n.* 有责任，有义务

11. unnecessary [ʌn'nesisəri] *adj.* 不必要的，不需要的；无益的；无用的

12. criteria[krai'tiəriə]*n.* 标准

13. investment [in'vestmənt] *n.* 投资（额）；（时间、精力等的）投入；
　　　　　　　　　　　　　　（可）投入资金的东西

14. prospective [prəs'pektiv]*n.* 将来的，未来的

Notes

1. Companies have to clearly know what enterprise resource is planning before thinking of implementing them. The catch word of ERP implementation is speed. The faster it is implemented, the quicker and better are the advantages and delivery in terms of results.

公司不得不在考虑如何利用资源前知道如何进行企业资源规划。ERP 应用的重点就是速度。如果能越快执行,那么在配送上的优势就会越迅速越明显。

2. Though the companies are at liberty to create security for their respective information ,there will not be any protection for the (pool of) records in the common database. However this has helped largely in many aspects.

尽管公司拥有为他们各自信息设置安全保障的权利,但对于公共数据库中的记录却没有任何保护措施。然而这个在很多方面都能有所帮助。

Topics for Discussion

1. What are the issues that an organization has to address after defining Enterprise Resource Planning?
2. What's the significance of ERP implementation?
3. What are the steps involved in completing the lifecycle of ERP implementation?

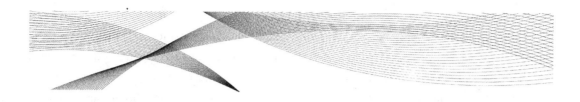

Unit 18

Material Resource Planning

MRP usually means Material Requirement Planning. While Material Resource Planning is customarily called MRP Ⅱ.

The Material Requirements Planning (MRP) system provides the user with information about timing (when to order) and quantity (how much to order), generates new orders, and reschedules existing orders as necessary to meet the changing requirements of customers and manufacturing [1]. The system is driven by change and constantly recalculates material requirements based on actual forecast orders. It makes adjustments for possible problems prior to their occurrence, as opposed to traditional control systems, which looked at more historical demand and reacted to existing problems [2]. Material Resource Planning (MRP Ⅱ) evolved from Material Requirements Planning when it was recognized that most major data needed to manage a manufacturing or distribution firm could be obtained from the Material Requirements Planning information. The ability of a Material Resource Planning system to meet the various needs of manufacturing, materials, and marketing personnel within a changing business environment contributes to its growing implementation by manufacturing companies.

1. Dependent and Independent Demand

The logic of the Material Requirements Planning system is based on the principle of dependent demand, a term describing the direct relationship between demand for one item and demand for a higher-level assembly part or component. For example, the demand for the number of wheel assemblies on a bicycle is directly related to the number of bicycles planned for production; further, the demand for tires is directly dependent on the demand for wheel assemblies. In most manufacturing businesses, the bulk of the raw material and in-process inventories are subject to dependent demand. An important characteristic of dependent demand items that affects timing is known as lumpy demand. Since most manufacturers assemble their products in batches or specific lot sizes to fulfil customer requirements, dependent demand items at lower levels do not exhibit uniform usage but are subject to extreme fluctuation. This creates situations in which no demand exists for weeks, and then a large quantity is required. While demand for the end drills is constant, the plant produces them in various lot sizes, thereby creating discontinuous and discrete demands. Applications by corporations of the just-in-time (JIT) philosophy will help smooth lumpiness to a certain extent since JIT argues for running smaller lot sizes [3]. Lumpy demand is handled in Material Requirements Planning through the calculation of future requirements at all levels of the assembled product. Dependent demand quantities are calculated, while independent demand items are forecast. Independent demand is unrelated to a higher-level item that the company manufactures or stocks. Generally, independent demand items are carried in finished goods inventory and subject to uncertain end-customer demand. Spare parts or replacement requirements for a drill press are an example of an independent demand item (See Figure 18.1).

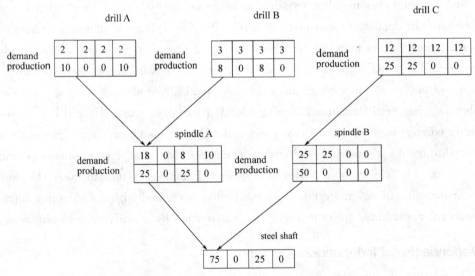

Figure 18.1 Lumpy demand in manufacturing for three types of drills

2. Material Resource Planning

In essence, Material Resource Planning (also termed closed-loop Material Requirements Planning) has the effect of extending the Material Requirements Planning scheduling into all major functions of the firm [4]. Material Requirements Planning provided firms with the ability to schedule and manage priorities. As the accuracy in Material Requirements Planning increased, firms realized they could use these numbers in their business and financial plans. There was no longer a need for two sets of numbers. Operating and financial data are not kept on one system. Further, top management can use Material Resource Planning as a system since it affects and is affected by sales, inventories, cash flow, production levels, and purchasing activities. Further, it ties key functional groups into the planning cycle. For example, the marketing group can use data from master production schedules to plan and promise customer orders. The engineering group's impact on the system has become more visible since changes in design now are reflected by the information system. If drawings are not completed on time, the schedule delay will be visible on the Material Resource Plan. Lastly, this plan permits firms to ask "what if" questions and analyze the effects of various factors on the overall operation.

3. Model System

A model Material Resource Planning system is shown in Figure 18.2. The business plan prepared by top management is based on certain expectations of sales from forecasts, firm orders, or a combination of sales forecasts and firm orders [5]. The master production schedule refers to the products that are actually going to be produced in a particular time period.

Demand inputs on the typical firm can originate from several sources: customers, warehouses, service parts, safety stock, and interplant orders. Except for make-to-order firms, the marketing forecast is adjusted periodically and reviewed by the plant manager as well as functional managers from the marketing, manufacturing, and materials groups. The marketing forecast is then translated into a production plan. This plan establishes an aggregate production rate which considers planned inventory increases or decreases. In a make-to-order company, production planning adjusts the customer order backlog; in a make-to-stock firm, the inventory levels are adjusted.

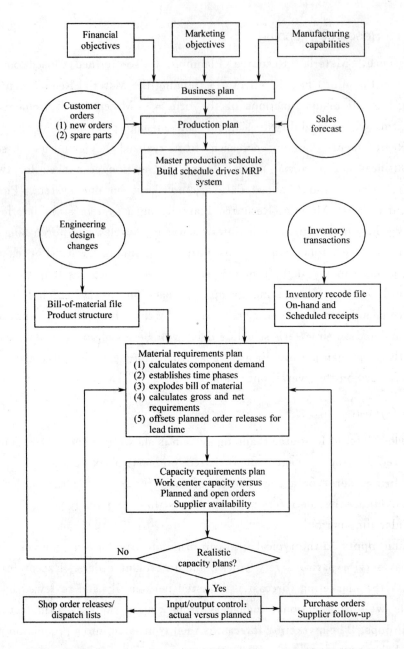

Figure 18. 2 Flowchart for a model Material Resource Planning system

4. Master Production Schedule

While the production plan is a general plan, the master production schedule is the shop-build schedule which drives the Material Requirements Planning system. The master production schedule is stated in bill-of-material numbers, and is used to generate the material requirements plan, and also generates the capacity requirements plan. This master schedule also lists all the end items (the items as sold by various users) by date (planned shipping period) and their quantity [6].

The master production schedule gives management an approximation of long-term capacity utilization, labour needs, the impact of new product plans in the shop load, and current priority status.

5. Bill-of-Material File

This contains information about all parts and shows the dependent demand relationship of subassemblies or end items (finished product) down to components and raw material level. For example, a bill of material for a screwdriver would show the plastic handle, forged shaft, and steel from which the shaft was made. If users are to obtain valid system outputs, the bill-of-material file must be accurate and up to date, and must be suitably defined for customers, manufacturing, and purchasing. Users must ensure that the latest engineering changes are incorporated into the bill of material.

6. Inventory Record File

This contains a record of the actual inventory level of each item and part as well as lead times. Inventory accuracy is critical in avoiding erroneous system outputs. Most users strive for 95%-99% accuracy and monitor actual inventory through cycle counting, which involves periodically counting inventory.

7. Material Requirements Plan

The function of this plan is to explode the master schedule against the bill-of-material file to determine the gross requirements necessary to make the product. These gross requirements are then compared to inventory on hand to determine net requirements. The net requirements at the higher level become gross requirements at the next lower level, and so on, down through the bill of material. These requirements are offset for lead time by subtracting the lead time from the date of the net requirements. The term projected requirements refers to the number of items necessary to make up the next-higher assembly (for example, 40 skateboards require 80 axles). The term scheduled receipts refers to material already on order or scheduled to come in.

The inventory of the item is represented by the term on hand. Planned order release (net requirements) means the number of items that manufacturing must make or purchasing must buy to meet higher-level requirements [7]. Level 0 is the highest level and represents the end item. Lead time is the time required to acquire an item after it is ordered or manufactured.

8. Capacity Requirements Plan

This part of the system enables manufacturing to determine what capacity will be required by work centers during each time period to meet the master production schedule. The Material Requirements Planning system will indicate which items are required and the timing of the items. The actual work load is then compared to work center capacity. If the available capacity falls short in meeting the master schedule, a decision must be made either to reduce the schedule or to expand capacity by working overtime, subcontracting, or purchasing additional capacity.

9. Input/Output Control

This part of the system monitors the levels of work into and out of each work center. Control is achieved by ensuring on-schedule job flow through various work centres. If a job slips behind schedule, its priority should be increased. When input to the factory begins to exceed output, this indicates that the production schedule has been overstated and should be reduced or the capacity expanded.

10. Dispatch lists and vendor follow-up lists

These help manufacturing and purchasing supervisors to determine accurate priorities. The dispatch list will print out jobs requested to be run and jobs available to be run, and the sequence in which to run them. Dispatch lists, usually generated daily, continually revise priorities on the shop floor. Follow-up lists give the purchasing department a tool to ensure that suppliers will deliver on time by providing information about requirements on a short- and long-term basis.

11. Advantages

Material requirements and Material Resource Planning systems offer users multiple benefits. From a broad perspective, this type of system provides a tool for total business planning of sales, production, cash flow, and so forth. It also provides a tool for marketing and provides better customer service through higher on-time completion dates, accurate order promise dates, and follow-up information. Other productivity enhancers include more professional purchasing, lower inventories, improved planning by shop supervisors, and increased direct labour productivity. By use of the computer, Material Resource Planning manipulates massive amounts of data to keep schedules up to date and priorities in order and valid.

The technological advances in computing and processing power, the benefits of on-line capabilities, and reduction in computing cost make computerized manufacturing planning and control systems such as Material Resource Planning powerful tools in operating modern manufacturing systems productively.

New Words and Expressions

1. recalculate[ri'kælkjuleit]*vt.* 重新计算
2. implementation [ˌimplimen'teiʃən]*n.* 执行
3. logic['lɔdʒik]*n.* 逻辑，逻辑学，逻辑性
4. bulk [bʌlk]*n.* 大小，体积，大批，大多数，散装;*vt.* 显得大，显得重要
5. lumpy ['lʌmpi] *adj.* 多块状物的，粗笨的
6. originate from   发源于
7. translate [træns'leit]*vt.* 翻译，解释，转化，转变为，调动;*vi.* 翻译，能被译出
8. aggregate ['ægrigeit]*n.* 合计，总计，集合体;*adj.* 合计的，集合的，聚合的
9. backlog['bæklɔg]*n.* 大木材，订货
10. approximation [əˌprɔksi'meiʃən]*n.* 接近，走近，[数] 近似值
11. screwdriver['skru:draivə]*n.* 螺丝起子
12. explode[iks'pləud]*vt.* 使爆炸;*vi.* 爆炸，爆发，破除，推翻，激发
13. gross [grəus]*adj.*总的，毛重的;*n.* 总额
14. receipt[ri'si:t]*n.* 收条，收据，收到;*v.* 收到
15. dispatch [dis'pætʃ]*vt.* 分派，派遣;*n.* 派遣，急件
16. vendor['vendɔ:]*n.* 卖主
17. supervisor['sju:pəvaizə]*n.* 监督人，管理人，检查员，督学，主管人
18. manipulate [mə'nipjuleit]*vt.* （熟练地）操作,（巧妙地）处理
19. computerize [kəm'pju:təraiz]*vt.* 用计算机处理，使计算机化

Notes

1. The Material Requirements Planning（MRP）system provides the user with

information about timing (when to order) and quantity (how much to order), generates new orders, and reschedules existing orders as necessary to meet the changing requirements of customers and manufacturing.

MRP 系统为用户提供时间(何时订购)以及数量(订购多少)方面的信息,生成新订单,并且可以重新计划现有的订单以满足顾客和市场需求的不断变化。

2. It makes adjustments for possible problems prior to their occurrence, as opposed to traditional control systems, which looked at more historical demand and reacted to existing problems.

与那些只注重过去需求并对现有问题起反作用的传统控制系统相对的是,MRP 系统能够在可能性问题发生之前做出相应的调整。

3. Applications by corporations of the just-in-time (JIT) philosophy will help smooth lumpiness to a certain extent since JIT argues for running smaller lot sizes.

由于 JIT 致力于小批量的运转,具有 JIT 理念的公司的应用有助于适当地平滑块状效应。

4. In essence, Material Resource Planning (also termed closed-loop Material Requirements Planning) has the effect of extending the Material Requirements Planning scheduling into all major functions of the firm.

本质上,MRP(亦称为 Material Requirements Planning)能够把物料需求计划的编制拓展到公司的所有主要部位。

5. The business plan prepared by top management is based on certain expectations of sales from forecasts, firm orders, or a combination of sales forecasts and firm orders.

高管理层所准备的商务计划是基于对预期销售、确定订货或者结合两者作出的。

6. This master schedule also lists all the end items (the items as sold by various users) by date (planned shipping period) and their quantity.

综合图表也按日期(计划运送周期)和数量罗列了所有的成品(不同客户所销售的物品)。

7. Planned order release (net requirements) means the number of items that manufacturing must make or purchasing must buy to meet higher-level requirements.

计划订单(净需求)是指那些为满足更高水平需求而必须制造或购买的物品清单。

Topics for Discussion

1. Could you give us the examples of dependent and independent demand?

2. As the accuracy in Material Requirements Planning increased, what will the

firms benefit from them?

3. What content will bill-of-material file include and what's the function of it?

4. From different perspective, what are the advantages of the Material Requirements Planning and Material Resource Planning systems?

Passage B

A Preliminary Definition for MRP III

1. Introduction of MRP

Material Requirements Planning, or MRP, has been officially around since the 1960's, with the advent of the use of computers in the manufacturing environment, though the basic principles involved in MRP are an integral part of the manufacturing process itself. However, by defining what "MRP" is, companies and software vendors are able to adapt a standardized set of methods by which they can schedule delivery of raw materials against the manufacturing schedule, thus keeping their assembly lines moving while at the same time minimizing the amount of inventory on-hand.

The ideal adaptation of the MRP process has, in the past, been considered to be a "just in time" scenario, when raw materials arrive just as they are required on the assembly line. Obviously, a system like this has the potential of being thrown "out of balance" by even the slightest problems; therefore, manufacturers build in "safety stock" or "lead time" factors to prevent material shortages from ever causing a "line stop". But safety stock and long lead times increase on-hand inventory, requiring larger warehouses to store raw materials, or even work in process, with no immediate benefit. Plus, it ties up the company's liquid capital in non-liquid inventory, which typically depreciates, gets damaged, spoils, and/or becomes obsolete within a relatively short period of time.

Obviously, there is a "happy medium" somewhere in between a true "just in time" system, where a single late or missing delivery can have drastic consequences, and a "just in case" system, where piece part inventories "turn" slowly, and often become wasted as obsolete inventory or spoilage. Somehow we must find the best inventory position, where the potential for material shortages is well-balanced with the need to minimize on-hand inventories, and minimize lead times. Finding this balance point, however, has never been a traditional component in an MRP system, or even an "MRP II" system.

Using Bandwidth Management —The concept of Bandwidth Management involves the use of statistics, based on known history, to define Control Limits that determine

222

the normal ranges for inventory levels, lead times, production rates, backlog, and orders placed by customers. It is possible to establish such a balance, between a minimum inventory on-hand and a consistently operating assembly line; therefore, we at S. F. T., Inc. propose to define the requirements for an "MRP III" system, which (among other things) includes the principles of *Bandwidth Management* as an integral component of the process, as well as a "Whole Business Planning" feedback loop to minimize the impact of an improper demand forecast on obsolete and excess inventory, plant capacity, and customer lead times.

2. The Development of MRP

MRP began as a relatively simple, yet important analysis of manufacturing processes and production schedules, combined with bills of material and/or resources, to predict what the requirements would be for various components and/or manufacturing processes in order to meet the current master schedule [1]. In addition, MRP applies component and process lead times to these requirements, along with various other "modifiers" (economic order quantities, safety stock, shrink factors, and so on) to generate recommended build schedules for non-master scheduled assemblies, and recommended purchasing orders for components. Existing schedules are not modified by a "standard MRP" process, though reports that make recommendations to re-schedule or cancel existing build schedules or purchase orders may be included in a "standard MRP" system. In essence, the "MRP" system merely performs an analysis of existing conditions, and reports back to you what the requirements are, and optionally recommends changes to existing purchase and production schedules to meet the requirements of the master schedule. It has been my experience that a "standard MRP" package, when properly implemented, will meet the needs of most customers that have consistent production schedules, adequate resources for the "critical paths" in the manufacturing process, and adequate delivery performance by vendors for the various component parts. However, in most cases, the MRP system doesn't seem to work so well. Either the component deliveries are consistently not on time, or the master schedule is constantly being changed, resulting in wildly fluctuating parameters. Typically, to make up for such conditions, safety stock limits will be increased until the warehouses are full of "just in case" inventory. Eventually, design changes in finished product cause a lot of this inventory to become "obsolete", or require some kind of retrofit in order to be usable again. This costs money. Further, in the electronics manufacturing industry, component prices typically go down over time, such that a warehouse full of old inventory will ultimately increase the cost of manufacturing a product above that of the competition, since the actual cost of components will be higher when purchased several weeks or months in advance.

3. From MRP to MRP II

To assist planners in tracking some of the problems associated with inventory control, some kind of "feedback loop" is needed in the MRP process, not only to automatically re-schedule certain items (when possible), and avoid excessive manual effort in controlling the process, but to detect and report performance that is "out of spec" (such as a vendor performance report to track on-time delivery performance)[2]. This "feedback loop" is the defining factor for an "MRP II" system. Though many systems claim to be an "MRP II" system, few actually fit the mold exactly. Still, with automatic rescheduling capabilities for work orders and/or repetitive build schedules, and "reschedule action" reports for purchase orders and outside contracting, the amount of actual analysis is reduced significantly. Other information, such as vender performance reports and process utilization reports, also help to measure the "performance to plan" capability of the manufacturing plant.

Even when the production plan is running at optimum performance, companies still often have serious problems with the manufacturing process. "hidden cost" issues associated with manufacturing increase the total cost of manufacturing, but are extremely hard to track. Some of these "hidden costs" can be caused by excessive P. O. rescheduling or excessive "crash buy" programs, excess and/or obsolete inventory, or planning problems that cause incorrectly stocked finished goods (too much of one, not enough of the other) that result in shortages. Another "hidden cost" issue might be frequent line stops related to a "limiting process" (such as a wave solder machine or component inserter), as well as material shortages and excessive "kitting" of common components. In addition, potential revenue losses from excessively long customer order lead times, or poor on-time customer delivery performance, are real problems, but very difficult to track and measure. As such, none of these problems are tracked nor reported by any "standard MRP" or "MRP II" system. To help solve these problems, and improve the company's competiveness and profitability, beyond existing capabilities, the MRP system must go beyond the standard definition of "MRP II", into what we at S. F. T. Inc. refer to as "MRP III".

4. Defining an MRP III Process

We at S. F. T. Inc. therefore propose to define a "whole business" MRP process that goes beyond simple component/assembly relationships, that goes beyond resource requirements, that goes beyond vendor performance and component shrink factors and safety stocks. The "MRP III" process begins with an Accurate Demand Forecast, for it is this Demand Forecast that drives the remainder of the business. Using the best possible demand forecast, a *Master Schedule* is developed. Ideally the total number of master scheduled items will be minimized, so that the MRP system can appropriately generate build schedules for components and "accessories" automatically, and will be derived directly from the Demand Forecast with little or no changes.

From the *Master Schedule*, the "MRP III" system derives the individual component and assembly requirements, and recommends new purchase orders, just like a "standard MRP" system, and also generates recommended purchase order reschedules, and automatically reschedules non-master scheduled assemblies based on the availability of components/resources and material requirements, just like an "MRP II" system. The "MRP III" system also monitors and reports vendor performance and "performance to plan" by the assembly line, similar to an "MRP II" system. However, to minimize the total amount of "detail information", the "MRP III" system concentrates on only reporting those items that fall outside of the allowed tolerances, thus minimizing the number of reported items.

When the MRP system has been fully integrated with the Order Management system, it becomes possible to calculate "available to promise" inventory, based on a combination of existing order backlog, the current inventory, and the projected availability of a product over time as it is built from the current production schedule. In this way, if a customer orders a product within lead time, and delivery is already promised to another customer, order management personnel can use this information to negotiate a realistic delivery schedule with the customer. Also, delivery re-schedules would become easier to manage, since order management personnel can view the current "available to promise" inventory, and use this information to determine when partial or full shipments could be re-scheduled. In all likelihood, there will be available inventory to ship ahead of schedule, should the customer need to perform a "crash buy". An "MRP III" system must therefore include the ability to view the "available to promise" inventory, based on current inventory, current backlog, and the current production plan.

Finally, the "MRP III" system bases its operating parameters on the principles of Bandwidth Management, dynamically adjusting parameters such as lead times and "ideal inventory" according to the historic data (when needed), and measuring performance to a set of statistically derived "control bands", rather than fixed parameters. The "MRP III" system then generates exception reports for those items that fall outside of the control bands, and automatically maintains as much of the manufacturing planning process as possible, with little or no human intervention.

A process such as "MRP III" would help to eliminate certain kinds of errors that currently plague manufacturing businesses on a nearly universal level. By far, the greatest single factor in ruining a perfectly good manufacturing plan is the tendency for the Demand Forecast to change on a regular basis, typically inside planning lead time. Or, the Demand Forecast may be completely useless for manufacturing purposes, forcing the person responsible for the master schedule to literally generate his own forecast in an attempt to predict what the demand actually will be. Often times, a combination of both of these conditions exists, where the marketing forecast is so inaccurate as to make it useless, forcing the master scheduler to perform this task of generating a forecast. And, without some kind of forecast, there is no master schedule. And, without a master schedule, there is no "MRP". Any "MRP" system without a demand forecast analysis capability is thus severely limited in its ability to help reduce overall inventory and simultaneously meet the requirements of the production plan.

Still, with all of the potential for automating the manufacturing planning process, people still need to use their skills and judgment within critical points in the planning process. Using "exception planning" will minimize the amount of items that people need to look at. This "exception planning" process is derived directly from *Bandwidth Management*, so that only those items that need attention will be addressed. It is still the planner's responsibility to implement purchase order re-scheduling or "crash buy" programs, outside contracting, and so forth, and (potentially) any manufacturing schedules oriented around a process or piece of equipment that is considered a "critical path" in the manufacturing process. The "MRP III" system must therefore supply as much useful information to the planner as possible, to help him make informed decisions, yet also limit this information to only those items that may actually require his attention.

5. How the Demand Planning Tool Helps to Implement S.F.T. III

The Demand Planning Tool, a product of S. F. T., Inc., is a combined effort of

226

over 5 years of development work, and is designed primarily to allow the user to quickly generate a more accurate forecast, maintain this forecast along with a long-term business plan, and perform daily or weekly *Demand Analysis* to measure current performance (actual data) to the forecast. It contains a number of screens, graphs, and reports to make this process as easy and fast as possible. The *Demand Planning Tool* employs the principles of *Bandwidth Management* to measure exceptions to the plan on a daily basis. By using *Bandwidth Management*, the number of exceptions to the plan is minimized, and therefore the plan becomes stable. A stable plan minimizes the negative impact of forecast changes inside of lead time on the manufacturing process, and allows the master scheduler to more effectively use the MRP system, with much fewer problems. The *Demand Planning Tool* forms a major part of the total "MRP III" system, as outlined above, by analyzing the DEMAND SIDE of the equation. The resulting *Demand Forecast* forms the input to the entire manufacturing process. The *Demand Planning Tool* can also track on-time delivery performance for customer orders, thereby measuring the overall system performance of the manufacturing environment, by comparing the actual shipment date to the customer's requested ship date.

New Words and Expressions

1. potential [pə'tenʃ(ə)l] *adj.* 可能的；潜在的

2. obsolete ['ɔbsəliːt]*adj.* 已废弃的；已不用的

3. backlog ['bæklɔg]*n.* 积压未办的事

4. schedule ['ʃedjuːl;(美)'skedʒjul] *n.* 目录，一览表，清单

5. recommend[rekə'mend]*vt.* 推荐，介绍

6. assembly [ə'sembli]*n.* 集合

7. consistently[kən'sistəntli] *adv.* 坚固，坚实，一致，始终如一，连贯

8. component [kəm'pəunənt]*adj.* 组成的，合成的，成分的，分量的

9. associate [ə'səuʃieit]*vt.* 联合，结交；加入

10. availability [əˌveilə'biliti] *n.* 有效性，可利用性[率]

11. negotiate [ni'gəuʃieit]*vt.* 议定，商定，通过谈判使……

12. statistically[stə'tistikli]*adv.* 统计上地，统计地

13. parameter [pə'ræmitə]*n.* 变数，特性；补助变数

14. maintain [men'tein]*vt.* 保持；维持；继续

15. overall ['əuvərɔːl]*a.* 全部的，全体的，从头至尾的，一切在内的

Notes

1. MRP began as a relatively simple, yet important analysis of manufacturing processes and production schedules, combined with bills of material and/or resources, to predict what the requirements would be for various components and/or manufacturing processes in order to meet the current master schedule.

MRP 作为一个相对简单但却对生产过程及产品计划具有重要分析的系统,与物料资源计划相结合,能够针对当前主导计划预测所需要的各种部件或者制造过程。

2. To assist planners in tracking some of the problems associated with inventory control, some kind of "feedback loop" is needed in the MRP process, not only to automatically re-schedule certain items (when possible), and avoid excessive manual effort in controlling the process, but to detect and report performance that is "out of spec" (such as a vendor performance report to track on-time delivery performance).

为了协助计划者与库存控制相关的问题解决,一些"反馈回路"被应用于 MRP 过程,不仅自动再调整特定的物料项目(如果可能的话)、避免控制过程里的过度体力劳动,而且察觉并上报那些不合规格的作业(例如一个卖家按时配送的过程)。

Topics for Discussion

1. What's the adaptation of the MRP process and its relationship with the "just in time" system?

2. From part three, to help solve these problems, and improve the company's competiveness and profitability, what will the MRP system go beyond the standard definition of "MRP II", into what we at S. F. T. Inc. refer to as "MRP III"?

3. How to define an MRP III process from our passage?

4. How the *Demand Planning Tool* helps to implement MRP III?

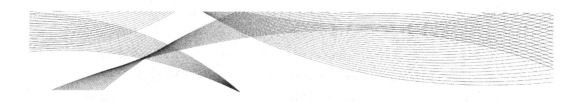

Unit 19

Passage A

Third-party Logistics

1. Outsourcing and 3PL

Third-party logistics （3PL） refers to the outsourcing of transportation, warehousing and other logistics-related activities which were originally performed in-house, to a 3PL service provider [1]. More and more corporations across the world are outsourcing their logistics activities due to various factors, some of which are outlined below.

A third-party logistics service is something more than subcontracting or outsourcing. Typically, subcontracting or outsourcing covers one product or one function that is produced or provided by an outside vendor. Examples include automobile companies subcontracting the manufacture of tires, or construction companies subcontracting roofing, or retail companies outsourcing the transportation function. Third-party logistics providers cut across multiple logistics functions and primarily coordinate all the logistics functions and sometimes act as a provider of one or more functions. The primary objectives of third-party logistics providers are to lower the total of cost of logistics for the supplier and improve the service level to the customer. They act as a bridge or facilitator between the first party （supplier or producer） and the second party （buyer or customer）.

2. The Motivation of Third Party Logistics

There are several reasons for the growth of third-party logistics over the past decade. The transportation and distribution departments of some of the major corporations have been downsizing in order to reduce operating costs. The most logical area to reduce costs is advisory functions such as operations research, followed by support functions such as transportation or warehousing. The area where companies want to strengthen by investing more is their core competency. Though it may sound like a fad it had been a reality at some of the major corporations. The other reason is from file customer side. Customers demand an exceptional service but are not willing to pay extraordinary price for it... This requires file use of faster and frequent transportation services and flexibility in inventory levels. A third-party logistics provider will be in a position to consolidate business from several companies and offer frequent pick-ups and deliveries, whereas in-house transportation cannot. Other reasons are as follows:

(1) The company's core business and competency may not be in logistics.

(2) Sufficient resources, both capital and manpower, may not be available for file company to become a world-class logistics operator.

(3) There is an urgency to implement a "world-class" logistics operation or there is insufficient time to develop the required capabilities in-house.

(4) The Company is venturing into a new business with totally different logistics requirements.

(5) Merger or acquisition may make outsourcing logistics operations more attractive than to integrate logistics operations.

In recent years there has been some concern expressed by file users of third-party service providers that riley are not being given the expected levels of service and business benefits. Users have also indicated that service providers are insufficiently proactive in their approach to the contracted operations—which they only aim to provide the minimum and fail to enhance file operations they are responsible for. On the other hand, service providers claim that they are seldom given the opportunity to develop new ideas and offer improvements, because users are not prepared to give them adequate information of their complete, supply chains. One consequence of this has been file idea of using an additional enterprise or organization to oversee and take responsibility for all the outsourced operations a user might have. This has become known as fourth-party logistics.

The need to take a total supply chain approach means that a different type of service provider and a different type of RFQ/ITr approach are required. The idea is to aim to provide solutions, not just services. It is important to recognize that there are often several different organizations or participants in a supply chain, that there is a need to develop partnerships and there should be opportunities to integrate and rationalize along the supply chain.

Thus, solutions can be developed by the co-venture of fourth-party service provider, to offer:

(1) A total supply chain perspective;

(2) Visibility along the supply chain;

(3) Measurement along the supply chain;

(4) Open systems;

(5) Technical vision;

(6) Flexibility;

(7) Tailored structures and systems.

3. Benefits of Relying on 3PL

Due to globalization, corporations across the world are increasingly sourcing, manufacturing and distributing on a global scale, making their supply chains very complex for them to manage. However, these activities can be outsourced today to experienced 3PL providers who have global operations and offer complete supply chain solutions with their sophisticated IT capabilities and state-of-the-art transportation and material handling equipment and warehousing facilities. Logistics outsourcing is also used to complement the logistics activities the corporations do not have competency in, and to increase the geographic reach[2] ⋯ When a corporation expands its business overseas, it may not be conversant with the customs duties, tax structures, rules and regulations, import/export policies of the government, and culture of the foreign country. A 3PL provider, who has long been operating in that country, will be better able to carry out the logistics operations [3].

Logistics may not be one of the core activities of a corporation. So, inefficiency may creep in if it is looked upon as a secondary activity. 3PL providers are now offering a number of value-added services such as customs clearance, freight forwarding, import/export management, distribution, after sales support, reverse logistics and so on. By outsourcing all these, corporations may focus on their core competencies and on improving cycle time and delivery performance, thereby increasing customer satisfaction[4]. This may also reduce costs as the 3PL providers can get the advantage of the economies of scale, which is otherwise not available to the corporations. By outsourcing logistics, corporations can reduce their asset base, and deploy the capital

231

released for other productive usage.

Electronic retailing has got incredible growth since the late 1990s. Many firms around the world with virtually no distribution systems rely mainly on 3PL providers to deliver their merchandise at the customer's doorstep. This has resulted in a significant growth in the order fulfillment sector of the 3PL service industry.

4. Evolution of 3PL

The concept of logistics outsourcing can be traced quite far back in history. In Europe, a number of logistics service providers can trace their origins back to the middle Ages. Tracing the evolution of 3PL in recent decades, we find that, in the 1950s and 1960s; logistics outsourcing was limited to transportation and warehousing [5]. The transactions were mainly short-term in nature. In the 1970s, the emphasis was on improved productivity, cost reduction and long-term contracts, while value-added services such as packaging, labeling, systems support and inventory management were on offer in the 1980s. Since the 1990s, outsourcing has picked up momentum, and more value-added services are being offered. Some of them are import/export management, customs clearance, freight forwarding, customer service, rate negotiation, order processing, assembly/installation, distribution, order fulfillment, reverse logistics, consulting services that include distribution network planning, site selection for facility location, fleet management, freight consolidation, logistics audit etc.

5. 3PL Market

Currently, the logistics cost around the world is about $2 trillion. For any country, the logistics cost is pegged between 9% and 20% of GDP. Take India for example, the figure is about 13%, given the GDP of over $475 billion and the logistics cost of about $62 billion.

The 3PL market across the world is increasing at a rapid rate. According to Armstrong and Associates, the world 3PL revenues in 1992, 1996 and 2000 were $10 billion, $25 billion and $56 billion respectively. According to another research finn IDC, the 3PL revenue was $141 billion in 2003, and it will touch $300 billion in 2006 growing at a compounded annual rate of 17%. The world's largest 3PL providers in terms of revenues are Europe-based (DHL being the largest in the world after its acquisition of Exel plc in December 2005), but the largest market is the US, which was about $80 billion in 2003 accounting for nearly 60% of the world market [6].

New Words and Expressions

1. advisory[əd'vaizəri] *adj*. 有权发言的,顾问的
2. competency['kɔmpit(ə)nsi] *n*. 胜任;能力
3. flexible['fleksəbl] *adj*. 容易适应新情况的
4. minimum['miniməm] *n*. 最小量,最低限度
5. strengthen['streŋθən] *v*. 更强
6. conversant [kən'və:sənt] *adj*. (与 with 连用)精通……的;熟悉……的;内行的
7. asset['æset] *n*. (常用复数)资产;财产;有用的资源,宝贵的人(物);优点,益处
8. sector['sektə] *n*. 部分,部门,[计]扇区,地区,象限,扇形
9. evolution [ˌi:və'lu:ʃən,ˌevə-] *n*. 进化;演化;发展
10. trace [treis] *vt*. (与 along,through,to 连用) 跟踪,追踪
11. momentum [məu'mentəm] *n*. 动量;总冲量;推进力;势头
12. clearance['kliərəns] *n*. [商]结算,清算,纯益;净利;票据交换
13. IDC   美国国际数据集团 IDG 下属的市场调研公司
14. DHL   敦豪国际快递公司
15. Exel   英运公司(DHL 收购的英国物流公司)
16. outsourcing   外包。公司把原来自己员工做的工作,委托外面公司做
17. core competence   核心能力。对公司而言,一个公司有一些特殊的技能知识
18. pickup   集货。运送行业到客户处收集货物然后由火车载回站所
19. pickup & delivery service reliability   收送货服务可靠度
20. pickup allowance   免接费
21. in-house   公司内部。有些活动在组织或公司内实行,而非由外部的厂商制作

Notes

1. Third-party logistics （3PL） refers to the outsourcing of transportation, warehousing and other logistics-related activities which were originally performed in-house，to a 3PL service provider.

第三方物流是指物流公司把原本由自己承担的运输、仓储及其他相关物流活动承包给物流服务供应商,即第三方物流服务供应商。

2. Logistics outsourcing is also used to complement the logistics activities the corporations do not have competency in，and to increase the geographic reach…

物流外包也被用来作为公司对没有竞争力的物流活动的补充,使公司可以把业务拓

展到较远的地方。

3. A 3PL provider, who has long been operating in that country, will be better able to carry out the logistics operations.

由于第三方物流供应商一直在该国运营,因此将能够更好地开展物流业务。

4. By outsourcing all these, corporations may focus on their core competencies and onimproving cycle time and delivery performance, thereby increasing customer satisfaction.

通过把所有这些业务外包,公司可以把注意力集中在自己的核心竞争力上,还可以集中精力改善产品流通周期和交货服务,因此将提高客户满意度。

5. Tracing the evolution of 3PL in recent decades, we find that, in the 1950s and 1960s logistics outsourcing was limited to transportation and warehousing.

历数最近几十年来第三方物流的演变过程,我们注意到,在 20 世纪五六十年代,物流外包仅限于运输和仓储。

6. The world's largest 3PL providers in terms of revenues are Europe-based (DHL being the largest in the world after its acquisition of Exel in December 2005), but the largest market is the US, which was about $80 billion in 2003 accounting for nearly 60% of the world market.

就收入而言,全世界最大的第三方物流供应商总部设在欧洲(敦豪国际快递公司2005 年 12 月兼并了英运公司后成为全球第一大第三方物流供应商),但是最大的市场却在美国。2003 年美国第三方物流总值约 800 亿美元,占全球市场的 60%。

Topics for Discussion

1. Why do companies outsource their logistics activities? Please break into groups of four persons and discuss the following topics. Try to base your discussion on some research online. Be prepared to give a presentation in class.

2. A third-party logistics provider will be in a position to consolidate business from several companies and offer frequent pick-ups and deliveries, whereas in-house transportation cannot. What are the other reasons?

3. What international 3PL providers are operating in China? What services do they offer?

Passage B

International Logistics

While an effective logistics system is important for domestic supply chain integration, it is absolutely essential for successful global manufacturing and marketing. Domestic logistics focuses on performing value-added services to support supply chain integration in a somewhat controllable environment. Global logistics must accommodate operations in a variety of different national, political, and economic settings while also dealing with increased uncertainties associated with the distance, demand, diversity, and documentation of international commerce [1].

1. Stages of International Development

The continuum of global trade perspectives ranges from export/import to local presence to the concept of a stateless enterprise. The following discussion compares conceptual and managerial implications of strategic development.

(1) Export/Import: A National Perspective

The initial stage of international trade is characterized by export and import. A participating organization is typically focused on internal operations and views international transactions in terms of what they will do for domestic business. Typically, when firms are committed to an export/import strategy, they use service providers to conduct and manage operations in other countries. A national export/import business orientation influences logistical decisions in three ways.

Firstly, sourcing and resource choices are influenced by artificial constraints. These constraints are typically in the form of use restrictions, local content laws, or price surcharges. A use restriction is a limitation, usually government imposed, that restricts the level of import sales or purchase. For example, the enterprise may require that internal divisions be used for material sources even though prices or quality are not competitive. Local content laws specify the proportion of a product that must be sourced within the local economy. Price surcharges involve higher charges for foreign-sourced product imposed by governments to maintain the viability of local suppliers [2]. In combination, use restrictions and price surcharges limit management's ability to select what otherwise would be the preferred supplier.

Secondly, logistics to support export/import operations increases planning complexity. A fundamental logistics objective is smooth product flow in a manner that facilitates efficient capacity utilization. Barriers resulting from government intervention make it difficult to achieve this objective.

Thirdly, an export/import perspective attempts to extend domestic logistics systems and operating practices to global origins and destinations. While a national perspective simplifies matters at a policy level, it increases operational complexity since exceptions are numerous. Local managers must accommodate exceptions while remaining within corporate policy and procedure guidelines. As a result, local logistics management must accommodate cultural, language, employment, and political environments without full support and understanding of corporate head-quarters.

(2) International Operations: Local Presence

The second stage of international development is characterized by establishment of operations within a foreign country. Internal operations include combinations of marketing, sales, production, and logistics. Establishment of local facilities and operations serves to increase market awareness and sensitivity. This is often referred to as gaining local presence. At the outset of a local presence strategy, foreign operations typically use parent company management and personnel, and practice home country values, procedures, and operations. However, over time, business units operating within a foreign market area will adopt local business practices.

This adoption typically means hiring host country management, marketing, and sales organizations and may include the use of local business system. As local presence operations expand, the host country philosophy will increasingly emerge; however, the company headquarters' strategic vision remains dominant. Individual country operations are still measured against home country expectations and standards.

(3) Globalization: the Stateless Enterprise

The stateless enterprise contrasts sharply to operations guided by either an export/ import or international perspective.

Stateless enterprises maintain regional operations and develop a headquarters structure to coordinate area operations. Thus, the enterprise is stateless in the sense that no specific home or parent country dominates policy. Senior management likely represents a combination of nationalities. Denationalized operations function on the basis of local-marketing and sales organizations and are typically supported by world-class manufacturing and logistics operations. Product sourcing and marketing decisions can be made across a wide range of geographical alternatives. Systems and procedures are

236

designed to meet individual country requirements and are aggregated as necessary to share knowledge and for financial reporting.

While most enterprises engaging in international business are operating in stages one and two, a truly international firm must focus on the challenges of global operations. Such globalization requires a significant level of management trust that transcends countries and cultures. Such trust can only grow as managers increasingly live and work across cultures.

2. Managing the Global Supply Chain

To meet the challenges discussed above, management must evaluate the complexity of the global supply chain and focus on five major differences between domestic and international operations:

(1) The Performance Cycle Structure

The performance cycle structure is the major difference between domestic and global operations. Instead of 3 to 5 day transit time and 4 to 10 day total performance cycles, global operational cycles are measured in weeks or months. For example, it is common for automotive parts from Pacific Rim suppliers to take 60 days from replenishment order release until physical order receipt at a U. S. manufacturing facility[3].

The reasons for a longer performance cycle are communication delays, financing requirements, special packaging requirements, ocean freight scheduling, slow transit time, and customs clearance. Communication may be delayed by time zone and language differences. Financing cause's delays since international transactions often require letters of credit. Special packaging may be required to protect products from in transit damage since containers typically are exposed to high humidity, temperature, and weather conditions. Once a product is containerized, it must be scheduled for movement between ports having appropriate handling capabilities. This scheduling process can require up to 30 days if the origin and destination ports are not located on high-volume traffic lanes or the ships moving to the desired ports lack the necessary equipment [4]. Transit time, once the ship is en route, ranges from 10 to 21 days. Port delays are common as ships wait for others to clear harbor facilities [5]. Customs clearance may further extend time. Although it is increasingly common to utilize electronic messaging to pre-clear product shipments through customs prior to arrival at international ports, the elapsed performance cycle time is still lengthy [6].

The combination and complexity of the above factors causes international logistics performance cycles to be longer, less consistent, and less flexible than is typical in domestic operations. The reduced consistency, in particular, increases planning difficulty. The longer performance cycle also results in higher asset commitment because significant inventory is in transit at any point in time.

(2) Transportation

The U. S. initiative to deregulate transportation during the early 1980's has extended globally. Three significant global changes have occurred:

- international ownership and operation,
- privatization, and
- cabotage and bilateral agreements.

Historically, there have been regulatory restrictions concerning international transportation ownership and operation rights. Transport carriers were limited to operating within a single transportation mode with few, if any, joint pricing and operating agreements. Traditionally, steamship lines could not own or manage integrated land-based operations such as motor or rail carriers. Without joint ownership, operations and pricing agreements, international shipping was complicated. International shipments typically required multiple carriers to perform freight movement. Specifically, government rather than market forces determined the extent of services foreign-owned carriers could perform. Although some ownership and operating restrictions remain, marketing and alliance arrangements among countries have substantially improved transportation flexibility. The removal of multi-model ownership restrictions in the U. S. and in most other industrialized nations served to facilitate integrated movement.

A second transportation impact on global operations has been increased carrier privatization. Historically, many international carriers were owned and operated by government in an effort to promote trade and provide national security. Government-owned carriers often subsidize operations for their home country businesses while placing surcharges on foreign enterprises. Artificially high pricing and poor service often made it costly and unreliable to ship via such government carriers. Inefficiencies also resulted from strong unionization and work rules. The combination of high cost and operating inefficiencies caused many government carriers to operate at a loss. A great many such carriers have been privatized.

Changes in cabotage and bilateral service agreements are the third transportation factor influencing international trade. Cabotage laws require passengers or goods moving between two domestic ports to utilize only domestic carriers. Cabotage laws were

238

designed to protect domestic transportation industries even though they also served to reduce overall transportation equipment utilization and to increase related efficiency. The European Community has relaxed cabotage restrictions to increase trade efficiency. Such reduced cabotage restrictions will save U. S.

(3) Operational Considerations

There are a number of unique operational considerations in a global environment.

First, international operations typically require multiple languages for both product and documentation. A technical product such as a computer or a calculator must have local features such as keyboard characters and language on both the product itself and related manuals. From a logistics perspective, language differences dramatically increase complexity since a product is limited to a specific country once it is language-customized. For example, even though Western Europe is much smaller than the U. S. in a geographic sense. It requires relatively more inventory to support marketing efforts since separate inventories may be required to accommodate various languages. Although product proliferation due to language requirement has been reduced through multipurpose packaging and postponement strategies, such practices are not always acceptable. In addition to product language implications, international operations may require multilingual documentation for each country through which the shipment passes. Although English is the general language of commerce, some countries require that transportation and customs documentation be provided in the local language. This increases the time and effort for international operations since complex documents must be translated prior to shipment. These communication and documentation difficulties can be somewhat overcome through standardized electronic transactions.

The second operational difference in global commerce is unique national accommodation such as performance features, power supply characteristics, and safety requirements. While they may not be substantial, the small differences between country requirements may significantly increase required SKUs and subsequent inventory level.

The third operating difference is the sheer amount of documentation required for international operations. While domestic operations can generally is completed using only an invoice and bill of lading, international operations require substantial documentation regarding order contents, transportation, financing, and government control. The table lists and describes common forms of international documentations.

Globalization is an evolving frontier that is increasingly demanding supply chain integration. As international business develop itself, the demand for logistical competency increases due to longer supply chain, less certainty, and more documentation. While the forces of change push toward borderless operations, supply chain management still confronts market, financial, and channel barriers. The barters are exemplified by distance, demand, diversity, and documentation. The challenge is to position an enterprise to take advantage of the benefits of global marketing and manufacturing by developing world-spanning logistical competency.

New Words and Expressions

1. continuum [kən'tinjuəm] *n.* 连续统一体,闭联集
2. characterize['kæriktəraiz]*v.* 表现……的特色,刻画的……性格
3. orientation [ɔ(:)rien'teiʃən] *n.* 方向,方位;定位;倾向性;向东方
4. sourcing *v.* 采购
5. viability [ˌvai'biliti] *n.* 生存能力,发育能力
6. coordinate [kəu'ɔːdinit] *v.* 调整,整理
7. aggregate['ægrigeit]*v.* 聚集,集合,合计
8. transcend [træn'send]*v.* 超越,胜过
9. replenishment[ri'pleniʃmənt] *n.* 补给,补充
10. elapse [i'læps]*v.* 过去,消逝;流逝
11. deregulate [diːregjuleit] *v.* 解除管制
12. privatization [ˌpraivitai'zeiʃən] *n.* 私有化
13. cabotage['kæbətidʒ] *n.* 沿海贸易权;沿海航行权
14. bilateral [bai'lætərəl]*adj.* 有两面的,双边的
15. subsidize['sʌbsidaiz] *v.* 资助,津贴
16. proliferation [prəuˌlifə'reiʃən] *n.* 增殖
17. sheer [ʃiə] *adj.* 纯粹的,绝对的,彻底的
18. incidence['insidəns] *n.* 影响范围
19. supply chain integration 供应链一体化
20. artificial constraint 人为的限制
21. local content laws 地方法律法规
22. prior to 在前,居先
23. asset commitment 资产需求

Notes

1. Global logistics must accommodate operations in a variety of different national,

240

political, and economic settings while also dealing with increased uncertainties associated with the distance, demand, diversity, and documentation of international commerce.

全球物流必须适应在不同国家、政治和经济环境中运作,同时,还要处理国际商务中与距离、要求、多样化以及单证相联系的日益增加的不确定因素。

2. Sourcing and resource choices are influenced by artificial constraints. These constraints are typically in the form of use restrictions, local content laws, or price surcharges. A use restriction is a limitation, usually government imposed, that restricts the level of import sales or purchase. Local content laws specify the proportion of a product that must be sourced within the local economy. Price surcharges involve higher charges for foreign-sourced product imposed by governments to maintain the viability of local suppliers.

采购和资源选择被人为的限制所影响。这些限制以使用限制、地方法律法规,或者价格额外费为典型表现。使用限制是一个通常由政府施加的限制,用来限制进口的销售或购买的水平。地方法律法规指定一种产品中必须在当地经济中被采购的比例部分。价格附加费是政府对外国采购产品收取更高的费用,为了保持当地供应商的生存能力。

3. For example, it is common for automotive parts from Pacific Rim suppliers to take 60 days from replenishment order release until physical order receipt at a U. S. manufacturing facility.

例如,为了从环太平洋地区的供应商处拿到汽车零件,从发出补充存货订单到美国的制造厂收到实际的订货通常需要 60 天。

4. This scheduling process can require up to 30 days if the origin and destination ports are not located on high-volume traffic lanes or the ships moving to the desired ports lack the necessary equipment.

如果出发港和目的港没有位于交通流量较高的航线上,或者驶往预定港口的船舶缺乏必要的设备,那么这种进展过程可能需要长达 30 天的时间。

5. Port delays are common as ships wait for others to clear harbor facilities.

港口的延迟是经常性的,因为船舶需要等待其他船使用港口的设施。

6. Although it is increasingly common to utilize electronic messaging to pre-clear product shipments through customs prior to arrival at international ports, the elapsed performance cycle time is still lengthy.

虽然现在越来越普遍地利用电子信息传输技术在产品还没有抵达国际港口之前,就事先办好清关手续,但是,上述过程所耗费的时间仍然很长。

Topics for Discussion

1. What will a national export/import business orientation influence logistical decisions?

2. What's a fundamental stage of international development?

3. To meet the challenges discussed above, management must evaluate the complexity of the global supply chain, and so what major differences will they focus on between domestic and international operations?

4. What's your understanding of globalization?

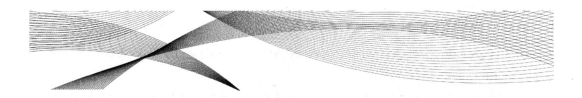

Unit 20

Passage A

Global Trade Drives 3PL Provider's Expansion (I)

The juggernaut of free trade and globalization of manufacturing and retail sourcing is unstoppable. But the speed with which this globalization is reshaping supply chains has been startling, especially for the third- party logistics providers whose job it is to support these supply chains [1].

"3PLs that expect to be competitive with major customers all have stepped up their strategic plans for global expansion," says Richard Armstrong, president of the Wisconsin-based 3PL research firm, Armstrong & Associates. "Their customers are telling them where they need to be to support rapid global business expansion."

This trend has lighted a fire under the world's 3PLs, including the U. S. -based companies that to a large extent have depended on the North American economy to fuel their growth. Until the end of the 1990s, 3PL annual revenue growth in the U. S. alone was climbing at around 10 to 15 percent year after year. International activity consisted mainly of cross-border NAFTA movements or management of export and import freight. In the last two years, however, setting up operations in Europe, Latin America and Asia have become a priority for those U. S. -based 3PLs that want to ride the globalization wave.

"Growth for 3PLs in emerging markets such as China and India should be between 20 to 30 percent over the next few years," says Ken Chay, corporate director of marketing for APL Logistics. "Average worldwide 3PL growth estimates for that same time horizon are only about 10 percent. Everybody knows where the action will be." [2]

1. Growth drivers

Global growth strategies for U. S. -based 3PLs are being driven by both their own plans, and by customer demand.

"Customers that we just served domestically are asking us to help them with their growing global activities," says Chay. "It is not just a matter of their being pleased with our domestic service, so they are willing to try our international services. Increasingly, they want to connect their global sourcing and inbound logistics operations with their domestic warehouse and distribution. As a global 3PL, we can bridge those two ends of the supply chain. "[3]

Mark Rhoney, vice president of marketing and strategy for UPS Supply Chain Solutions, says customers are coming to his company looking for their own global growth opportunities.

"Our path to global growth is showing these customers that outsourcing more functions optimizes their global flexibility to react to new market trends," says Rhoney, who adds that global customers are finding this flexibility by having 3PLs streamline vendor management into the manufacturing process, managing supplier compliance and consolidating shipments for easier transport and customs clearance.

At the same time, Rhoney says, UPS SCS is driving its own global destiny. "Global expansion has been part of the company's growth strategy for more than a decade," he says. "The most rapidly growing part of business, for both package delivery and for supply-chain services, is wholly outside the U. S. " UPS SCS was involved in expanding its global footprint primarily through acquisitions since 1995. These acquisitions of forwarders, customs brokers and other operations around the world were driven by customers asking UPS SCS to be in more places to support them. "In the early days of the globalization trend, those customers tended to be U. S. -based multinationals," says Rhoney. "Now, the customer base is much more diverse and includes companies with no ties to the U. S. " Chay agrees that the large U. S. -based 3PLs have been preparing themselves for increased globalization for some time. "We all anticipated the shift to manufacturing in China," he says, "but we were all surprised by how quickly the shift has occurred. " Global sourcing of consumer goods, especially from China, is the center of growth for APL Logistics. This sourcing function takes in many activities throughout the supply chain. At origin, APL provides freight forwarding, purchase order management, quality assurance, vendor-managed inventory, information based services, scanning, documentation and container consolidation. It manages

244

International Ocean and air as a freight forwarder. At destinations in the U. S, Europe and elsewhere, APL handles import activities such as customs brokerage, portside flow through warehouses and deconsolidation as well as full domestic warehouse distribution through a system of shared and contract warehouses. At destination points, APL Logistics also provides domestic truckload and intermodal services. China, however, has increasingly become the big growth engine for APL Logistics. The company has been in the market for more than 20 years, and was among the first to have the so-called wholly foreign-owned enterprise (WFOE) license. Its logistics activities there grew out of the APL liner service to China that goes back 150 years.

The next services that APL Logistics (and virtually all foreign 3PLs) would like to perform in China are domestic transportation and distribution operations. Right now, however, China does not allow foreign investment in logistics operations or domestic 3PL.

"The opportunities for direct 3PL activity in China will be enabled by the World Trade Organization schedule over the next five to 10 years," says Chay. "The logistics opportunities will open up gradually on a laddered basis. "

Consultant Richard Armstrong sees these domestic Chinese distribution opportunities as one of the most important competitive battles for the 3PL industry in the years ahead. "China will become a huge consumer market in which all truly global 3PLs will need to operate," says Armstrong. He adds that likely U. S. -based candidates include all of those companies that have been successful there supporting the export trade, such as APL Logistics, UPS SCS, FedEx and a few others.

"But these U. S. companies will be going up against the big Japanese players such as SembCorp Logistics, Yamato, Nippon Express, as well as the well-known European-based 3PLs," says Armstrong. "It is going to be a donnybrook. "

In the meantime, China still represents opportunities for U. S. -based 3PLs beyond exporting consumer products and electronics to the U. S. and Europe. For example, Joe Mulvehille, vice president of international for C. H. Robinson Worldwide says that although export forwarding from China is its primary business activity in that region, its export to Asia from the U. S. and other parts of the world grew significantly.

"Moving raw materials to China and other parts of Asia to support their manufacturing base is becoming huge," he says. "When the restrictions on foreign ownership and operations within China are reduced, this inbound business will flourish even more. "

2. Beyond China

Ironically, the success of the China trade is helping some 3PLs to expand their businesses in other parts of the world. APL Logistics' Chay says that many customers have learned caution about relying too heavily on China from such events as the West Coast port shutdown, the SARS epidemic and repeated terrorist scares. An increasing number of companies are diversifying their risk, and APL Logistics helps them develop a "plan B" sourcing strategy if for any reason China were suddenly shut off.

"China will remain the dominant location, but many companies want backup plants or sourcing points in places like India, Vietnam, Mexico and farther south in Latin America," says Chay. "When we have a deep customer relationship, we can engage them in discussions about sensitive subjects such as contingency planning."

Asian manufacturing and sourcing are not the only trends fostering global 3PL growth. According to UPS's Rhoney, opportunities abound.

"From a 3PL perspective, there are opportunities in every marketplace," he says. "New consumer markets are growing in emerging economies in Latin America and Eastern Europe. Outsourcing is more accepted in Europe, so there are more opportunities than even in the U. S."

Rhoney also believes that in all geographies, but especially outside the U. S., there are special opportunities for 3PLs in certain industries. He points to high-tech companies that source, manufacture and distribute on a global basis. High-tech has always been a large user of UPS's airfreight and express services because of the importance that speed plays in reducing inventory costs, avoiding obsolescence and introducing new products.

"High-tech is just now beginning to look at outsourcing more broadly to 3PLs," says Rhoney. He says that customers in the high-tech sector are using UPS SCS for vendor-managed inventory, managing inbound supply into contract manufacturers and streamlining post-sales functions such as service parts, returns management and repair and refurbishment.

New Words and Expressions

1. NAFTA: North American Free Trade Agreement   n. 北美自由贸易协议
2. juggernaut['dʒʌgənɔːt]n. 使人盲目崇拜并为之牺牲的事物;不可抗拒的力量
3. revenue['revinjuː]n. 收入,国家的收入,税收

4. freight [freit]*n.* 货物，船货，运费，货运

5. inbound['inbaund] *adj.* 开向本国的；归航的；入境的，入站的

6. warehouse['wɛəhaus]*n.* 仓库，货栈，大商店 *vt.* 储入仓库

7. optimize['ɔptimaiz]*v.* 使最优化

8. streamline['striːmlain]*vt.* 使成流线型；使(企业、组织等)简化并更有效率

9. vendor['vendɔː]*n.* 卖主

10. compliance [kəm'plaiəns]*n.* 服从；遵守

11. consolidate [kən'sɔlideit]*vt.* 统一；合并

12. shipment ['ʃipmənt]*n.* 装船，出货

13. acquisition[ˌækwi'ziʃən]*n.* 获得，获得物

14. forwarder['fɔːwədə]*n.* 代运人，运输业者，转运公司

15. broker['brəukə]*n.* 掮客，经纪人

16. shift [ʃift]*n.* 移动，轮班，移位，变化，办法，手段

17. scanning['skæniŋ]*v.* 扫描

18. documentation [ˌdɔkjumen'teiʃən]*n.* 文件[证书等] 的提供

19. truckload ['trʌkləud]*n.* 一货车的容量

20. intermodal [ˌintə(ː)'məudl]*adj.* 联合运输的

21. donnybrook['dɔnibruk]*n.* 〈口〉闹哄哄的殴斗，大混战

Notes

1. The juggernaut of free trade and globalization of manufacturing and retail sourcing is unstoppable. But the speed with which this globalization is reshaping supply chains has been startling, especially for the third- party logistics providers whose job it is to support these supply chains.

制造业和零售采购业的自由贸易与全球化的巨大力量是势不可挡的。但是全球化改造供应链的速度一直是很惊人的,特别是对于第三方物流供应商来说,他们的工作就是支持这些供应链。

2. "Average worldwide 3PL growth estimates for that same time horizon are only about 10 percent. Everybody knows where the action is. "

同一时期内,全世界第三方物流平均增长速度估计只有10%,所以每个人都知道战斗会在哪里打响。

3. "Increasingly, they want to connect their global sourcing and inbound logistics operations with their domestic warehouse and distribution. As a global 3PL, we can bridge those two ends of the supply chain. "

逐渐地,他们想要把自己的全球采购和进货物流业务与国内的仓储和分销业务联系起来。作为一个全球第三方物流商,我们能把这两端连接起来。

Topics for Discussion

1. Growth for 3PLs in emerging markets such as China and India should be between 20 to 30 percent over the next few years . So what's the most important role for 3PL?

2. From a 3PL perspective, there are opportunities in every marketplace. So could you tell us some examples of it?

3. What will the customers in the high-tech sector use UPS SCS for?

Passage B

Global Trade Drives 3PL Provider's Expansion (II)

1. Picking Winners

Armstrong believes the global winners among U. S.-based 3PLs will be those companies that have both strong financial backing and the capability to broaden services. He says UPS SCS is one such 3PL doing all the right things.

"UPS SCS did over $2bn in sales in 2003, and half of that revenue was earned outside the U. S. ," says Armstrong. "They are cross-selling the UPS express services and the UPS SCS 3PL services to move each other forward. This year, they will probably have a couple billion dollars in free cash flow to build their businesses even further. "

Rhoney confirms that more than half of the 3PL's revenue is derived from activity outside the U. S. borders by performing more than 60 services, including international trade management, order and inventory management, distribution, supply-chain design and management, transportation network management, and service parts logistics. The company is also growing its global business through acquisition and through partnerships with other service providers.

"We are increasingly the general contractor utilizing our own assets and those of local providers," says Rhoney. "This approach gives the customer more flexibility. Local and regional players still have a role to play because of their niche services or local network but we generally are engaged to play a broader role than just a local market. "

Another 3PL that Armstrong sees making strides in the global arena is Penske Logistics, the subsidiary of Penske Truck Leasing, which is a joint venture of General Electric and Penske Corporation.

Vince Hartnett, president of Penske Logistics says that his company will derive about 25 percent of 2004 revenue outside the United States. European operations are the most important international market segment for them, followed closely by Mexico and the rest of Latin America. The Asian business is just developing. "

We see a convergence of services, not just specific functions such as warehousing or transportation management," says Hartnett. "Customers have complex supply chains, and they want a 3PL that can provide integrated solutions."

With customers such as Ford, Detroit Diesel, Whirlpool and many others, the company is finding that automotive and industrial manufacturers are among the most promising targets for their global efforts.

"We have a lot of experience supporting their complex supply-chain activities, such as managing inbound flows of components and materials," says Hartnett, who says that this customer base increasingly is looking far outside of the U.S. for sourcing and manufacturing. "This surge in demand for global sourcing services has happened just in the last 24 months," he says.

Becoming a global 3PL requires companies to acquire new capabilities and to provide new services. For example, Hartnett points out that nearly all of their customers' supply chains used to be limited to specific regions, such as North America, the European Union or the Mercosur countries of Argentina, Brazil and Chile. Cross-border procedures in each of these regions are well established and relatively trouble-free.

"Now we are seeing companies extend their sourcing base outside of these regions, especially to Asia, where cross-border movements are more difficult," says Hartnett, who adds that the company is expanding its capabilities to meet these needs in two ways. First, Penske Logistics is developing additional skills and expertise internally to provide what its customers need for inter-regional operations in areas such as customs and duties. "We also excel at providing lead logistics management of other best-in-class service providers to handle tasks beyond our core competencies."

For example, in Brazil, Penske has a joint venture with Cotia Trading, which has been in the international trade financing business in that region for 25 years. The Cotia Penske operation in Brazil has customers such as Ford and French retailer Carrefour.

"We tap into the expertise of partners where it provides the exact services our customers need," says Hartnett. "This lead logistics approach also allows us to grow more rapidly in the global sphere."

2. More Acquisitions

Armstrong also expects to see more U.S. 3PLs growing their global businesses by making strategic acquisitions, especially in Europe where there is an abundance of mid-sized, private 3PLs with solid market niches.

"These companies are more affordable than the very large global companies, and often do better financially," says Armstrong. "These acquisitions allow U.S.-based 3PLs to gain new skill sets and to expand geographic coverage very quickly."

250

One U. S. -based 3PL that has developed through acquisitions is C. H. Robinson Worldwide. It has made its mark in global logistics through acquisitions such as its purchases of international freight forwarder C. S. Greene in 1992, European motor carrier Transeco in 1993, South American 3PL Comexter Group in 1998 and French 3PL Norminter in 1999.

According to C. H. Robinson's Mulvehill, global logistics revenue from outside the U. S. borders is now about 14 percent of the company's total logistics top line.

"This international business is growing faster than the domestic portion, but from a much lower base," [1] says Mulvehill.

While he agrees that acquisitions such as Norminter have been important, he points out that the company is also growing simply by offering more services to more points around the world. The company already has 12 offices in Western Europe and two in Eastern Europe that provide truckload service and pan-European distribution capability.

"Our core competency is over-the-road truckload service," says Mulvehill, "but we are also expanding ocean and group age services worldwide. One of the cornerstones of our growth strategy that has communicated to our investors is that we are aggressively expanding our global network."

Economies in Latin America have been volatile for the last three years, so Mulvehill says that the 3PL business there has been flat. C. H. Robinson provides trucking in the Mercosur countries, but the largest part of their Latin American business is still import and export air and ocean freight forwarding.

"Brazil is probably our strongest Latin American market, but this business is still not growing at the high rates we are enjoying in Europe and Asia," says Mulvehill.

In growing the global 3PL business, Mulvehill says, the company has learned how to operate differently from how it does in the fast-paced U. S. market.

"Operations tend to be more manual," he says, "and the infrastructure is not as well developed as in the U. S. and Western Europe. We have learned patience, and we have learned that customer relationships are often more important than the written contracts."

Armstrong predicts that only a handful of U. S. 3PLs will actually become truly global and compete head-on with the major foreign 3PLs such as Exel, DHL and Kuehne & Nagel.

"Within five years, there will be as few as five or six 3PLs that will offer true global reach, manage shipments of all sizes and provide a complete spectrum of supply-chain management services," [2] says Armstrong. "It is hard to predict how many of these will be U. S. -based companies, but the competition will be fierce."

New Words and Expressions

1. backing['bækiŋ]n. 支持，后援
2. inventory['invəntri]n. 详细目录，存货，财产清册，总量
3. niche [nitʃ]n. 适当的位置；称心的职务
4. stride [straid]n. 大步；阔步
5. arena [ə'ri:nə]n. 竞技场，舞台
6. subsidiary [səb'sidjəri]adj. 辅助的；附属的；次要的
7. convergence [kən'və:dʒəns]n. 集中，收敛
8. expertise [,ekspə'ti:z]n. 专门技能；专门知识
9. retailer[ri:'teilə]n. 零售商
10. acquisition [,ækwi'ziʃən] n. 收购
11. affordable[ə'fɔ:dəbl]adj. 担负得起费用（损失、后果等）的，
    花费得起的，经受得住；
12. pan[pæn]n. 摇镜头，拍全景
13. volatile['vɔlətail]adj. 易变的，短暂的；非永久性的
14. manual['mænjuəl]adj. 手的，手动的，手工的，体力的
15. infrastructure['infrə'strʌktʃə]n. 基础；基础结构[设施]
16. head-on   adj. , adv. 迎面的(地)，直接的(地)
17. spectrum['spektrəm]n. 范围，系列

Notes

1. "This international business is growing faster than the domestic portion, but from a much lower base,"
但从更低基准上说，国际间的商业活动比国内的部分发展要快。

2. "Within five years, there will be as few as five or six 3PLs that will offer true global reach, manage shipments of all sizes and provide a complete spectrum of supply-chain management services,"
"在五年内，将真正会有五到六个能提供全球性的第三方物流组织，它们管理所有货物的尺寸并提供一个供应链服务管理的全部范围。"

Topics for Discussion

1. Armstrong believes the global winners among U. S.-based 3PLs will be thosecompanies that have both strong financial backing and the capability to broaden services. After reading this, please talk about your opinion.

2. So with the growing of global businesses, what does the "more acquisitions" mean in part two?

3. In growing the global 3PL business, what has the company learned to operate in the fast-paced U. S. market?

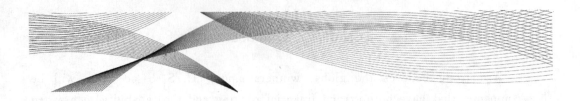

Unit 21

Passage A

Green Logistics

1. Introduction: The Issue of Green Logistics

The two words that make up the title of this chapter are each charged with meaning, but combined; they form a phrase that is particularly evocative. Logistics' are at the heart of modern transport systems. As has been demonstrated earlier, the term implies a degree organization and control over freight movements that only modern technology could have brought into being [1]. It has become one of the most important developments in the transportation industry. Greenness' has become a code-word for a range of environmental concerns, and is usually considered positively. It is employed to suggest compatibility with the environment, and thus, like 'logistics' is something that is beneficial. When put together the two words suggest an environmentally-friendly and efficient transport and distribution system. The term has wide appeal, and is seen by many as eminently desirable. However, as we explore the concept and its applications in greater detail, a great many paradoxes and inconsistencies arise, which suggest that its application may be more difficult than what might have been expected on first encounter.

In this chapter we begin by considering how the term has been developed and applied in the transportation industry. Although there has been much debate about green logistics over the last ten years or so, the transportation industry has developed very narrow and specific interests. When the broader interpretations are attempted it will be shown that there are basic inconsistencies between the goals and objectives of

254

'logistics' and 'greenness'. We conclude this chapter by exploring how these paradoxes might be resolved.

2. Development and Application of Green Logistics

In common with many other areas of human endeavor, greenness' became a catchword in the transportation industry in the late 1980s and early 1990s. It grew out of the growing awareness of environmental problems, and in particular with well-publicized issues such as acid rain, CFCs and global warming. The World Commission on Environment and Development Report (1987), with its establishment of environmental sustainability as a goal for international action, gave green issues a significant boost in political and economic arenas. The transportation industry is a major contributor to environmental degradation through its modes, infrastructures and traffics. The developing field of logistics was seen by many as an opportunity for the transportation industry to present a more environmentally-friendly face. During the early 1990s there was an outpouring of studies, reports and opinion pieces suggesting how the environment could be incorporated in the logistics industry. It was reported that the 1990s would bethe decade of the environment'.

As we look back on the decade we can observe that interest in the environment by the logistics industry manifested itself most clearly in terms of exploiting new market opportunities. While traditional logistics seeks to organize forward distribution, that is the transport, warehousing, packaging and inventory management from the producer to the consumer, environmental considerations opened up markets for recycling and disposal, and led to an entire new sub-sector: reverse logistics. This reverse distribution involves the transport of waste and the movement of used materials. While the term 'reverse logistics' is widely used, other names have been applied, such as 'reverse distribution', 'reverse-flow logistics', and 'green logistics'.

Inserting logistics into recycling and the disposal of waste materials of all kinds, including toxic and hazardous goods, has become a major new market. There are several variants. An important segment is customer-driven, where domestic waste is set aside by home-dwellers for recycling. This has achieved wide popularity in many communities, notably because the public became involved in the process [2]. A second type is where non-recyclable waste, including hazardous materials, is transported for disposal to designated sites. As land fills close to urban areas become scarce, waste has to be transported greater distances to disposal centre. A different approach is where reverse distribution is a continuous embedded process in which the organization (manufacturer or distributor) takes responsibility for the delivery of new products as well as their take-back. This would mean environmental considerations through the whole life-cycle of a product (production, distribution, consumption and disposal). For example, BMW is designing a vehicle whose parts will be entirely recyclable.

How the logistics industry has responded to the environmental imperatives is not unexpected, given its commercial and economic imperatives, but by virtually overlooking significant issues, such as pollution, congestion, resource depletion, means that the logistics industry is still not very "green". This conclusion is borne out by published surveys. Murphy et al (1994) asked members of the Council for Logistics Management what were the most important environmental issues relating to logistics operations. The two leading issues selected were hazardous waste disposal and solid waste disposal. Two thirds of respondents identified these as being of "great" or "maximum" importance. The least important issues identified were congestion and land use, two elements usually considered of central importance by environmentalists. When asked to identify the future impact of environmental issues on logistical functions, again waste disposal and packaging were chosen as leading factors. Customer services, inventory control, production scheduling-logistical elements-were seen to have negligible environmental implications.

By the end of the 1990s much of the hyperbole and interest in the environment by the logistics industry had been spent. A count of the number of articles with an environmental orientation in three journals between 1997 and 1998 revealed that they represented an insignificant proportion of all articles. Most of the articles that were identified as having an environmental content dealt with hazardous waste transport issues.

At the beginning of the 21st Century the logistics industry in general is still a long way from being considered green. Reverse logistics has been its major environmental pre-occupation. While this is an important step, recycling being one of the important elements in sustainability, many other environmentally significant considerations remain largely unaddressed. Are the achievements of transport logistics compatible with the environment?

New Words and Expressions

1. evocative [i'vɔkətiv]*adj*. 唤[引]起……的（of）
2. compatibility [kəmˌpæti'biliti]*n*. 适合，适应（性）

3. environmentally-friendly　对环境无害的,环保的

4. paradox['pærədɔks]n. 似乎矛盾的论点,似非而可能是的论点,诡辩

5. orientation [ˌɔ(:) rien'teiʃən]n. 向东

6. identify [ai'dentifai]vt. 使等同于;认为一致(with)

7. publicize['pʌblisaiz] vt. 宣传;公布;广告

8. disposal [dis'pəuzəl]n. 布置,安排;陈列

9. distribution [ˌdistri'bjuːʃən] n. 分配,分发;配给;配给物;分配装置;
配给方法

10. sub-sector　子行业

11. congestion [kən'dʒestʃən]n.(交通的)拥挤;(货物的)充斥;(人口)稠密

12. commercial [kə'məːʃəl]adj. 商业的

13. designate['dezigneit]vt. 标出;表明;指定

Notes

1. The two words that make up the title of this chapter are each charged with meaning, but combined; they form a phrase that is particularly evocative. "Logistics" are at the heart of modern transport systems. As has been demonstrated earlier, the term implies a degree organization and control over freight movements that only modern technology could have brought into being.

组成这章标题的两个词单独各有其意思,但合并在一起,它们组成了这样一个特别的词。"物流"是现代交通运输的核心。在早期,这个词意味着现代技术在货物运输上达到的组织和控制程度。

2. Inserting logistics into recycling and the disposal of waste materials of all kinds, including toxic and hazardous goods, has become a major new market. There are several variants. An important segment is customer-driven, where domestic waste is set aside by home-dwellers for recycling. This has achieved wide popularity in many communities, notably because the public became involved in the process.

物流中废料回收和废物(包括有毒品和危险品)处理领域是一个主要新兴的市场,其形式有多种。其中一个重要的部分是鼓励顾客将家庭废料进行回收处理。这一方案现已在许多社区取得了广泛的支持,主要是因为公众自己参与到过程里。

Topics for Discussion

1. What's the important issue for green logistics?

2. As we explore the green logistics in greater detail, why it suggest that its application may be more difficult than what might have been expected on first encounter?

3. How many different types for Inserting logistics into recycling and the disposal of waste materials of all kinds? Could you list some typical ones?

4. In the future, are the achievements of transport logistics compatible with the environment?

Passage B

The Green Paradoxes of Logistics in Transport Systems

If the basic characteristics of logistical systems are analyzed, several inconsistencies with regards to environmental compatibility become evident. Four basic paradoxes are discussed below.

1 . Costs

The purpose of logistics is to reduce costs, notably transport costs. In addition, economies of time and improvements in service reliability, including flexibility, are further objectives [1]. Corporations involved in the physical distribution of freight are highly supportive of strategies that enable them to cut transport costs in the present competitive environment. The cost-saving strategies pursued by logistic operators are often at variance with environmental considerations, however. Environmental costs are often externalized. This means that the benefits of logistics are realized by the users (and eventually to the consumer if the benefits are shared along the supply chain), but the environment assumes a wide variety of burdens and costs. Society in general, and many individuals in particular, are becoming less willing to accept these costs, and pressure is increasingly being put on governments and corporations to include greater environmental considerations in their activities.

Although there is a clear trend for governments, at least in their policy guidelines, to make the users pay the full costs of using the infrastructures, logistical activities have largely escaped these initiatives. The focus of much environmental policy is on private cars (emission controls, gas mixtures and pricing). While there are increasingly strict regulations being applied to air transport (noise and emissions), the degree of control over trucking, rail and maritime modes is less. For example diesel fuel is significantly cheaper than gasoline in many jurisdictions, despite the negative environmental implications of the diesel engine. Yet trucks contribute on average 7 times more per vehicle-km to nitrogen oxides emissions than cars and 17 times more for particulate matter. The trucking industry is likely to avoid the bulk of environmental externalities it creates, notably in North America.

The external costs of transport have been the subject of extensive research. Early gross estimates suggested congestion costs to account on average for 8.5% of the GDP and from 2.0% to 2.5% for safety. Recent estimates in Europe suggest that annual costs amount to a figure between 32 and 56 billion ECU. Cooper et al (1998) estimate the costs in Britain at 7 billion ECU, or twice the amount collected by vehicle taxation.

The hub-and-spoke structure has characterized the reorganization of transportation networks for the past 20 years, notably for air and rail and maritime freight transportation. It has reduced costs and improved efficiently through the consolidation of freight and passengers at hubs. Despite the cost savings in many cases, the flows, modes and terminals that are used by pursuing logistical integration are the least sustainable and environmentally friendly. The hub-and-spoke structure concentrates traffic at a relatively small number of terminals. This concentration exacerbates local environmental problems, such as noise, air pollution and traffic congestion.

In addition, the hub structures of logistical systems result in a land take that is exceptional. Airports, seaports and rail terminals are among the largest consumers of land in urban areas. For many airports and seaports the costs of development are so large that they require subsidies from local, regional and national governments. The dredging of channels in ports, the provision of sites, and operating expenses are rarely completely reflected in user costs. In the United States, for example local dredging costs were nominally to come out of a harbor improvement tax but this has been ruled unconstitutional and channel maintenance remains under the authority of the US Corps of Army Engineers. In Europe, national and regional government subsidies are used to assist infrastructure and superstructure provision. The trend in logistics towards hub formation is clearly not green.

The actors involved in logistical operations have a strong bias to perceive green logistics as a mean to internalize cost savings, while avoiding the issue of external costs. As underlined earlier, a survey among the managers of logistical activities pointed out that the top environmental priority is reducing packaging and waste. Managers were also strongly against any type of governmental regulation pertaining to the environmental impacts of logistics. These observations support the paradoxical relationship between logistics and the environment that reducing costs does not necessarily reduce environmental impacts.

2. Time / Speed

In logistics, time is often the essence. By reducing the time of flows, the speed of the distribution system is increased, and consequently, its efficiency. This is achieved in the main by using the most polluting and least energy efficient transportation modes. The significant increase of air freight and trucking is partially the result of time constraints imposed by logistical activities. The time constraints are themselves the result of an increasing flexibility of industrial production systems and of the retailing sector. Logistics offers door-to-door (DTD) services, mostly coupled with just-in-time (JIT) strategies. Other modes cannot satisfy the requirements such a situation creates as effectively. This leads to a vicious circle. The more physical distribution through logistics is efficient, the less production, distribution and retailing activities are constrained by distance. In turn, this structure involves a higher usage of logistics and more ton-km of freight transported. There is overwhelming evidence for an increase in truck traffic and a growth in the average length of haul, and although McKinnon (1998) has suggested that JIT is not greatly increasing road freight volumes (italics added), it cannot be considered a green solution. The more DTD and JIT strategies are applied, the further the negative environmental consequences of the traffic it creates.

3. Reliability

At the heart of logistics is the overriding importance of service reliability. Its success is based upon the ability to deliver freight on time with the least threat of breakage or damage. Logistics providers often realize these objectives by utilizing the modes that are perceived as being most reliable. The least polluting modes are generally regarded as being the least reliable in terms of on-time delivery, lack of breakage and safety. Ships and railways have inherited a reputation for poor customer satisfaction, and the logistics industry is built around air and truck shipments... the two least environmentally-friendly modes.

4. Warehousing

Logistics is an important factor promoting globalization and international flows of commerce. Modern logistics systems economies are based on the reduction of inventories, as the speed and reliability of deliveries removes the need to store and stockpile [2]. Consequently, a reduction in warehousing demands is one of the advantages of logistics. This means however, that inventories have been transferred to a certain degree the transport system, especially the roads. This has been confirmed empirically. In a survey of 87 large British firms cited by McKinnon (1998), there had been a 39 per cent reduction in the number of warehouses and one third of the firms indicated an increased amount of truck traffic, although the increase was thought to be small in most cases. Inventories are actually in transit, contributing still further to congestion and pollution. The environment and society, not the logistical operators, are assuming the external costs.

Not all sectors exhibit this trend, however. In some industrial sectors, computers for example, there is a growing trend for vertical disintegration of the manufacturing process, in which extra links are added to the logistical chain. Intermediate plants where some assembly is undertaken have been added between the manufacturer and consumer. While facilitating the customizing of the product for the consumer, it adds an additional external movement of products in the production line.

5. E-commerce

The explosion of the information highway has led to new dimensions in retailing. One of the most dynamic markets is as e-commerce. This is made possible by an integrated supply chain with data interchange between suppliers, assembly lines and freight forwarders. Even if for the online customers there is an appearance of a movement-free transaction, the distribution online transactions create may consume more energy than other retail activities. The distribution activities that have benefited the most from e-commerce are parcel-shipping companies such as UPS and Federal Express that rely solely on trucking and air transportation. Information technologies related to e-commerce applied to logistics can obviously have positive impacts. For instance, the National Transportation Exchange (NTE) is an example where freight distribution resources can be pooled and where users can bid through a Web Site for using capacities that would have otherwise been empty return travel. So once again, the situation may be seen as paradoxical.

The consequences of e-commerce on Green Logistics are little understood, but some trends can be identified. As e-commerce becomes more accepted and used, it is changing physical distribution systems. The standard retailing supply chain coupled with the process of economies of scale (larger stores; shopping malls) is being challenged by a new structure. The new system relies on large warehouses located outside metropolitan areas from where large numbers of small parcels are shipped by vans and trucks to separate online buyers [3]. This disaggregates retailing distribution, and reverses the trend towards consolidation that had characterized retailing earlier. In the traditional system, the shopper was bearing the costs of moving the goods from the store to home, but with e-commerce this segment of the supply chain has to be integrated in the freight distribution process. The result potentially involves more packaging and more tons-km of freight transported, especially in urban areas. Traditional distribution systems are

262

thus ill fitted to answer the logistical needs of ecommerce. The dimension, outcome and paradox of green logistics are shown in Table 21.1.

Table 21.1　Paradoxes of Green Logistics

Dimension	Outcome	Paradox
Costs	Reduction of costs through improvement in packaging and reduction of wastes. Benefits are derived by the distributors.	Environmental costs are often externalized.
Time Flexibility	Integrated supply chains. JIT and DTD provide flexible and efficient physical distribution systems.	Extended production, distribution and retailing structures consuming more space, more energy and producing more emissions (CO_2, particulates, NOx, etc.).
Network	Increasing system-wide efficiency of the distribution system through network changes (Hub-and-spoke structure).	Concentration of environmental impacts next to major hubs and along corridors. Pressure on local communities.
Reliability	Reliable and on-time distribution of freight and passengers.	Modes used, trucking and air transportation, are the least environmentally efficient.
Warehousing	Reducing the needs for private warehousing facilities.	Inventory shifted in part to public roads (or in containers), contributing to congestion and space consumption.
E-commerce	Increased business opportunities and diversification of the supply chains.	Changes in physical distribution systems towards higher levels of energy consumption.

How green are logistics when the consequences of its application, even if efficient and cost effective, have led to solutions that may not be environmentally appropriate?

New Words and Expressions

1. retailing [ˈriːteiliŋ] n. 零售业
2. compatibility [kəmˌpætiˈbiliti] n. 适合，适应(性)
3. reliability [riˌlaiəˈbiliti] n. 可靠性，安全性；可信赖性；确实(性)；强度
4. externalize [eksˈtəːnəˌlaiz] vt. 给……以外形；使客观化，使形象化，使具体化
5. infrastructure [ˈinfrəˈstrʌktʃə] n. 基础；基础结构[设施](尤指社会、国家赖以生存和发展的)
6. maritime [ˈmæritaim] adj. 海上的；海运的；沿海的；生在沿海地带的
7. congestion [kənˈdʒestʃən] n. (交通的)拥挤；(货物的)充斥；(人口)稠密
8. sustainable [səˈsteinəbl] adj. 可以忍受的，足可支撑的，养得起的
9. concentrate [ˈkɔnsentreit] vt. 集中；使……集中于一点

10. terminal['tə:minl] *n.* 终端，终点；极限

11. dredging['dredʒiŋ] *n.* 挖泥作业；清淤；疏浚（工程）；拖锚（走）

12. unconstitutional['ʌnkɔnsti'tju:ʃənəl] *adj.* 违反宪法的

13. maintenance['meintinəns] *n.* 维持；保持

14. internalize [in'tə:nə,laiz] *vt.* 使变成内部的

15. constraint [kən'streint] *n.* 约束，压抑，拘束

Notes

1. The purpose of logistics is to reduce costs, notably transport costs. In addition, economies of time and improvements in service reliability, including flexibility, are further objectives.

物流的目的是为了降低成本，尤其是运输成本。此外，对于时间经济性、服务可靠性以及灵活性的提升都是更长远的目标。

2. Logistics is an important factor promoting globalization and international flows of commerce. Modern logistics systems economies are based on the reduction of inventories, as the speed and reliability of deliveries removes the need to store and stockpile.

物流是促进国际化全球化商流的重要因素。随着迅捷、可靠的配送业务取代了存储和堆放，现代物流体系经济便基于减少库存。

3. The standard retailing supply chain coupled with the process of economies of scale (larger stores; shopping malls) is being challenged by a new structure. The new system relies on large warehouses located outside metropolitan areas from where large numbers of small parcels are shipped by vans and trucks to separate online buyers.

标准供应链以及经济规模扩大的过程（更大的商店、大型购物中心）正在被一种新的结构所挑战。这种新的体系基于建设在大都市的大型仓库，在那里，货车或者卡车将运送大量的托盘给在线购买者。

Topics for Discussion

1. What are the basic paradoxes of logistics in transport systems?

2. How to understand the consequences of e-commerce on Green Logistics?

3. How to solve the inconsistencies with the regards to the environmental compatibility at present?

4. What's the development process for E-commerce, and could you tell the typical events that happened in different phase?

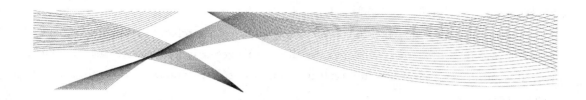

Unit 22

Passage A

Reverse Logistics

1. What is Reverse Logistics

Logistics is defined by The Council of Logistics Management as:

The process of planning, implementing, and controlling the efficient, cost effective flow of raw materials, in-process inventory, finished goods and related information from the point of origin to the point of consumption for the purpose of conforming to customer requirements.

Reverse logistics includes all of the activities that are mentioned in the definition above. The difference is that reverse logistics encompasses all of these activities as they operate in reverse. Therefore, reverse logistics is:

The process of planning, implementing, and controlling the efficient, cost effective flow of raw materials, in-process inventory, finished goods and related information from the point of consumption to the point of origin for the purpose of recapturing value or proper disposal.

More precisely, reverse logistics is the process of moving goods from their typical final destination for the purpose of capturing value, or proper disposal.

Remanufacturing and refurbishing activities also may be included in the definition of reverse logistics. Reverse logistics is more than reusing containers and recycling packaging materials. Redesigning packaging to use less material, or reducing the energy and pollution from transportation are important activities, but they might be better placed in the realm of "green" logistics. If no goods or materials are being sent "backward," the activity probably is not a reverse logistics activity.

Reverse logistics also includes processing returned merchandise due to damage, seasonal inventory, restock, salvage, recalls, and excess inventory. It also includes recycling programs, hazardous material programs, obsolete equipment disposition, and asset recovery.

2. Respondent Base

Companies included in this research are manufacturers, wholesalers, retailers, and service firms. In some cases, a firm may occupy more than one supply chain position. For example, many of the manufacturers are also retailers and wholesalers. The supply chain position of the research respondents is depicted in table 22.1.

Table 22.1 Supply Chain Position

Supply Chain Position	Percentage of Respondents
Manufacturer	64.0%
Wholesaler	29.9%
Retailer	28.9%
Service Provider	9.0%

Most of the firms included in the research are very large companies. Nearly half of the firms have annual sales of $1 billion or larger.

3. Interest in Reverse Logistics

Awareness of the art and science of logistics continues to increase. Additionally, great interest in reverse logistics has been piqued. Many companies that previously did not devote much time or energy to the management and understanding of reverse logistics have begun to pay attention [1]. These firms are benchmarking return operations with best-in-class operators. Some firms are even becoming ISO certified on their return processes. Third parties specializing in returns have seen a great increase in the demand for their services.

In addition to this research project, several other academic endeavors focusing on the reverse flow of product are in process. Leading-edge companies are recognizing the strategic value of having a reverse logistics management system in place to keep goods on the retail shelf and in the warehouse fresh and in demand.

4. Size of Reverse Logistics

A conservative estimate is that reverse logistics accounts for a significant portion of U. S. logistics costs. Logistics costs are estimated to account for approximately 10. 7 percent of the U. S. economy. However, the exact amount of reverse logistics activity is difficult to determine because most companies do not know how large these are. Of the firms included in this research, reverse logistics costs accounted for approximately four percent of their total logistics costs. Applying this mean percentage to Gross Domestic Product (GDP), reverse logistics costs are estimated to be approximately a half percent of the total U. S. GDP. Delaney estimates that logistics costs accounted for $862 billion in 1997. The estimate of this research, based on the respondent sample, is that reverse logistics costs amounted to approximately $35 billion in 1997. The magnitude and impact of reverse logistics varies by industry and channel position. It also varies depending on the firm's channel choice. However, it is clear that the overall amount of reverse logistics activities in the economy is large and still growing.

Within specific industries, reverse logistics activities can be critical for the firm. Generally, in firms where the value of the product is largest, or where the return rate is greatest, much more effort has been spent in improving return processes [2]. The auto parts industry is a good example. The remanufactured auto parts market is estimated (by the Auto Parts Remanufacturers Association) to be $36 billion. For example, 90 to 95 percent of all starters and alternators sold for replacement are remanufactured. By one conservative estimate, there are currently 12,000 automobile dismantlers and remanufacturers operating in the United States.

Rebuilding and remanufacturing conserves a considerable amount of resources. According to the ARPA, about 50 percent of the original starter is recovered in the rebuilding process. This may result in saving several million gallons of crude oil, steel, and other metals. ARPA estimates that raw materials saved by remanufacturing worldwide would fill 155,000 railroad cars annually. That many rail cars would make a train over 1,100 miles long.

5. Return Percentages

The reverse logistics process can be broken into two general areas, depending on whether the reverse flow consists primarily of products, or primarily of packaging. For product returns, a high percentage is represented by customer returns. Overall customer returns are estimated to be approximately six percent across all retailers.

Return percentages for selected industries are shown in Table 22.2. In each case, return percentages were established by several different firms.

Clearly, return rates vary significantly by industry. For many industries, learning to manage the reverse flow is of prime importance.

Table 22.2　Sample Return Percentages

Industry	Percent
Magazine Publishing	50%
Book Publishers	20%-30%
Book Distributors	10%-20%
Greeting Cards	20%-30%
Catalog Retailers	18%-35%
Electronic Distributors	10%-12%
Computer Manufacturers	10%-20%
CD-ROMs 18%-25% Printers	4%-8%
Mail Order Computer Manufacturers	2%-5%
Mass Merchandisers	4%-15%
Auto Industry (Parts)	4%-6%
Consumer Electronics	4%-5%
Household Chemicals	2%-3%

New Words and Expressions

1. encompasses [in'kʌmpəs]vt. 围绕，围住，包围

2. in-process　进程内

3. merchandise['məːtʃəndaiz]n. [集合词]商品，货物

4. manufacturer [ˌmænju'fæktʃərə]n. 制造商，厂主；制造厂

5. benchmark['bentʃˌmɑːk]n. 水平点；基准

6. best-in-class　同级别最佳，同类产品中最佳

7. leading-edge　居领先优势的

8. respondent[ris'pɔndənt]adj. 回答的；有反应的；响[感]应的

9. household['haushəuld]n. [集合词]家属，家眷；家庭，一户

10. retail['riːteil]n. 零售

11. replacement[ri'pleismənt]n. 代替，替换

12. gallon['gælən]n. 加仑(美加仑＝3.7853 公升；英加仑＝4.546 公升)

13. reverse[ri'vəːs]vt. 颠倒；反转；翻转[案]

268

14. distributor [dis'tribjutə]*n.* 分发[配，布]者，散布者

Notes

1. Awareness of the art and science of logistics continues to increase. Additionally, great interest in reverse logistics has been piqued. Many companies that previously did not devote much time or energy to the management and understanding of reverse logistics have begun to pay attention.

人们对物流的科学性和艺术性的意识在逐渐增加。此外，对于回收物流的极大兴趣已经受到激励，许多曾经未对管理和回收物流投入时间精力的企业现在也开始进行关注。

2. Within specific industries, reverse logistics activities can be critical for the firm. Generally, in firms where the value of the product is largest, or where the return rate is greatest, much more effort has been spent in improving return processes.

在特殊的工业中，回收物流已成为公司的关键性活动。通常来说，企业会对价值最大或者回报率最大的产品改进更多。

Topics for Discussion

1. From part one, what kind of processing does reverse logistics include?

2. In the table, how to depict the supply chain position by the research respondents?

3. What is the difference in the return percentages established by several different firms? What extra information can you get from it?

4. What's the size and importance of reverse logistics? Could you combine the text content and your own understanding to describe it?

Passage B

Reverse Logistics in theUrban Environment

In the literature available on logistics in an urban environment, or "City Logistics", to which it is often referred, little mention is made of reverse logistics. City logistics implies that goods transport to the inner city is consolidated in a distribution terminal outside the city and thereafter distributed by one logistics provider to urban areas.

Environmental impacts of logistical activities are most severe when population densities are highest; i. e. in cities. Urban freight transport deals largely with the distribution of goods at the end of the supply chain, so deliveries are likely to be frequent, but limited to carrying small loads. Possibilities for the extension of the traffic infrastructure within cities are limited and unsustainable [1].

Taniguchi et al. (2003) proposed three basic pillars as the guiding principles for green city logistics: mobility, sustainability and live ability. These pillars ought to support and enhance the goals and objectives of logistics, such as efficiency, congestion alleviation and energy conservation. The harmonization of efficiency, environmental friendliness and energy conservation is vital for ensuring sustainable development of freight transport in urban areas. Thus, the goal of city logistics should be to deliver and collect the goods for activities produced in a city in an efficient way, without disrupting the sustainable, mobile, livable and environmental friendly character of the city.

The environmental impact of the transportation requirement of logistics can be alleviated somewhat by consolidating freight and balancing "back-haul" movements. Making use of spare capacity on the return leg of a delivery journey makes more efficient use of valuable resources such as fuel and driver time by finding loads that need to be shipped between similar areas as those visited by the returning vehicle. Higher load balance helps reduce the number of empty trucks on the road, alleviate traffic congestion and cut down pollutant emissions.

Four basic physical network types for retail organizations to handle returns were identified by the authors of *The Efficiency of Reverse Logistics* study. Different elements of each of these basic forms might be utilized by retailers to obtain a full solution to their returns management issues:

Type A : *Integrated outbound and returns network*

270

Utilizing backhauling, companies own fleet takes returns from retail outlets to the Regional Distribution Centre (RDC). The sortation and potential refurbishment processes are carried out at the RDC. This works well if the frequency of delivery to stores is high, and volume of returns is also high.

Type B : *Non-integrated outbound and returns network*

A separate network is used for managing returns, typically a third party logistics supplier (3PL) taking returns (on an "as and when" required basis) from stores to a separate location where the reverse logistics activities are undertaken by the retail organisation. This works well if the level of returns varies in volume but is generally low.

Type C : *Third party returns management*

Total management of returns is outsourced to a third party contractor. The retailer benefits in that no expertise is required to be developed in-house-the 3PL provides the necessary returns management processes, with supporting technologies and refurbishment and disposition programs.

Type D : *Return to suppliers*

Goods returned to the suppliers are exchanged for credit. Retailers have little responsibility for returns in this scenario. However, there may be additional costs in terms of vehicle kilometers, as the goods have to return to the supplier before disposition.

Geroliminis et al. (2005) present several examples of sustainable city logistics and green logistics schemes that have been used in various cities around the world. Of the 17 examples cited, five have particular relevance to this review:

• **Copenhagen** —City Goods Ordinance for capacity management

In early 2002, Copenhagen implemented a compulsory certification scheme (City Goods Ordinance) in the medieval city centre with requirements of capacity utilization and engine technology. The aim was to reduce the environmental impact from goods traffic in the city centre and make the narrow medieval streets more accessible by increasing the utilization of vans driving into the heart of the city, thus reducing the number of vehicles.

• **Berlin—Goods Traffic Platforms (Public Private Partnership)**

Within Berlin city limits, 45 million tons of goods are distributed by trucks and smaller delivery van each year, with an expected future increase in these figures. The main objective of this project was to reduce the frequency of deliveries through cooperation between various recipients (e. g. adjacent shops being supplied by the same carrier) and a combination of deliveries to a single recipient. Results indicate that Goods Traffic Platforms are successful tools, as they contribute to the reduction of congestion during loading or unloading of vehicles.

- **Stockholm—logistical centre for coordinated transport**

The logistical centre was set up in 2003; its main objectives were to reduce energy use and CO_2 emissions through coordinated transport to the district residents, municipal institutions such as schools, day-care and elderly-care centers, as well as private companies operating in the district.

The centre is responsible for delivering online purchased goods, dry cleaning services, and food and beverages. Reports indicate that the centre has the potential for becoming an integrated distribution system for locally produced food, coming directly from approximately 300 local farmers.

- **Tokyo—Advanced Information System**

Although parcel delivery companies can efficiently implement full-load transport of large trucks between cities, the delivery and pick-up of cargo within the city is relatively inefficient [2]. To improve the existing situation, a cooperative parcel pick-up system using the internet was tried in Otemachi (Tokyo downtown area) in 2002. Requests were made online, and a logistics service provider collected the bundled demand for each building. The demand on roadside parking was reduced as were the number of kilometers travelled by freight vehicles.

The EC's Urban Freight Transport and Logistics brochure gives an overview of research from the Fourth and Fifth Framework programs, together with policy implications and requirements for future research (EC, 2006).

One outcome of the "Best Urban Freight Solutions" project was a series of recommendations on the following themes:

- Statistical data, data acquisition and analysis regarding urban freight transport
- City access, parking and access time regulations and enforcement support
- E-Commerce and urban freight distribution (home shopping)
- Road pricing and urban freight transport
- Urban freight platforms (single company platforms, freight villages, urban distribution centers)
- Intelligent transport systems
- Public Private Partnerships

Building on the structure and experience gained from this project, BESTUFS II aims to strengthen and extend the promotion and dissemination of "City Logistics

Solutions" in Europe and beyond, e. g. by establishing new links with other networks, groups and other international experts that interface with urban freight transport issues (BESTUFS, 2006). While some aspects of reverse logistics are implicit within the scope of this project, no explicit mention is made of the impact of reverse logistics on city logistics.

The START project (Short-Term Actions to Reorganize Transport of goods) has partners in the cities of Bristol, G teborg, Ljubljana, Ravenna and Riga. The project deals with making goods distribution more energy efficient by combining access restrictions, incentives and the development of consolidation centers. The Exel/DHL transshipment centre trial in Bristol is being continued under this program which has seen a successful reverse logistics system created for the return of recyclables (packaging, cardboard and paper) from retail business in the city centre.

New Words and Expressions

1. density ['densiti] *n.* 稠密；浓厚
2. pillar ['pilə]*n.* 柱（子）；支柱
3. congestion [kən'dʒestʃən]*n.* (交通的）拥挤；（货物的）充斥；（人口）稠密
4. utilize [ju:'tilaiz]*vt.* 利用（亦作：utilise）
5. sortation [sɔː'teiʃən]*n.* 分类
6. accessible [ək'sesəbl]*adj.* 能接近的，容易会见的；可亲的
7. ton [tŋ]*n.* 时髦，时兴，流行
8. coordinate [kəu'ɔːdinit] *n.* 同等者[物]；同位
9. cargo ['kɑːɡəu] *n.* (pl. cargoes, cargos)船(装)货，货物；载运的货物
10. freight [freit]*n.* [英]（船运的）货物；[美]（水上、陆上、空中运输的）货物
11. partnership ['pɑːtnəʃip]*n.* 合伙 [营，股]；伙伴关系；全体合伙[合股]人
12. transhipment [træn'ʃipmənt]*n.* (=transshipment)转运，转船

Notes

1. Environmental impacts of logistical activities are most severe when population densities are highest; i. e. in cities. Urban freight transport deals largely with the distribution of goods at the end of the supply chain, so deliveries are likely to be frequent, but limited to carrying small loads. Possibilities for the extension of the traffic infrastructure within cities are limited and unsustainable.

当人口密度较高时,物流活动的环境影响就是很严重的问题,例如在城市中出现的此类问题。城市货物运输即是大量处理供应链终端物品配送,因而属于交货频率较高但负载量小的物品运输。城市交通基础设施的扩充有所限制而且不持续。

2. Although parcel delivery companies can efficiently implement full-load transport of large trucks between cities, the delivery and pick-up of cargo within the city is relatively inefficient.

尽管包裹运输公司能高效处理城市间的满载运输,但在城市内的货物配送方面效率很低。

Topics for Discussion

1. What's the function of reverse logistics in the urban environment?

2. What are the differences of reverse logistics in each country written above?

3. In which way will the environmental impact of the transportation requirement of logistics be alleviated? Can you give us more things in details?

Unit 23

Passage A

What is a 4PL (I)

You will get no argument that the increasing complexity of logistics management coupled with the explosion of information technology has created fertile ground for a "super manager" of sorts for intricate supply chains. Moreover, academicians, consultants and third-party logistics providers, not to mention customers, say that the need for such an entity is growing all the time. Its job: to supervise all aspects of the supply chain of a manufacturer or distributor and to be the sole point of contact between that company and its array of logistics and information service providers.

What gets the hairs bristling on the necks of the 3PLs and consultants is when you start to narrow down who is more perfectly suited for the super manager's role. And there are sensitivities at work here. For example, using the term "4PL"—for fourth—party logistics provider—instead of the more palatable handles of "logistics integrator" and "lead logistics provider" rankle the 3PLs to no end. That is particularly so when the 4PL concept is presented as a product from, and the holy ground of, the consulting firms. It certainly derives from that community; 4PL was coined and trademarked by Andersen Consulting. On the other hand, consultants take umbrage to the charge that they have attempted to manufacture a market by coining, trade marking, and then relentlessly flogging the future of the 4PL. An old-fashioned turf battle is brewing. And you don't have to scratch too far below the surface to get a reaction, particularly from the 3PLs that have invested in technology, human resources and alliances in order to present a single point of contact for operation of a customer's supply chain. Those leading firms include Menlo Logistics, Ryder System, Federal Express, UPS Logistics,

GATX Logistics, Exel and Schneider Logistics.

But first, here's the deal from the Andersen side of the equation, according to James W. Moore, an associate partner with Andersen Consulting.

"The pace of change has been accelerating, the complexity has been accelerating, and our sensation—and we're not alone in this—is that there's a role emerging for a complexity manager," says Moore. This complexity manager—call it a 4PL or logistics integrator or lead logistics provider or super manager—would be, in Moore's words, an "on-purpose entity with shared risk/reward and would have multi-function management responsibility, including supply-chain planning, some information technology capabilities, the more traditional transportation and distribution disciplines, and a multi-provider management function."

That's what Andersen is doing in the United Kingdom, Moore says, where it is serving as a 4PL for Thames Water. "That's a cooperative venture where we perform their supply-chain operations for them. They are the largest water utility in the U.K."

Expanding into the 4PL role constitutes an interesting shift for Andersen, as the consultancy's general position has been on the front end of a logistics solution: The troops typically go in to a customer location, collect information, and perform due diligence and provide a white paper solution. A logistics firm usually then manages the business.

The leading 3PLs have a different take on the 4PL phenomenon. "The 4PL to me is nothing more than the lead logistics provider, and that name has been around for quite some time," says Rodger Mullen, vice president and general manager of Schneider Logistics [1].

The root of the issue, says Mullen, is that whenever service providers go into a logistics outsourcing project, the customer these days essentially wants one company and one point of contact to do it all. "However, given the way logistics organizations exist today, there isn't really one company that has all the core competencies to do everything that a truly global customer wants to do. In order to get to that total end-to-end solution, the lead logistics provider or 4PL in essence contracts with different providers, assembles those end-to-end solutions, manages them and serves as the single point of contact to the shipper." Schneider has been providing that comprehensive, single-point-of-contact service for GM's Service Parts Division and has several other irons in the fire, Mullen says [2].

"There's a lot of talk about how the concept of the 4PL developed, but one theory is that the consulting firms really wanted to figure out a way to create an ongoing revenue stream to supplement their project work, and therefore they coined the phrase 4PL, which basically meant that they were going to manage the 3PLs on a continuous basis for a client such as a manufacturer or distributing company," offers Todd Carter of GATX. "That's maybe the more cynical theory. The more optimistic theory is that because of the growing criticality of information in managing the supply chain, it was a natural progression. "

Jim Fields, director of business development for Menlo Logistics, sees it this way. "The 4PL terminology has grown out of the consulting industry in what I think was really an attempt to create a market and position the company as the logical party between customer and the 3PLs," says Fields. As that go-between, the 4PL would be in position to manage what many consider is the most important aspect of the operation— the customer relationship.

On the practical front, however, Fields questions the need for an additional player here. "I don't think the 4PL role references anything more than what 3PLs and some of the largest integrators have been doing — being the single point of integration of information flow and operational responsibility for an entire enterprise or a defined portion of that enterprise," he says [3]. Menlo provides re-engineering services, performs systems integration and subcontracts with and manages third-party service providers for a number of customers, he says. "And if the scope of your outsourcing contract is such that you will be acting as the sole conduit or the sole responsible party for the outsourcing of this scope of work and are the sole point of responsibility back to the customer ... well, if you want to call that 4PL or 5PL or systems integrator, the principle is the same, the responsibility is the same, and the operation is the same. "

Bringing another company into the mix as a super manager of sorts raises the cost-versus-value question, says Fields. "This puts another layer of cost into the supply chain, and the challenge is to understand what kind of value is created by having this other group aside from the 3PLs. Does this company bring enough value to justify itself? I don't think it does. "

New Words and Expressions

1. trademark['treidmɑ:k]n. 商标；vt. 贴上商标，登记……商标
2. intricate['intrikit]adj. 复杂的，错综的，难以理解的
3. distributor [dis'tribjutə]n. 销售者，批发商
4. bristle['brisl]vi. (毛发等)竖起，发怒

5. justify['dʒʌstifai]vt. 证明……有道理[应该]，为……辩护

6. palatable['pælətəbl]adj. 愉快的；宜人的；惬意的

7. rankle['ræŋkl]vt. 激怒

8. coin [kɔin]vt. 造字，杜撰新词语；造币；铸币

9. umbrage['ʌmbridʒ]n. 生气

10. relentless[ri'lentlis]adj. 无情的

11. flog [flɔg] vt. 鞭打，鞭策，迫使，驱使，严厉批评

12. turf [təːf]n. 地盘

13. brew [bruː]v. 酿造，酝酿

14. equation [i'kweiʃən]n. 相等，平衡，综合体，因素，方程式，等式

15. venture['ventʃə]n. 冒险，投机，风险

16. ongoing['ɔngəuiŋ] adj. 正在进行的

17. stream [striːm]n. 溪，川，流，一股，一串，河流

18. cynical ['sinikəl]adj. 愤世嫉俗的，冷嘲热讽的；玩世不恭的

19. terminology [ˌtəːmi'nɔlədʒi]n. 术语；专门名词

20. go-between   n. 媒介者，中间人

21. re-engineering['riːendʒi'niəriŋ] n. 重建，改建；再设计

22. subcontract [sʌb'kɔntrækt]n., v. 转订的契约[合同]，转包工程

23. versus['vəːsəs] prep. 对(指诉讼，比赛等中)，与……相对

24. conduit['kɔndit]n. 管道，导管，沟渠，泉水，喷泉   .

Notes

1. The leading 3PLs have a different take on the 4PL phenomenon. "The 4PL to me is nothing more than the lead logistics provider, and that name has been around for quite some time," says Rodger Mullen, vice president and general manager of Schneider Logistics.

主要的第三方物流供应商们对第四方物流现象持有不同的观点。施奈德物流的副总裁兼总经理 Rodger Mullen 这样说道："第四方物流对我而言只不过是个首要的物流供应商，而且这个名字已经见过世面相当长时间了。"

2. Schneider has been providing that comprehensive, single-point-of-contact service for GM's Service Parts Division and has several other irons in the fire, Mullen says. Mullen 讲到，施奈德物流一直致力于为通用汽车的配件部门提供全面的、单一接口的服务，而且我们同时还有其他的活动要完成。

3. "I don't think the 4PL role references anything more than what 3PLs and some

of the largest integrators have been doing — being the single point of integration of information flow and operational responsibility for an entire enterprise or a defined portion of that enterprise," he says.

他说:"第四方物流角色作为一个整个企业或者该企业的某个特定部分的信息流与运作职责的单点集成,我并不认为它涉及比第三方物流供应商和一些最大的集成商们一直以来所做的事情更多的地方。"

Topics for Discussion

1. What does the concept of 4PL come from?
2. What's the difference between 3PL and 4PL from the content?
3. What is the main research part of 4PL from the text?
4. How to see the 4PL correctly?
5. How to deal with 4PL and 3PL correctly and could you give a general idea about their strengths and weakness? Please discuss it with your classmates.

Passage B

What is a 4PL (II)

Prof. John H. Langley, Dove Distinguished Professor of Logistics at the University of Tennessee, understands the friction between the 3PLs and consultants, but he sees a new demand developing in the logistics arena as changes in supply-chain practices cause supply-chain managers to place value on three emerging competencies. One competency is in managing the activities of more than one third-party logistics provider, and there are both operational and strategic elements to this, he says.

A second competency is managing the availability and utilization of knowledge. "The natural reaction of most people is to say, 'I can be responsible for my own knowledge, thank you,' but I think, given how quickly things are changing today, that it's not unreasonable to actually hire an expert to manage the knowledge — to process information, utilize it and make it available — in the same way you might have legal counsel to make you aware of the latest developments of a legal nature that impact your business."

The third competency focuses on information technology. "Things are changing so quickly today in the IT sector that you really have to have not only a capable party but one that has core competency in knowing what systems are available and how to utilize and integrate those systems with other capabilities." [1]

These three competencies clearly exceed what might normally be expected from a 3PL, the professor explains. "That in my mind would justify the business case for a fourth-party provider," says Langley. "The question that comes up is — and it's a valid question from a customer firm or a 3PL — am I suggesting they cannot do these things themselves? I'm not suggesting that, but I'm suggesting that certain competencies are needed. If you are a 3PL and you have them, great, you should be going full speed ahead." He adds that no reason exists why a 3PL could not bring these competencies into its service portfolio by subcontracting.

Andersen clearly hopes to see a fruitful market for consultancies in the 4PL arena - at least for their consultancy — but backs off from confrontational language and talk about a turf war.

"I don't see it as a struggle between the consultants and the 3PLs, and we certainly

280

don't view ourselves as competitors to 3PLs," says Moore. "With a new role like the 4PL, a role that is mostly global, information technology rich, asset-free... I don't think that puts us in conflict with 3PLs. We're consultants."

The key thing that is happening in the supply chain is that time now is often more important than geography, he explains. "The management of time and the associated optimization of the use of time throughout a supply chain is oftentimes a skill set provided by information technology people and consultants, more so than the third-party logistics firms have in past," he points out. "Certainly the 3PLs are catching up, but the primary role we see for the 4PL is the management of complexity and time."

"We all agree in this business that information has become as important and sometimes more important than the actual physical movement of the product," says Todd Carter of GATX. "Information on orders, on inbound material, on shipment accuracy, inventory control ... all of this is highly critical information. And as that information becomes even more critical, the reliance on information itself and the systems to manage it has become increasingly more important, which has really led to this role of a logistics integrator."

Carter acknowledges that a 4PL/logistics integrator could be either a consultant or the lead logistics provider, depending on the customer's most pressing needs. "The role of the lead logistics provider is knitting together for a manufacturer or distributing company the services of various transportation and warehousing companies and third-party service providers," he says. "The first question we have to ask is whether there is potential value in a company acting in the role of a lead logistics provider or 4PL."

If one thinks that the answer to that question is yes, as Carter does, the next consideration is who might be best positioned to be of value to particular manufacturers and distributors. "Certainly 3PLs bring the advantage of operating experience: We've lifted the boxes and kicked the tires, we know how things are supposed to operate and we know what to do if operations break down. But, typically, compared to the consulting firms we may be weak on management talent, organizational talent or process re-engineering. So depending on what you're after from a 4PL, you might look one way or the other."

Clearly the first and foremost mission of a 4PL would be to integrate the information and operations, he says. "Whether the second mission is to provide some management organizational talent or really hit on productivity and quality within the operation probably would drive who would do a better job as a 4PL, the former being a management consultancy, the latter being one of the top 3PLs that is entering the 4PL market."

Menlo's Fields responds to suggestions that the consultancies are better positioned to handle the information flow and to oversee system re-engineering by pointing out that his company and the leading 3PLs have brought new talent into the equation through hiring and via alliances. "We have some of the best consultants in the world ... engineers and Ph. D. s and MBAs ... and these people are just like the people who work for the consulting firms. And consulting firms have engineers who are very competent people," says Fields. "The difference between us and a big consulting company is that whenever we are asked to consult, we generally are asked to operate. And that's a key differentiation. I'm not out there arguing that we should be hired ahead of consulting companies, because we work directly with consulting companies. I will say that we have this added advantage: When we consult for our customers, we also have to operate and manage the solutions, so our solutions have to be very credible."

Schneider also has brought more consulting talent in-house, according to Mullen. "We've really beefed up our engineering staff, so when we get a proposal, we are able to go to the possible customer's site and collect data and information and really come up with what we call our own solution and one that we feel has integrity on the operation front," he says. "And we've grown our engineering staff to be consultative in nature, not only on the front end. As you start managing the business, there are also other opportunities as well."

Langley doesn't foresee a single provider type emerging as the only or even the best kind of provider of 4PL/logistics integrator services. It will be a mix of 3PL-type firms and consulting firms, he says, and he would not rule out the technology sector itself as becoming the provider of 4PL services. "Think about it: When you have the Ernst & Young, the Andersen and the Deletes positioning themselves as potential 4PLs alongside the operating companies like Ryder and Exel, there's no reason why you couldn't have Manugistics or i2 Technologies emerge in a 4PL role," he says. "We also have some of the e-commerce type of companies that are bordering on providing those kinds of services as well. The leadership could come from a number of directions, and probably over the long term, we will see the direction established by multiple types of providers."

Fields agrees. "This is a huge market, and the projects are going to take all different kinds of shapes and forms and structures," he says.

Moore indirectly acknowledges that the movement from designing solutions to managing programs constitutes a significant shift within Andersen. "The lines between a lot of providers are blurring, and I think many consultants are trying to take a longer operating role in the supply chain," says Moore. However, he points out that the leading 3PLs haven't exactly been passive in the current logistics environment when it comes to forging new alliances and business relationships and might well be qualified for the 4PL role in certain logistics operations.

"In logistics today there are a lot of relationships among competitors where they have come together in alliances to work for a particular customer," [2] says Moore. "You end up partnering with a variety of people in this space now. The supply-chain space with the addition of the e-economy is getting very complex, so you have a classic cohabitation."

"Logistics outsourcing is becoming analogous to the information technology sector of the economy, he explains. Alliances and joint ventures are more prevalent in the IT sector, but as the supply-chain sector becomes more information-rich and thus more akin to the IT world, it's natural to expect a progression of alliances and joint efforts, say Moore. And while alliances often are difficult to work with (and ownership of client relationships remains an issue), he says, they are a necessary evil, a faster way to get capability on board an enterprise."

"In IT outsourcing, there's a concept that has been developed over the past 10 years related to best of breed," [3] says Moore. "Depending on the supply-chain situation and the weight and importance of the discipline you bring to the party, the overall manager serving the role of the 4PL in a best-of-breed contract could be a consultancy or it could be an asset-free associate of a 3PL. Some of the very large 3PLs are developing some pretty strong capabilities."

The most successful high-tech firms are rich with alliance relationships that include companies that often are direct competitors with each other, Moore points out. "And if you look at the 3PL landscape, they are developing a large suite of alliance relationships as well. There's an increasing maturity in the entire industry."

Several of the leading 3PL firms have achieved 4PL/logistics integrator relationships with a select customer or two, but the concept remains largely theoretical in nature.

"It's a tough sale," admits GATX's Carter. "One of the things that a 4PL's client gives up when they enlist the services of a 4PL is the day-to-day touching of providers, so it's really a leap of faith for somebody to go to a systems integrator and basically relinquish control and contact with the logistics service providers — the transportation companies, warehouse companies, freight payment service firms, packaging specialists—that make the supply chain work. In true systems integrator environment that contact goes away and is managed through the integrator/4PL."

From the more candid customers, 3PLs hear about other considerations. "The natural business argument from the manufacturer's perspective is that the 4PL scenario can create tremendous exit barriers," Carter says. "These customers ask, 'How can you get rid of an integrator or 4PL when they basically own the commercial relationship with the service providers?' There are some pretty important decisions involved here."

Looking into the future, Langley sees two things happening. "We will see the emergence of some relatively comprehensive providers that have the ability to provide the needed information technology and knowledge as well as access to a wide range of logistics services, and these comprehensive providers will give customers truly integrated packages."

There also will be a continued market for highly focused niche kinds of operations of all types, particularly in transportation and warehousing. If you look at the marketplace in one respect you might think that if the larger companies have their way, there won't be room for anyone else. But I think just the opposite will be true. As the large companies improve their capabilities that will actually do two things: improve the market position of those companies, and create a lot of identifiable niches where more specialized services are needed."

This might develop along the lines of the tier system in the automotive industry, he suggests. "You might find some of the Tier II and III companies providing valuable services to the 3PLs directly and may have customer bases of their own."

The logistics business is ripe for change, Langley adds. "Five or 10 years ago, we thought there were some identifiable directions for the logistics business. But right now the logistics arena is such an exciting environment, and there are so many different types of opportunities. If you look at the extent of the investment capital being ploughed into some of the large firms — Federal Express, Ryder, UPS, Menlo, Exel — a lot of companies are trying to take a huge position in the marketplace."

New Words and Expressions

1. emerge [i'mə:dʒ]*vi.* 显现，浮现，暴露，形成
2. competency['kɔmpit(ə)nsi]*n.* 资格，能力，[律]作证能力
3. friction['frikʃən]*n.* 摩擦，摩擦力
4. portfolio [pɔ:t'fəuljəu]*n.* 文件夹；公事包；纸夹
5. consultancy [kən'sʌltənsi]*n.* 顾问（工作）

6. differentiation [ˌdifərenʃi'eiʃn] n. 区别，差别；划分

7. credible['kredəbl,-ibl] adj. 可信的，可靠的

8. in-house [in'haus] adj., adv. 内部的

9. blur [bləː] v. 使模糊；使看不清

10. forge [fɔːdʒ] v. 结盟，建立联系

11. cohabitation [ˌkəuhæbi'teiʃən] n. 同居，同居生活

12. analogous [ə'næləgəs] adj. 类似的，相似的，可比拟的

13. prevalent ['prevələnt] adj. 普遍的，流行的

14. akin [ə'kin] adj. 性质相同的；类似的

15. theoretical [θiə'retik(ə)l] adj. 理论的

16. enlist [in'list] v. 征募，谋取（支持、赞助等）

17. relinquish [ri'liŋkwiʃ] v. 放弃

18. candid ['kændid] adj. 无偏见的，公正的，坦白的，率直的

19. scenario [si'nɑːriəu] n. 情景；场面

Notes

1. "Things are changing so quickly today in the IT sector that you really have to have not only a capable party but one that has core competency in knowing what systems are available and how to utilize and integrate those systems with other capabilities."

在 IT 时代，事物往往会变化很迅捷以致于你不仅仅要有才能，还应该具备知晓系统是否可行以及如何运用和综合系统各项功能的能力。

2. "In logistics today there are a lot of relationships among competitors where they have come together in alliances to work for a particular customer,"

在当今的物流行业里，存在许多因为一个特别顾客需求而使得竞争者联合共赢的关系。

Topic for Discussion

1. "With a new role like the 4PL, a role that is mostly global, information technology rich, asset-free …"After reading this, what's your understanding of it ?

2. "We all agree in this business that information has become as important and sometimes more important than the actual physical movement of the product" What does it mean? Can you tell us the importance of information in an enterprise?

3. What are the competencies of 4PL for supply-chain management?

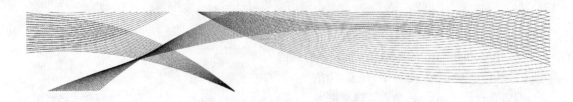

Unit 24

Passage A

The Introduction to RFID

This paper describes the basic components of a Radio Frequency Identification (RFID) system and explores the technology, applications, and competitive advantages of RFID technology and its uses for Automatic Identification Data Collection (AIDC).

1. Introduction

Traditional bar-coding technology provides an economical solution for Automatic Identification Data Collection (AIDC) industry applications. However, this technology has a primary limitation: each bar-coded item has to be scanned individually, thus limiting the scanning speed. Extra costs are incurred through the use of manual labor or automating the scanning process. And when the scanning is manually performed, there is the added possibility of human error. As a result of these limitations, RFID technology has been making inroads in AIDC applications.

RFID offers greater flexibility, higher data storage capacities, increased data collection throughput, and greater immediacy and accuracy of data collection. An increasing number of companies in a variety of markets worldwide are embracing RFID technology to increase quality and quantity of data collection in an expeditious manner, a feat not always possible with bar-coding systems [1]. The technology's enhanced accuracy and security makes it an ideal data collection platform for a variety of markets and applications, including healthcare, pharmaceutical, manufacturing, warehousing, logistics, transportation and retail.

2. Components of an RFID System

A basic RFID system consists of these components:

(1) A programmable RFID tag/inlay for storing item data consisting of:

- an RFID chip for data storage;
- an antenna to facilitate communication with the RFID chip.

(2) B. A reader/antenna system to interrogate the RFID inlay.

3. The RFID Tag

RFID tags are categorized as either passive or active. Passive tags do not have an integrated power source and are powered from the signal carried by the RFID reader. Active tags have a built-in power source, and their behavior can be compared to a beacon. As a result of the built-in battery, active tags can operate at a greater distance and at higher data rates in return for limited life driven by the longevity of the built in battery and higher costs. For a lower cost of implementation, passive tags are a more attractive solution.

The RFID tag consists of an integrated circuit (IC) embedded in a thin film medium. Information stored in the memory of the RFID chip is transmitted by the antenna circuit embedded in the RFID inlay via radio frequencies, to an RFID reader. The performance characteristics of the RFID tag will then be determined by factors such as the type of IC used, the read/write capability, the radio frequency, power settings, environment, etc.

The information stored in an RFID chip is defined by its read/write characteristics.

For a read-only tag, the information stored must be recorded during the manufacturing process and cannot be typically modified or erased. The data stored normally represents a unique serial number which is used as a reference to lookup more details about a particular item in a host system database. Read-only tags are therefore useful for identifying an object, much like the "license plate" of a car.

For a read/write tag, data can be written and erased on demand at the point of application. Since a rewriteable tag can be updated numerous times, its reusability can help to reduce the number of tags that need to be purchased and add greater flexibility and intelligence to the application. Additionally, data can be added as the item moves through the supply chain, providing better traceability and updated information. Advanced features also include locking, encryption and disabling the RFID tag.

RFID systems are designed to operate at a number of designated frequencies, depending on the application requirements and local radio-frequency regulations:

- Low Frequency (125kHz)
- High Frequency (13.56MHz)
- Ultra High Frequency (860~960MHz)
- Microwave (2.45GHz)

Low-frequency tags are typically used for access control & security, manufacturing processes, harsh environments, and animal identification applications in a variety of industries which require short read ranges. The low frequency spectrum is the most adaptive to high metal content environments, although with some loss of performance. Read ranges are typically several inches to several feet.

High-frequency tags were developed as a low-cost, small-profile alternative to low-frequency RFID tags with the ability to be printed or embedded in substrates such as paper [2]. Popular applications include: library tracking and identification, healthcare patient identification, access control, laundry identification, item level tracking, etc. Metal presents interference issues and requires special considerations for mounting. Similarly to the low-frequency technology, these tags have a read range of up to several feet.

UHF tags boast greater read distances and superior anti-collision capabilities, increasing the ability to identify a larger number of tags in the field at a given time. The primary application envisioned for UHF tags is supply chain tracking. The ability to identify large numbers of objects as they are moving through a facility and later through the supply chain, has an enormous opportunity for ROI in retail such as reduction of wasted dollars in inventory, lost sales revenues due to out of stock inventory, and the elimination of the human factor required today for successful barcode data collection [3]. There is a large number of additional markets with demand for UHF RFID technology such as transportation, healthcare, aerospace, etc.

Microwave tags are mostly used in active RFID systems. Offering long range and high data transfer speeds at significantly higher cost per tag making them suitable for railroad car tracking, container tracking, and automated toll collection type applications as a re-usable asset.

New Words and Expressions

1. application [ˌæpliˈkeiʃən]n. 使用，运用，适用，应用，用途
2. scanning[ˈskæniŋ]n. 细看，审视

3. healthcare　保健

4. interrogate [in'terəgeit] *vt.* 讯问，质问，详问

5. battery['bætəri] *n.* 电池，电池组

6. database['deitəbeis] *n.* 数据库，基本数据

7. traceability [ˌtreisə'biləti] *n.* 可描绘，可描写，可追溯

8. disable [dis'eibl] *vt.* 使无能（from doing, for）；使伤残

9. envision [in'viʒən] *vt.* 想象；预见；展望

10. elimination [iˌlimi'neiʃən] *n.* 淘汰，排除；排泄，消去

11. significantly　*adv.* 意味深长地，值得注目地

12. limitation [ˌlimi'teiʃən] *n.* 限制

Notes

1. An increasing number of companies in a variety of markets worldwide are embracing RFID technology to increase quality and quantity of data collection in an expeditious manner, a feat not always possible with bar-coding systems.

在全世界各个不同的市场中，越来越多的公司在积极快速地应用 RFID———一种用传统条码技术所不能实现的技术，来提高数据收集的质量和数量。

2. High-frequency tags were developed as a low-cost, small-profile alternative to low-frequency RFID tags with the ability to be printed or embedded in substrates such as paper.

作为低频 RFID 标签的替代选择，高频标签被设计成低成本、小外形的产品，而且能够印刷或镶嵌在诸如纸这样的基板上。

3. The ability to identify large numbers of objects as they are moving through a facility and later through the supply chain, has an enormous opportunity for ROI in retail such as reduction of wasted dollars in inventory, lost sales revenues due to out of stock inventory, and the elimination of the human factor required today for successful barcode data collection.

（UHF RFID）能够识别那些运动当中的，正通过某个设备并将流经整个供应链的大量对象，因而对提高零售业的投资回报率无疑是个巨大的机遇，比如它可以减少库存资金浪费，避免由于没有库存而导致销售收入损失，并消除条码数据成功采集所要求满足的人为因素。ROI＝return on investment

Topics for Discussion

1. After collecting the related information, what's your idea of the RFID? Please give us your opinion about it.

2. What are the components of an RFID System?

3. What's the basic composition of RFID tag? Could you tell the main parts of it? You can discuss it with your mate in group.

Passage B

Benefits and Applications of RFID

1. Benefits

The primary benefits of RFID technology over standard barcode identification are:
- Information stored on the tag can be updated on demand
- Large data storage capacity (up to 4k bits)
- High read rates
- Ability to collect data from multiple tags at a time
- Data collection without line-of-sight requirements
- Longer read range
- Greater reliability in harsh environments
- Greater accuracy in data retrieval and reduced error rate

2. About Barcodes

As barcodes approach their "middle ages" (it's been 30 years since a pack of gum was scanned at a Marsh grocery store in Ohio), they are as "alive" and useful as ever. And while RFID provides advantages, the demise of the barcode is greatly exaggerated. The Auto-ID Center, the research and development group that formulated and standardized much of the RFID technology evolution did not set out to make barcodes extinct. According to its spokesperson, "The Auto-ID Center does not advocate replacing barcodes as barcode-based systems such as the UPC are a standard automatic identification technology in many industries and will be an important complimentary technology for many years."

3. Applications

3.1 Library Information Systems

Tracking a library's assets and loan processing is very time-consuming and traditional bar-coding systems help to improve the process. However, RFID technology offers additional enhanced features:

291

Efficient processing—When each library item contains an embedded RFID tag on a printed label, its availability can be tracked much more efficiently (versus manual tracking). Library items can be checked in and out much faster than manual barcode or human readable data processing. In fact, with RFID, processing returned items no longer requires any human intervention at all. RFID enables libraries to provide certain services around the clock, without incurring additional costs.

Security—If a tagged library item has not been checked out, any attempt to remove it from the library premises will be detected via the RFID antenna at the entrance gate, hence the RFID tag doubles as a EAS antitheft device [1].

Inventory management—Book inventory that previously took weeks or months to execute can now be shortened to hours using RFID tagging. Using a portable RFID device, a librarian needs only to walk through a corridor of book shelves to check the status of the books available. The RFID reading device reads item information from the books' IC chips and then automatically interfaces with library inventory software systems to update the appropriate databases. In addition, it can notify the operator immediately if an item is not in its designated location.

3.2 Supply Chain Management

Key challenges faced by companies in their supply chain, is the visibility, tracking and traceability of materials and products as well as the quality and quantity of data collected in real time. RFID to increase data collection throughput and accuracy enable companies to identify materials, products and trends in supply chain with greater accuracy in real-time, compared to data collection technologies utilized to date [2]. Once RFID technology is fully integrated, minimal human effort is required in this process thus reducing errors and costs. By providing accurate, real-time data and information, RFID solutions enable companies to capture "live" data, converting it to meaningful information and automating all associated transactions and processes.

3.3 Healthcare

Erroneous patient data, including administering incorrect medications or dosages, is a major factor resulting in serious and in some cases, fatal medical mishaps. According to the Institute of Medicine:
- Between 44,000-98,000 Americans die from medical errors annually
- Only 55% of patients in a recent random sample of adults received recommended care with little difference found between care recommended for prevention to address

292

acute episodes or to treat chronic conditions

- Medication-related errors for hospitalized patients cost roughly $2 billion annually

These statistics have dramatically increased the demand for fail-safe accuracy in managing patient care; RFID is providing an effective solution. In RFID-equipped hospitals, patients wear wristbands with RFID tags containing encoded medical information. All prescription bags contain an embedded RFID tag containing details of the medication. Before any medication is administered to a patient, an RFID reader verifies the information between patient's tag and the prescription bag's tag. Information about the patient's medical allergies or other relevant patient care criteria is also highlighted on the RFID host computer. This secure patient-data system greatly reduces the possibility of human error thereby preventing a majority of unnecessary medical mishaps.

4. RFID Summary

Over the past few years, RFID technology has been attracting considerable attention. Giants such as Wal-Mart, Target, Best Buy, U. S. Department of Defense (DoD), Tesco, REWE and Metro Group have announced RFID mandates instructing their top suppliers to start utilizing RFID technology as part of a supply chain compliance program. In January 2005, there were in excess of 400 major companies worldwide required to use RFID technology. As a result of the current RFID supply chain mandate schedules, an estimated 50,000 + suppliers who will ultimately be affected by these plans and RFID solutions are a large driver for future business growth. The long-term focus in the United States will be on the retail and DoD adopters, who have to be compliant in the near future. Eventually, they will move beyond compliance only, and attempt to use RFID to increase efficiency and start gaining return on their investment. This will almost certainly mean more upgrades and additional spending on enterprise solutions.

New Words and Expressions

1. expedient [iks'pi:diənt] *adj.* 有利的;*n.* 权宜之计
2. waybill['weibil] *n.* 乘客名单
3. configuration[kənˌfigju'reiʃən] *n.* 结构,构造,配置,外行
4. expenditure [iks'penditʃə,eks-] *n.* 支出,花费

5. profitability [ˌprɔfitə'biliti] *n.* 收益性，利益率

6. database['deitəbeis] *n.* [机] 数据库

7. manipulation[məˌnipju'leiʃən] *n.* 处理，操作，操纵，被操纵

8. mining['mainiŋ]*n.* 采矿，矿业

9. retail['riːteil]*n.* 零售；*adj.* 零售的；*vt.* 零售，转述；*vi.* 零售；*adv.* 以零售方式

10. strategy['strætidʒi] *n.* 策略，军略

11. leverage['liːvəridʒ] *n.* 杠杆作用

12. inventory['invəntri] *n.* 详细目录，存货，财产清册，总量

13. rolling stock *n.* 全部车辆

14. consignee [kɔnsai'niː]*n.* 受托者，收件人，代销人

15. entail [in'teil] *vt.* 使必需，使蒙受，使承担，遗传给 *n.* [建]限定继承权

16. costly['kɔstli] *adj.* 昂贵的，贵重的

17. portfolio[pɔːt'fəuljəu] *n.* 文件夹；公事包；纸夹 绘图纸；文件 部长职务

18. trigger['trigə] *vt.* 引发，引起，触发；*n.* 板机

19. bypass ['baipɑːs] *n.* 旁路；*vt.* 设旁路，迂回

20. outsourcing ['autˌsɔːsiŋ] [商] 外部采办，外购

21. bundle['bʌndl] *n.* 捆，束，包；*v.* 捆扎

22. subsidiary [səb'sidjəri] *adj.* 辅助的，补充的

23. affiliate [ə'filieit]*v.* (使…) 加入，接受为会员

24. asset['æset]*n.* 资产，有用的东西

25. sophisticate[sə'fistikeit] *n.* 久经世故的人；*v.* 篡改，曲解，使变得世故

26. dilemma [di'leməˌdai-] *n.* 进退两难的局面，困难的选择

Notes

1. If a tagged library item has not been checked out, any attempt to remove it from the library premises will be detected via the RFID antenna at the entrance gate, hence the RFID tag doubles as a EAS antitheft device.

如果试图将一个被贴上标签的图书馆物件未经登记带出图书馆，那么在出入口就会由 RFID 天线探测出来，因此 RFID 标签作为一个电子标签防盗系统还起到了安全保障的作用。(double 指其不仅有标签识别功能，还有防盗功能) EAS = Electronic Article Surveillance，电子标签

2. RFID to increase data collection throughput and accuracy enable companies to identify materials, products and trends in supply chain with greater accuracy in real-time, compared to data collection technologies utilized to date.

主语是 RFID to increase data collection throughput and accuracy，谓语动词为 enable，compared to data collection technologies utilized to date 为比较状语，译为：与到目前为止所使用的其他数据采集技术相比。

Topics for Discussion

1. What are the primary benefits of RFID technology over standard barcode identification?

2. Could you explain what barcodes are and just give us some common types of it.

3. In your understanding, what other fields will RFID technique apply for?

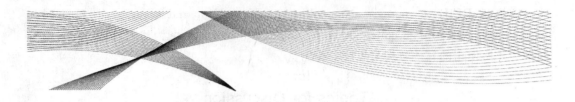

Unit 25

Case Study 1-1　The Best Way to Measure a Supply Chain：At Lexmark，Cash is King

There are all kinds of ways to measure the performance of a supply chain, but only one really gets to the heart of the matter. And that's cash.

Lexmark International, Inc. has embraced that philosophy in a big way. The $5bn maker of laser and inkjet printers chose cash-to-cash cycle time as one of its primary metrics, when it launched a sweeping program to boost customer service, reduce inventories and drive supply-chain efficiency [1].

Based in Lexington, Ky., Lexmark was born in 1991 as a spin-off from IBM. It went public in 1995 and has since carved out a substantial market share in printers both for business and retail consumers. But the competition is intense, especially from industry leader Hewlett-Packard Co., and margins can be challenging. So Lexmark decided to take a close look at the financial end of the organization, and how it affects key supply chain processes.

Supply chain analytics have a way of turning into abstruse mathematical formulas and numbing statistics. But nothing is simpler than the cash-to-cash measurement. In essence, it's the period of time between paying a supplier and getting that money back in the form of revenue. (To calculate the actual amount, add inventory days of supply and days sales outstanding, and then subtract day's payable outstanding.) By reducing cycle time, a company firms up its balance sheet, improves cash flow and cuts working capital requirements [2].

296

Together, the three components that make up the cash cycle-inventory, receivables and payables-can present an accurate picture of supply chain performance. Take the inventory measurement. Excess stocks could signal problems with forecasting, raw-materials planning, supplier reliability or distribution processes. Day's sales outstanding, in the form of high receivables, could mean snags in order fulfillment and invoicing. And high accounts payable are a symptom of poor relations with suppliers, or a company's inability to leverage its buying power.

In 2001, around the time of its 10th birthday as a stand-alone company, Lexmark set out to correct some of these flaws. Its strategy would focus on three key elements: customers, cash and total supply chain costs. Customer service was the most important of the three "Cs", but Lexmark was also seeking a balance between cash and cost, says Donna Covington, vice president of customer services. Both elements could be addressed from the perspective of cash-to-cash cycle.

In the "deep-dive" phase of its initial assessment, Lexmark's purchasing organization scrutinized payables, finance looked at receivables, and existing information about inventories was added to the mix [3]. The company then benchmarked its performance against major players both inside and outside its industry. By identifying the leaders, it could get a handle on how much work there was to be done. Says Covington: "It helps you to understand the difference between continuous improvement and breakthrough thinking."

The benchmarking effort was undertaken with the help of Miami, Fla.-based Adjoined Consulting Inc., a specialist in inventory management. The consultant helped Lexmark to select companies that had demonstrated leadership in key performance metrics, says John A. White III, managing officer of strategy. Industries surveyed included consumer electronics, computer hardware, communications equipment, household appliances, packaged goods and apparel accessories.

"It became obvious that Lexmark had a continued desire to improve its supply chain operation," White says. "They are a learning organization."

The effort was collaborative from the start. All Lexmark divisions and locations around the world were included. Getting everyone on board was a time-consuming process, Covington acknowledges, "but you save time in the execution portion." Lexmark's suppliers, including contract manufacturers and logistics service providers, were also brought into the program at an early stage.

1. New Product Intros

Under the direction of Covington, who has responsibility for all supply chain operations, Lexmark moved ahead on multiple fronts. New-product introduction was a priority. The company set up cross-functional teams to attack product design and development. Goals included more design flexibility to allow for product differentiation at the point of distribution, fewer "touches" during final assembly and distribution, early review of size and weight specifications to lower shipping costs, and optimization of pallet configuration at the factory, to streamline handling at the distribution center.

Lexmark was determined to ease the transition of data between phases of new-product development. In companies with strict corporate "silos," that can be tough to achieve [4]. So the supply chain development team launched a series of weekly Transition Management Team (TMT) meetings. Attendees included representatives of development and manufacturing engineering, tooling, supply chain management, demand and supply planning, information technology, packaging design and software development. The team was also given oversight of parts purchasing for both old and new products. In that area, the goal was twofold: to minimize inventories of product reaching the end of life, and avoid stock outs.

Regular "milestone" meetings, held before the ordering of components with long lead times, helped to synchronize the transition from outgoing to incoming products. For the first time, the purchase and production of end-of-life items could be executed by the entire group, based on demand as well as status of the replacement product.

Part commonality was another important consideration. Good planning at the outset can maximize the number of old parts and add-on features that can be reused in later models, Lexmark says. The practice might add to the bill of materials cost up front, but it pays off in greater efficiencies down the line.

Under Covington's direction, supply chain management became intimately involved in new-product introduction. Planners sought to devise a controlled production schedule that could reach desired volumes in the shortest time possible.

Again, corporate silos can frustrate such efforts. So the supply chain, engineering, quality assurance and manufacturing departments of Lexmark came up with a common Product Quality Process (PQP). It lays out a series of milestones for the various steps of a production line. Each station must meet certain quality and volume goals before it can advance to a higher level of production. That forces the entire operation to focus on product quality. And it helps Lexmark to do a better job of managing outside contract manufacturers, who make the majority of the company's hardware.

Further collaboration takes place at the stage just prior to sale. All parts of the supply chain are involved in the design of product that can be customized to meet the needs of individual regions or customers. For example, Lexmark came up with a packaging design that allows the distribution center to reprogram a printer's memory without removing the machine from its box. The company also cut down on the size and number of unique parts required for each configuration. One solution was as simple as creating a snap-on attachment with the company's logo, instead of molding it into the plastic. Unique identifiers that couldn't be removed were reduced in size and designed to be easily replaced.

2. Customized Headaches

Customization is great for the end user, but it creates numerous headaches throughout the supply chain. Factories can only turn out so much product of a given configuration, making for short product lifecycles that are difficult to manage. Producers face the dual risk of investing in too much capacity or suffering lost sales due to inadequate supply.

One solution is to make a machine that isn't as unique as it appears. Lexmark is able to offer multiple models with a common printer engine. A handful of additional components can turn a regular printer into a premium model with a host of features, including LCD screen and network portal. Minor modifications can also yield printers with various price points and software configurations for the same market. And they have allowed Lexmark to experiment by quickly launching or withdrawing new products according to changing buyer tastes.

By altering the way in which product moves to market, Lexmark realized further efficiencies in the cash-to-cash cycle. The idea was to minimize physical "touch points" in the supply chain, while reducing the amount of inventory in storage.

Direct shipment, an idea that has been growing in popularity among many manufacturers, was one answer. Lexmark's traditional supply chain consisted of multiple links, including supply inventory, product customization, and cross-docks. Most of those middle stages are eliminated with the shipment of printers direct from the plant to retailers, resellers and distributors, bypassing Lexmark's own DCs. Between 2002 and 2004, direct shipments of customized product increased by 2,100 percent, and factory-direct movements rose 975 percent.

Product postponement and direct shipment can be viewed as contradictory strategies. Where, after all, will a printer be configured for customers if it doesn't stop at a Lexmark facility? But Covington says the dual approach presents no conflict. Direct shipment is used for basic printers with relatively low price points and destined for retail shelves. There, she says, keeping down costs is paramount. And demand for retail models is fairly predictable.

New Words and Expressions

1. scrutinize['skrutinaiz]*vt*. 细察，细阅；仔细审查
2. laser['leizə]*n*. 激光
3. spin-off   *n*. 副产品；让产易股，抽资脱离
4. margin['mɑ:dʒin]*n*. 盈余，利润；毛额
5. numbing['nʌmiŋ]*adj*.使麻木的，使失去感觉的
6. snag [snæg]*n*. 障碍
7. invoicing['invɔisiŋ] *n*. 货品计价
8. stand-alone   *n*. 单机，卓越
9. benchmark['bentʃˌmɑ:k] *n*. 基准，规范
10. appliance [ə'plaiəns] *n*. 用具，器具
11. apparel [ə'pær(ə)l]*n*. 衣服，装饰
12. intro['intrəu] *n*. 介绍
13. pallet['pælit] *n*. (运货用的)托台，扁平工具，棘爪，货盘
14. configuration [kənˌfigju'reiʃən] *n*. 构造，结构，配置，外形
15. silo ['sailəu]*n*. 筒仓，地窖，[空]竖井，(导弹)发射井
16. oversight['əuvəsait]*n*. 监督，监视，看管；疏忽，漏失，失察，失错
17. twofold['tu:fəuld]*adj*.两部分的，双重的
18. commonality [ˌkɔmə'næliti]*n*. 共同或普通的性质或状态
19. outset['autset]*n*. 开端，开始
20. devise [di'vaiz]*vt*. 设计；计划；发明
21. attachment [ə'tætʃmənt]*n*.附件，附加装置，配属
22. identifier [ai'dentifaiə]*n*. 标志[标识，识别]符
23. premium['primjəm]*n*. 高级，优质
24. bypass['baipɑ:s;(US)'baipæs] *vt*. 回避

Notes

1. Lexmark International, Inc. has embraced that philosophy in a big way. The

$5bn maker of laser and inkjet printers chose cash-to-cash cycle time as one of its primary metrics, when it launched a sweeping program to boost customer service, reduce inventories and drive supply-chain efficiency.

利盟国际非常拥护这一理论。当这个拥有 50 亿美元资产的激光和喷墨打印机制造商启动一项全面的计划来改善顾客服务、降低库存和提升供应链效率时,它就把现金周期模型作为其最主要的业绩衡量方式之一。

2. (To calculate the actual amount, add inventory days of supply and days sales outstanding, and then subtract day's payable outstanding.) By reducing cycle time, a company firms up its balance sheet, improves cash flow and cuts working capital requirements.

(要计算实际的数量,就可以把存货供应天数和应收账款天数相加,再减去应付账款天数。)通过降低循环周期时间,公司可以加强其资产负债表,改善现金流并删减营运资本要求。

3. In the "deep-dive" phase of its initial assessment, Lexmark's purchasing organization scrutinized payables, finance looked at receivables, and existing information about inventories was added to the mix.

在评估的"深潜"阶段,利盟国际的采购组织细查到期应付款项,财政部门着眼于应收款项,而库存的当前信息也被增加到考虑范围之中。

4. Lexmark was determined to ease the transition of data between phases of new-product development. In companies with strict corporate "silos", that can be tough to achieve.

利盟国际决定要使新产品开发过程中的数据转换更加顺利。在有着严格垂直管理组织结构的公司内,这一点是很难实现的。

Topics for Discussion

1. What's the best way to measure a supply chain?

2. What kind of controlled production will the planners seek to reach desired volumes in the shortest time possible?

3. Where, after all, will a printer be configured for customers if it doesn't stop at a Lexmark facility?

4. Further collaboration takes place at the stage just prior to sale. All parts of the supply chain are involved in the design of product that can be customized to meet the needs of individual regions or customers. Can you give us some examples?

Case Study 1-2　The Best Way to Measure a Supply Chain: At Lexmark, Cash is King

1. Two Supply Chains

High-end printers, loaded with extra features, are better candidates for postponement. In such cases, "you want to be able to customize at the last minute with applications for specific industries," Covington says. In fact, Lexmark supports two distinct supply chains, one a "no-touch" operation for inkjet printers sold in retail stores, the other a conduit for laser and multi-function machines that can cost up to $5,000 apiece, and are purchased by resellers or distributors.

The streamlining of Lexmark's supply chain has also led to channel consolidation. By reducing its shipping points, the company can make better use of economical full container and truck loads. Covington says Lexmark had previously cut down on the number of carriers, with which it did business, boosting its buying clout with the rest. Today, regional reps no longer have the power to pick their own vendors. Transportation purchases are made through a worldwide logistics council, which also selects logistics service providers (LSPs) for each region.

Every business that doesn't demand cash up front struggles with slow-paying customers. So a look at Lexmark's accounts receivable was inevitable. Again, centralization of processes was the result.

Lexmark embraced a single worldwide credit policy. It covers which customers will be extended credit, how much credit will be permitted without executive review, and the criteria for credit suspension [1]. All actions are guided by a series of strict trigger points and accounts-receivable metrics.

On paper, Lexmark has long followed the practice of prompt invoicing. Whether those invoices were accurate was another matter. A steady worsening of days sales outstanding suggested that they weren't. So another cross-functional team, consisting of representatives from customer management and order fulfillment, was assigned to the problem. They reviewed the entire billing process, from purchase order to receipt of payment.

The team even visited customers who had reported high levels of inaccurate invoices. In one case, it turned out that the customer wasn't using the shipping documentation provided by Lexmark for the receipt of product. The customer was mixing up orders on the receiving dock, making it difficult to come up with an accurate report of receipt. Other reasons for invoice discrepancies included picking error within the distribution operation, mistaken reports, notification by customers at the end of credit terms instead of when the error appeared, and the inability of Lexmark's customer-service department to handle claims quickly.

In response, Lexmark stepped up the number of quality audits for outbound shipments. With the proper data finally in hand, it saw the opportunity to redesign the warehouse in order to cut down on fulfillment errors. Parts with similar numbers were shifted in order to reduce picking error. And pallet-sizing rules for mixed pallet shipments were tweaked to reduce customer confusion.

In the end, Lexmark revamped and shortened its entire internal claims process. Personnel from order management and distribution became the central point of contact for problems reported by customers. Taken together, those efforts have led to a 300 percent reduction over five years in the average length of time needed to reduce claims, Lexmark says.

At the same time, the company shifted the focus of receivables management from past due to pre-collection, to ensure that customers were adhering to their contracted payment terms. As an incentive to the Lexmark sales team, bonuses were tied partly to customers' payment histories.

What Lexmark owes is just as important as what others owe it. Here, the company took an opposite approach. It sought longer payment terms from suppliers and other vendors, while identifying those offering the highest return. Lead buyers within the company were matched with top global suppliers to negotiate extended payment terms. The overall intent was to offer one face to suppliers on a worldwide basis, rather than rely on procurement specialists within each division.

The payment-term extension wasn't simply dictated to suppliers, says Covington. For one thing, it was more easily implemented with new suppliers, who didn't have a history with the company. Longer terms could therefore be negotiated up front, without complaint.

For veteran suppliers, the demand was sugar-coated. Lexmark offered to work with them to improve the overall supply chain efficiency of all parties. "We're not trying to stick our partners," Covington says. "We want to talk about how can you shrink or shorten the pipeline." Everyone benefits from fewer inventories in the system, she adds.

Lexmark was successful in implementing the new policy with suppliers new and old. The program has led to a 51 percent improvement in average payment terms, it says.

The company also made greater use of supplier-managed inventory (SMI). Also known as vendor-managed inventory, SMI puts more responsibility on the shoulders of the supplier, who holds title to product or parts until the last possible moment. The practice lightens the load on Lexmark's books, and ensures that the company is only buying the product that it needs. It has also shortened the time during which production is locked in for a particular model. As for suppliers, they get a "very large say" in the setting of inventory targets and how stocks are replenished, Covington says.

2. The Inventory Trend

Like consumer goods producers, Lexmark would like to see inventories go in just one direction: down. Since 2001, it has reduced inventory levels by 32 percent. To make that happen, the company launched several initiatives. They included a better planning process, greater visibility of inventory throughout the supply chain, SMI programs and direct shipment to customers.

On the planning side, the company shifted from a monthly to weekly process. The move has allowed it to react more quickly to changing consumer demand [2]. And it has kept inventories low, with product flowing to end customers in smaller lots and shipment quantities.

Adjoined Consulting helped Lexmark to devise a strategy for better inventory management. According to White, the effort ranged over such considerations as customer service, forecasting and demand management, continuous improvement, sourcing and product design. "Inventory is a cross-functional impact area," he says. Multiple controls are necessary for handling supplier contracts, calculating lead times and assessing optimal inventory levels.

The method of determining precise inventory levels is far from perfect. Lexmark looks at the history of all product segments in order to predict sales for new and existing items. The exercise requires deep collaboration with customers, says Covington, including some access to point-of-sale data from retailers.

"We're trying to take that data all the way back through the supply chain on a weekly basis," she says, adding that the company can adjust to shifting patterns of

304

consumption in a relatively quick manner.

One of Lexmark's major customers is Clearwater, Fla. -based Tech Data Corp. , a large distributor to retailers and online consumers. Revenues were $19. 8bn in the fiscal year ending Jan. 31, 2005. Tech Data recently awarded Lexmark the title of Best Supply Chain Innovator, based on work the partners have done to reduce touches in the supply chain. According to Tech Data, the effort has led to significant savings in warehouse space, management costs, and labor and freight charges.

Tech Data participated in Lexmark's direct ship program, buying from the manufacturer overseas and shipping to its own logistics centers in full container loads, says Brooke Powers, vice president of supply chain management and purchasing. The key was buying enough product to justify the effort economically and fill containers-not a problem for a distributor the size of Tech Data.

One consideration is product value. The program works best for less expensive printers with relatively low price volatility, Powers says. The company must be able to justify the extra time it takes to get printers from manufacturers in Asia, as opposed to buying them from Lexmark in the U. S.

Other suppliers of Tech Data are now embracing a similar strategy of direct shipment for certain items. "Lexmark has really caught the front of the wave," says Powers. "They've been increasing the number of products that they add [to the program]. " At the same time, he says, the distributor will continue to rely on domestic sourcing for around half its total volume, in order to minimize order lead times and lessen the impact of potential supply-chain disruptions.

For Lexmark, the final piece of the puzzle is a renewed focus on the customer. Previously, the company had lacked a consistent view of its customer base across all departments. Now, a series of cross-functional teams, drawing on customer service, supply-chain management, sales and marketing and order management, work closely with retailer customers on every aspect of order fulfillment. At the same time, Lexmark is segmenting its customers according to their importance to the company's bottom line.

The results have been dramatic, and company-wide. In just four years, Lexmark has seen a 45 percent decline in cash-to-cash days, a 300 percent increase in cash flow from operations, and a 32 percent reduction in days of inventory.

But Lexmark isn't satisfied yet. It continues to experience intense pricing pressure from competitors, especially for its lucrative ink cartridges. According to Covington, there's more work to be done on customer service through multiple sales channels. And the supply chain can be made even more efficient. She says the company is on track to achieve another 15 percent reduction in its cash-to-cash cycle this year.

"We're looking at our touch points, the number of distribution centers, our infrastructure and how we can simplify and reduce cycle time," [3] Covington says. "That's a continued challenge."

New Words and Expressions

1. clout[klaut]*n.* (影响他人决定的)力量，权势
2. audit['ɔːdit]*n.* 审计，稽核，查账
3. tweak [twiːk]*v.* (对机器、汽车或系统)做小小的改进
4. revamp['riː'væmp] *v.* 修补，修改
5. incentive [in'sentiv]*n.* 刺激；鼓励，动机
6. bonus['bəunəs]*n.* 奖金，红利
7. owe [əu]*v.* 欠，应感激，应该把……归功于(to)
8. veteran['vetərən]*n.* 老资格；老手，富有经验的人
9. stick [stik]*v.* 刺，戳
10. shrink [ʃriŋk]*v.* 收缩，(使)皱缩，缩短
11. pipeline['paipˌlain]*n.* 管道，传递途径
12. replenish[ri'pleniʃ]*v.* 补充存货
13. segment['segmənt]*v.* 分割
14. lucrative['luːkrətivˌljuː-]*adj.* 有利的；赚钱的

Notes

1. Lexmark embraced a single worldwide credit policy. It covers which customers will be extended credit, how much credit will be permitted without executive review, and the criteria for credit suspension.

Lexmark 包括了全球的贷款政策。它包括了什么样的顾客能持久信贷，多少的贷款可不经行政检查，以及中止信贷的标准。

2. On the planning side, the company shifted from a monthly to weekly process. The move has allowed it to react more quickly to changing consumer demand.

在计划这部分，公司从月计划转变为周计划。这个变化让它能对变化的顾客需求迅速做出反应。

3. "We're looking at our touch points, the number of distribution centers, our infrastructure and how we can simplify and reduce cycle time,"

"我们正在寻找触点、配送中心数量、我们的基础设施以及简化和减少周期时间的方法。

Topics for Discussion

1. From the first part, how can the company make better use of economical full container and truck loads?

2. At some time, why will the company shift the focus of receivables management from past due to pre-collection?

3. On the planning side, why will the company shift from a monthly to weekly process?

4. From Covington's saying, what will be the continued challenge? Could you imagine it from what you've learned from or out of text?

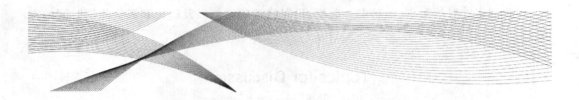

Unit 26

Case Study 2-1   HP Invents New Framework
for Managing Supply Chain Risk

In 2000 Hewlett-Packard faced a supply crisis. The flash memory used in its highly profitable printers also was being used by fast-growing cell-phone makers and HP was unable to obtain sufficient supply to meet its demand. As a result, the company failed to ship about 250,000 printers, which translated into a revenue loss in the tens of millions of dollars. Moreover, to ensure supply HP was forced to sign a three-year fixed-quantity, fixed-price contract with significant non-performance penalties for what historically has been a highly volatile component [1].

This experience served as the catalyst for HP to develop a framework for measuring and managing supply chain risk. Known today as Procurement Risk Management (PRM), the framework, which encompasses both process and technology, has become a key initiative at the company and is being applied to about $6bn of spending annually across numerous HP business units. Incremental savings to date total more than $100m.

The task of developing the risk management solution fell to a research and development team led by Venu Nagali, distinguished technologist at HP. "One of the first things we did when we started this program was to look out and see how other manufacturers were managing supply chain risk," says Nagali. "To our surprise we found that few manufacturers had any processes at all in place." Indeed, he adds, the team found numerous high-profile cases where failing to manage supply risk had resulted in significant losses of revenue and of shareholder value. These failures fell into three primary categories: price risk, demand risk and availability risk. "These three-demand, cost and availability-is the key uncertainties that have to be measured and managed," says Nagali [2].

All industries experience these uncertainties, but they can be especially volatile in the high-tech sector where HP is the biggest single purchaser of many components, including memory, hard disk drives and LCD panels. "It is good to be number one in any given market, but that also forces you to take on substantial risk, just by virtue of the large volume of components you have to buy," says Nagali. Additionally, high-tech components are among the most volatile in terms of cost and availability. Nagali offers an example of DRAM memory used by HP, which dropped in price by more than 90 percent in 2001 only to more than triple in 2003. "Except for the electricity market," he says, "I have not seen a market with more price volatility than high-tech."

Availability also is often uncertain. In addition to general disruptions caused by natural disasters or political acts, Nagali notes that in periods of high demand, suppliers place original equipment manufacturers like HP under allocation "whereby they supply only a fraction of an OEM's total demand." [3]

The final variable, demand, is intensified by high-tech's notoriously short product life cycles. "If your product is successful, it lasts for six to nine months," says Nagali. "If it is a failure, it can last less than a month."

1. Wall Street Model

Since Nagali and many of his team members had prior experience working with risk management in financial markets, they studied the Wall Street model carefully. While many of the principles were applicable to the supply chain, the underlying stratagems used on Wall Street were not easily transferable. "Financial engineering practices enable the management of cost uncertainty through such instruments as call and put options," says Nagali. "But such instruments are not available for high-tech components." Financial risk management also fails to address demand and availability uncertainties, he says.

Conversely, current supply chain management practices emphasize the management of demand and availability uncertainties through inventory buffering strategies, but have little if any focus on managing component cost uncertainties. "The philosophy seems to be that all the risk can be pushed onto suppliers," says Nagali. "But what is not really well understood is that suppliers charge a premium to manage that risk. This is a hidden cost. "

The bottom line, he says, is that in the supply chain, demand, cost and availability uncertainties all are equally important and correlated. This means that they all need to be managed together.

"What we had to do was invent a completely new framework for managing risk," says Nagali. "It was not possible to simply take the math from Wall Street and apply it. " This framework also required new technology, since existing supply chain management and Enterprise Resource Planning software do not support risk management.

The first challenge that the team tackled was how to measure and account for uncertainty in each of the three areas: demand, cost and availability. To do this, they developed new algorithms that are embedded in a software solution called HP Horizon. This solution begins with a typical point forecast, which it analyzes and corrects for biases. Then, using historical forecasts and current demand trends, the software builds statistically significant scenarios that calculate how high and how low demand could go, attaching to each scenario a probability number. Generally, the low number defines the 10th percentile, where the chance of demand falling below this level is only 10 percent. The high number defines the 90th percentile, which has only a 10 percent likelihood of being exceeded. Between these two numbers is an 80 percent range that is expected to encompass most demand.

The same type of tool is used to develop a high, low and middle range for the cost variability of component parts, typically looking six months out. "We have developed proprietary analytics that model the unique cost dynamics of high-tech components," says Nagali, "but these analytics also could be adopted to forecast the cost uncertainty of other manufactured commodities, such as plastics, chemicals or steel. "

Determining availability uncertainty has been more difficult to automate. "What we are trying to gather from this scenario is the likelihood that we will be able to meet our demand without any contracts-just by going to the spot market," says Nagali. Unfortunately, he says, there are not enough data points to build a model at this time, so HP determines this variable through interviews with market specialists.

2. Measure

Once uncertainties have been calculated, with probabilities assigned, the question becomes how to use this information to make decisions differently, says Nagali. "The answer to this question is the more powerful aspect of PRM and it involves developing a portfolio of procurement contracts designed to share risks with suppliers," he says.

310

"The risk sharing nature comes about by HP taking ownership of the risks that we can bear more cheaply and asking suppliers to take risks that they can more easily manage."

For the segment of demand where uncertainty is low, for example, HP enters into fixed-quantity, fixed-price contracts for a reasonably long period of time. "This is different to what manufacturers do now, which is simply to send a full point forecast to suppliers-just a forecast, not a commitment," he says. By just sending a forecast, "manufacturers are pushing the entire demand risk onto suppliers, which is unfair," says Nagali.

Using PRM, "what HP now does is to say to suppliers, here is a segment of demand that HP can absolutely commit to, guaranteed'," he says. In return for that guarantee, suppliers are willing to give HP a price discount because the commitment allows them to manage their capacity more efficiently. "Committed volumes can be scheduled during non-peak times, and inventory carries no risk," says Nagali. Additionally, on high-volume deals, suppliers can modify fabrication lines to significantly reduce costs. "One printer supplier modified a conventional process based on HP's binding, forward commitment," says Nagali. "The resulting cost reductions yielded an additional 15 percent savings to HP, over and above volume discounts."

Less certain demand is satisfied through flexible quantity agreements. "Flexible agreements are the most common supplier arrangement in our industry, so creative modifications of these agreements are usually easy to pull together with suppliers," says Nagali. Suppliers often provide pricing discounts for committed upside volumes, he says, especially when the volumes have growth potential. Discounts typically increase as more volume is purchased. Making some of these commitments binding eliminates supply risk and provides further cost savings. "A significant percentage of HP's memory requirements are met through these binding but flexible agreements," says Nagali. "Contract horizons generally match HP's product lifecycle times and/or supplier capacity lead-times. The longer the horizon, the deeper the price discounts and the more binding the supply commitments." [4]

For demand with high uncertainty neither HP nor the supplier makes commitments. "Demand that is least likely to materialize can often be satisfied through the open or spot market," says Nagali. "As these sources dry up, secondary-sourcing options can be used such as brokers, auctions and product recycling programs." These approaches mean higher prices, but are often a better solution than carrying inventory, he says. And, the supply risk associated with these approaches often is less than expected. In one instance, HP's customer support teams realized significant inventory savings by recovering critical parts from unsold products. They also found consistent supply for low volume microprocessor demand through auctions, saving on inventories subject to severe price erosion, he says.

New Words and Expressions

1. principle ['prinsəpl]*n*. 原理，原则
2. incremental [inkri'mentəl]*adj*. 增加[量，值]的，逐渐增长的，递增的
3. numerous['nju:mərəs]*adj*.[修饰单数集合名词]由多数人形成的，人数多的
4. correlate['kɔrileit]*n*. 相关的人[物]
5. purchaser['pə:tʃəsə]*n*. 买主；购买者
6. enterprise['entəpraiz]*n*.（艰巨、复杂或冒险性的）工作，事业；
   企业；事[企]业单位
7. percentile [pə'sentail] *adj*. 百分比的，按百等分排列[分布]的
8. yield [ji:ld] *vt*. 生出，出产；产生
9. whereby [(h)wɛə'bai][疑问副词]根据什么
10. discount['diskaunt] *n*. 折扣
11. microprocessor [maikrəu'prəusesə(r)]*n*.〈计〉微处理器，单片机
12. horizon [hə'raizn]*n*. 地平(线；圈)，水平(线)

Notes

1. Moreover, to ensure supply HP was forced to sign a three-year fixed-quantity, fixed-price contract with significant non-performance penalties for what historically has been a highly volatile component.

另外，为了保证供应，惠普被迫为了某个从历史发展来看一直变化很大的部件签订了三年的固定数量、固定价格和巨额违约赔偿金的协议。

2. Indeed, he adds, the team found numerous high-profile cases where failing to manage supply risk had resulted in significant losses of revenue and of shareholder value. These failures fell into three primary categories: price risk, demand risk and availability risk. "These three—demand, cost and availability—is the key uncertainties that have to be measured and managed," says Nagali.

实际上，他补充道，研究小组发现了数目众多的由于未能管理好供应风险而导致收益和股东价值重大损失的知名案例。这些失误可分成三大类：价格变动风险，需求变动风险和现有风险。Nagali 说，"需求、成本和可获得性，是需要被估量和管理的最重要的三种不

312

确定性。

3. Availability also is often uncertain. In addition to general disruptions caused by natural disasters or political acts, Nagali notes that in periods of high demand, suppliers place original equipment manufacturers like HP under allocation "whereby they supply only a fraction of an OEM's total demand."

可得性也经常是不确定的。除了由于自然灾害或整治行动导致的一般的中断以外，Nagali 指出，在高需求阶段，供应商会把像惠普这样的 OEM 制造商置于配给位置，"所以他们只供应一个 OEM 制造商总需求的一小部分"。

4. "Contract horizons generally match HP's product lifecycle times and/or supplier capacity lead-times. The longer the horizon, the deeper the price discounts and the more binding the supply commitments.

合约时间范围通常与惠普产品的生命周期时间和/或供应商能力提前期相匹配。时间范围越长，价格就越优惠，供应承诺就越具有约束力。

Topics for Discussion

1. What's the first challenge the team tackled in order to measure and account for uncertainty in each of the three areas?

2. What's the main reason for the coming up of HP invents new framework and how to determine the availability uncertainty?

3. Why it is said that "For demand with high uncertainty neither HP nor the supplier make commitments"? Can you get the main idea from it?

Passage B

Case Study 2-2   HP Invents New Framework for Managing Supply Chain Risk

1. Optimizing the Portfolio

The next challenge for the PRM team was to help users determine an optimal contract portfolio for enabling specific business objectives. To meet this goal, the team developed additional new software called HP Risk, which provides contract valuation analytics. Since many contracts are in place at any given time, the HP Risk engine must look not only at current demand, price and availability of components, but also at the specific structure and terms of other contracts in effect, says Nagali. "Effectively, this software builds scenarios that show you how your world would look with one set of contracts versus another set of contracts. Then it helps you determine which set of contracts best meets your objectives," he says.

Objectives vary from one business unit to another, Nagali adds. "In some business units cost saving is the biggest objective, while it others it may be assurance of supply or cost predictability. " Using the PRM portfolio approach, "we can enable any combination of objectives," he says.

Innovations in the HP Risk suite of PRM software have resulted in five patent applications thus far, but Nagali emphasizes that the solutions are very user friendly. "The entire math is hidden," he says. "The user just has to click on a few buttons. "

For Nagali, "coming up with the math and embedding it in the software was the easy part of this project. " A much bigger challenge, he says, was the people and process issues around getting PRM embedded in the HP organization.

Adding to this challenge, he says, is the fact that few employees, particularly in the supply chain, have any training in risk management, nor do they possess the skill sets or concepts needed to effectively manage this area [1].

Further, existing ERP and SCM systems do not support decision-making that is future looking. And metrics for assessing risk management do not exist. "There are metrics for almost every other thing, but not for supply chain risk," says Nagali. "Most metrics in the supply chain are about how long or how many, not about how much risk

314

I am taking over the next six months."

Finally, the PRM process is extremely cross-functional. "For risk management to work, you need to have procurement, finance, sales and marketing, and the supply chains all working in vertical alignment,"[2] says Nagali. "Each has different information that is important to the process." At HP, he says, "we now have a cross-functional process where business-unit teams routinely look at risks and ask themselves, how are we going to manage this?"

The cross-functional process at HP is simple in structure but rigorous in execution. "Strategy and governance for a particular commodity typically includes approving procurement objectives, establishing metrics and reviewing performance of any existing portfolio of deals," says Nagali. Strategy and governance for product specific commodities is managed at the business level, while commodities common across products are managed more centrally.

Nagali's team serves as a consultant to introduce HP business units to PRM, to help them develop pilots and to train people on the software. More than 750 HP professionals have been trained in PRM concepts, says Nagali. Typically, it takes a business unit one year to two years "before they are ready for us to totally get out of the way and go it alone," he says. "At that point we give them the software and turn it over."

2. Range of Benefits

During the past five years, HP has implemented PRM for key strategic commodities as well as for procurement of certain indirect materials and services like advertising. "This wide range of applications illustrates the power and generality of the PRM approach," says Nagali. The process has enabled more than $100m in incremental savings, or savings over what would have been achieved through other methods without PRM.

Benefits can be categorized into four areas:

• Material costs savings

HP has obtained incremental material cost discounts up to 5 percent for standard components and an even higher discount for custom components, indirect materials and services. These discounts are a result of HP's quantity commitments, which lower supplier demand risks while enabling more efficient planning and production processes.

• Cost predictability

By including specific pricing terms in contracts, including price caps and floors where indicated, HP has been able to proactively manage cost uncertainty and protect margins.

- Assurance of supply (AoS)

Managing component demand and availability uncertainties is a key objective for PRM at HP. PRM deals has improved AoS for several commodities even under conditions of an industry-wide shortage. For example, during an industry-wide shortage for memory that occurred in 2004, the PRM deals executed by a particular HP business unit ensured that they obtained 100 percent of their demand.

- Inventory cost reductions

The precise measurement of demand uncertainty using PRM software enables HP to optimize inventory levels internally and externally at supplier sites. Such optimization has cut inventory-driven costs by several percentage points for commodities implementing the PRM framework.

Suppliers also have benefited, says Nagali. "The quantity commitments that HP makes to suppliers, as opposed to just exchanging non-binding forecasts, has lowered supplier's demand risks," he says. "Suppliers of several strategic commodities have locked-up a significant portion of their capacity through PRM deals with HP."

These cascades through the supply chain, he says, with some suppliers making commitments to their suppliers based on HP's quantity commitments to them. The result is a significant drop in order volatility and a reduction of the "bullwhip effect".

Today PRM is considered a competitive advantage by HP senior management, says Nagali. "HP has an ambitious program to continue leading the industry and setting the industry standards in this important new business discipline."

New Words and Expressions

1. optimize ['ɔptimaiz]*vi*. 表示乐观
2. component [kəm'pəunənt]*adj*. 组成的,合成的,成分的,分量的
3. predictability [pri,diktə'biliti]*n*. 可预言
4. assess [ə'ses]*vt*. 估定(财产,价值等)
5. portfolio [pɔːt'fəuljəu]*n*. (皮制的)文件夹;公事包
6. illustrate ['iləstreit]*vt*. 举例说明;例证
7. demand [di'mɑːnd]*vt*. 要求,请求
8. framework ['freimwəːk]*n*. 骨架,结构框
9. volatility [,vɔlə'tiliti]*n*. 挥发性 [度]

10. ambitious [æm'biʃəs]*adj.* 志向远大的；有雄心壮志的；豪迈的；有野心的

Notes

1. Adding to this challenge, he says, is the fact that few employees, particularly in the supply chain, have any training in risk management, nor do they possess the skill sets or concepts needed to effectively manage this area.

他说，增加这个挑战难度的是：特别在供应链里，很少有员工进行过风险管理的培训，或者他们也没有掌握在这个领域里能有效管理的技术或概念。

2. "For risk management to work, you need to have procurement, finance, sales and marketing, and the supply chains all working in vertical alignment.

对于工作的风险管理，你需要将采购、财政、销售、市场以及供应链纵向一体化地联合考虑。

Topics for Discussion

1. From the text, what's the next challenge for the PRM team for enabling specific business objectives?

2. Adding to this challenge, the fact is that few employees, particularly in the supply chain, have any training in risk management, nor do they possess the skill sets or concepts needed to effectively manage this area; is that true?

3. Nowadays, why the Today PRM can be considered as a competitive advantage by HP senior management?

Appendixes

附录 A　汉英物流术语解释

物品	Article	经济活动中涉及实体流动的物质资料
物流	Logistics	物品从供应地向接收地的实体流动过程。根据实际需要,将运输、储存、装卸、搬运、包装、流通加工、配送、信息处理等基本功能实施的有机结合
物流活动	Logistics Activity	物流诸功能的实施与管理过程
物流作业	Logistics Operation	实现物流功能时所进行的具体操作活动
物流模数	Logistics Modulus	物流设施与设备的尺寸基准
物流技术	Logistics Technology	物流活动中所采用的自然科学与社会科学方面的理论、方法,以及设施、设备、装置与工艺的总称
物流成本	Logistics Cost	物流活动中所消耗的物化劳动和活劳动的货币表现
物流管理	Logistics Management	为了以最低的物流成本达到用户所满意的服务水平,对物流活动进行的计划、组织、协调与控制
物流中心	Logistics Center	从事物流活动的场所或组织。应基本符合下列要求:(1)主要面向社会服务;(2)物流功能健全;(3)完善的信息网络;(4)辐射范围大;(5)少品种、大批量;(6)存储、吞吐能力强;(7)物流业务统一经营、管理
物流网络	Logistics Network	物流过程中相互联系的组织与设施的集合
物流信息	Logistics Information	反映物流各种活动内容的知识、资料、图像、数据、文件的总称
物流企业	Logistics Enterprise	从事物流活动的经济组织
物流单证	Logistics Documents	物流过程中使用的所有单据、票据、凭证的总称
物流联盟	Logistics Alliance	两个或两个以上的经济组织为实现特定的物流目标而采取的长期联合与合作
供用物流	Supply Logistics	为生产企业提供原材料、零部件或其他物品时,物品在提供者与需求者之间的实体流动

生产物流	Production Logistics	生产过程中,原材料、在制品、半成品、产成品等,在企业内部的实体流动
销售物流	Distribution Logistics	生产企业、流通企业出售商品时,物品在供方与需方之间的实体流动
回收物流	Returned Logistics	不合格物品的返修、退货以及周转使用的包装容器从需方返回到供方所形成的物品实体流动
废弃物物流	Waste Material Logistics	将经济活动中失去原有使用价值的物品,根据实际需要进行收集、分类、加工、包装、搬运、储存等,并分送到专门处理场所时所形成的物品实体流动
绿色物流	Environmental Logistics	在物流过程中抑制物流对环境造成危害的同时,实现对物流环境的净化,使物流资源得到最充分利用
企业物流	Internal Logistics	企业内部的物品实体流动
社会物流	External Logistics	企业外部的物流活动的总称
军事物流	Military Logistics	用于满足军队平时与战时需要的物流活动
国际物流	International Logistics	不同国家(地区)之间的物流
第三方物流	Third-Part Logistics (TPL)	由供方与需方以外的物流企业提供物流服务的业务模式
定制物流	Customized Logistics	根据用户的特定要求而为其专门设计的物流服务模式
虚拟物流	Virtual logistics	以计算机网络技术进行物流运作与管理,实现企业间物流资源共享和优化配置的物流方式
增值物流服务	Value-added logistics service	在完成物流基本功能基础上,根据客户需求提供的各种延伸业务活动
供用链	Supply Chain	生产及流通过程中,涉及将产品或服务提供给最终用户活动的上游与下游企业,所形成的网链结构
装箱单	Packing List (sometimes as packing note)	列出运输所需的资料,例如发票、买方、收货人、原产地、航班日期、装货港口/机场、卸货港口/机场、交货地点、装运标志/货柜编号、货品重量/体积,以及全部有关货品的详情,包括装箱资料
空运提单	(AWB) Air Waybill	航运公司。这是用于空运货物的一种运货单。空运提单说明运输的条件,作为交付货品的收据,但不是所有权证明文件或可转让的文件
运输商空运提单	(HAWB) House Air Waybill	航空公司。这是空运代理行发出的空运托运单,提供货物说明及记录,但非所有权证明文件
条码	Bar Code	由一组规则排列的条、空及字符组成的、用以表示一定信息的代码。同义词:条码符号 bar code symbol[GB/T 4122.1-1996 中 4.17]
汇票	Bill of Exchange, or Draft (B/E)	这是无条件的书面指示。出口商在该指示中要求进口商即时或在未来日期支付某一金额给抬头人或持票人

本票	Promissory Note	这是可转让的财务文件,证明海外买方须付款给持票人
信托收据	(T/R) Trust Receipt	银行凭此文件向买方发放货品(货品仍属银行所有)。买方取得货品后,必须将货品与本身其他资产分别开来,随时准备银行收回
提单	(B/L) Bill of Lading	航运公司。这是货品拥有人与运输公司之间的合约。顾客通常需要提单的正本,以证明货品属他所有,有权提取货品。提单分两种:不可转让的直接提单,以及可转让或付货人指示提单(亦是所有权证明文件),后者可在货物过境时买卖或交易,以及用于多种融资交易
跟单信用证	D/C Documentary Credit	这是按买方要求开立的银行文件,证明开证银行向卖方保证,只要符合跟单信用证所列的具体要求,便会支付某一金额
备用信用证	Standby Credit	客户与其银行作出的安排,使客户享有在该银行兑现某一金额内的支票的便利。或出口商与进口商的安排,承诺若完成不了合约内容,出口商需要赔偿进口商部分损失,这又叫履约保证书。通常用于大宗的交易如原油、肥料、鱼苗、糖及尿素等
托收指令	Collection Instruction	这是出口商向其银行发出的指示,授权银行根据合约条款代出口商收款
电子数据交换	Electronic Data Interchange	通过电子方式,采用标准化的格式,利用计算机网络进行结构化数据的传输和交换
有形损耗	Tangible Loss	可见或可测量出来的物理性损失、消耗
无形损耗	Intangible Loss	由于科学技术进步而引起的物品贬值
国际铁路联运	International Through Railway Transport	使用一份统一的国际铁路联运票据,由跨国铁路承运人办理两国或两国以上铁路的全程运输,并承担运输责任的一种连贯运输方式
国际多式联运	International Multimodal Transport	按照多式联运合同,以至少两种不同的运输方式,由多式联运经营人将货物从一个国境内的接管地点运至另一国境内指定交付地点的货物运输
大陆桥运输	Land Bridge Transport	用横贯大陆的铁路或公路作为中间桥梁,将大陆两端的海洋运输连接起来的连贯运输方式
班轮运输	Liner Transport	在固定的航线上,以既定的港口顺序,按照事先公布的船期表航行的水上运输方式
海运提单	Sea Waybill	货运代理行。这是货物收据,内含付货人与航运公司之间的运输合约。海运提单是不可转让的文件,并非所有权证明文件
租船运输	Shipping By Chartering	根据协议,租船人向船舶所有人租赁船舶用于货物运输,并按商定运价,向船舶所有人支付运费或租金的运输方式
船务代理	Shipping Agency	根据承运人的委托,代办与船舶进出港有关的业务活动
货运担保	Shipping Guarantee	货运代理行。这是通常由航运公司预先印备的表格,由进口商银行向航运公司担保交还运输文件正本,顾客便可凭这文件提货,而不必出示提单正本。这文件通常与信托收据一并使用,以保障银行对货物的控制权

国际货运代理	International Freight Forwarding Agent	接受进出口货物收货人、发货人的委托,以委托人或自己的名义,为委托人办理国际货物运输及相关业务,并收取劳务报酬的经济组织。理货 Tally 货物装卸中,对照货物运输票据进行的理(点)数、计量、检查残缺、指导装舱积载、核对标记、检查包装、分票、分标志和现场签证等工作
装运通知	Shipping Advice	由出口商(卖主)发给进口商(买主)的
装运须知	Shipping Instructions	由进口商(买主)发给出口商(卖主)的
国际货物运输保险	International Transportation Cargo Insurance	在国际贸易中,以国际运输中的货物为保险标的保险,以对自然灾害和意外事故所造成的财产损失获得补偿
报关	Customs Declaration	由进出口货物的收发货人或其代理人向海关办理进出境手续的全过程
进出口商品检验	Commodity Inspection	简称"商检"。确定进出口商品的品质、规格、重量、数量、包装、安全性能、卫生方面的指标及装运技术和装运条件等项目实施检验和鉴定,以确定其是否与贸易合同、有关标准规定一致,是否符合进出口国有关法律和行政法规的规定
普及特惠税制度产地来源证表格甲(即特惠税证)	Certificate of Origin Generalised Systems of Preferences (GSP) Form A (or as Form A)	该文件证明出口国产品根据普及特惠税供给国的普及特惠税制度享有进口税优惠(减税或免税)。一般来说,货品必须同时符合受惠国的产地规则与供给国普及特惠税制度的产地标准,才可获发表格甲。中国香港目前是加拿大及挪威普及特惠税制度下的受惠者。而中国则是澳大利亚、欧盟、加拿大、捷克、日本、波兰、俄罗斯、斯洛伐克等国的普及特惠税受惠者
经济订货批量	Economic Order Quantity	通过平衡采购进货成本和保管仓储成本核算,以实现总库存成本最低的最佳订货量
定量订货方式	Fixed-Quantity System(FQS)	库存量下降到预定的最低的库存数量(订货点)时,按规定数量(一般以经济订货批量为标准)进行订货补充的一种库存管理方式
定期订货方式	Fixed-interval system(FIS)	按预先确定的订货间隔期间进行订货补充的一种库存管理方式
电子订货系统	Electronic Order System(EDS)	不同组织间利用通信网络和终端设备以在线联结方式进行订货作业与订货信息交换的体系
配送需求计划	Distribution Requirements Planning (DRP)	一种既保证有效地满足市场需要又使得物流资源配置费用最省的计划方法,是 MRP 原理与方法在物品配送中的运用
配送资源计划	Distribution Resource planning (DRPⅡ)	一种企业内物品配送计划系统管理模式。是在 DRP 的基础上提高各环节的物流能力,达到系统优化运行的目的

附录 B 英汉物流术语解释

ATA Carnet	暂时过境证	这是国际海关文件,用来申请将货品(如国际交易会的展品、货办及专业设备)暂时运进《暂时过境证海关公约》的缔约国时免缴关税
Bar Code	条码	由一组规则排列的条、空及字符组成的、用以表示一定信息的代码。同义词:条码符号 bar code symbol[GB/T 4122.1-1996 中 4.17]
Certificate of Origin	产地来源证	这是证明货品制造地点、性质/数量/价值的证明书。工业贸易署及五个贸易机构
Import/Export Declaration	进出口报关单	这是在货物进出港口时向海关关长递交的报关声明书,用于申报货品的详情,包括付运货品的性质、目的国、出口国等,其主要作用是汇编贸易统计资料
Import/Export Licensee	进出口证	这是由有关政府部门签发的文件,授权某些受管制货品进口及出口
International Import Certificate	国际进口证	这是目的地政府签发的声明,证明进口的战略物品会在指定的国家出售。中国香港只为符合出口国的规定而发出国际进口证
Delivery Verification Certificate	货物抵境证明书	这是由目的地政府签发的声明,证明指定的战略物品已抵达指明的国家。中国香港只为符合出口国的规定而发出货物抵境证明书
Landing Certificate	卸货证明书	这是目的地政府签发的声明,证明指定的商品已抵达指明的国家。中国香港的卸货证明书由政府统计处签发。申请时需提交下列文件:进口报关单及收据、提单、海运提单及舱单、供应商发票,以及装箱单(若有)
Customs Invoice	海关发票	这是进口国海关指定的文件,说明货品的售价、运费、保险、包装资料、付款方式等,以便海关估价
Commercial Invoice	商业发票	这是出口商要求进口商根据销售合约支付货款的正式文件。商业发票应说明所售货品的详情、付款方式及贸易条款。商业发票也在货物清关时使用,有时供进口商安排外汇时使用
Consular Invoice	领事发票	这是有些国家要求的文件,载明付运货品的详情,例如托运人、收货人、价值说明等。此文件由驻外国领事馆人员签署证明,供该国海关人员核实付运货品的价值、数量及性质
Customized Logistics	定制物流	根据用户的特定要求而为其专门设计的物流服务模式
(D/R)Dock Receipt or Mate's Receipt	码头收货单或大副收据	付货人/运输公司。这是确定码头/货仓已收妥待运货物的收据。码头收货单是拟备提单所需的文件,但不是处理付款事宜时按法律规定必须具备的文件
External logistics	社会物流	企业外部的物流活动的总称
Electronic Data Interchange	电子数据交换	通过电子方式,采用标准化的格式,利用计算机网络进行结构化数据的传输和交换

Fumigation Certificate	熏蒸证书	这是虫害防治证明书,证明有关产品已经过获认可的熏蒸服务商所提供的检疫及付运前熏蒸程序。美国、加拿大和英国的海关都要求来自中国香港及中国大陆的实木包装材料附有熏蒸证书
Health Certificate	卫生证明书	这是在出口农产品或食品时,由主管国家发出的文件,证明农产品或食品符合出口国的有关法例,以及在付运前检验时完整无损、适合人食用
House Bill of Lading (Groupage)	运输商提单(拼箱提单)	这是由货运代理商发出的提单,很多时都不是所有权证明文件。付货人如选用运输商提单,应在采用信贷服务前向银行说明是否可接纳作信用证用途。与个别托运相比,拼箱提单的优点包括包装较少、保费较低、过境较快、损失风险及费用较低
Inspection Certificate	检验证明书	由独立公证人(检验公司)或出口商就买方或有关国家要求的付运货品规格(包括品质、数量及/或价钱等)发出的报告
Insurance Policy / Certificate	保险单/保险证明书,分保单	保险单是证明付运货品已投保的保险文件,详述有关保险额的资料。保险证明书证明付运货品已受保于某一开口保单,保障货品在付运途中免受损失或损害
Intangible Loss	无形损耗	由于科学技术进步而引起的物品贬值
Logistics Network	物流网络	物流过程中相互联系的组织与设施的集合
Logistics Information	物流信息	反映物流各种活动内容的知识、资料、图像、数据、文件的总称
Logistics Enterprise	物流企业	从事物流活动的经济组织
Logistics Documents	物流单证	物流过程中使用的所有单据、票据、凭证的总称
Logistics Alliance	物流联盟	两个或两个以上的经济组织为实现特定的物流目标而采取的长期联合与合作
Phytosanitary Certificate	植物检疫证	国际间通常规定进口的植物或种植物料须附有出口国发出的植物检疫证,证明付运货品大致上没有疾病或害虫,并符合进口国现行的植物检疫规例。在中国香港应向渔农处申请植物检疫证
Packing List	出口商	详列付运货品装箱资料的文件
Pro Forma Invoice	估价发票	这是货物付运时由供应商提供的发票,作用是通知买家即将付运商品的种类、数量、价值及进口规格(重量、大小及类似的特点)。估价发票不是用来要求买方付款的,但可用于申请进口证、安排外汇或其他财务安排
Production Logistics	生产物流	生产过程中,原材料、在制品、半成品、产成品等,在企业内部的实体流动
Product Testing Certificate	产品测试证明书	这是证明产品在品质、安全、规格等各方面均符合国际或个别国家技术标准的证明书
Quotation	报价单	指售货的报价,应清楚说明价钱、品质详情、货品数量、贸易条款、交货条件、付款方式
Returned Logistics	回收物流	不合格物品的返修、退货以及周转使用的包装容器从需方返回到供方所形成的物品实体流动

Sales Contract	销售合约	是买方与卖方之间的合约,订明交易细则,具法律约束力,因此在签署前最好先征询法律意见
(S/O) Shipper Order	付货通知单或出仓纸	文件===功用==负责拟备件者。这是说明货物详情及付货人各项要求的文件,是拟备其他运输单据(如提单、空运提单等)所需的基本文件
Supply Logistics	供用物流	为生产企业提供原材料、零部件或其他物品时,物品在提供者与需求者之间的实体流动
Supply Chain	供用链	生产及流通过程中,涉及将产品或服务提供给最终用户活动的上游与下游企业,所形成的网链结构。
Tangible loss	有形损耗	可见或可测量出来的物理性损失、消耗
Value-added Logistics Service	增值物流服务	在完成物流基本功能基础上,根据客户需求提供的各种延伸业务活动
Waste Material Logistics	废弃物物流	将经济活动中失去原有使用价值的物品,根据实际需要进行收集、分类、加工、包装、搬运、储存等,并分送到专门处理场所时所形成的物品实体流动

附录 C 汉英物流常用词汇

中 文	英 文
工具柜	Tool Cabinet
工具车	Tool Wagon
工作台	Work Bench
零件盒	Working Accessories
整理架	Hanger Rack
周转箱	Container
平托盘	Flat Pallets
网箱托盘	Grille Box Pallets
箱式托盘	Box Pallets
柱式托盘	Post Pallets
物流台车	Roll Pallets
集装袋	Flexible Freight Bags
集装箱	Containers
杠杆式手推车	Hand Truck
手推台车	Platform Truck
手动托盘搬运车	Manual Pallet Trucks
手动升降平台车	Scissor Lift Table
电动托盘搬运车	Electric Pallet Trucks
电动托盘堆垛车	Electric Pallet Stacks
前移式叉车	Reach Fork Lift Trucks
内燃式叉车	Engine Fork Lift Trucks
电瓶叉车	Electric Fork Lift Trucks
叉车属具	Attachments of FT
侧面叉车	Side Fork Lift Trucks
低位拣选叉车	Order Picking Trucks
高位拣选叉车	Order Picking Trucks
牵引车	Tow Tractor
固定平台搬运车	Fixed Platform Trucks
集装箱叉车	Container FLT
轻型货架	Light Duty Rack

中　文	英　文
工业货架系统	Industrial Rack System
托盘货架系统	Pallet Rack System
移动货架系统	Mobile Rack System
滑动式货架	Slide Rack
悬臂货架	Cantilever Racking
托盘单元式	Pallet Unit AS/RS
盒式单元式	Fine Stocker AS/RS
高架叉车仓库	Rack Fork Stocker
有轨堆垛机	Stacker Crane
无轨堆垛机	Rack Fork
高层货架	High Level Rack
入出库输送机	O/R Conveying Systems
自动搬运车	Automatic Guided Vehicle
剪叉式升降台	Aerial Work LT
车载式升降台	Car-carrying LT
自行剪式升降台	Self-propelled LT
升缩高空作业车	Self-propelled Articulated Booms
折臂高空作业车	Self-propelled Telescopic Booms
悬臂起重机	Cantilever Cranes
梁式起重机	Beam Cranes
桥式起重机	Overhead Travlling Cranes
门式起重机	Gantry Cranes
带式输送机	Belt Conveyors
链式输送机	Chain Conveyors
滚道输送机	Roller Conveyors
悬挂输送机	Overhead Chain Conveyors
单轨输送机	Overhead onorail Conveyors
垂直输送机	Elevator Conveyors
生产输送机	Production Line
分拣输送机	Sorting & Picking System
吊索具	Current Collector Sleave
移动供电装置	Sliding Power Devices
遥控装置	Remote Control

中　文	英　文
电机减速机	Motors
制动器	Brake
链传动元件	Element of Chain
滚道传动元件	Element of Rolls
工业用门	Industrial Door
环保车辆	Cleaning Equipment
电瓶·充电机	Battery & Charger
称量装置	Load Weighing Devices
条码用材	Material of Label
条码打印机	Barcode Printer
数据采集终端	Data Collection Terminal
质量检测仪	Quality Testing
无线管理系统	Wireless Network
电子标签系统	Electronic Labeling System
自动化元器件	Element of Automation
正本	Original
副本	Copy
客户	Customer
卖主	Vendor
买主	Vendee
发货人	Consignor
收货人	Consignee
托运(收货)人的代理人[通知人]	Notify
承运人	Carrier
启运地	Departure
航班	Flight
日期	Date
航空公司	Airline Company
代理	Agent
货币	Currency
保险	Insurance
收货件数	No. of Pieces RCP (reception)
费率	Rate

中　文	英　文
对承运人申报的价值	Declared value for carriage
对海关申报的价值	Declared value for customs
装卸	Loading and unloading
包装	Package/packaging
销售包装	Sales package
定牌包装	Packing of nominated brand
中性包装	Neutral packing
运输包装	Transport package
托盘包装	palletizing
集装化	Containerization
散装化	In bulk
配送	Distribution
拣选	Order picking
组配	Assembly
仓库	warehouse
库房	Storehouse
自动化仓库	Automatic Warehouse
冷藏区	Chill space
冷冻区	Freeze space
集装箱码头	Container terminal
国际铁路联运	International through railway transport
国际多式联运	International multimodal transport
大陆桥运输	Land bridge transport
班轮运输	Liner transport
租船运输	Shipping by chartering
报价单	Quotation
销售合约	Sales Contract
估价发票	Pro Forma Invoice
商业发票	Commercial Invoice
装箱单	Packing List
检验证明书	Inspection Certificate
产品测试证明书	Product Testing Certificate
卫生证明书	Health Certificate

中　文	英　文
植物检疫证	Phytosanitary Certificate
运输商提单（拼箱提单）	House Bill of Lading (Groupage)
海运提单	Sea Waybill
货运担保	Shipping Guarantee
装箱单	Packing List (sometimes as packing note)
进出口报关单	Import/Export Declaration
进出口证	Import/Export Licence
卸货证明书	Landing Certificate
海关发票	Customs Invoice
单元货载	Unit load
单元货载系统	Unit load system
支柱	Upright
护脚	Upright protectors
装箱	Vanning
垂直输送机	Vertical conveyor
窄巷道电动堆高机	Very narrow aisle truck
仓库	Warehouse
无线管理系统	Wireless Network
工作台	Work Bench
零件盒	Working Accessories

附录 D 英汉物流常用词汇

英　文	中　文
Acrial Work LT	剪叉式升降台
Agent	代理
Airline company	航空公司
Anchoring	膨胀螺钉
Assembly packaging	集合包装
Attachments of FT	叉车属具
Automatic Guided Vehicle	自动搬运车
Average inventory	平均存货
Barcode Printer	条码打印机
Battery	电瓶
Battery & Charger	电瓶·充电机
Beam	横撑,横梁
Beam Cranes	梁式起重机
Belt Conveyors	带式输送机
Block pattern row pattern	整齐码放
Bonded warehouse	国际物流中心保税仓库
Box Pallets	箱式托盘
Brake	制动器
Brick pattern	砌砖式码放
Buffer stock	缓冲储备
Cantilever Cranes	悬臂起重机
Cantilever Racking	悬臂货架
Cantilever Shelving	悬臂架
Car-carrying LT	车载式升降台
Cargo freight	货物
Carrier	承运人
Carrying	搬运
Chain Conveyors	链式输送机
Charger	充电机
Cleaning Equipment	环保车辆

英　　文	中　　文
Cold chain system	冷冻链系统
Common carrier	公共承运人
Container	周转箱
Containers	集装箱
Container terminal	集装箱中转站
Container FLT	集装箱叉车
Contract carrier	契约承运人
Contract logistics	契约物流
Copy	副本
Counterbalance truck	平衡式电动(柴油、电动、瓦斯)堆高机
Customer	客户
Current Collector Sleave	吊索具
Currency	货币
Cycle inventory	周期存货
Dagonal bracing	斜撑
Date	日期
Data Collection Terminal	数据采集终端
Declared value for carriage	对承运人申报的价值
Declared value for customs	对海关申报的价值
Delivery	配送
Departure	启运地
Devanning	拆箱
Dock leveller	月台调整板
Dock shelter	月台门封(充气式、非充气式)
Drive-in pallet racking	直入式重型物料钢架
Dry cargo	干货
Dunnage	填充
Elevator Conveyors	垂直输送机
Electric Pallet Trucks	电动托盘搬运车
Electric Pallet Stacks	电动托盘堆垛车
Electronic Labeling System	电子标签系统
Element of Automation	自动化元器件
Engine Fork Lift Trucks	内燃式叉车

英　文	中　文
Electric Fork Lift Trucks	电瓶叉车
Element of Chain	链传动元件
Element of Rolls	滚道传动元件
Export processing zone	加工出口区
Fill rate	供应比率
Fixed Platform Trucks	固定平台搬运车
Flat Pallets	平托盘
Flexible Freight Bags	集装袋
Flight	航班
Floor utilization percentage	地面面积利用率
Flow(dynamic) racking	重型流力架
Flow(dynamic) rack shelving	轻型(料盒、纸箱)流力架
Forklift truck	叉车
Frame	支柱组
Frame feet	脚底板
Frame joint	柱连杆
Freight container	货物集装箱
Gantry Cranes	门式起重机
General cargo	一般货物
Grille Box Pallets	网箱托盘
Hand pallet truck	油压拖板车
Hand Truck	杠杆式手推车
Hanger Rack	整理架
High Level Rack	高层货架
Horizontal bracing	横撑
Industrial Rack System	工业货架系统
Industrial vehicle	工业车辆
Industrial Door	工业用门
Insurance	保险
Intermodal transportation	复合一贯运输
Lashing	捆扎加固
Levelling plate	垫片
Light Duty Rack	轻型货架

英　文	中　文
Load efficient	装载效率
Load Weighing Devices	称量装置
Loading and unloading	装卸
Logistical utilities	物流效用
Logistics	物流
Materials handling	物料搬运
Material of Label	条码用材
Mezzanines floor	积层架
Mini-load AS/RS	料盒式自动仓库系统
Mobile dock leveller	月台桥板
Mobile Rack System	移动货架系统
Mobile shelving	移动柜
Motors	电机减速机
Net unit load size	净单元货载尺寸
Notify	托运(收货)人的代理人〔通知人〕
No. of Pieces RCP（reception）	收货件数
Operation area	理货区
Order picking truck	电动拣料车
Order shipped complete	订货完成率
Original	正本
Overhead Chain Conveyors	悬挂输送机
Overhead onorail Conveyors	单轨输送机
Order Picking Trucks	高位拣选叉车
Packaged cargo	包装货物
Packaging	包装
Pallet	托盘,(木质)栈板
Pallet container	栈板笼架
Pallet pool system	通用托盘系统
Pallet racking	传统式重型物料钢架
Palletization	托盘化
Palletizing pattern	托盘装载方式
Physical distribution model	物流标准
Pick up	货物聚集

英　文	中　文
Picking	拣货,拣选作业
Pictorial marking for handling	货运标识
Pinwheel pattern	针轮式码放
Plan view size	平面尺寸
Plastic bin	物料盒
Plastic pallet	塑胶栈板
Platform	物流容器,站台,月台
Platform Truck	手推台车
Post Pallets	柱式托盘
Pallet Unit AS/RS	托盘单元式
Pallet Rack System	托盘货架系统
Powered pallet truck	电动拖板车
Production Line	生产输送机
Push-back pallet racking	后推式重型物料钢架
Quality Testing	质量检测仪
Rack	货架
Rack Fork	无轨堆垛机
Rack Fork Stocker	高架叉车仓库
Rack notice	标示牌
Rate	费率
Reach Fork Lift Trucks	前移式叉车
Reach truck	前伸式电动堆高机
Remote Control	遥控装置
Returnable container	通用容器
Roll container	笼车
Roll Pallets	物流台车
Roller conveyor	滚筒式输送机(带)
Safety pin	插销
Safety stock	安全储备
Scrubber	洗地机
Self-propelled LT	自行剪式升降台
Self-propelled Articulated Booms	升缩高空作业车
Self-propelled Telescopic Booms	折臂高空作业车

334

英　文	中　文
Shed	临时周转仓库
Shelving	轻量型物料钢架
Shuttle car	梭车
Slat conveyor	条板式输送机（带）
Sliding Power Devices	移动供电装置
Slotted-angle shelving	角钢架
Sorting	分类
Sorting & Picking System	分拣输送机
Special cargo	特殊货物
Spot stock	现场储备
Stacker Crane	有轨堆垛机
Stacker crane	自动存取机高架吊车
Stacking	堆垛
Stockout frequency	缺货频率
Storage	存储
Support bar	跨梁
Surface utilization percentage	表面利用率
Sweeper	扫地机
Table trolley	物流台车
Third party logistics service provider	第三方物流服务商
Tow Tractor	牵引车
Tool Cabinet	工具柜
Tool Wagon	工具车
Transit inventory	中转存货
Transportation	运输
Transportation package size by modular coordination	运输包装系列尺寸
Tray conveyor	盘式输送机（带）
Truck terminal	卡车货运站
Turntable	转盘（变更输送方向）

附录E 物流常用缩略词和组合词

缩 略 词	原 词	释 义
A	Accepted	承兑
AA	Auditing Administration	(中国)审计署
AAA		最佳等级
ABS.	Abstract	摘要
a/c，A/C	Account	账户、账目
a/c，A/C	Account Current	往来账户、活期存款账户
A&C	Addenda and Corrigenda	补遗和勘误
Acc.	Acceptance or Accepted	承兑
Accrd. Int	Accrued Interest	应计利息
Acc.	Account	账户、账目
Acct.	Accountant	会计师、会计员
Acct.	Accounting	会计、会计学
Acct. No.	Account Number	账户编号、账号
Acct. Tit.	Account Title	账户名称、会计科目
A/C no.	Account Number	账户编号、账号
ACE	Air Cushion Equipment	气垫设备
ACN	Air Consignment	航空托运单
Acpt.	Acceptance or Accepted	承兑
A/CS Pay.	Accounts Payable	应付账款
A/CS Rec.	Accounts Receivable	应收账款
ACT	Advance Corporation Tax	预扣公司税
ACU	Asia Currency Unit	亚洲货币单位
A.C.V	Actual Cash Value	实际现金价值
a.d.，a/d	After Date	开票后、出票后
AD/ADV	Advertising	广告
ADDS，ADS	Address	地址
ADMIN	Administrative	行政的
ADRS	Asset Depreciation Range System	固定资产分组折旧法
Adv.	Advance	预付款
ad.val，A/V	Ad Valorem To（According Value）	从价

缩　略　词	原　　词	释　　义
AGCY	Agency	机构
AGNT	Agent	机构
Agt.	Agent	代理人
Agt.	Agreement	协议、契约
AGV	Automatic Guided Vehicle	自动导引车
AIM	Automated Inventory Management	自动库存系统
AIR，AIRML	Airmail	航空
AIRD	Airmailed	航空
AIRG	Airmailing	航空
AIRFRT	Airfreight	航空
AJE	Adjusting Journal Entries	调整分录
AMIS	Automated Mask Inspection System	自动伪装检验系统
AMT	Amount	金额
Amt.	Amount	金额、总数
Ann.	Annuity	年金
A/P	Account Paid	已付账款
A/P	Account Payable	应付账款
A/P	Accounting Period	会计期间
A/P	Advise and Pay	付款通知
APPT	Appointment	约会、预约
A/R	Account Receivable	应收账款
A/R	at the rate of	以……比例
A.R	All risks	金额
ARR，ARV	Arrive	到达
A/S，a/s	After Sight	见票即付
A/S，acc/s	Account Sales	承销账、承销清单，售货清单
ASAP	As soon as possible	尽快
ASR	Acceptance Summary Report	验收总结报告
AS/RS	Automatic Storage Retrieval System	自动存取机/系统，自动存取仓储系统，自动仓库系统
ass.	Assessment	估征、征税
Assimt.	Assignment	转让、让与
ASST	Assistant	助理

缩　略　词	原　词	释　义
ATC	Average Total Cost	平均总成本
ATM	At the money	仅付成本钱
ATM	Automatic Teller Machine	自动取款机(柜员机)
ATS	Automated Trade System	自动交易系统
ATS	Automatic Transfer Service	自动转移服务
Atty.	Attorney	代理人
Auct.	Auction	拍卖
Aud.	Auditor	审计员、审计师
Av.	Average	平均值
AVL	Automated Vehicle Location	自动车辆定位
AVI	Automated Vehicle Identification	自动车辆识别
a. w.	All Wool	纯羊毛
A/W	Air Waybill	空运提单
A/W	Actual Weight	实际重量
AWB	Air Waybill	空运提单
BA	Bank Acceptance	银行承兑汇票
bal.	Balance	余额、差额
Banky.	Bankruptcy	破产、倒闭
b. b.	Bearer Bond	不记名债券
B. B. , B/B	Bill Book	出纳簿
B/B	Bill Bought	买入票据、买入汇票
b&b	Bed & Breakfast	住宿费和早餐费
b. c.	Blind Copy	密送的副本
BC	Buyer Credit	买方信贷
B/C	Bills for Collection	托收汇票
B. C.	Bank Clearing	银行清算
Bd.	Bond	债券
B/D	Bills Discounted	已贴现票据
B/D	Bank Draft	银行汇票
b. d. i.	Both Dates Inclusive，Both Days Inclusive	包括头尾两天
B/E	Bill of Entry	报关单
b. e. , B/E	Bill of Exchange	汇票
BEP	Breakeven Point	保本点、盈亏临界点

缩略词	原词	释义
b/f	Brought Forward	承前
BF	Bonded Factory	保税工厂
Bfcy.	Beneficiary	受益人
B/G，b/g	Bonded Goods	保税货物
BHC	Bank Holding Company	银行控股公司
BIS	Bank of International Settlements	国际清算银行
bit	Binary Digit	两位数
BIZ，BSNS	Business	生意,业务
BKG D	Background	背景
Bk.	Bank	银行
Bk.	Book	账册
BLDG	Building	建筑物、大楼
B/L	Bill of Lading	提单
B/L original	Bill of Lading Original	提货单正本
bldg.	Building	大厦
BMP	Bank Master Policy	银行统一保险
BN	Bank Note	钞票
BO	Branch Office	分支营业处
BO	Buyer's Option	买者选择交割期的远期合同
BOM	Beginning of Month	月初
b. o. m.	Bill of Materials	用料清单
BOO	Build-operate-own	建造—运营—拥有
BOOM	Build-operate-own-maintain	建造—运营—拥有—维护
BOOT	Build-operate-own- transfer	建造—运营—拥有—转让
b. o. p.	Balance of Payments	收支差额
BOT	Balance of Trade	贸易余额
BOY	Beginning of Year	年初
b. p. ，B/P	Bills Payable	应付票据
Br.	Branch	分支机构
BR	Bank Rate	银行贴现率
b. r. ，B/R	Bills Receivable	应收票据
Brok.	Broker or Brokerage	经纪人或经纪人佣金
b. s. ，BS，B/S	Balance Sheet	资产负债表

缩　略　词	原　词	释　义
B/S	Bill of Sales	卖据、出货单
B share	B Share	B 股
B. T. T.	Bank Telegraphic Transfer	银行电汇
BUS	Business	商业、生意
BV	Book Value	票面价值
CAD	Cash Against Document	凭单据付款
CC	Freight Collect	到付
CHG	Charge	费用
CFR	Cost and Freight	成本加运费价
CFS	Container Freight Station	集装箱货运站
CIF	Cost, Insurance and Freight	成本、保险加运费价
CIFC	Cost, Insurance, Freight and Commission	成本、保险加运费价及佣金
CLI	Shipper's Letter of Instruction	委托书
CLK	Clerk	(办公室)职员
CNEE	Consignee	收货人
CNF	Cost and Freight	成本加运费价
CO	Company	公司
COD	Cash on Delivery	货到付款
COMM	Commission	佣金
CORP	Corporation	(有限)公司
CNEE	Consignee	收货人
CR, CRED	Credit	信用,贷方,银行存款
CRP	Continuous Replenishment Program	连续库存补充计划
C/W	Chargeable Weight	计费重量
D/A	Documents Against Acceptance	承兑交单
Data PRO	Data Processing	数据处理
D/C	Documentary Credit	跟单信用证
DEPT	Department	部
Dest	Destination	目的地
DIR	Director	董事
DIV	Division	分工、部门
DOZ	Dozen	一打
D/P	Documents Against Payment	付款交单

缩 略 词	原 词	释 义
D/R	Dock Receipt or Mate's Receipt	码头收货单或大副收据
DRP	Distribution Requirements Planning	配送需求计划
DRPII	Distribution Resource Planning	配送资源计划
DVC	Delivery Verification Certificate	货物抵境证明书
ECR	Efficient Customer Response	有效客户反应
EDI	Electronic Data Interchange	电子数据交换
EQPT	Equipment	装备
ERP	Enterprise Resource Planning	企业资源计划
ETA	Estimated Time of Arrival	估计抵达时间
ETC	And so on	等等
ETD	Estimated Time of Departure	估计出发时间
ETS	Estimated Time of Sailing	估计起航时间
EXP	Experience	经验
EXP	Export	出口
EXP'D	Experienced	有经验的
EXT	Extension	延伸、扩展
FCL	Full Container Load	整箱货
FLT	Flight	期订货方式
FQS	Fixed—Quantity System	定量订货方式
FIS	Fixed—Interval System	定期订货方式
FOB	Free on Board	离岸价
FR. BEN	Fringe Benefits	额外福利
F/T	Full Time	全日制
G/W	Gross Weight	毛重
HAWB	Home Air Way Bill	空运分单
HQTRS	Headquarters	总部
HOWB	Home Ocean Way Bill	海运分单
HR	Hour	小时
HRLY	Hourly	每小时
HS	High School	高中(学历)
IATA	International Air Transport Association	国际航协
IIC	International Import Certificate	国际进口证
IMMED	Immediate	立即

缩 略 词	原 词	释 义
IMP	Import	进口
INCL	Including	包括
IND	Industrial	工业的
INEXP	Inexperienced	无经验的
INT'L	International	国际性的
INV	Invoice	发票
JR	Junior	初级
JRREV	Irrevocable	不可撤销的
KNOWL	Knowledge	知识
KG，KGS	Kilogram，Kilograms	千克
L/C	Letter of Credit	信用证
LGV	Laser Guided Vehicle	激光引导无人搬运车
LIC	License	许可证
LOC	Location	位置、场所
L/T	Long Ton	长吨
LRP	Logistics Resource Planning	物流资源计划
LV/LVL	Level	级/层
MACH	Machine	机器
MANUF/MF	Manufacturing	制造
MAWB	Master Air Way Bill	空运主单
MECH	Mechanic	机械的
MGR	Manager	经理
M-F	Monday-Friday	从周一到周五
MO	Month	月
MOWB	Master Ocean Way Bill	海运主单
MAX	Maximum	最大量,最大数
MIN	Minimum	最小量,最小数
M/T	Metric Ton	公吨
MRP	Material Requirements Planning	物料需求计划
NEC	Necessary	必要的
N/W	Net Weight	净重
NT	Net Weight	净重
OT	Overtime	超时

缩　略　词	原　　词	释　　义
PAYMT	Payment	支付,付款
PCL	Full Container Load	整箱货
PCT	Percent	百分比
PERM	Permanent	永久性的
PLS	Please	请
PP	Freight Prepaid	预付
PREF	Preference	(有经验者)优先
PREV	Previous	有先前(经验)
P/T	Part Time	非全日制
OR	Quick Response	快速反应
REFS	References	推荐信
REL	Reliable	可靠的
REPS	Representative	(销售)代表
REQ	Required	需要
SAL	Salary	工资
SCM	Supply Chain Management	供应链管理
SECTY	Secretary	秘书
SH	Shorthand	人手不足
SHPR	Shipper	托运人
S/O	Shipper Order	付货通知单(俗称落货纸或出仓纸)
SPEC	specification	规格
SR	senior	资深
SS，S/S	steam ship	轮船
STG	pound sterling	英镑
STMTS	statements	报告
SZ	size	尺寸
TECH	technical	技术上
TEL/PH	telephone	电话
TEMP	temporarily	临时性(工作)
TEU	Twenty—feet equivalent unit	换算箱
TPL	Third—part logistics	第三方物流
T/R	Trust Receipt	信托收据
TRANS	transportation	交通

缩 略 词	原 词	释 义
TRNEE	trainee	实习生
TYP	typing/typist	打字/打字员
UNAVLBL	unavailable	无货的,无法利用的
USD	us dollar	美元
VMI	Vendor managed inventory	供应商管理库存
WCS	Warehouse Control System	仓储控制系统
WK	week/work	周/工作
WPM	words per minute	打字/每分钟
WMS	Warehouse Management System	仓储管理系统
WT	weight	重量
YR(s)	Year(s)	年

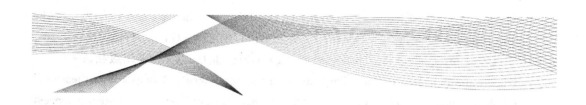

References

[1] C. Jotin Khisty and B. Kent Lall. Transportation Engineering：An Introduction (3rd Edition). *Pearson Prentice Hall*, *Pearson Education Inc.*, Upper Saddle River, New Jersey 07458, 2003.

[2] 彭志忠. 物流英语. 济南：山东大学出版社,2008.

[3] 张庆英. 物流工程英语. 北京：化学工业出版社,2005.

[4] 包胜华. 物流工程专业英语. 北京：国防工业出版社,2006.

[5] 景平. 物流英语. 上海：上海财经大学出版社,2004.

[6] 周宁. 物流英语. 北京：北京电子工业出版社,2007.

[7] 段云礼. 物流英语阅读教程. 天津：南开大学出版社,2005.

[8] 乐美龙. 现代物流英语. 上海：上海交通大学出版社,2005.

[9] Dennis W Krumwiede , Chwen Sheu . A model for reverse logistics entry by third-party providers. College of Business, Idaho State University, Pocatello, ID 83209-8020, USA；College of Business, Department of Management, Kansas State University, Manhattan, KS 66506, USA.

[10] Majed Al-Mashari Abdullah Al-Mudimigh , Mohamed Zairi. Enterprise Resource Planning：A taxonomy of critical factors . Department of Information Systems, College of Computer；ECTQM, University of Bradford, Emm Lane, Bradford B094JL, West Yorkshire, UK.

[11] Majed Al-Mashari Industrial Management and Data Systems. Enterprise Resource Planning (ERP) systems：a research agenda.

[12] John L Burbidge. Production Flow Analysis for Planning Group Technology：For Planning Group Technology. Oxford University Press, USA, 1997.

[13] John L Burbidge. Production Flow Analysis for Planning Group Technology. Journal of Operations Management, 1991, 10(1)：5-27.

[14] R Reed. The role of material flow systems. Industrial and Commercial Techniques Limited, 1968.

[15] Rolf T Wigand. Electronic Commerce: Definition, Theory, and Context . The Information Society: An International Journal, 1087-6537, 1997, 13(1):1—16.

[16] 张庆英. Introduction to transportation engineering. 北京:电子工业出版社,2007.

[17] Kini Anil,Choobineh Joobin. Trust in electronic commerce : definition and theoretical considerations. Proceedings of the Hawii International Conference on System Sciences, Big Island, USA,January 6-9 1998(4): 51—61.

[18] Kenneth C Laudon, Jane P. Laudon. Management information systems: Managing the Digital Firm (8th Edition). Prentice Hall, Upper Saddle River, NJ, USA, 2003.

[19] Gordon B Davis, Margrethe H Olson. Management information systems: conceptual foundations, structure, and development (2nd th Edition). McGraw-Hill College, New York, NY, USA, 1984.

[20] Gordon B Davis. Management information systems: a fifteen-year perspective. ACM SIGMIS Database, 1982, 13(4): 10—11.

[21] W Lawrence Neuman. Social research methods: Qualitative and quantitative approaches (5th Edition). Allyn and& Bacon, 2002.

[22] http://www. rfidjournal. com/

[23] http://www. readwriteweb. com/archives/

[24] http://www. materialflowsystems. com/

[25] http://www. intelligententerprise. com/020114/502infoscl _ 1. jhtml.

[26] http://papers. ssrn. com/sol3/papers. cfm? abstract _ id=1317682

[27] http://www. bitpipe. com/tlist/Warehouse-Management. html

[28] Christina Soh, Sia Siew Kien, Joanne Tay-Yap. Enterprise Resource Planning: cultural fits and misfits: is ERP a universal solution? Communications of the ACM, 2000, 43(4): 47—51.

[29] Management information systems: a fifteen-year perspective. University of Minnesota, New York, NY, USA.

[30] Majed AI-Mashari. Enterprise resourse planning (ERP) systems: a research agenda. Industrial Management and Data Systems, 2002, 102(3): 165—170.

[31] www. supplychainbrain. com